LJ EVANS

This book is a work of fiction. While reference might be made to actual historical events or existing people and locations, the events, names, characters, places and incidents are either the product of the author's imagination or are used fictitiously, and any resemblance to actual persons, living or dead, business establishments, events, or locales is entirely coincidental.

MY LIFE AS A COUNTRY ALBUM Copyright © 2014 by LJ Evans

Published by LJ Evans Books

www.ljevansbooks.com

Cover Design © Designed by Grace
Cover Image © Iris Productions
Editing: Jenn Lockwood Editing

Publishers' Cataloging-in-Publications
Evans, L. J., 1970- author.
LJ Evans Books, [2014] I Series: My life as an album series ; v. I.
LCSH: Neighbors--Fiction. I Dating (Social customs)--Fiction. I Man-woman relationships-- Fiction. I Teenagers--Death--Fiction. I Diabetes in adolescence--Fiction. I Football stories. I GSAFD: Love stories. I LCGFT: Romance fiction. I Sports fiction. I Bildungsromans. I BISAC: FICTION / Coming of Age. I FICTION / Family Life / General. I FICTION / Friendship. I FICTION / Romance / Contemporary. I FICTION / Romance / New Adult. I FICTION / Romance / Sports. I FICTION / Southern. I FICTION / Small Town & Rural. I FICTION / Women.
LCC: PS3605.V3684 M913 2014 I DDC: 813/.6--dc23

ISBN 13: 978-1521091807
ISBN 10: 1521091803
ASIN: B06ZZMWKPL

Printed in the United States of America

Playlist

Playlist available at: http://bit.ly/mlaacaspoti

Featuring Taylor Swift

Prolouge: Out of the Woods 1. Mary's Song (Oh My, My, My)
2. I'm Only Me When I'm With You 3. Stay Beautiful
4. A Perfectly Good Heart 5. Better Than Revenge
6. You Belong With Me 7. Mean 8. White Horse
9. The Way I Loved You 10. Change 11. Tim McGraw
12. Our Song 13. Superman 14. The Moment I Knew
15. Dear John 16. I Knew You Were Trouble
17. Ours 18. Stay Stay Stay 19. Treacherous
20. Sad Beautiful Tragic & Long Live 21. Red
22. A Place in This World 23. Begin Again 24. State of Grace

Message from the Author

Thank you for taking the time to read my story. This book was inspired by music and love, so I hope that you are inspired by those same things as you read the words. In all my books, my characters learn how to live their lives resiliently. They find a way to get through life's challenges with grace, humility, strength, and—most importantly—LOVE.

A lot of authors at this point will give you a long list of their social media sites, places to leave reviews, and a laundry list of their other books, but the truth is, I don't want to give you those things… not yet.

I'd rather you get to reading. I'd rather you fall in love with my characters, their worlds, and the love, laughter, and *family* that is held within these "pages."

So… here it is… Cam's coming-of-age story filled with all the people she adores… I'll touch base with you again AFTER you've read the story…

Happy Reading!

LJ EVANS

♫ where music & stories collide ♫

Sigh…okay. Some of you want all that information now, so if you do, please feel free to look at the back in the Second Message from the Author.

 *Dedication*

To my family who has supported my writing from the crazy fan fiction of my childhood to the hopes and dreams of adulthood. I could not have done this without all of you: my loving husband, creative daughter, determined sister, and supportive parents.

# The End

Out of the Woods

"Are we out of the woods yet

Are we in the clear yet

Good!"

- Swift & Antonoff

It happened when we were out and about looking at apartments that we couldn't afford. It was a failed attempt to reclaim some of our Polaroid moments of color and passion that had disappeared months ago with your kidneys. The sun streamed through a set of picture windows and highlighted you in a halo of light that captured my breath. In that moment, caught in the shimmery white, you almost looked like the football god you once were and not the weaker version of yourself you'd become. You gave me your slow, heart-melting smile as you grabbed my hand and twirled me around in the empty space until I was held tight against your chest, feeling like the only girl in your world. You swayed me back and forth, slow and sensual, and for a second, we forgot it all. We forgot the realtor, the year of doubt, and the harsh reality of the future. I let out a breath into your neck and thought maybe, just maybe, we were in the clear. We'd held onto each other through it all. You tipped my chin up, and I was caught, as I'd always been, in the sparkle of your beautiful, green and gold mosaic eyes. The only eyes that ever made me feel alive.

You kissed me, reaching down to the depths of my heart where you'd forever claimed every last tile on the walls of my soul. The realtor cleared his throat, but we just ignored him like we'd ignored everyone for that picture-perfect six months we'd been away at college. You smiled against my lips, and I couldn't help but smile back. You whirled me out of your arms and then dragged me up the stairs at a jog.

I was smiling, still caught in that precious moment, when you turned to me again and whispered, "Cami," and I listened because I always listened when you said my name that way and not the short version, Cam, that we both preferred. And this time, my heart melted for a totally different reason when your mosaic eyes turned to me with an indescribable look. It was like a switch had been thrown from that brief second of life below until now. Then you said something that would tear at me for the rest of my life. You said, "I love you, Camdyn," before you crumpled to the floor.

An ambulance ride later, we were at the hospital. Again. How many times had we been there this year? It didn't actually matter because I already knew. I already knew that this time it was going to be different.

You see, it was the only time in our entire life you'd called me Camdyn.

Chapter One

The Beginning: Mary's Song
(oh my, my, my)

"And our daddies used to joke about the two of us
Growing up and falling in love and our mamas smiled
And rolled their eyes."
- Swift, Rose, Maher

People who don't know us, people like the therapist I saw not long ago, they always ask me the most ridiculous question. They ask me how you and I met. And I know, it is only ridiculous to us because we obviously know the story, but my tolerance for stupidity and my quick mouth running ahead of my brain, always has me replying with an equally ridiculous answer. I respond with a cryptic, "'Mary's Song'!" And when they look at me puzzled, I just wave a disgusted hand and say, "Just listen to that song, and then you'll know."

You'd be grinning and laughing that deep, skin-tingling, Jake laugh of yours if you ever heard me say that. You'd tousle my plain, brown hair and say something smart-ass about me comparing our life to a country song. Not that you minded country music. We live in Tennessee after all and have a great many country artists on our playlists. You'd just find it humorous that I was comparing us to any song. Especially knowing me; knowing that I'm not really a girly girl who gets all romantic and mushy expecting you to sing to me like Patrick Swayze in *Dirty Dancing.*

But I still can't help it because it's the only response I know to that moronic question. When I think of our beginning, those lyrics are the first thing that pops into my head. It has two kids who are a couple years apart living next to each other and playing in their tree house, inseparable. It has them growing up with stolen kisses and tangled hands in truck rides out to the creek… or the lake in our case. And you know it's true that the essence of that song is the inexplicable connection between the two kids. And that definitely was us. Will always be us.

I think *THE* moment your parents remember most as cementing our childhood connection is the "tree house incident." I'm almost certain that you'd agree. Do you remember the hushed tone they'd take when speaking about it, as if some alien spaceship had landed in the middle of Tennessee? It really wasn't the beginning of us… but it was the moment that made your parents scratch their heads and wonder about the nature of the universe and God and what things were meant to be.

I know I shouldn't remember it as clear as I do, seeing as I was only four while you were seven, but I guess the "tree house incident" isn't something you forget, even if you are only four. If I close my eyes, I can almost relive it moment by moment in my head. I remember it was my nap time, and I hated nap time just like I pretty much hated anything that kept me from your side. So, what did I do? I sneaked out of my house and went searching for you in "our" backyard. And of course, people who don't know us look at me puzzled again, because we didn't live together in the same house, but we did share a backyard. That's because it's really two yards, but our daddies tore down the fence that separated them before we were ever born, so we've always had this one big rectangle of suburbia that our families share like we pretty much share everything.

Focus, Cam. That's what you'd tell me. Because it's one of my worst traits, the way my thoughts and actions lead me down a completely different path than the one I start on. I could claim a disability I'm sure, but my family isn't really a making-excuses-for-your-actions kind of family. Anywho, that day—the day of the "incident"—there was a ladder propped up against the aging oak tree where our daddies had begun building a tree house for us. And like always, my body had clambered halfway up the ladder before my brain caught up. And when my brain did catch up, it was because my body was soaring through the sky. There was nothing holding me but the thick Southern summer air. And then… Then what? Then I was in your arms, all smiles.

Everyone thought I should have been frightened, falling from a ladder like that at four. But I wasn't. That moment of free falling filled my little body with electric energy as if I was a baby bird spiraling from its nest for the first time. What did scare me, however, was the look you gave me as I beamed up at you. It was the first time I remember you being angry with me. Definitely not the last. But the first. Your eyes turned this deep, deep lake green, and you yelled at me as much as you could with your seven-year-old voice and your adorable, dark, shaggy hair shaking about you.

"You could've been killed!" And even though you were furious and only a little kid yourself, you pulled me into a hug. At that point, I didn't know better, so I squirmed away from your surprisingly strong arms just like I would my mama's a minute later.

So? People would say. So, you caught me from falling. What's so crazy about it that our parents call it the "tree house incident" in whispers? Well, it's really about how you came to be in our yard, standing by that tree ready to catch me that gets everyone going.

Your mama, Marina, was two seconds behind you, and she hauled me to my house shaking like a kitten in a bath. She was babbling to my mama in that rapid-fire way of hers, "Jake and I were just eating lunch at the counter as always, when all of a sudden, he got this awful look on his face like he might throw up. He ran out the back door quick as a June bug, and I followed. And what do I see? Cami flying off of the ladder, and Jake catching her."

"Oh my lord!" my mama exclaimed, pulling me and then you against her, to which, of course, we both objected and yanked ourselves away. "How on Earth did he know?"

Your mama and mine regarded us as if we were *La Chupacabra* itself because, as you well know, the golden granite bar in your kitchen has no view of our tree house. None at all. So, the question became: how on Earth had you known that I was out there? That I was climbing that ladder? That I needed saving? At that time, we didn't care for the wild look in our mamas' eyes, so we really did take off as quick as a couple of June bugs. And where did we go?

Right back up the tree. To the place that became our little haven many times later in life.

People don't believe me when I tell them that story. They don't believe that I can remember it in such vivid detail when I was only four. They don't believe that you took off from your house to save me without seeing me on the ladder. They think I made some kind of noise or something that you heard. Maybe. Maybe I did. All I know is that it wasn't the last time we saved each other in crazy, unknown ways, was it? People can believe it or not. But it's true. Cross my heart and hope to die, stick a hundred needles in my eye.

That's another thing, isn't it? I never had to tell you I was telling the truth. You just knew. Just like I knew when you were telling the truth. It was the same whether we lied over stupid things like who ate the last MoonPie or more serious things like wounded hearts. No matter what, we just knew. I think that's why you chose not to talk to me about some things later. So you wouldn't have to pretend to lie, and I wouldn't have to pretend not to know.

♩ ♩ ♩

The "tree house incident" is your parents' favorite story about "us" from our childhood, but it's not my mama's. Did you know that? My mama's story always starts before I was even born. Before you were even born. When I was little, she used to tell it to me daily over our breakfast cereal because I'd plead with her until she caved. I'd say, "Tell me how Jake made me," and she'd grin.

Mama would say, "Well, Marina and I met in college. We were roommates and best of friends. That's how it all really started."

And I'd roll my eyes and say, "Mama, not that part."

And she'd say, "Cami, the good things in life all have roots that start somewhere else."

You know how hard it was for me to sit still when I was little. Even now, it still is. But I'd try my best because I knew the good part was coming. The part with you in it. I'd sit with my spoon waggling around and my foot going crazy kicking the table leg while Mama got all dreamy in her story-telling mode.

Mama would say, "When Marina and I met Jake and your daddies, it could have all gone south, but it didn't. We all got along so well that it was just meant to be." I didn't get that when I was little, but I guess it could truly have gone haywire right then because sometimes couples just don't get along, right? We certainly haven't liked all of each other's boyfriends and girlfriends. So, I guess it was meant to be that our daddies were as keen on each other as our mamas.

"Mama, tell me the part about Jake making me!" I'd demand, squirming in my seat, torn between wanting to hear the rest of the story and wanting to be done so that I could go find you. Mama would just smile her knowing smile at me.

"We were really lucky when we went to buy our first houses that there were these two beautiful places sitting right next to each other," she'd start again.

"Because now Jake and I get to play together in one big yard," I'd roll my eyes at her again, but she'd just smile. Making me be patient. That's Mama. She never gave in to me. Still doesn't.

"And it was just the kind of town we wanted to raise our children in. Enough country left to be part of Tennessee, but big enough for your daddies to make a living selling cars." And I guess we were lucky that they'd put down roots in a place that allowed us to run wild in the country mud and then visit a mall all within the same fifteen minutes.

"As the first child to come along, Jake was a big deal, you know. Marina and Scott named him Jake Carter Phillips with the Carter being after your daddy."

"Mama!" I'd kick the table leg harder and more incessantly.

"Sweet tea and stories both take time, Camdyn."

In the home movies from that time, you were the hit of both families. You were this dark-haired beauty with kaleidoscope hazel eyes that were always more green than brown. I know, you'd razz me again for calling you a beauty, but you were. Even then. Like some gift that the gods laid down on Earth to torture us mere mortals with. You wouldn't disagree with that, would you? You'd called yourself a god more than once in our life. Your mama even punished you once for it… focus, Cam. Save that story for later.

Back to Mama's story… "Jake was a big deal for your daddies because as soon as he started throwing that football of his, it was always straight as an arrow and right on target.

It was like some tall tale legend come to life, but Jake was a big deal for me because…"

"—he made me!" I'd interrupt, and mama would laugh.

"I was lying on the couch, that one right over there, sadder than I'd ever been," she'd go on.

When she first started telling me this story, I'd stop her to ask why she was sad. Later, I knew it was because she'd lost a baby before me, so I didn't even breathe a word because I didn't want to hear about her or the lost baby. I wanted to hear about you.

"That dreamy little boy came over, laid his tiny hands on my tummy and said, 'Drea. You be happy real soon.' And he was right. It wasn't even two weeks later that I found out I was pregnant with you. That Jake, he must have willed you into existence."

And just like "Mary's Song" gets stuck in my head, that picture of you gets stuck in my head too, because you'd always been like that: able to will things into existence like my mama swears you willed me into being. You were smooth as the lake on a still day even at two. So, how was any young girl ever going to keep from giving you their heart when you grew up into a muscled, dark-haired football hero with a sharp wit and a super-sized batch of kindness?

I always asked my mama the same question at this point. I asked, "And how'd you know I was a girl?"

Mama would wink at me and lean in real conspiratorial like, her brown eyes twinkling. "Well, that would be Jake again. One day he felt you kicking in my tummy, and he simply said, 'That baby girl can't wait to meet me,' and so we all knew it was true. You were a girl."

Swear to God that's what my mama has always told me you said. My parents didn't even come up with a boy name. I guess you were waiting for me then just like I had to wait for you later. And three years and two weeks after you were born, I came along. Camdyn Marina Swayne. My middle name, Marina, being after your mama.

From that moment in my mama's stomach, when you said I was waiting to meet you, I was always waiting to meet you. Always waiting for your mosaic eyes to light upon me. It felt like that was the only time I ever was truly alive... when you were watching me.

Some kids do crazy stunts to get their parents' attention, but the only person whose attention I ever wanted was yours. Did you realize that? Or did you just tolerate the crazy neighbor kid who couldn't seem to leave your side? I don't think you minded. I think we were always meant to be together. Remember, I could tell when you were lying.

Anyway, everything I did, from my very first memory, was in order to get you to look at me, laugh at me, or just sit next to me. The first time I actively remember using my wily ways to get your attention must have been right around the same time as the "tree house incident." We were eating Popsicles out on the steps of your parents' porch, licking the gooey sweetness faster than a dog at a water bowl, when I realized that you had your eyes on the boys playing football on the street. I knew that as soon as you were done, you were going to be off that step and on the street with them.

Even as young as you were, the boys in the neighborhood loved it when you threw the ball to them.

You were destined to have a football in your hands at all times. And, even though later I would be an absolute tomboy, footballs and my hands were always like north poles of magnets trying to come together. That was one game that I just couldn't ever really play.

At that moment, all I knew was that I didn't want you out on the street with the boys. I wanted you with me. So, what did I do? Well, I just put my sticky little hand into yours and squeezed so hard that you exclaimed, "Cam!"

That drew our daddies' attention. My daddy winked at yours and said, "Look at those two, stuck like glue. Someday we'll be griping about the cost of a white wedding!"

Your daddy chuckled, but our mamas, swaying on the porch swing, looked down and saw two dirty, sticky messes and just rolled their eyes. "Don't be wishing any such thing," my mama scolded, but my daddy was still grinning.

You pulled me up and said with disgust, "Let's get another Popsicle."

But you know what? You didn't drop my hand, not even though you were seven and grossed out by girls. Instead, you held it all the way into the house to the freezer where we stood for a long time cooling off before we raided it again with those sticky, dirty hands.

It wasn't until after eighth grade, when your life changed, that you'd say to me, "I'm never getting married or having kids, Cami. I wouldn't do this to another kid." And I'd know that you were serious because you only called me Cami when you really wanted to make sure I was paying attention. And you never, ever called me Camdyn. Only that once. God... Did you realize that? Did you do it on purpose? I'm almost sure you didn't. It doesn't matter, I was always Cam. And I liked it that way because I fit in with the boys that way. Cami was a girl name. Cam... well that was just me. Me with you.

As we grew up, and even after your little sister came along two years after me, it was mostly you and I playing together. You didn't seem as interested in her. Poor Mia. Mia Andrea Phillips with the Andrea after my mama. Mia was always such a good kid, and later, a good friend to me when you were away.

One of the reasons we were together so much was because your mama looked after me while my mama was working at the hospital and our daddies were at the car dealership. As a website designer, your mama could do her work and bake chocolate chip cookies all at the same time. Even then, your home was my home. Sometimes my memories are so blended together that I can't remember whose house things happened in.

It didn't matter to me whose house we were at as long as we were together; which is also probably why I hated school so much, especially before I started kindergarten, because you went away for the majority of the day. I think I was at my worst then. Well... maybe not. I can think of some times later when I was worse. Your poor mama! Only the good Lord knows how she put up with me as she did. I can remember her chasing me down the block on more than one occasion. When she'd catch me, she'd always say, "Where do you think you're going young lady?"

I'd look at her as if she was an ogre, and I'd always say, "I'm goin' with Jake."

She'd laugh, and pick me up, kicking and screaming. "Someday, young lady, you'll have another young man you're following, and all I can say is, have mercy on his soul."

It's astounding that Marina and my mama didn't agree to lock me in a closet during the day. I was bitter, grumpy, and mean. But once you came home, I was all sweet smiles.

We'd find ourselves on your bed tucked up liked two 'possums. You'd read me whatever silly book that your first or second grade teacher would send home with you or I'd hold the flash cards up for you to practice your math facts. It didn't matter to me what I was doing as long as I was doing it with you.

Once you were done with your homework, we'd be out on the street riding our bikes, playing tag, having mud fights, and, basically, finding anything and everything to get us dirty. Now that I'm grown up, and I think of all the wackos that live out there preying off young kids, I'm surprised our mamas let us take off like that. But our community felt safe. Our street felt safe. And when I was with you, I was always safe. Whenever I got hurt, there you were, with an arm around me and that heavenly scent of yours, like warm chocolate cookies and boy. Like home.

The boys on the block came along with us a lot. At least, that's how I thought of it: them with us. I think they thought of it as some annoying little brat they had to drag with them. You didn't. One time Paul Lambert found me tagging after you, and he said, "Cripes, Jake, did you have to bring the baby with you? We're hunting 'coons after all!"

And do you remember what you did? You punched him so hard in the gut that he landed in the mud of the creek bed.

Everyone just stared at him and you and me for a long time. Then you turned and headed down the creek, and I followed, but not before sticking my tongue out at Paul. No one ever complained about me again, at least not when I was around. Someday, you'd punch Paul over me again, but for a different reason. I promise, I'll stay focused and save that story too.

When I finally did get to go to school, I didn't hate it quite as much because at least we'd walk together and sometimes I'd see you at lunch… and I'd find other ways to be with you. But still, school was never my favorite place. My poor mama and daddy got called down to the school quite a bit because of my focus issues. And anger issues. Especially if I knew you were outside at recess, and I was still inside.

"Mrs. Morris, I have to go to the bathroom," I'd say to my first-grade teacher, and she'd size up the desperate nature of my pee need. So, I'd squirm and hold my privates as if it was going to burst.

As soon as she relented, I'd be out the door and on the playground finding you. You were usually on the field, throwing a football, or, less frequently, on the basketball court. I'd jump right into the middle of whatever you were doing, and all the fourth-grade boys would roll their eyes, but no one would say anything derogatory. Not after you'd punched your best friend over me.

"Jake, your little friend is here again." You'd look at me and smile, and I'd feel like I was home.

"What'd you say this time?" you'd ask me, eyes flashing with as much of a smile as your lips.

"Pee break."

You'd rub my hair and put your arm around my neck and drag me back to class. Sometimes, you'd even grab my hand even with the boys looking on. When you got to my class, you'd look at my pretty first-grade teacher and say with your feather smoothing smile, "So sorry, ma'am. I promise it won't happen again."

But Mrs. Morris knew better. I swear sometimes she let me go because she knew I wouldn't stop until I'd seen you. She may be the only teacher who ever understood that, so, "Thanks, Mrs. Morris, wherever you are!"

After school, I always went to your house. Some kids remember their mama or daddy helping them to write their name, but for me, it was you. Sometimes I wonder why you didn't ever put up a stink about it. Why'd you help the five-year-old neighbor kid long after your own homework should have been done? It's still an unsolved mystery to me.

Am I painting you like some sort of angelic savior? Probably. But to a kid three years younger than you, you pretty much were. I know. I know. If you were reading this, you'd probably toss something at me—probably a football— and call me a liar because you weren't perfect. There were lots of times, especially as we got older, that it seemed you were downright mean to me. Cruel. But I know you didn't intend it to be that way. It was just more difficult later. There were more expectations of how we should be together. Or not be together.

You'd probably also remind me that I was always the first one to criticize you, the first one to spot your weaknesses and imperfections. I could always tell when your throws were off, or when you'd missed an opening that cost a touchdown, and I'd tell you to your face. Just like I'd tell you, bluntly, that you'd strung the fishing pole wrong or that your hair was too long. I was never afraid to tell you that you were wrong. Or an idiot. Which you could be sometimes.

You hated math facts. You'd get so frustrated while memorizing them that you'd throw the flash cards at me. And what would I do? I'd just pick them up, shove them in your face and say, "Go ahead, be a butthead, doesn't bother me." And I'd just wait for you to say the math fact. So, no, you weren't perfect, but you were mine. At least, that's how I considered it when we were little.

And even though I hated it when you'd play football because it was a game I didn't play, I was an unremitting coach and referee when you did play. Do you remember the first time you and Wade, a boy two years older than you, got into it about whether a catch had been made in bounds? You were right in each other's faces and were a breath away from going to blows when I slammed the ball out of your hands, which wasn't an easy thing to do, and said, "It was out of bounds, idiot. Third down."

Wade smirked because I'd called in his favor. Your mosaic eyes regarded me as if you wanted to toss me into the creek, but I cut you off.

"One word, and I'll kick your ass out of the game," and I put my hands on my hips daring you to argue with me.

That made you grin, and you ruffled my hair as you walked away, calling back, "Don't swear!" After that, everyone always listened to the six-year-old referee. I was the official game caller because everyone knew I'd call it fair… even if it was against you.

So, I guess instead of responding with "Mary's Song," I could tell people all of this. But who would want to listen to all of that when it's so much easier to listen to that Taylor Swift song and know just exactly how we knew each other? It doesn't say it all, but it gets close. And maybe it would have stayed even closer to that if you hadn't gone ahead and got hormones before I did. In any event, for a long while, we went to school together, did homework together, played together, often ate together, and many, many nights my parents had to come pick me up off your bed where we'd fallen asleep together.

You know that other country song by Tim McGraw, the one about the boy asking the daddy not to take the girl? Well, I guess that could have been us too.

Chapter Two

I'm Only Me When I'm With You

"And sometimes we don't say a thing;

just listen to the crickets sing.

Everything I need is right here by my side."

-Swift, Orrall, Angelo

So, once people realize we've known each other since we were babies, the next question is usually something like, "But when did the two of you really, you know, hook up?" And that is a much harder question to answer because whether we were out at the lake listening to crickets, or in the tree house counting stars, we were always together. All I ever needed was you. You at my side. Even when you drove me crazy, like you were prone to do, I never wanted to be without you. It always felt like I wasn't quite myself until somehow our day brought us right next to each other again.

I guess the easier question to answer goes something like this, "When weren't you together?" That question I can answer with one godforsaken word. Hormones. That's when we weren't together. When hormones kicked in, wouldn't you agree? Your hormones first. Mine later. I swear those pesky little things are both the best and worst of people.

I first noticed yours on the way home from the creek one spring day. You and Paul were sniggering about balls. You both were having laughing fits over it, and the worms we'd just spent the afternoon catching were spilling out of our pails like escapees from the apple basket. I didn't like you messing with the bait we'd just spent hours collecting, so I punched you hard in the arm.

"Geez, Cam. That hurt." But you didn't punch back. You never did.

Paul sniggered again, "At least it wasn't in the balls."

And you were both in fits of boy laughter all over, worms escaping over the sides of the cans and all.

That night, as Mama came in to say goodnight and tuck me in the best I'd let her, I asked, "Mama, what the heck is wrong with Jake these days? He keeps talking about balls and nuts and looking at girls all funny."

My mama stared at me like I had four heads. And because she did that a lot, I didn't really think anything about it. She started to say something. Stopped. Started again. It was like she was the catfish we'd caught that night, trying to breathe air when it never knew how.

Finally, Mama burst out with that one word. "Hormones!" and when I looked puzzled, mama just kept on going. "All that's wrong with Jake is a good, old-fashioned case of adolescent hormones!"

With Mama working at the hospital, I thought hormones were a disease. "How do we fix it?" I asked calmly. This gave my mama a good chuckle. She never answered me, just shook her head and left the room. It took me a while before I realized what she'd meant. But, come to find out, part of your problem was a disease, we just didn't know that right away, did we? So, I guess for now, we'll blame it all on the hormones.

Those annoying little critters were definitely in the air the summer before you entered eighth grade. That was the summer the pool at the high school had been finished, and it was the new place to hang out if you were under fourteen. That first day we rode our bikes there, my mama loaded up that stupid pink backpack my grandmother bought me with water, snacks, sun screen, blah-blah, and made me take it with me! A PINK backpack! I still shiver at the thought.

The pink backpack was my grandmother's lame attempt to make me into a girly girl. I bet you'd think that was funny now. Someone trying to turn Cam into a girl. Well. Maybe you wouldn't laugh now. But, going into eighth grade, the thought of me being a girly girl would have made you pee your pants. Somehow my grandmother had gotten the idea that because I was going into fifth grade, I would suddenly have a desire for skirts, fancy shoes, and boobs. I didn't want any of that. I didn't want anything that was going to slow me down from keeping up with you. And at that point, that was tennis shoes, shorts, t-shirts, and messy brown ponytails.

So, what did I do when Mama handed me that pink backpack full of supplies? Well, I stomped my foot and threw this huge tantrum. "I'll just take my old backpack!"

"That revolting, wet-rat smelling thing with holes? I threw it away," Mama responded calmly.

"Well, I'm not taking that P-I-N-K one!" I stomped again with my hands on my hips. She met my furious look with a tranquil one of her own. She was used to my fits of anger, but she had her hands on her hips too, so I knew she meant business as much as I did.

"If you don't take it, you don't go," she replied, leaving it on the floor by my feet. She knew I'd take it because she knew there was no way I was letting you go to the pool without me.

I sighed deeply, grabbed it, and headed out the door where I promptly got a little of my normal Cam revenge by dragging it through the dirt down our driveway. I knew that when we came home, my mama was going to be as mad as a hive of bees that's been poked at, but I didn't care. At least this way it had lost some of its pink sheen. My poor mama… I really wasn't an easy child, was I?

Where was I? Oh yeah, pool. I met you at your porch and was ready to punch you if you said something about the P-I-N-K backpack, but you didn't really notice. Instead, we grabbed our bikes, rode to the pool, paid our two dollars, and entered a brand new world. There were kids from our school all over the place. Most, parent free, like us.

"No Blake. No Wade," I said in disgust. And you didn't disagree. We knew where they were. They were at the lake. The new high school pool might entice wannabe teenagers, but all the cool high school kids still hung out at the lake. And that's where we really wanted to be.

You shrugged and tousled my hair, "At least it's somewhere wet. And… no parents."

And you were right. It was hot, sticky, and basically a normal summer in Tennessee, so we'd rather be at some sort of water than nowhere. We set up with your friends, Paul and Craig, in between the diving boards and the snack bar. My friend Wynn, who was basically the only girl at school who would put up with my craziness, came with her sister, Kayla. What a mistake that turned out to be! But when I first saw Wynn, I didn't know that. I was just super glad to see her.

Wynn wasn't quite the tomboy I was, and she was starting to get boobs and thought that was the beginning and end, but she'd still play chicken and Marco Polo and splash the boys, so it was okay. She had pretty strawberry blonde hair and pale blue eyes with this pale white skin that made me think of cupcakes, but it also meant she got sunburnt really easily, so she always smelled of sunscreen, almost year-round.

That first day at the pool, we let out all our craziness. We jumped and dove, hit balls, threw Frisbees, and basically acted like monkeys escaped from the zoo. The lifeguards yelled at us probably a million times, but never kicked us out. We splashed everyone. Not on purpose, but we were always intense and competitive when it came to any game we played, weren't we? The few grown-ups who had braved the pool with their little ones frowned and pulled their toddlers away. But we didn't care. The pool was our new kingdom, and we were set to rule it with panache.

The best thing about the pool for me ended up being the diving boards. They had two; one at five meters and another at seven and a half meters. They didn't want "little kids" like me on the high board, but I slipped up there anyway. I did all kinds of wild stunts off the boards. Paul and Craig thought I was insane, and sometimes you did too, but I think you thought the diving board was safer than anything else I'd frequently jump from.

After my first flight from the tree house, I'd been addicted to that feeling of free falling. I would do anything to just get a moment of air time. It drove you nuts. You were always saving me from jumping off the roofs of cars, beds of trucks, the shed, a tire swing, whatever would give me a few seconds of that floating feeling. You must have thought I was a pain in the ass more than once, but you never showed it to me back then. Not when we were little.

The lifeguards must have realized I could handle it too because after the first few times of screaming at me, they'd just shrug and let me go. That moment, me on the diving board, was life changing. It started something really good which probably kept me sane during our teenage years and the angst I went through over you… the angst that started, ironically enough, also at the pool.

I had just gotten out of the water after one particularly kick-ass stunt, and Paul and Craig were clapping me on the back when I noticed you weren't there to critique me. It seemed you hadn't watched my dive at all. I thought maybe you'd gone to the bathroom or to the snack bar, but you hadn't. You were still there, you just weren't watching me. And, of course, that made my stomach turn as if I'd eaten bad sushi.

Who were you watching? You were watching Kayla. Well, really you were watching her boobs. No way, you'd say, right? But you'd grin, like you always did when you knew I was razzing you about something true. Let's face it, boobs were still pretty much all eighth-grade boys could think about, and Kayla's very tan pair were barely covered by her teeny tiny pink bikini. P-I-N-K! Pink! Ugh! I already hated pink, so you can imagine how I felt about the color after that.

Kayla did not have Wynn's strawberry complexion because they weren't really related at all, completely different parents who'd wound up marrying each other. Kayla was all gorgeous, bikini-model-like blonde, and she knew it, and you'd just discovered it. You were eyeing her bikini like it was the last MoonPie and you couldn't wait to dig in.

Kayla worked that bikini well. She had her perfectly manicured hand on your arm, with her hip stuck out just so, and she was giggling at something you said while tossing back her shiny hair. And you smiled. You smiled at her so beautifully. The smile that I thought was just for me and could smooth the ruffles on the angriest wild cat… meaning me. Your smile kept dropping down to her chest which was moving as she laughed and was barely staying inside that stupid-colored bikini.

Wynn, Paul, and Craig were taunting me to go back and try my backflip off the board again because they didn't think I could repeat its greatness, but I was lost in that moment with you staring at Wynn's stunning sister while I was left on the side of the pool, wet as a seal, in board shorts and a one piece. With no boobs. And no shiny blonde hair. Mine was dark brown. Kind of mousy, but after the summer, it would have enough reddish highlights to be classified as chestnut, but no way was it the blonde perfection of Kayla's. And my gray eyes? Well, they paled into insignificance against her bright, clear sky blue ones.

Everything went perfectly still, like when you're under the water. The sounds were muffled and things were in slow motion as I walked towards the two of you. You didn't raise your eyes from her chest to me. You didn't even register I was there. You hadn't seen my backflip. You didn't know how great it had been. My insides twisted faster and faster. So, without thinking, which is what always got me into trouble, I stuck out my hand and pushed Kayla into the pool as I walked by.

You started laughing. You were, after all, a teenage boy. You weren't even mad. But after one little glance in my direction, you turned back to the pool to where Kayla had emerged from underneath the water. She was mad enough for both of you. Her hair was flattened to her head, and she had mascara running down her face, but you held out your hand to her and easily lifted her up with all your muscled boy-ness. I wanted to scream. I crossed my hands over my non-existent chest and just watched, realizing my mistake as soon as her pink-toenailed feet hit the sidewalk because now you couldn't keep your eyes off her pale pink bikini top or bottom because they were both very, very see-through.

"Oh my God, you are such a freak!" Kayla yelled at me. She pushed my shoulder, and you didn't come to my defense like you normally would. You were mesmerized by the sight of the dark hair through her bikini bottom.

Wynn had hurried up to the two of us, and she realized just as I had why your eyes were basically popping out of your head. I looked Kayla up and down as best I could even though I was a good couple inches shorter than her and replied snottily, "At least I'm not showing everything I own to the entire town."

"Jesus, Cami!" Wynn breathed out in a frustrated voice. Kayla looked down at herself and turned about five different shades of red. Wynn shoved Kayla's matching pink cover-up at her. She scrambled into it and couldn't look at you again which made me happy. For the moment.

"We're leaving, Wynn," Kayla said in a haughty tone that only big sisters and mamas seem to be able to perfect. "You can thank your mutant friend for spoiling our day."

Kayla stomped over to pick up the rest of her things and shoved them in her designer bag before storming out of the pool area. Wynn wasn't happy. So, I was already feeling contrite. My only girl friend was really pissed off at me.

"I'm sorry, Wynn."

"I just don't understand you sometimes," was all she said as she followed Kayla out. It wasn't the last time Wynn would say that to me. Truth was, sometimes I didn't understand me either. I couldn't tell you why I did the spontaneous stuff I did. It was just my body working faster than my brain.

When I turned to you, I thought you'd be just as angry at me as Wynn was, but you were still beaming like you'd made a touchdown. You put your arm around me and rubbed my hair in that way that always sent tingles from my scalp to my toes. "Thanks for that, Cam. I owe you big time."

And that's when I found out quick enough that the pool was my enemy, at least, where you were concerned. That was the first day you found out that your godlike status had moved from the football-boy world to the girl world.

Ugh! See! Hormones. On the bike ride home, all you, Paul, and Craig could talk about was Kayla Nichols in her see-through bikini. I'd just given you the gift of porn and didn't know it. What I did know was that we had to get out of that stupid pool and into the lake, but I just didn't know how to make it happen. It took care of itself after just a few weeks, but I didn't know that, that day.

I refused to go with you to your house when we got there. It didn't register to you why. You still had Paul and Craig with you and probably needed to go lock yourselves in the bathroom in your house. Who knew? I didn't want to think about it. I heard you all talk about stuff you shouldn't be talking about in front of me, but I didn't really want to imagine any of it. Made me a little nauseous, really, at the age of ten.

That was the first day that I really started to look at myself not just as a kid, but as a GIRL. I went home and stood staring into my mirrored closet door. And what I saw was a tomboy in a one-piece bathing suit with buds for breasts. They were there, coming in, but they weren't the mounds that Kayla had. And I'd started to get hair in places I didn't want to think about and kind of grossed me out, but even if I'd worn Kayla's bikini, there wouldn't have been anything to see when it got wet. At the moment, all I knew was that I hated Kayla for being able to keep your attention. Not that I wanted a pale pink bikini. It wouldn't have withstood the dives that I wanted to do from the seven-meter platform, but I realized then that you liked girls and for the first time I realized that you wanted girls in a way you didn't want me.

I pounded my pillow so hard that night that it burst on one end, showering my room with downy feathers that felt like my reality coming apart. I didn't know how to fit into that new world you were suddenly fascinated with like a cat is to a laser. I thought of my grandma and her pink backpack she'd given me. I could start right then being a girly girl if I wanted, but I knew that would exclude me from another part of your life. The part you still lived in more: the boy part. The riding bikes, fishing, hiking, football-playing part that I was much more comfortable being in.

The next day, I was quiet on our way to the pool. You still didn't notice. You, Paul, and Craig were wondering what kind of bathing suit Kayla would be in today. Still snickering and all boy talk. When we got off our bikes, I punched your shoulder like I always did when it was difficult to get your attention.

"What the hell, Cam?"

"If you'd get your head away from your jockstrap for five minutes, you'd realize that I'm still beating you two to one at the 100 butterfly. Don't you think that's a hell of a lot more important than a bikini?"

"Jesus, Cam. Don't talk like that," you said and then just stared at me.

I crossed my arms over my non-existent chest. Cussing was a big thing with you and your boys now that you were in middle school. It was like you'd crossed some invisible line into what you thought manhood was all about. But if I cussed or repeated any of your gross boy comments, you hated it.

"So, you're wussing out on me? I can declare myself swim champ this year? Sounds awesome! Guess you'll be the one shoveling poop for a month, because that was our bet. Winner gets a month off poop duty. And remember, my dog's twice the size of yours, so there's a lot of it in our yard."

You narrowed your eyes at me. I'd caught your attention. "No way in hell am I on poop duty." Your voice was deep and challenging. My spine tingled. I'd gotten you back even if it was for just a few seconds.

It didn't last long. I lost you again when we went inside. The three of you were surrounded by pretty faces. Kayla, her equally blonde friend, Brittney, and their horde of girly friends flocked to you. They liked to ooh and ahh and toss their hair at the three gorgeous boys of summer. Especially you. You were a tanned summer god who could play football, flex strong muscles, and show off washboard abs that you didn't even have to work at getting. Paul and Craig were pretty too. But everyone knew you were the real god.

You stood about two inches taller than Craig and had a smile that lit up a room. And your eyes! Those mosaics that flashed and laughed and made a girl feel like they were the only one that mattered. And you were nice. Paul and Craig were pretty crass. You were smooth like ice cream. You'd always been. You'd practiced on my mama.

I got in the pool, and Wynn was quickly at my side. I'd called last night to apologize. She'd said, "I know you think Jake's yours, but what eighth grader is going to pick a fifth grader to be his girlfriend?" I hadn't argued. I didn't tell Wynn that I didn't want to be your girlfriend. The thought of kissing you at that point made me want to eat a lightning bug. But I also knew that I didn't want you kissing Kayla Nichols.

"Hey, pretty boy, you ever gonna get in the pool or shall I just race undefeated?" I shouted out at you.

You dove in so fast it splashed all the girls. They screamed their high-pitched girly screams, but couldn't stop smiling at you anyway. It was like a herd of boy band fans. When you reached me, you dunked me under the water. I couldn't really put up much of a fight. You were bigger and stronger than me. I didn't really want to fight. You were mine again, if only for the length of the pool.

I came up spurting but grinning just in time to hear you tell Wynn to call start. I barely had time to catch a breath and get into position before she screamed go. I raced alongside you. You were bigger and stronger, but the water and I had a certain relationship that you didn't. The water seemed to move me forward like a surfer on top of the waves. You had to fight it. In the end, you still won that match.

When we got back to the start, we had parents screaming at us because we'd knocked little kids out of the way and the lifeguard came and told us to take it easy. But you were grinning at me. At me! So, everything was right in my world. They could have told me that we were banned for life, and it wouldn't have mattered.

Your gaze didn't stay with me for long though. Every time you came up for air, the girls surrounded you. That's when I gave them their name. The gaggle of geese. Flocking around you like birds to seed. Stupid, white, pretty birds. Mean. But pretty. Geese are mean. You ever noticed that? They'll chase after you and bite you even if you're feeding them. Plus, the sound was just like a gaggle. Loud, obnoxious, and never shut up.

That day, Paul and Craig didn't even bother joining our races. They usually did even though neither of them could kick either of our asses. Maybe that's why. Paul nor Craig wanted to get shown up by a little girl in front of the gaggle. Plus, let's face it, they loved the girl attention.

That night on the bike ride home, I brought the whole pool issue up.

"We're never going to finish our races at the pool. The lifeguards are yelling at us constantly, the parents are whiny, and the girls won't stop touching you."

You grinned at me. You were enjoying your newfound super power. Football may still be number one, smooth talking number two, but now girl magnet was number three. "I know. I'm a king among men, what can I say?"

I reached out and pushed your shoulder causing you to nearly swerve your bike into the fence. You just laughed at me.

"We need to go to the lake to get some peace and quiet."

You turned serious. Probably because you knew that once I got a burr up my derriere, I never let it go until I got what I wanted. "Our parents will kill us if they find out we've gone to the lake," you reminded me.

"Who's gonna tell? At least we won't be bothered by your gaggle of geese in their itty-bitty bikinis."

You were all smiles again. It had really gone to your head. Admit it. That summer you were all ego. Well, not just that summer, for several summers!

"They'll get used to seeing me in all my suntanned glory and back off," you said. I probably could have reached out and touched your ego that day.

I shrugged, doubting that they'd ever leave you alone. Geese didn't leave the bread sitting there. They tore it to shreds. They fought over it viciously and the winner got the remains. I wasn't sure I liked the thought of you being the remains. And I certainly didn't want to be left with the crumbs of you.

Over the next couple weeks, it was more of the same. We hardly got to swim, we were behind on our racing goal for the summer, and I was in the lead in the poop bet. Finally— thankfully— you grew a little tired of the attention. I mean, it was good to be flirted with and touched, but they were also a little light in the conversational category. They talked shoes and TV dramas and who had kissed who. You wanted to talk football and NASCAR and, well, the who had kissed who was okay. So, we hatched a plan with Paul and Craig to go to the lake instead of the pool.

Our parents would have skinned us alive and hung us out to dry if they'd known what we were doing. Unsupervised lake? With the teenagers there partying and whooping it up? Well, it wasn't exactly a parent's dream come true, was it?

For me, that first day at the lake was magical. The high school kids didn't hit the lake till later in the day. Maybe they were sleeping off their hangovers or making plans for that night, who knows, but they weren't there till the afternoon. And the lake wasn't really big enough to attract serious boaters or water-skiers. So, all in all, it was pretty quiet.

We were a lot farther from town and our houses, but it was all good. We had your cell phone in case of emergencies, but we'd almost die before we used it and have our parents find out. We didn't want to ruin a good thing.

The lake had a warm breeze and the smell of the trees and flowers. One hundred and ten percent better than the chlorine, suntan lotion, and hot dog stench at the pool. We measured the distance across at the short end and had our new racing grounds. We didn't have Wynn. I missed that a little. Just a little. But there was no way I wanted Wynn to know where we were and bring the flock of gaggling girl geese with her. Plus, Wynn would probably say something to her mama, and it would all be over because then my mama would know. Wynn wasn't the best secret keeper in the world back then.

We raced all day. Hardly used sunscreen. Ate lunch on the shore. And we didn't have to fight with babies, parents, or lifeguards. It was a little piece of heaven. You beat me every single race that day, and yet I was still smiling. I told you that it was because you weren't distracted by boobs. You laughed and ruffled my hair, but didn't disagree.

We were both starving by the time we left at almost six o'clock. We'd eaten everything we'd brought with us by about one. When we were at the pool, you were constantly back and forth to the snack bar, so we'd never really gone hungry. That day you acted cranky and a little disoriented on the way home. I had to keep you from making a couple wrong turns down the dirt roads, and you growled at me like my dog, Sparky, when the cable guy came to our house.

When we got home, dinner was waiting on your table, and we scarfed it down like we hadn't eaten in a week. As soon as you had food, you perked right back up. When I made a couple wisecracks about your GPS failing you, you looked at me funny like you didn't even know what I was talking about. Even in my stupid ten-year-old brain, that seemed strange.

So, I just started packing lots of extra food. Energy bars, bananas, extra sandwiches, and Gatorades. I don't think I really realized that anything serious was wrong with you. I just thought you'd been super hungry. My mama thought I was trying to save money and was all smiles. If she'd known I didn't give a rat's patootie about the money, that I just wanted to keep you from being cranky with me, she might have been a little more hesitant to send me off with such a pile.

Slowly, as the summer got hotter, the lake got busier earlier in the day. More teenagers came bringing their music and beer. Most of them left us alone because, even as middle schoolers, you and your boys seemed like kids to them. But a few of them, Wade and Blake especially, because they were the ones who played football with you on our block, began to watch our races. And even participate. It became a new adventure. They hated being beaten by a "little" girl. But I was quick as lightning in the water. I didn't always win, but I came close, and sometimes I did win.

Unfortunately, they also brought their girlfriends with them. That was a distraction for you again because these girls had more curves than the wannabes at the pool had.

They were also a lot more experienced, and better at flirting, and you were the god you were even at thirteen. The only good thing is that the lionesses weren't really interested in a man-cub, even though you were the god you were.

But you were interested. Or rather, your hormones were. One day, while you were particularly distracted by the music wafting from Wade's car and the teenage girls in their short-shorts and bikini tops dancing around full of alcohol, I was left alone longer than I could stand. I got angrier than a bull stabbed in its… well… that would be more boy humor. I'd gone from competing with a gaggle of geese to a group of lionesses. And if the geese outshone me, the lionesses might as well have eaten me alive, the little grasshopper I was.

So, that day, while you were honing in on your flirtation skills, I was alone, with no kaleidoscope eyes watching me. And I only felt alive with you or when I was in the air. So… that left me eye-balling the cliff hanging over the lake. It seemed to be a little higher than the seven and half meter board at the pool, but to me, that just added to the challenge and excitement. It would mean I'd be in the air for longer.

I left you on the beach, found my way barefooted through the trees, up the cliffside and out onto the edge. I looked down into the water and could feel the breeze on me already. It was a hot, sticky breeze, but I knew it would lift me up and away, and for three seconds I'd feel as if you were watching m,e whether you were or not.

I closed my eyes and pictured the dive. I just wanted a forward pike with a twist. At that point, I didn't know what the move was called. I just could picture in my head what I wanted my body to do.

I pushed off the edge, and just as I felt my feet leave the ground, I heard you. That inner sense of yours had tuned in at the last minute, and you screamed, "Cami! Nooooo!"

But it was too late. I was already rotating through the air, feeling alive and feeling the breeze. I unfolded, arms first into the water. I took my time coming up to the surface, and when I did, you had swum out to me. You grabbed my shoulders and shook me so hard my eyeballs rattled.

"What the hell were you thinking?!"

"You're hurting me," I said as you pushed your fingers harder into my arms and continued to shake.

"You God damn fool!"

I looked up at you feeling alive from my dive. Alive from your eyes on me. I'm sure I was all smiles. I felt right down to my bones that it had been a damn good dive. But you weren't interested in critiquing my dive at all. You were all rant and no rave.

"You can't dive here at the lake! You don't know how low it is or what the hell is under the water. You could have broken your neck. You could be dead!"

You were raging, and your fingers were still digging into me, and I still didn't care.

Blake swam out to join us. "She okay?"

"I'm fine!" I said with a grin the size of Texas on my face.

You were still glaring at me, and Blake noticed the whiteness of your fingers pressed into my skin. He reached out and tore your fingers from my arms.

"Dude. You're gonna leave a mark. Let her go. She's okay. She's Super Girl."

You released me, but then you brought me up against your chest and hugged me so tight, like you had when you'd caught me flying from the tree house ladder. Your chin rested on top of my head. This time, I definitely didn't push you away. Instead, I let my hands wrap around you as you held onto me like you'd never let me go. And I was lost. That was the only place I could ever call home. Ever.

We stayed late at the lake that night. Wade and Blake had brought their tiny barbeque out with them and cooked burgers, and we'd even gotten permission to stay out with them. Well…our parents thought we were "going to the lake with them," not "staying at the lake with them." Paul and Craig had to go home. Gee, darn. So, it was just you and I and the rest of the teenagers.

After we'd eaten, Blake brought out his guitar and started dazzling the ladies with his country rock music, which didn't sound too bad, but what did I know? I couldn't carry a tune any more than I could throw a football. Anyway, the lionesses were otherwise engaged, and you and I went over to our favorite tree. The one that looked like it was holding its arms up to the sky in a victory dance. We lay down on the grass below it. The sun went down, and the lightning bugs came out. The air smelled like summer. But all I could smell was you. The sweaty boy smell that somehow didn't disgust me at all. It smelled like grass and earth and summer and cookies.

You put your hands behind your head, and I laid my head on your inner arm. We stared at the stars as they started to sprinkle the sky almost as if the lightning bugs buzzing through the grass had been caught up in the great beyond. We were quiet for a long, long time. Finally, you broke our silence.

"You have to promise me, you won't do that again, Cami." You said it in your voice that had changed to its deep, deep ember over the summer. I knew you were serious because you called me Cami. So, I just nodded, my heart in my throat.

"I mean it. I don't know what I'd do if something happened to you." I couldn't have responded if I wanted to because, at ten, I didn't even begin to understand the flood of emotion those words gave to my body just beginning its own hormone overdrive.

"Let me hear you say it," you said while never looking at me, just looking at the sky as it turned from gray to midnight blue.

"I promise I won't dive off the cliff again," I said quietly. Solemnly. And you knew I was telling the truth because I never broke promises to you. And right then, I had no intention of breaking that promise. But later on, that was a different story. And I guess that story is for later.

Blake ruined the moment when he called out to us, "Come on lovebirds, time to pack it in."

"You're perverted, Blake," you hollered back as you pulled me to my feet. And I guess to you, at thirteen, that did seem perverted. As if you'd think twice about a ten-year-old whose boobs had barely started to form.

But I took off so fast towards Blake that you started teasing me on the ride home in the back of his pickup truck about having a crush on him. And sure, Blake's shaggy blonde hair and baby face was on top of a really built body, but I wasn't interested in him. There was only one boy I'd ever be interested in. And right then, his mosaic eyes were looking at me with laughter. What more could a girl want?

At our houses, Blake stopped long enough for you to lift me off the tailgate and holler, "Adios, Super Girl," before tearing off the down the street. I winced as your hands touched my bruised arms from earlier, and the wince didn't escape your notice even though I tried to play it off.

"I'm sorry I hurt you," you said with emotion in your voice.

"I'm sorry you did too," I said back. You hugged me one more time. Just a one armed, sideways hug before letting me go and ruffling my hair. We headed to our respective porches. I stopped with my hand on the doorknob when your voice called out to me.

"Cam."

"Yeah?"

"It was a really beautiful dive."

I was all smiles when I walked through the door because I knew that, no matter what happened, you would always understand what drove me.

Chapter Three

Stay Beautiful

"There's pretty girls on every corner
That watch him as he's walking home."
- Swift & Rose

The gaggle of geese must have sung "Stay Beautiful" about you as much as I did. It's that song that talks about the boy with the jungle eyes and music smiles that all the girls watch as he goes by. The gaggle quickly realized what I'd always known: that you were beautiful—inside and out. And on top of that, you were going to be a superstar. And while all the girls were daydreaming about you, somehow, over the summer, my dreams slowly started to change too. When we'd begun the summer at the pool, I hadn't really wanted you in a boy-girl sort of way. I just didn't want anyone else to have you. But eventually, I realized that there was more to it than that.

While life was bringing me a little more into focus as a girl, I still had bumps for breasts, and hips that seemed to be there but not really. I didn't know it then, but I was not ever destined to be a "curvy" girl. And truth was, I wasn't even comfortable with the little curve that was there. Even though I knew that you still couldn't keep your eyes off Kayla and her friends' bumps and curves, I couldn't imagine you seeing mine.

♫ ♫ ♫

Somehow, our parents found out about the lake, and weren't even mad. They just made sure you had your cell phone, and that I loaded us up with supplies. So, with the blessing of parents, more and more of the gaggle of geese made their way to the lake too. As if almost being eighth graders somehow made them adults. They weren't. They liked to think they were though. I guess I'd understand that in three years, when I was in eighth grade and wanted you to see me as the adult that I wasn't.

We still split our time between the lake and the pool, though, because you wouldn't let me dive at the lake, and I had gotten bitten by the diving bug. It was kind of nice to keep the gaggle on their toes. Where was Jake going to be? We could escape for a portion of the time from the girls who thought that you were a piece of apple pie and couldn't get enough. Bad thing was that I couldn't have Wynn there if I didn't want Kayla there.

But you and Kayla had become a thing, sort of. Kayla had lots of things because she and her friend, Brittney, were the queen bees of middle school. Lovely, popular, but with a mean side that could twist a knife in anyone with words said with a smile. Not to you, of course. To you, they were like sweet tea on a hot day.

It was okay. I learned to put up with the flock of gaggling geese as long as they weren't yet lionesses. I got to dive when we were at the pool. And that kept me alive inside while you were flirting with the girls, draping your arm around their shoulders, and tossing them playfully into the water, only to pull them up and rescue them from their damsel-in-distress calls. It was all a little sickening. Even Wynn thought so, and she was all girl.

One day, I caught you kissing Kayla behind our tree. I was looking for you to start our 100 freestyle, and there you were with one arm around her waist and the other behind her head to protect it from the gnarly tree bark. I saw a flick of tongue, and she pressed her bikini covered breasts into your bare chest. I just stared for a moment, like I was caught watching a movie that I didn't want to see the ending to, but couldn't turn away from.

She opened her eyes and saw me. She pushed you away. "We've got company. Your kid sister is here."

She sauntered by me with a snarky smile. "Freak," she whispered as she went by. It was all I could do to keep from sticking my leg out and tripping her, but you hated it when I was mean to your gaggle. So, I restrained myself. I was learning restraint because you were teaching it to me. My parents should have paid you money for teaching me something they never had succeeded at.

I pretended to puke as you joined me. "Do you have to ruin our tree by stinking it up with your skanky love motions?"

You were one big beaming smile, and you ruffled my hair, but your eyes were on Kayla's ass. I sighed. A deep, disgusted sigh. You chuckled.

"You'll get it. Give yourself three years, and you'll be Kayla with some boy kissing you by the tree."

You pushed my shoulder with yours. I was ready for it and pushed back. The pushing match turned into a wrestling match. It wasn't really a fair fight. I mean, I was strong. Strong for a girl because I was in super good shape. After all, I had to be able to keep up with you and your boys. But you were still three years older, and all muscled football player.

So, the result was me in the mud by the lake with you straddling me with my wrists caught in your hands. Okay. I may have been just a kid, but wowie, wow, wow was that enough to make my hormones and insides go boom, boom, boom. You were your normal, gorgeous self. Tall, dark, muscled and grinning like you'd won the kingdom with your lance.

Kayla caught sight of us, you tickling me while I was held in the mud, and she smiled her fake little smile before calling out. "God, Jake, I'm not letting you touch me now with all that mud on you."

It worked like a charm. You were off of me and after her in a flash. Trying to catch her to share your mud with her. And when you caught her, because she let you, you rubbed your body on hers, and she screamed as if she hated it, but we both knew she loved every second of it.

And in those moments, the lake was not necessarily heaven for me. You may not have seen me as your little sister, but you certainly didn't want to stick your tongue down my throat and rub your chest along my small, small, infinitesimal boobs. I just lay there in the mud by the side of the lake staring at the puffy, white clouds stretched out across the pale, blue silk.

Wynn came up and suggested we move the tubes out on the lake. We floated silently in the hazy sunshine while Kayla's playful screams and shouts reached us, breaking the quiet of the day like a dog yapping in the middle of the night.

"She's so pathetic," Wynn said with surprising repugnance. This was new. Wynn had always secretly worshipped Kayla, wanting to be the beautiful bombshell Barbie that Kayla was.

"Thanks, Wynn," I said, because you have to agree it was a nice thing for my best friend to say.

"I mean it. If I ever act that way with a boy, just go ahead and put a bullet to my head."

"It works though."

She turned her tire so she could watch your and Kayla's antics on the shore. I hated to watch. It made my guts turn in ways I could never make sense of.

"Yeah, but you know that none of the guys really respect her."

That was true too. Paul and Craig talked smack about her on our bike rides home every night, and you didn't really argue with them or discourage it. It was like you knew you could get her to do anything you wanted her to do, and that wasn't a challenge or respectable.

"They fight over her all the time," Wynn said quietly.

"Your parents?"

She nodded. "HER dad, and MY mom." There was some bitterness to it, and I realized why Wynn was no longer the worshipping stepsister. Kayla was causing problems in a home that had been stitched together and wouldn't be that hard to rip apart. We continued again in silence for a long time while she watched Kayla's drama.

The good thing about the lake was still our races. I was on poop duty last year, and I was determined not to be this year, but you and Paul had started pumping iron to get in better shape for the football season. Eighth grade was a big deal. The high school coaches were all watching you and seeing exactly what position they'd have you starting in the following year, so it was important to you. Football in Tennessee is like Coke and bubbles. Can't have one without the other.

In any event, I still didn't really stand a chance against you in the long haul, but I was still beating Craig. He wasn't a jock. I wasn't even sure why he still hung out with you two. He was into computers and video games and was constantly talking about how he was going to make the first real flying car that would be marketable to the masses.

Craig was annoying. He was like a gnat buzzing in your ear all day long. But you and Paul still hung out with him even though you were nothing alike. A lot of the times, I was stuck with him because you were off flirting. I tried to be nice. He was your friend after all, but sometimes, you just have to push a guy like that into the lake to see what reaction he'll give you. He never had one. He just dried off and moved on. What kind of guy does that?

Near the end of the summer, football practice kicked back up. I usually rode with you from the lake to practice. I'd watch from the stands and criticize everything you and the coach had done on the ride home. After all, I'd been watching you play football since I could stand.

I wasn't the only one that came to watch though. There was your gaggle. To be honest, you weren't the only cute guy on the team. Paul held his own with his Harry Stilesness and some of the other football players had mighty fine asses that drew the girls in as well.

But even though all the girls would "claim" ownership of one guy or another so that no one was stepping on their "turf," in truth, they all would have dumped that crush in a heartbeat if they thought they had a chance with you.

You threw like a god. You ran in touchdowns. You could block with one hand. And when you took off your helmet and shook out your dark, wavy locks to wink up at the stands, it was like a collective sigh went out amongst the girls sitting there. Movie reel perfect. You wouldn't even contradict me, would you? You'd just smile that self-assured smile and ruffle my hair.

Kayla had dibs on you, but I could tell her best friend, Brittney, would have tossed her panties your way in eighth grade and said to hell with Kayla. She was always watching you, even when you were with Kayla. Truth be told, she was actually prettier by far than Kayla, but not quite as obnoxious and flirty. The guys said she was a man killer. Quiet and deadly. I could see that about her. But you were interested in the flirty one. So, Brittney just stood by on the sidelines and watched with a knowing smile, as if she had looked into a crystal ball and could see the future. It made me nervous for you. And me.

♫ ♫ ♫

It was after the gaggle had started appearing to drool over you at football practice, and near the end of summer, that things started to go really haywire with you physically. There was one day that really stands out amongst the rest to me.

We'd left our bikes at home when we'd gone to football practice, and we'd just gotten rid of your gaggle and headed towards our block when it started. You were carrying most of your pads and gear. I was carrying your helmet when all of a sudden you bumped into me. At first, I thought you were just playing our little bumper car game that usually ended up in a wrestling match on the ground, but when I looked up, your eyes were all out of focus. I grabbed your arm and called your name. You looked at me, but it was with a faraway look. I sat you down on a neighbor's lawn and grabbed a Gatorade from my backpack, practically force feeding it to you. It took a while, but you came back a little.

"What the hell, Jake?"

"I'm just dizzy. Dehydrated."

But you were still slurring your words, and you were still out of it. We both knew it was more than being dehydrated. In fact, you were drinking more liquids than ever. You were always thirsty. And ever since that first day at the lake earlier in the summer, you'd been having these spells, and lately, they'd been getting worse.

"You need to tell your mama. Or my mama," I said thinking of mama's job at the hospital.

"No way. I tell anyone, and they pull me out of football make a big stink that I can't play until I'm checked out. That's bullshit. I'm fine. The Gatorade helped."

I just stared at you. I knew you weren't fine the same way you knew I wasn't fine when you'd saved me from the tree house or saw me dive off the cliff. So, I just stared. You squirmed a little, drank some more Gatorade, and then sighed at me when I was still glaring at you like a tiger eyeing its prey.

"After season. I promise," you finally said. And I knew you would keep your promise. Just like I'd kept all my promises to you. But I made a silent promise to myself that I'd have lots of food, Gatorade, water, whatever on hand just in case you needed it.

♩ ♩ ♩

You harassed me about the dirty pink backpack loaded with crap after that, but I think you did it as your way of telling me you hadn't forgotten your promise to me. Or thanking me for bringing it. Or both. I just took the pestering and moved on. Paul said it was like I was storing up for an invasion, but he was always the first to deplete my resources which pissed me off because I was saving them for you.

You and I would exchange a look during Paul's harassment that spoke volumes. I never gave up my silent vigil, watching your every move for a sign that something was wrong. Kind of like our cat, Sadie, had watched her kittens tumble about… watching to see if something bad came around.

I never gave a thought to what would happen if I wasn't there keeping watch. After all, I practically lived with you during the summer. We even spent many a night sleeping out in the tree house with Mia as our chaperone. Not that our parents would have thought we needed a chaperone. Not then. Not when even you didn't think we needed a chaperone.

I just had no notion that we'd be separated. Dinner was at my house or your house, and even with the gaggle texting you the whole time, you never shooed me away. Sometimes, when you were in the bathroom, I'd look at the text and want to throw the phone against the wall because Kayla was so obvious and stupid and full of drama. You knew it. But you liked having someone to practice kissing on.

And according to Wynn, Kayla bragged all the time about what a good kisser you were. Why wouldn't you be? You were good at everything else. It seemed only logical that the smooth as ice cream boy would be smooth as silk on the lips too. And you were. I'd find that out later. Go ahead and laugh, snicker. I know you're doing it with that knowing smile of yours. I wish I could punch your shoulder right now…

Anyway, back to the point at hand. One of the things that started chipping away at our time together came a couple weeks after that big dizzy spell, right before school started. You know what I'm talking about, right? I can tell you it in one word: Coach.

We were at the pool, and I was doing a dive from the high board. It was a particularly difficult backward twist that I hadn't quite perfected but loved doing because I felt like it kept me in the air longer. When I emerged from the water, instead of being there to criticize my move, you were talking to an older man. All I felt was relief that at least it wasn't a girl. I swam over to the poolside where you both looked down at me.

"I hear you're Cam," the older man said. I liked the look of him. He was wrinkled in a nice way, from smiling. And he had gray hair that was losing its last battle with color and would soon be white. But he didn't look too old, like my grandma on my mama's side who seemed like she was just about to step into an urn reserved for her.

He squatted down and stuck out a hand, not afraid to shake my wet one. "I'm Coach Daniels," he announced.

I looked from you to Coach and shook his hand, but I still wasn't following what was going on yet.

"Coach Daniels has a competitive dive team," you filled in the blanks for me.

"The Vikings?" I asked. I'd heard of them. I remembered you reading a little about their success in the paper. There'd been some story about this big time Olympic coach opening up a dive school, but I hadn't really paid much attention. He was still raising money to build his own facility and was using the high school pool as home base for now. But I wasn't diving for medals; I was diving for air time.

"You've heard of us?" His smile grew.

I just nodded and pulled myself fully out of the pool. He looked me over. Not in a creepy way either, but more like he was seeing where my muscles were and where they needed to be shored up.

"Cam, he loved your dive." I looked at your face and your amazing kaleidoscope eyes, and they were shooting fireworks of excitement. I didn't see you like that very often. Mostly playing football. Sometimes when we came up with some crazy stunt to punk our parents.

"Thank you?" I said questioningly because I was still a little behind on what you thought was so exciting.

"Young lady," I winced, and Coach changed tactics, "Cam. That was the best damn dive I've seen in a couple of years."

I just stared at him and then at you like you'd both lost your freakin' minds. The best dive? It had been really awful. I'd made a huge splash going into the water and my twist really hadn't been completed. I told you both that and Coach's grin just got wider and wider.

"That's amazing! Most divers your age can barely tell me the name of that dive let alone what they did wrong."

"Well, I'm not sure what the dive is called, but I can sure as hell tell you what was wrong with it."

"Cam! Don't swear," you said. I just rolled my eyes at you. You'd been swearing so much this last year that I didn't think I'd be able to keep it out of my vocabulary even if I wanted to try. Which I didn't. My mama and daddy had been called to the school three times last year because of my language, which I thought was an improvement over my lack of self-restraint, but I'd still been grounded. Homework and reading only for a week each time. I didn't care. I still got to do homework and reading with you, so what did it matter?

"I'd like to come by your house. Talk with your parents. Get you on my team," Coach told me.

"Really?" I said with genuine surprise.

"Really!" he said with a smile.

♫ ♫ ♫

So that night, Coach came by my house. You were there. Like you would have been anywhere else, right? You'd bounded into my house and read my parents the article on Coach from our local newspaper's website. Then you brought up all these Olympic stats on him and rattled off names of famous divers he'd worked with.

My parents were trying to play catch up, bewildered. "I don't understand. Where has Cami been diving?" my mama asked.

"At the pool," you and I said in unison, but our eyes met, thinking of my cliff dive.

"From the high board? Jesus, Cami. You could have gotten seriously hurt doing that," my daddy said with a sad shake of his head.

"No, sir. She's really good," you came to my defense.

So, when Coach came in, they were already a little dazzled and off-centered. And Coach completely bamboozled them. They would have been ready to hand him the keys to the house if he'd asked.

"That's settled then. I'll see you on Monday at the high school, right after school lets out?" he said.

It was then that it hit me. Right after school. Not only was school starting, and we'd be drawn apart all day for that, but now, if I was diving somewhere, it meant that I wouldn't be at your football practice. I wouldn't be able to watch for signs of dizziness or fainting or crankiness.

"Um. Thanks, but no thanks," I replied and ducked my head.

"What?" everyone in the room said at once, including you.

"I just think I have other things to do after school." But I couldn't meet anyone's eyes, especially yours.

"Like what?" mama said, eyes narrowing in on me with suspicion.

I looked up at you; my eyes begging you to understand that I couldn't leave you. Sure, I loved diving, but I could do that no matter what. If something happened to you when I wasn't watching, I'd die. And you did get it, but you didn't smile. Instead, your eyes darkened and you gave me your hard, unrelenting stare you normally reserved for your opponents on the field.

"Can I talk with Cam for a minute?" you asked. My parents just nodded, and you led me out to our backyard. Without a word, you climbed the ladder to our tree house, and I followed.

We lay down and looked out the window at the stars as the crickets made music. You didn't say anything for a really, really long time.

"You need to do this, Cami." And you used my name wrong so I knew you were serious, but I didn't care.

"No, I don't."

"If you don't do it, I'll never forgive you."

I looked over at you, and you were watching me in a funny way. A way that made my stomach do flip-flops that they never did when I dove.

"I can't." I barely breathed it out, but you heard me.

"Then I'll quit football so that you will."

Now, even being the stupid girl that I was, I knew there weren't many things a country boy would give up football for. Football was a living, breathing entity in Tennessee, just like in many Southern states. And you were the god of the football team. And now you were saying you would give up that godlike status so that I would dive. It wasn't a little thing. It was huge.

"No! Out of the question." I was stubborn and unhappy.

"What if I promise, promise, promise to keep myself hydrated and at the first signs of dizziness, I'll sit out?"

"You won't."

We both knew you wouldn't. You were quiet again. You were staring into my eyes, trying to guess exactly how stubborn I was willing to be on this. I was willing to die being stubborn about this. Diving didn't mean anything. You meant everything. Finally, you said real quiet, "What if I promise to talk to my parents and go see a doctor?"

I looked up at you and saw the depth of your emotion in your shining green eyes.

"I don't want to go to a stupid dive school anyway. They'll want me to dive their way, and you know me, I'm not any good at following rules."

"I think Coach Daniels is different, Cam. I think you'd have a lot of say. Shit. You're only ten, and he already respects you." You put your hands behind your head and turned back to looking out at the stars. "You're like a dolphin in the water, Cam. You. The water. You're one. It's amazing to watch. It's beautiful."

My hungry little heart thumped at those words. You. Calling me beautiful. Even if it was only the way I swam. I scooted over so that my head was on your inner arm and stared out at the night with you. The thought of diving for someone else was an interesting perspective. To feel like I was good at something. To know that you thought I was good enough to do this. It was a little intoxicating. But my insides were still all twisted up at the thought of leaving you at practice and something happening.

I guess I knew, even then, that at some point I wasn't going to be able to stop what was happening to you with anything in my dirty pink backpack full of food supplies. So, if this was a way to get you to go see the doctor, then what did I really have to lose? Ha. That's a joke now, looking back. I had everything to lose.

"You'd really go to the doctor?"

You just nodded. But I felt it. And I knew you were telling the truth like I always did. It was a low blow in some ways because you knew that I wanted you to go to the doctor because I was worried about you, but on the other hand, it made me realize just exactly how much you wanted this for me.

We realized we'd have to go back inside to talk to the grown-ups, so I jumped out of the tree house from the window with you growling at me not to, and we went back inside. Coach Daniels was so excited he picked me up and swung me around so that my feet actually floated. My parents just stared like they weren't sure who I was and really weren't sure about this crazy, happy dude in their living room.

You said you'd see me in the morning, and our eyes met for a long time. I could see the mixed feelings in yours. You were still excited for me. The brightness was still there, but you were worried too. I just had this aching feeling that our lives were changing even more, and this time, I couldn't blame it on the hormones.

♩ ♩ ♩

On Monday, after school, I saw you just enough to wave as you got into your mama's car, and I got into mine. You winked at me. We had both caught hell from our parents once you'd gone home and told them what had been going on.

My mama, the hospital administrator, filled me with a million horror stories of what could have happened, what could be wrong, and how dangerous it was to keep quiet about someone's health. Your parents railed on you about how stupid it was to risk your health and your future for a stupid game. Even though both our daddies knew it wasn't a stupid game. They were right, you know. We had to find that out the hard way... God, if we could only go back. Do it again, right? Life doesn't give you do-overs, no matter how much people talk about second chances. It doesn't happen.

You had to skip practice, and my punishment was that I couldn't go with you to the doctor. I wanted to. Instead, I was on my way to meet Coach Daniels for the first time at the high school pool.

It helped a lot that he was really excited to see me. He talked non-stop about all this potential he saw in me. It was a little infectious. There were other kids there too. Some younger, some older. Boys and girls. But they all looked at me a little enviously as Coach told them about me in ranting raves. He put me through some dives. I didn't know any of the names, so he showed me videos on his phone. I could do a lot of them. Not well, but I could get through the motions.

"Shit. I have to put in a ten meter," he muttered almost to himself. Then he saw me watching him with a smile, and added, "Sorry, little lady. Didn't mean to cuss. I know you are trying to break the habit."

It made me like him even more. Right there. The fact that he was laughing with me. That he wasn't trying to change me. That he was going to change the build of his dive school just for me. Instead of me having to change for him. That was all kind of cool. And even though I'd liked the look of him before, I really felt like I could trust him now. That was a big step for me because trust was usually something I reserved for just one person.

I didn't have much time to think about you until practice was over. Coach kept me real busy. And I think over the next few years, my mama became Coach's biggest fan because he was able to take that energy of mine and leash it into something positive. Something no one had really been able to do, even you. My mama was waiting for me in the parking lot. I slid into the car with wet hair and a smile.

"So, looks like it went good," she said.

"I think I'm in love," I told her.

She laughed. "He's a little old for you, honey." Which brought my mind immediately back to you, and my smile was wiped away.

"Any news on Jake?"

She shook her head. "Let's go find out."

I don't think I breathed the whole way home. We saw your mama's car parked out front, and we skipped our door to go in yours. My eyes went immediately to you. You didn't look happy, but you didn't look devastated either, so I felt like I could breathe a little again. Like I'd been given a small shot of oxygen to tide me over until the next break.

"So, what's the verdict?" my mama asked in her professional tone that she took at the hospital.

"Type 1 Diabetes," your mama said with a frown.

We all just stared at each other. It was then that I noticed the needles and monitors and little bottles spread out on the table. There was a printed-out schedule and a pamphlet on food choices. I met your eyes again, and you kind of shrugged.

"Football?" I whispered.

"Don't be silly, Cami. Of course, he can continue to play football. Diabetes isn't debilitating. As long as they take care of themselves, people with diabetes can do everything anyone else can do," my mama responded, still in her business tone.

"Is that true?" I asked you. I guess I should have just believed my mama. I mean, she was around this stuff all the time, but until I heard it from you, I couldn't believe it. I guess maybe I should have listened closer to the grown-ups then and less to you, but I didn't. Instead, my eyes went back to yours.

You nodded in agreement with Mama, and the noose around my heart lightened just a bit more. I knew you weren't happy. I knew that this was a game changer, but it wasn't like you had to give up anything you really loved. Maybe just the MoonPies and the rest of the junk food we raked in.

♪ ♪ ♪

All of that meant our lives took on a new pattern. I still had a supply of food and drinks in my backpack. You had needles and a monitor. Instead of me watching your practice, we both went to practice and then met at the corner between the high school and the middle school to walk home and do homework like normal. But we were both a little different now. I had something besides you to focus on. You had something besides football and girls to focus on. It was like our lives had stretched a little in opposite directions from each other. But when we laid on your bed, side by side, talking about our day while you texted the gaggle of geese and did homework, for those few hours, it was the same.

Chapter Four

A Perfectly Good Heart

"Why would you wanna make the very first scar?"

-   Swift, James, Verges

𝓛𝓲𝓴𝓮 𝓲𝓽 𝓸𝓻 𝓷𝓸𝓽, 𝔂𝓸𝓾 𝔀𝓮𝓻𝓮 the first to break my heart. You used to tease me that you'd beat the crap out of any boy who did. Ha. You were the only one to break it. Ever. You left all the scars that are now embedded there like the notches on our victory tree. The first time you broke it, you didn't even know. Not for a long time. Not till I spelled it out for you, and it took me a long time to have the guts to say it to your face. I was afraid that if I told you, you'd leave me behind more than you already were.

It was in your freshman year that I first had the courage to tell you. And it all began and ended with Kayla.

We'd been pulled in different directions over the course of the last couple years because of my time on the competitive dive team, and your football. But it got worse as you entered high school and started as the quarterback on the JV football team.

Us spending so much time apart, was a hard pill for me to swallow. I hated that I wasn't able to protect you or to cheer you on. With my meets, I missed a lot of football games. And you missed a lot of my meets, but we were always there for each other if we could be. We definitely were each other's biggest fans… and biggest critics. I was always telling you what you hadn't seen on the field, and you were always telling me when my legs weren't in the right position, or I splashed too much.

It was a mixed blessing that you didn't need me watching over you quite as much because you had your needles and your monitor, but there were still days when all your levels got off, and I was typically the first one to notice it. I could tell by the things you'd say or the scowl you'd get on your face. Even your mama was impressed by how quickly I knew you needed a shot or food or pure sugar.

You'd been my protector for so long, that I think you resented it a little that I was your protector in those cases. Sometimes you'd gripe at me for watching you like you were a baby, but mostly, you were grateful when I handed you a candy bar when you needed it most.

In order to keep our time apart down to a minimum, I was usually the first one out of the pool, dried off, and at the boys' locker room waiting for you to come out after football practice. I'd always breathe a sigh of relief when I saw your grin, knowing that all was good in our world. I can't believe that you even tolerated having the sixth-grade tomboy pick you up at the locker room. I mean, I'm sure the boys thought you had the responsibility of walking me home, but it didn't feel like that to me. To me, it felt like I was watching over you.

Do you remember the time you came out of the locker room with a black eye, and I was all over it like ants on a chocolate cake? You laughed it off, explaining that you'd "accidentally" gotten elbowed by this sophomore, Brian, as he was trying to block you. We both knew the truth though. Brian was just pissed because you'd taken his quarterback position on the JV team as a freshman. The coaches didn't even bat an eye at passing you over the freshman football team. In fact, there was a long discussion about putting you directly on the varsity team. But they had a halfway decent varsity quarterback, and I think they were afraid of you getting hurt or burning out before they could really use you, the god of football.

There was no question in my mind that Brian had done it on purpose, so as Brian came out of the locker room, I didn't even think. I just reacted. I balled up my fist, reached up and cracked him one across the jaw. I mean, I was tall for a sixth grader, but Brian was a lot taller, so the jaw was what I could reach.

His head flew back and hit the brick wall with a crack. He tried to shake it off. But all the kids around him started laughing hysterically, and he stepped toward me with a face so red that it could have been marinara sauce. You pushed me behind you.

"Fuckin' freak!" he growled.

You held me back without breaking a sweat, but I was using every ounce I had to get at him some more. My fists were flying, and I threw a few choice words his way. Paul had joined us by this time, and he was shielding me too. I'm sure to you and Paul it seemed like you were blocking him from me, but I felt the opposite. I knew I could get some prime kicks in to his nether regions for calling me a freak, and I was still royally pissed that he'd marked up your gorgeous face. But the thing was, Brian had dropped his gear and looked like he wanted to take me on.

Thinking back, I can imagine how asinine it must have looked. Sophomore football player raising fists at a scrawny girl with lean muscle but no mass. It was at that point that Blake also joined us. He leaned his elbow on my shoulder in a nonchalant, casual way that hid his acute readiness, and said, "What's up, Super Girl?"

You knew Blake was there but just continued to stare Brian down, "What ya gonna do, Bri? Beat up a sixth-grade girl? You'll look like more of an ass than you already do."

Brian glared at you and me and the number of built guys that were clearly on my side and realized he was losing the battle, so he grabbed his stuff and slammed his way out of the building.

"Jesus, Cam," you breathed out as he left.

"He's such a shithead," I muttered.

"Don't cuss." You grabbed my arm, hauled me out the door, and dragged me down the street toward home before I could shake you off. You were quiet for a long time. I knew you were angry with me, but I wasn't really sure why or just how mad. We'd always taken care of each other, right? And you'd been mad at me before, but I always seemed to have this love-hate relationship with it. On the one hand, I didn't want you to be angry, but on the other hand, I loved that I had your full attention in those moments.

Finally, I couldn't take the silent treatment, so I said the only stupid thing I could think of which was, "Don't be mad."

I'd stopped, but you didn't. You kept going. I raced to catch up. When you did respond, you didn't even look at me.

"I know you don't think about what you do before you do it, Cam, but I can look after myself. What are people going to say if I rely on a little kid to fight my battles for me? I can beat the shit out of Brian wherever and whenever I choose, and I choose to beat him on the football field."

I knew you were right. You'd look like a wuss if I went around beating up everyone for you. But even though I knew that was true, it irked me that you'd called me a little kid. So, I decided I was as infuriated as you were.

I crossed my arms, dragged my feet, and added my own silence to yours. It took some time, but once we were almost home, you reached out and grabbed my right hand to take a look at it. I didn't realize it, but I'd bruised my knuckles on Brian's face. Who knew that hitting someone could impact you so quickly? That never happened to the heroes on TV. Reality sucked. And I hadn't even felt my hand when you and I were fighting, but now that you were holding it in yours, and I could see the worry in your eyes, I realized just how much it was throbbing.

"What am I going to tell your mama?"

I shrugged. "I'll just tell her I hit it on the diving board."

We went to your house, and you iced it for me while we did our homework together, but by the time I got home, someone had called my mama. Probably Brian's mama, because in my book he was just the type of sissy to complain to his mama about some little girl hitting him.

My mama was angrier than a bear stung by bees, but my daddy was trying not to smile while they talked to me about aggression and expressing myself in other ways. It was an old talk. I'd been shoving people on the playground for a long time. Mostly bullies. Regardless, I was grounded. For a week. Unfortunately for me, my parents had finally figured out what really mattered to me… you. So, the deal was no more studying at your house for a week.

It was probably the most time we'd spent apart in my entire life, even considering traveling for dive meets and your football games. We still got to walk home together, after dive and football practice, but you had to leave me at my door. I felt like a puppy whose owner was leaving to go to work.

And as if that wasn't already awful enough, what really ended up hurting, what my parents didn't realize would get to me even more than having to abstain from my daily Jake fix, was that this allowed Kayla to writhe her way into our alone time in her serpent-like way. She took to coming home with us and "studying" with you. She was obviously thrilled to find out that I couldn't home in on her time with you. And you might have liked a bit of alone time, too, because of all the kissing you were into these days. Of course, your mama was quick to pick up on this, and I was happy to find out that Mia was placed in your room as a chaperone.

Mia was going to be on my side. Well, I could easily manipulate her to be on my side, leaving you with as little kissy time as possible. I could make sure that she'd be blabbing to your mama if too much hot and heavy happened.

♫ ♫ ♫

After my grounding period was over, Kayla didn't stop accompanying us home. I tried not to hate her. For your sake. For Wynn's sake. Because Wynn was a good friend, and she was already having enough issues with Kayla and their parents. And on the upside, Wynn got to come with us too. I think maybe their parents finally found out where Kayla had been spending her afternoons, and they wanted to make sure there was a chaperone in the room as much as your mama had. Either way, it allowed me to spend time with Wynn and you, so I guess I should have been grateful to Kayla. I didn't see it like that then. All I saw was her taking you from me because you hardly had eyes for me when she was there.

She even got my spot on the bed next to you. Wynn and I were regulated to the floor. I'm sure my grades suffered that year because it was hard to study when all I could do was listen to the slobbering noises of your tangled tongues and her giggles. And, God, she giggled a lot. It was really rather stomach-churning.

Wynn and I would roll our eyes and sometimes make smooching noises just to irritate the two of you. Normally, you'd end up throwing a pillow or a pencil at us. Sometimes, when I really couldn't handle it, Wynn and I would grab the pillows and initiate a pillow fight with you. This always made Kayla angry because her hair and/or makeup would get messed up and that would send her off home with Wynn in tow. Wynn always felt like she'd won one for the team, though, and she'd give me the thumbs-up sign as she left the room. Sigh. Wynn was such a good friend.

Unfortunately, Wynn was huge into dance. Ballet. Shivers go down my spine even thinking about something as girly as that. Coach made me take a ballet class at one point, wanting me to see how the grace of dance could help my dives. I think I almost passed out from just the action of putting on the leotard and tights. I mean, my swim suit and the leo weren't that different. But tights? And those P-I-N-K ballet shoes? God. It felt like I was two years old. And the dance teacher and I definitely did not see eye to eye. Ballet and I lasted two weeks. That was all the teacher and I could take.

Wait. Focus. Back to Wynn and Kayla. Anywho, Wynn was really good at ballet. So, there were a few days a week that Wynn didn't get to come with us. You'd think their mama would have dragged Kayla along with them to the dance studio, but no such luck. Instead, Kayla was tagging along with us almost permanently. She was stuck to us like a Swahili bird to a giraffe which was probably what put the idea in my head at Halloween of things being stuck together. And what led to Kayla telling me to stop tagging along. Did you know she did that? I don't think you did.

This is how it got started. It was a Saturday close to Halloween, and it was raining sheets of hard, steady water such that even us outdoorsy kids weren't going to brave it. Instead, we were doing the rare thing of playing video games. Well, the boys and I were. It was Paul, Craig, you and I. Kayla and Wynn weren't around, thankfully. All of you boys were joking around about what you were going to "be" for Halloween because really, dressing up was not very cool anymore, so the suggestions were pretty crass. I was quiet because I knew if I said anything, you'd remember my age and who I was and tell them to knock it off, and the truth was that it was kind of funny listening to boy humor. It was an education at least.

At one point, you were joking around, and you said that you should dress up as Jesus Christ on the cross. You were kidding, but your mama chose that moment to walk through carrying a basket of laundry, and she almost dropped the basket.

"Jake Carter Phillips! That's blasphemy! We may not be the most religious of families, but I will not tolerate that kind of disrespect." Neither of our families attended church, which was pretty much a sin all on its own in Tennessee, but your mama was still all put out.

I didn't have the heart to tell her that, as most of the girls in the neighborhood already thought you were a god, it wouldn't be that much of a stretch for you to be dressed up as the savior. Or, at least, not that much more of a blasphemy than normal.

You looked a little chagrinned and told her you were just joshing, but then she stood there waiting to hear what else you had decided to dress up as. You didn't really want to dress up as anything, but I dove in.

"We're going as conjoined twins."

Your mama looked at me like she didn't know what to make of me. You, Craig, and Paul just stared at me like I'd gone insane. After your mama had looked at me for a long time, she just shook her head and left the room.

You were all over me after she left, wrestling me to the ground, and rubbing my head until I had electricity in my hair so bad that I could have charged your iPhone. But I loved it. And Kayla wasn't there to mess it up with some demanding little giggle or boobs sticking out of a tank top that showed more bra than it covered.

So, that's how we ended up joined at the hip on Halloween instead of you being Kayla's partner. I think she'd wanted you to be Robin Hood to her Maid Marian. Did she really think you were going to wear tights? You were a Southern football player and your football uniform was as close to tights as you'd ever get.

We always took Mia out trick-or-treating, and somehow and for some reason, Marina had taken my conjoined twins idea to heart and came up with an outfit for us. Neither of us could bear the thought of telling her that we'd rather be caught dead in our underwear than caught in a costume on Halloween as a freshman and a sixth grader. And even if we had, I honestly think she had done it as punishment for you saying you were going to be Jesus Christ and would have made you wear it anyway.

Either way, that was how we ended up tied together when we ran into Kayla. Since you hadn't agreed to be her Robin Hood, she'd changed gears and was wearing a sexy vampire outfit that really wasn't anything a respectable vampire would be caught dead in. I saw her look of surprise at us being tied so closely together. She and Wynn quickly joined our trip around the block with Mia.

I have to hand it to you. You played it all off really well. You somehow ended up the cool older brother who did anything to help the neighbor kid and his little sister. All the girls were oohing and ahhing over how sweet you were.

Ugh. I mean, you were sweet, but if Marina had been trying to lower your ego, it had seriously backfired.

After we'd done the block, shed our costume, and were going through the loot that you couldn't really eat, Kayla came up to me. She made sure you were busy with Mia so that you wouldn't hear us.

"Listen, freak. Jake won't say it because he's too nice, but you need to buzz out of the big kids' playroom. He doesn't want you there every day. So go join the circus or something, will you?"

Of course, I didn't believe her. Maybe it was true, but I didn't think so. And I'll have you know, you would have been proud of me because I didn't even punch her in the face. I really wanted to. But I didn't. She may have accidentally ended up sitting on a squished chocolate bar though, I won't confess to it, but it could have happened.

♫ ♫ ♫

Even after Kayla had told me to take a flying leap, I continued to tag along with you. I'd always been stubborn as a catfish on a hook. Kayla just didn't know that about me. She saw me as a pest to be rid of like a horse flicks at the flies. But when football ended, and you started waiting for me to finish practice before you walked home, I knew she'd been lying. You could have easily used that as an excuse to go home without me. To be rid of the fly buzzing about.

I think the fact that you wanted to wait for me irritated her to the ends of the earth, but she knew she couldn't say anything. So, she just tried to make out what a good "big brother" you were. Always minimizing me to the little kid status I was fighting so hard against.

The entire school year went by this way. I was really hoping you would get tired of her. Sometimes I thought you were finally done because your eyes flashed with irritation when she talked smack about people. But when she kissed you, you'd get that goofy look on your face like Santa had just given you an early Christmas present.

I did my best to put up with it. I really did. Wynn helped a lot, but near the end of the school year, on one of the days when Wynn was at ballet, I finally reached my breaking point.

You and Kayla were all kissy-kissy, and while the noise was obnoxious, what really got me was that I could see your hand inching up her top, and I really didn't want to see Kayla's boobs any closer than I'd already seen them in her see-through bikini a few years ago. I got up, threw your football at you, and stormed out, smashing the door against the wall on my way.

Your mama looked up in surprise as I reached the back door stomping and slamming things along the way like a bear caught in a car. "Everything okay?"

I looked at her with my heart on my sleeve. I couldn't help it. I think it was the first time your mama realized just exactly what I was feeling for you and just what I was going through. In response, I yelled, loud enough for you to hear, "I just couldn't stand the tonsil hockey anymore!"

And I continued my tantrum by slamming my way out the back door. I saw your mama get off the barstool so fast that I'm surprised it didn't leave skid marks on the floor. But it didn't make me feel any better knowing that she was going up to chew you out and shoo Kayla home. It would be just another mark against me in Kayla's book, and you'd be pissed too.

I climbed up to our tree house and waited. I knew you'd come eventually. Maybe not for a while, but you'd come because you'd know I was waiting there.

Dinner came and went. My mama didn't even call out. She assumed I was at your house. You climbed up once the air had turned chilly, and I was shivering. The first thing I saw was the sweatshirt you tossed at me. I grabbed it and pulled it on, deeply inhaling the scent of you as I pulled it over my face. Chocolate chip cookies, grass, and boy.

You sat down across from me. You seemed awkward, and I hoped to God that your mama hadn't said anything. But Marina would never give me away. I could trust her just like I could trust my mama. It was just that I liked that my mama was clueless about my feelings for you. I'd never admit them to her. Maybe because I wasn't so sure she'd be letting me spend so much time in your bedroom if she knew I didn't think of you as a brother. Little did she know, you'd never been a brother to me.

"So?" you said, finally breaking the silence.

"Sew buttons," I said half-heartedly using a saying from when I was five and you were eight. I picked at some invisible lint on your sweatshirt sleeve with my knees pulled up tight against the bumps that were still my breasts, trying not to draw a comparison to them and Kayla's mounds.

"What gives?" you asked.

"You really want me around for your make-out session? Never thought of you as a sick voyeur."

You laughed out loud and gave me that big ol' dazzling smile that stopped a million girls' hearts every day. Including mine.

"Where do you get these words?"

"From studying vocabulary with you!"

Your grin turned bigger, and I looked away just as my eyes welled up with tears. I swear. Tears! I wasn't a sissy, and it killed me. But you'd still noticed.

"Geez, Cam. What's up?"

"I can't do it anymore," I could barely say it because my lungs were so tight, and my heart felt like a windup toy that had been wound too far.

"I didn't know we were grossing you out. I didn't even really think about it. I'm sorry."

"It's not… I mean…" I couldn't finish.

You wouldn't take your eyes off me, I could feel them boring into me, but I refused to look at you with stupid tears in my eyes. Finally, you turned my face toward yours, but I still refused to look. I just closed my eyes. And the tears fell. You wiped them with a gentle thumb.

"You never cry. Not even when you broke your toe at the lake and rode your bike all the way home. Not even when you bruised your hand on Brian's face. So, what gives?"

I pulled your hands off my face and pushed you away a little. I kept my eyes closed because I was afraid that, if I opened them, I wouldn't have the courage to say what was trying to burst out of me.

"You're breaking my heart." It was a whisper. But it was said. And I couldn't take it back.

There was no noise. Nothing from you. You hadn't moved. Hadn't screamed in disgust. Hadn't run away. Finally, I couldn't stand it, and I risked looking at you. You were looking out at the stars. Our favorite pastime when we had too much on our minds.

After a long time, you breathed out, "I'm not trying to break your heart. I'm just a fifteen-year-old guy trying to get to third base."

You said it with a lot of sarcasm. And I couldn't tell what that meant. All I knew was that right then, you didn't see me as a girl. You just saw me as the kid next door who was a good friend, and it broke my heart a little more. I mean, I know I didn't dress like a girl, or act like a girl, or even have boobs like most girls, but somehow I'd always thought that you still knew I was a girl. This proved you didn't.

I scrambled away from you to the door. I was halfway down the ladder when you called out to me.

"Cami."

I halted. Like I would forever halt when you used the longer version of my name. You knew I'd stopped, because there was silence instead of the pounding of your boots on the tree house floor following me. You knew I'd stopped because I always did when you said my name like that, but you didn't say anything else. It was like that was all you could offer me at that time or like you didn't know what else to say.

I waited for a minute or so. It seemed like forever. I was still hoping you'd come sweep me up into your arms, but you didn't. I finished by jumping the rest of the way down the ladder and took off to my house. I let myself in, being careful to avoid the family room, and just hollered goodnight to my parents. I ran to my room where I promptly destroyed several more pillows while taking out my pent-up anger at Kayla, and you with Kayla, and at me for being so stupid as to cry over it all in a decidedly un-Cam-like way.

♫ ♫ ♫

The next day I prepared myself to do the only thing I could do after the fit I'd thrown, which was to go home on my own to my own room. There was no way I could go back into that room with you and Kayla playing tonsil hockey. But when I left practice and found you leaning on the brick wall outside the girls' locker room, Kayla and Wynn weren't there. I wasn't sure what that meant. I wasn't sure I could even face you. But you ruffled my hair, and it felt a little bit like normal. As we started off home, I said, "Where's your feathered friend?"

And even though you hated me calling the girls who followed you your gaggle of geese, you didn't react. Instead, you shrugged. "Not sure."

I was happy as a clam, as the saying goes. Although, how do you really know that a clam is happy? In this case, my heart was happily doing somersaults. Maybe that's what a clam is like, jigging it up on the inside, but all shell on the outside. That was me. I was thrilled to have you all to myself again even if it was only for one day. Because I was so happy, I didn't notice at first how quiet you were. You weren't depressed quiet, just thoughtful quiet.

I suggested that, after homework, we go out and play football with Paul, Wade, and Blake. You always came to life playing football. That's how we ended up on the street with you still treating me like the non-girl that I'd always been to you and the boys. But I didn't care. Kayla wasn't there, you were smiling again, and that was all that mattered for that day.

When Kayla didn't come with us the next day either, I knew you'd broken up. I was ready to truly celebrate. When I asked Wynn about it, she said that the two of you had a huge fight over me. Yippee me. Well, mostly. I did feel a brief flash of guilt. Maybe I would have felt guiltier if our families had been more religious, but I didn't. And the truth was, you really didn't seem so upset after that first day without Kayla.

It took another few weeks, when school was out and summer had started, before I grasped the fact that you weren't upset because you knew there was a long line of girls waiting to take her place. For me, I was determined that that summer would be the time that you would see me as a girl instead of just a kid that beat you at swimming. Stupid though it was, I know, I was finally hoping that you'd want to play tonsil hockey with me. After all, I had been the first girl in your line all along.

Chapter Five

Better Than Revenge

"The story starts when it was hot and it was summer and...

I underestimated just who I was dealing with."

- Taylor Swift

𝓘 may have been the first in your long line, but the one that came next caught me off guard. That's what makes me think of Taylor's song, "Better Than Revenge." It wasn't that I didn't suspect it. It was just that I wasn't prepared for how quickly she swooped in on her feathered wings and snapped you up. I wanted revenge. Big RED revenge. But it would be a long time before I got it. And in the meantime, I had to put up with the sneaky actress who was just another person who thought I was a freak.

For a brief moment, the summer started like H-E-A-V-E-N. And I was delusional enough to think it would stay that way. I was still a little naïve you see. I hadn't really learned what the long line of geese and lionesses meant.

Wade and Blake were going to be seniors, and they were spending the first part of the summer doing the college circuit to find out which ones they wanted to apply to in the fall. Paul was off at his grandparents in D.C., and Craig had decided he liked computers way better than losing to me in a race. So, for the first few weeks of summer, it was just the two of us at the lake. We'd never taken Mia. Poor Mia. Although, to tell you the truth, Mia was never really an outdoor girl. She was pretty much my opposite in that regard.

After we'd been out of school a week or so, I made Wynn take me bathing suit shopping, and I bought a cute bikini, hoping that this would make you see me like a girl. But that same day, I wore it to dive class and lost the top on impact with the water. Coach was real nice about it. Although, I think he turned a couple shades of white that I didn't know existed.

Anyway, I realized the bikini wouldn't stand up to the rigors of the competitions and wrestling at the lake either, so Wynn and I went back to the drawing board. We resorted to a tankini. Not a grown-up ugly thing meant to hide your cellulite, but a cute lime-green polka-dotted one that let my belly button peek out and had tantalizing strings holding the bottoms together.

My mama smiled when she saw it. It was a step in the girl direction she and my grandma had been dreaming about. My daddy not so much. He frowned so hard that I thought they'd have to unglue his eyebrows at the hospital. They had this whispered conversation where I could hear words like "appropriate" and "girl" and "get used to it."

Mama won. It was the first time in forever I'd wanted my mama to win a battle with my daddy over me. Normally I was hoping Daddy won like you hope for the lottery. You know there's a chance, but it's pretty much a long shot. But

I did put my cover-up on, trying to help, but I could see Daddy's furrow bury itself deeper in his forehead. It was a cute little white cover-up that was kind of like a dress although I never, ever wore dresses. Never. It was a sin to my earlier self. But I was trying to be a girl, and Wynn promised me it made me look very girly. It must have. That was why Daddy hated it so much.

The first day I wore the new suit to the lake, I loaded up my pink backpack, now really a grungy tan, with all the things I normally loaded mostly for you, and joined you out between our two porches where you were carrying your own backpack. I waited for you to notice the cover-up with my tankini polk a dots showing through, but you hardly glanced at me. We got on our bikes and took off toward the lake.

I knew that you had other things on your mind. Like getting your driving permit and trying to convince your parents to let you buy the '67 Camaro that Wade's brother was selling. But I couldn't help being a little put out that you hadn't noticed the girly gear I was wearing. Especially since I'd done it just for you. I tried to make myself feel better by thinking that once the cover-up was off, you'd really notice.

Instead, you dove right into the water, and yelled at me when I took my time actually putting on sunscreen, which I never did, but was doing in a lame effort to get you to notice me. I didn't know how to play the game as well as the gaggle of geese or the lionesses. You swam out to the makeshift wooden dock that a whole group of us had anchored to the middle of the lake last year and hollered at me again.

I sighed. Eventually. That's all I could think. Eventually, you'd have to really look at me. You were just used to not looking at me. I was always around, so it was just like your arm. You didn't always notice it, but it was still there. Little did you know that I was always looking at you. I could tell the moment my eyes were on you whether you'd gotten a new haircut or you'd shaved or you had on a new outfit because your mom had convinced you to go shopping. That wasn't as hard as it used to be, convincing you to shop, because you liked to look good for the ladies.

Anyway, I swam out to the platform, and we spent the morning splashing, jumping off of it, and racing each other across the lake and back. It was a lazy day. Warm. Not yet too muggy to be uncomfortable, but just enough to make everything feel sluggish and a bit dreamlike. The kind of dream that you don't want to wake up from because you knew you'd never get back to that happy place, but somehow you knew you couldn't stay in because alertness was tugging you into reality.

Near lunchtime, you took off for the shore to test your sugar level and fuel up. I lay out for a while more drinking in the heat of the wood beneath me and the sunshine above me like maple syrup into a hotcake. I lay there thinking of some way that I could get you to take notice of my little curves (helped out a lot by the padding of my tankini top).

You bellowed at me to come get some food. I'd been out on the platform for a while when I waded through the water back to shore. I'd pretty much given up on you, so I wasn't prepared for your reaction when I walked up.

You blanched. Face white like when you had your reactions to the insulin, and that's what I thought at first, but your mouth almost hit your chest in this look of shock, and I about burst with happiness thinking that you'd finally noticed my new suit, until you finally spoke.

"Shit. Cami. You're bleeding. All over," your voice was hoarse and shaken.

I looked down and realized I'd started my period. And it was running down my leg. Not a ton, but enough to be noticeable. Probably because I'd lain on the platform so long and not been in the water. Probably because the water was washing the blood out of my bottoms. Didn't matter. There it was.

I hadn't started my period before that. Many of my friends had, but not me, I felt like I was a late bloomer in every way, even though I know now I really wasn't that old. My mama said I might be even later because I was so athletic, but I had thought it was God's way of making sure you would never see me as a girl.

And now, here I was, registering my girlhood in the most personal way to you. There was no way in hell I was going to tell you that though. Instead, I played it off as if it was nothing even though my heart was pounding like it might take off of its own accord.

I laughed, grabbed my towel, and wrapped it around me. By this time, you'd noticed my belly button, too, and were having difficulty looking at me at all. Nothing could keep the little smile off of my face.

"Crap. We'll have to ride to the Quick Stop," I said, trying very hard to sound nonchalant, as if bleeding down my leg was something I'd experienced a million times.

"Are you all right?" You were worried and white, and I was cheering for myself inside. That little clam doing its jig again. I continued to play it off as well as I could.

"It's just my period, it's not like I stabbed myself in the stomach or anything."

You stared at me for a moment, then shook yourself out of your reverie. You loaded up your stuff while I loaded up mine, and we hit the bikes. We rode all the way to the Quick Stop in silence. It was the closest place that would have pads.

We parked our bikes, and you looked at me for a moment, hesitant, unsure. I hardly ever saw this side of you. You were forever the confident god of girls and football.

"Do you want me to pick something up for you while you go to the bathroom?" you asked, still looking like you might throw up at any moment.

"That would be great," I said casually.

I headed to the bathroom, and you headed to the personal hygiene products.

Luckily, I had another suit and some jean shorts in my bag. I got that out, ready to change once you showed up at the door. I was starting to get worried that you had actually passed out when you finally knocked.

"What took so long?" I groused, but it turned to a laugh at the look of complete bewilderment on your face.

"There were so many. I... I didn't know what to choose," you whispered. "I hope these are okay."

You shoved a brown bag at me, and I realized that the guy at the counter must have taken pity on the football hero buying feminine hygiene products because Lord knows you couldn't call them pads or tampons.

"It'll be fine, thanks," I said with a smile and shut the door in your face.

Thank God my mama had already shown me everything about these stupid female products. She even had a store of them waiting for me at home. It took me a few minutes to feel like I was cleaned up and had it on right, but I still wasn't comfortable.

I looked at myself in the mirror. I didn't look any different, but all of a sudden, I was different. And you knew it. God hadn't been taunting me at all. He'd actually helped me out. A lot. You wouldn't be able to believe I was anything but a girl now. After a few minutes, I realized I couldn't keep you waiting anymore. Even though having you worry about me was kind of making me all tingly inside.

I left the bathroom and froze. There you were. No longer worried at all. Instead, you were all smiles, and they weren't aimed at me. They were aimed at Brittney. Kayla's BFF who was nowhere near as cutesy and ditzy as Kayla. No way anyone could think of Brittney that way. Most especially me. Kayla might toss her hair and giggle, but Brittney was smart and manipulative.

Brittney had an ICEE in one hand, and the other hand was twisting the rope bracelet you had on your wrist. The one I'd made you last summer as part of Wynn's attempt to have me learn some girl things, and you'd worn it all year. It was a little beat up, but you said it was good luck.

For a second, I hoped that you weren't laughing about me. That you hadn't said anything about why we were at the Quick Stop. But then I knew better. You'd die before you'd blab one of my secrets to someone. Even someone who looked as good as Brittney.

Her hair was blonder than Kayla's. Ice blonde. But still Barbie-like. And it swung around her face like strands of silk, whereas my dark hair was always dry and brittle from too much chlorine. She always looked just girly enough to show off every beautifully perfect curve of hers, but not so girly as to be prissy and turn the boys off. She didn't look like someone who spent hours in front of the mirror even though I knew she had to in order to be that amazingly perfect every day.

I joined you.

"Well hello, Cami," she said with her fake, mean girl smile.

God, I wanted to punch her in her perfect nose for ruining everything. It had all finally been going my way. A fantastic lazy day with you being hit with a lightning bolt sign that said, "Cam is a girl, Cam is a girl, Cam is a girl."

Now, instead of seeing me as a girl, you were looking at Little Miss Model with your knowing, flirty smile. You leaned onto the Coke machine, placing your hand just above her head as she preened under your shadow. Then you turned and winked at me. She couldn't see it, but I knew that wink.

I rolled my eyes, and Miss Perfect thought I was doing it at her, so she got all squinty-faced.

"Guess where Brit was heading, Cam?"

I looked at her in her cover-up that barely covered her tush and wanted to strangle her a little more. Of course, she was heading to the lake.

"Well, a bunch of us are meeting up out at the lake. Jake says you were just here to stock up on some supplies before going back out?" she said, daring me to contradict it.

I shrugged.

"So, Cam. Looks like we won't be so lonely at the lake now."

I grimaced and shifted from foot to foot. Truth was, I wasn't feeling myself. I had dive practice in a couple hours and wasn't sure what the hell I was going to do or tell Coach, and sometime before then, I really wanted to talk to my mama. God was trying to tell me I was a girl, after all, and Mama was a girl.

To this day, I'll blame it on being my first time that my judgment was clouded right then, because I did the stupidest thing I've ever done... like a cow walking itself into the slaughterhouse. What I said was, "You go on. I want to go home and get out of the sun for a while before dive practice."

And you bought into that line. Of course, I had just bled all over the place in front of you, so maybe you thought I should go get out of the sun. Or maybe you wanted to put some distance between us to forget the gory sight. Or maybe you'd completely forgotten about it in the ten minutes I'd been in the bathroom and Miss Perfect had shown her boobs to you. Boobs I still didn't have.

God, I hated girls with boobs.

You grabbed your bike and walked it alongside Brittney who didn't have a bike, of course. Beautiful Barbie dolls didn't ride bicycles. I went the other way, towards home. You did look back at me once and wave. I waved back, but I was feeling more down than I'd ever felt before. I know. I know. Hormones. They were still playing havoc on us.

That weekend, I knew I needed help. If I was going to snag you before another goose did, I had to grab your attention once and for all. True, I was still three years younger than you. You were going to be a sophomore, and I was only going into seventh grade, but it could work, right? Okay... so, I was delusional back then? I'll just continue to blame it on the hormones.

I recruited Wynn to help me once again. Her and my grandma. My grandma was so thrilled that I wanted to shop for some girl clothes that she handed over her AMEX card as fast as a raccoon opens a garbage can. My mama was disgusted and told me that I was abusing her mama's good nature, but I promised her I really was going after girl clothes. I don't think she believed me until I came home.

Wynn and I spent an entire weekend at the mall. It was more time than I'd spent at the mall all year, probably in all my almost 13 years put together. But it was a pain that I knew would help me in the end. Like the zillion push-ups and pull-ups Coach made me do that tore my muscles apart in order to put them back together all that much stronger.

Wynn helped me with dresses and frilly tops. Wedges and boots with heels. She took me to her hairdresser and had my hair layered. She took me to the MAC makeup counter and had them do their thing on me. When we got home on Sunday, my mama burst into tears. Literally. She took a thousand pictures and sent them to my grandma, and Grandma called me crying. It was a little nauseating.

"Mama, I may look like a girl, but I'm still me, and this mushy stuff is more than I can take," I said with disdain as I stormed my way to my room with Wynn in tow.

Wynn helped me get my closet set up, then moved on to my bathroom to uncoil the flat iron we'd bought and write directions on my mirror for the makeup regimen so that I would be sure to do it. God, it seemed like a lot of work to be a girl. Being a boy, or at least a tomboy, was way easier. You got up, brushed your teeth, pulled your hair into a ponytail, threw on jeans and a tee, and were out the door in fifteen minutes. All this was going to take me forever.

After Wynn took off, because her family insisted on having a full sit-down family dinner on Sundays, I stared at myself in my sliding closet mirror. I didn't not like the look. It was still me. Just a me with a jean skirt instead of shorts and a lacey top instead of my t-shirt. The makeup, well, that would take some time to get used to.

After staring at myself, trying to decide what I thought about the new look, I decided that I had to see your reaction. Like I was bleeding all down my leg again and needed to know that you knew I was a girl. After all, your reaction was the only one that mattered. I called out to my mama and daddy that I was going next door. I heard my dad snicker and the slap that was my mama hitting his shaved head. I just rolled my eyes and let the screen door slam.

When I got to your porch, I heard a twitter, and I froze. Fear reached up from the pit of my stomach to place a stranglehold on my heart.

"Jake, I have to go." The voice drifted away into a sound that I had come to hate with a passion that could only be equivalent to our Tennessee Titans' hatred of the Ravens. It was the smacking and slurping which meant only one thing. More tonsil hockey. I smacked my head against the post silently. It was Brittney. She'd swooped in like a hawk, instead of the goose that I'd taken her for.

After I listened, yet again, to more smooching for more time than I thought I could handle, I stepped my newfound boots onto the step with a click. The noise brought two faces around. Yours and Brittney's. Her eyes were way more calculating than Kayla's had ever been. She knew exactly what I wanted, whereas Kayla had mostly seen me as her little sister's freaky friend who wouldn't leave you alone but wasn't really a threat in the girlfriend area.

"Well, well, it's the girl next door," she said with a smile and a Southern, daddy's girl sweetness that hid her true meaning from you and only you. Us girls, we understood each other. And even though you may not have thought of me as a girl back then, I still was one and Brittney knew it.

"Cam! Where you been all weekend?" you asked in a way that at least let me know you had noticed my absence. Maybe not enough to call out a search party, but you'd noticed.

I moved fully onto the porch and into the light better. Brittney saw it immediately. And she laughed. Her pretend I'm-being-nice laugh.

"Why Cami, don't you look beautiful. You're all done up. Who's the boy?"

You had your arm around her waist, and she'd turned so she was leaning her backside up against you. You let your chin rest on her head like you had once upon a time with me, and my insides turned nastily. My fists clenched.

"I don't know what you mean," I tossed and tried to look blasé in my new threads.

"I don't think I've ever seen you in a skirt. Turn around for us," Brittney continued. You hadn't said anything. You were eyeing me, but your hand was wandering up and down Brittney's arm in a distracted sort of way. She placed her hand on top of yours and played a little jingle on it that I guess was meant to be seductive. I surely didn't know anything about that yet. The art of seduction.

"Come on, Jake. Make her turn around for us. She looks so pretty, don't you think?"

Her asking you the thing I wanted most to hear from you, was enough to almost make me want to pound her head into the porch pillar, but I wouldn't let her see it get to me, so I just wiggled around and shook my booty like I was dancing to a country rock song. She laughed. You didn't. You were more serious.

"You look really good, Cam. Different. But good different." The smooth baritone of your voice washed over me.

I'd missed the look in your eyes as you said it because I was still turned around, so I whipped about to see if I could catch the remains of whatever it had been, but Brittney had already drawn your face down to hers for a kiss. If only I could shoot arrows with my eyes. If only I really was Super Girl like Blake teased.

"I've gotta go. But I'll see you tomorrow at the lake, mister." She kissed you long and hard, flashed her perfect white teeth at me, and then strolled gracefully off the steps and down the street. Her house was just a block over.

You watched her until she was out of sight, and I watched you. You had a different look on your face than you normally had watching Kayla. With Kayla it had always been a little about exploration and adventure. A game. A new game you were learning. With Brittney, there was a look of something else. Fascination? Determination? I don't know. I just knew it was different.

I slid past where you leaned against the house to get to the porch swing. You joined me, and we swung in silence for a while.

"So, who is he?" you asked, picking up on Brittney's assumption.

I shrugged.

"Come on. You can tell me," you teased, nudging my shoulder playfully.

I couldn't look at you. I wanted to shout, "You, you moron!" but Brittney had taken the steam out of me.

"So, Brittney, huh?" I said, changing the subject.

You looked out to where she'd disappeared and grinned. That grin of confidence that melted many, many a heart. Including mine. How could one boy be so damn perfect?

"I didn't realize that she's liked me for so long."

I rolled my eyes at you. "God, you're dense sometimes."

You looked at me in surprise, the smile still there. "You knew?"

"Everyone knew, idiot."

"Why didn't you tell me?"

Now there was a loaded question. "She couldn't have done anything about it anyway."

"What?"

I punched your arm, and you wrestled with me a little. It ended up with me on the floor of the porch in a very unladylike fashion. I was super glad I hadn't put on the pair of thongs that Wynn had tried to insist I wear.

You didn't even notice. You didn't even try to look up my skirt. You just sat on my stomach, crushing the air out of me like you'd done since I was barely walking.

"What are you talking about?" you asked.

"The girl code. Can't go after the guy your friend's been playing tonsil hockey with. Now get off me, you're crushing a rib."

You proceeded to tickle the hell out of me until, even in the dim light, you could see I was turning blue from lack of oxygen to the brain. Even then, you didn't get up.

"You should have told me."

"Why?"

"I like her better than Kayla. She's smart. And definitely not annoying. Just think how far I could have gotten this year."

"You're gross," I said, breathing heavily as you rolled off me and sat on the steps looking up at the stars. I watched you for a moment. My heart breaking with each beat that it took.

I rolled over and joined you. We sat there in silence for a while, shoulder to shoulder. Finally, I stood, jutted my hip out a little, and said with as much sauce as I could muster, "Gotta go. Big day tomorrow."

You grinned at me. "God help the boy you've set your eyes on."

"Well, you know. It is me."

I flaunted and then wiggled across your lawn in a bad imitation of Brittney's graceful sway. I flashed a smile back at you and said, "Did I do it right?"

"What?"

"God. You really are an idiot."

You picked up a pebble from the flower bed and tossed it at me. I ducked in plenty of time and finished wiggling back to my house, listening to you chuckle after me, wishing with all my heart for a whistle instead of a laugh.

So, my new look had been too late. At least for you. But I did make a splash at the Dairy Queen on Monday. We all went there after the lake. I had my new threads on, you had Brittney on. Vomit.

There were eighth grade boys and even high school boys that were taking a look at me. Wynn was pleased as a pumpkin. She felt like she had done her job. You were too busy feeling up Brittney to notice. And that was the only person I really wanted to notice me.

So, I just was me. Obnoxious, tomboyish me. Although, somehow combining my new look with my normal, boy-like talk, seemed to draw a crowd. Wynn was very grateful. She dove right in and picked up where I was silent. She wasn't stupid like Kayla, but she definitely knew how to appeal to the guys' hormones too. I didn't. Obviously. Well, maybe it was just your hormones that were like me and the football. Matching ends of magnets.

♫ ♫ ♫

That's the way our summer passed. With you and Brittney playing tonsil hockey... and more. Ew. All I know is that now there were times where you sent me home from the lake while you and Brittney stayed. On the blanket we used to use. Gross.

I had a crowd of boys willing to take me home. My daddy hated it. But he didn't have to worry. None of them even got to first base. I just wasn't that interested in doing that whole thing with any of them. They seemed childish and too eager. The couple of guys that tried to kiss me got smacked on the head and were quick to move on.

By the time school started, things were pretty much back to normal. Except Wynn had a boyfriend, and you had a girlfriend. And I had to focus on my diving in order to survive the torment inside me. Coach was thrilled. He hadn't seen me that focused since, well, ever. I started winning more competitions left and right. My parents were proud, and you were proud. But you would hug me and then text Brittney, which kind of blew the whole thing for me. Because, let's face it, I'd never cared if my parents were proud of me.

Chapter Six

You Belong with Me

"And you've got a smile that could light up this whole town

I haven't seen it in awhile, since she brought you down."

- Swift & Rose

The one thing about Brittney is that she never really got the Jake Phillips on the inside. She liked the outside Jake. She liked the captain-of-the-football-team-whose-gonna-be-someone-someday Jake. And when you were upset or fighting with her, she didn't get why it was me that you went back to, why I was the one who could make you laugh when you were down, or why our tastes were always exactly the same and often opposite of hers. She didn't get it because she never really got that you didn't belong to her. You belonged to me. And it was almost a year before she would figure that out.

At the end of summer and once football started, it was easier for me to ignore Brittney's attachment to you. Our families and I were your biggest cheering section. You got to play varsity as a sophomore as the quarterback. Your god-like status had turned into mega stardom in our little town. Of course, Brittney thrived on that. And she was cheering too, but as a cheerleader on the sideline. So, she had to cheer for everyone, versus I got to scream your name like crazy. Brittney would give me dirty looks. But I just ignored it.

She got me back though. As she was on the sidelines, she always got to be the first one to hug you when you came off the football field, and I had to settle for second. She didn't let it last long though. And she'd get the ultimate payback in dragging you off to an after-party to which, on no uncertain terms, was I allowed to go to as a mere seventh grader. Neither my parents nor you would have allowed me to go.

Not that I didn't try, but Mama had a sixth sense about me trying to sneak out now. She'd been around me for almost thirteen years. It was like you going to kindergarten all over again and me trying to follow behind. Mama still didn't lock me in my room, but I think she wanted to because I could be just as crabby and mean as I had when I was three and you were gone without me.

One good thing about Brittney was that she had a temper. And that meant she was mad at you about as much as she was in love with you. So, there were some weeks where I only had to walk home with her once or twice because on the other days she was throwing her daddy's-girl tantrum at you over something stupid. Or trying to make you "pay" for something. It was really lame. I was kind of surprised you put up with it so much. But maybe you'd gotten farther with her than you had with Kayla and weren't willing to let that go yet. Boy hormones and all.

But I'd gotten the picture. On the days Brittney walked home with us, with no chaperone sent by her mama, and your mama not really seeing the need these days as long as your door was left open, I went to my own house to do homework. It was crappy. And lonely. But it was better than sticking toothpicks in my eyes trying not to watch the two of you with your hands all over each other, and with no Wynn to distract me or take one for the team.

The times that the three of us were together (or even the three of us in a bigger group), Brittney and I would fight as much, if not more, than the two of you. We would argue about music, sports, anything. It was our ultimate goal in life to see which of us you would side with more. And we were definitely keeping score. I was winning. Well, Brittney probably didn't think so, but I knew that you'd only said that you liked Lady Gaga to appease her. You and I had made fun of that drama music many times. So, she thought she was winning, but I knew the truth about you like I always would. Just like I knew the truth about how you saying I was your little dolphin just drove her nuts, but she'd smile her wickedly sweet smile and agree.

The things you and Brittney fought over were stupid, high school drama things. Like the fact that Sherry Martin smiled at you in first period, or that you picked up Amber Whittaker's books for her after they hit the deck in the hallway. Or the time she got really drunk at a party and kissed Paul because you were talking to some random girl. Things that proved she was insecure and jealous, even though she tried so hard to pretend that she wasn't. She always made mountains out of molehills.

You would get frustrated and tell her that she had to trust you. You never screamed at her. I wanted to scream at her. God, I would have loved to have torn her hair out and banged her head on a sidewalk somewhere, but I think you enjoyed the fact that after you calmed her down, you'd get a little further into her pants. Sometimes, I think you provoked the fight by making sure she saw you with a girl so that you could do just that. Get a little further in the make up, make out sessions. Ergh. Still gives me the shudders.

I knew that you fought over me too. Like you and Kayla had, but again, you never did it in front of me. And Brittney never said anything to me like Kayla had. She tried the opposite tactic. She didn't want me to think that she was threatened by me. She was. There were times that you'd choose me over her. Coming to my meets versus taking her to a movie. Or, like you had with Kayla, staying to walk home with me after school even when football season was over. Things like that killed her. Just like they'd killed Kayla.

But Brittney had learned from your break up with her BFF, and she didn't want me to know that I was more than a fly on the windshield to her and her relationship with you.

In January, you turned sixteen and I turned thirteen. You and I were close in more ways than one. Our birthdays being only about two weeks apart. Both January babies. Winter babies. For two whole weeks, our mamas had thought that I'd be born on your birthday. But I was stubborn even then and wanted a bit of my own space, so I waited just a bit. I'm the thirteenth. You're the third. This year our parents had decided to throw us a joint party. A big shindig that would celebrate two rites of passages. We were holding it the weekend between our birthdays.

The day you turned sixteen, you got your driver's license, and our daddies drove home a cherried-out '67 Camaro for you. Okay. We may have not been rich by the standards of the folks who go to boarding school and attend debutante balls, but, for our little town, our families did okay. And a lot of cars came our daddies' way through the dealership. The Camaro was proof of that. They'd originally said it was too much car for you, but I think that was to throw you off the scent when you'd been talking about the dump that Wade's brother had owned.

Now we had a cool way to get everywhere. No more bikes required. Of course, sometimes we took the bikes just because you and I enjoyed bike riding. We'd take a ride down to the lake and over the hills and back to town just to clear our heads and let off steam. That was something else Brittney didn't like, but she was a cheerleader, not a tomboy, and at fifteen going on sixteen, she was never going to be seen on a bike.

The week you got your license, we were riding home in the Camaro, and Brittney started in on you about how you'd invited Amber to our party. I'm sure she was seething inside that I'd be the center of attention with you, but I had no doubt that she'd make sure she was glued to your arm all night.

Regardless, she didn't want to play second fiddle to me and some other girl. So, she was ranting and raving about how you inviting Amber made it seem like you were shopping around for a new girlfriend, and made her look like last year's news.

You were trying to keep your cool, but I could see your ears turning red which meant you weren't really playing it up this time, but were really seething inside.

I was sitting in the back seat watching the ping-pong match, thinking to myself, "What the hell do you see in this girl? She obviously doesn't know you at all. Doesn't know how loyal and trustworthy you are. Doesn't see how you are steeped in Southernly knighthood that had been passed down by Tennessee daddies for generations." Okay... you're right. I probably didn't think all of that. But it doesn't make it not true.

Finally, I couldn't keep quiet anymore. I just screamed out, "Would you stop the ABC Family drama?!"

To which both of you whipped around and said, "Butt out, Cami." In unison. Well, you said Cam.

And you went right back at it.

"Then grow up!" I quipped back.

Brittney turned on me, "Grow up! Says the child pretending to be an adult so she can tag along after Jake like the sick little puppy she is."

Silence, for a second settled down. I looked into the rearview mirror, and you wouldn't meet my gaze. The fact that you didn't defend me, when you always defended me, made my temper flare in a way it hadn't in a long time.

I pushed the front seat forward, slamming Brittney into the glove box. She caught herself with her hands and a cuss word, but I was reaching for the handle of the door, ignoring it.

"Let me out of the car," I said, pulling at the door.

"Jesus Christ, Cami," you said as you squealed to a stop with me halfway out of the car.

I didn't care. I got out, gave you both a one-fingered wave, and headed off down the street. I heard the engine cut out, but didn't really comprehend anything until you had me slung over your shoulder like a bag of cornmeal.

"Put me down!" I screamed, pounding your back with barely controlled anger from four years of pent up emotions, at the same time as I was trying to pull down my jean skirt so that my polka-dotted underwear wouldn't show to the world.

Brittney was out of the car with her arms crossed.

"She is not getting back in this car with me," Brittney said angrily. "She could have killed me slamming my head against the dash!"

"She is. And so are you," you muttered with a grunting male manhood that startled me. You were never all caveman chauvinist, but you seemed to have reached your estrogen limit.

"I am not," Brittney defied you.

"Well, she is," you said, and you flung me into the back of the car with such ferociousness that I bumped my elbow on the side of the car and had to slam my hands out to keep myself from hitting the floorboards.

"Are you choosing her over me?" The sarcasm and disdain in her voice could have dripped an acid hole in the sidewalk.

"I'm not choosing anybody," you growled. "She's my responsibility. I'm taking her home. I'd really like my girlfriend to come too, but if you can't handle that, it's on you."

Neither Brittney nor I were happy with this response. I didn't want to be your responsibility. I wanted to be the girlfriend. I wanted to choose to get in the car, not be there because you felt I had to be.

I tried to get out, "I am not your problem!" But you pushed me back into the back seat with one hand. And it hurt. When I looked up into your face, your beautiful eyes were so dark that I could hardly see the gold flecks. You were pissed. Probably as angry as you'd been the day I'd dove off the cliff at the lake. It stopped me. I shoved myself back against the seat and crossed my arms.

You looked across the top of the car to Brittney, still standing on the sidewalk like a diva gone wild.

"Well?" your voice was foreboding. I knew that even in my dreams I'd never go against that tone. A tone you had never, ever used with me, but I'd seen you use before slaughtering the opposition on the football field.

Brittney reached into the car, grabbed her designer bag, and stomped off down the street completing her diva image in my mind. I wanted to celebrate, but was still as pissed at you as you were at me.

You got in and burned rubber in the opposite direction. In the couple blocks it took to get home, you had calmed down enough to at least be driving sane, but one look at you in the mirror told me you were still fuming.

You drove into your driveway, and I jumped out from behind the passenger seat like a jack-in-the-box set free. I was feeling an odd burning sensation at the back of my eyes, and I had no intention of letting you see me cry again over you. Not ever, if I could help it. But you were quicker than me. You were around the car, and had grabbed me by the arm and dragged me, not to your house, but to mine before I could dig my heels in.

As we entered the house, I was screaming at you to let me go, and you had your lips set in a straight line that you usually reserved for your opponents on the football field. I tried to escape but you flung me on the couch, and when I went to leave, you sat on me.

All the commotion drew my mama into the room. She looked at you and at me with surprise registering all over her face.

"What on earth?"

"Tell your mama the kind of language and foul gestures you've been using today, Cami."

Cami. My heart sank. You were deadly serious. But I just glared at you and made the childish gesture of buttoning up my lips and throwing away the key.

I pushed at you again, but you didn't budge.

"Jake, what is this?" My mama moved forward because she clearly didn't like the way you were manhandling me, but I think she knew that I must have done something pretty drastic to push you over the edge like this. Even on the football field you hardly ever lost your cool. It was your cool head that was probably going to win you a scholarship.

"She's a nightmare, Andrea," you said with exasperation.

My mom broke out laughing, "And it's taken you this long to figure that out."

"She doesn't respect anyone's privacy, purposely provokes Brittney, and uses language that would make a trucker blush," you said in response.

"Camdyn?" Mama said, looking at me, waiting for my response.

"They fight all the time and then make up like jackrabbits going at it and expect me to sit there and take it all in stride," I finally huffed out. "And I don't swear all the time. Just when I'm angry."

Mama looked at both of us for a moment, and I think somewhere in her brain or heart or both, she started to see what was going on. Like your mama had the day I'd slammed out of your house while you were making out with Kayla.

"I see," she said, continuing to watch us. You were out of breath, but calming down, and I was trying to gasp for breath with you sitting on me, but no way were you getting me to admit that I was being crushed and couldn't breathe.

Mama walked over and touched your shoulder, looking down into your eyes with understanding and caring. "I think I'll take it from here, Jake honey. I think you both need some time to cool off."

You didn't even look at me, but you did stand up and say, "Fine," in a tone that said it was anything but, as you stormed out of the house.

I closed my eyes and gasped for air. It was bittersweet though, because the truth was, I already missed the weight of you on top of me. At least then I had you close to me. No Brittneys. No Kaylas. No sports. Just you and I.

My mom sat down next to me on the couch and waited a long time. She waited too long because I knew I couldn't leave until she'd said her piece, but I was so strung up emotionally, that I ended up crying. Silent tears. But tears. I hadn't wanted to cry in front of Jake or her. I hated tears. They were for weak-kneed fools and drama queen girls like Brittney, and I didn't want to be either. I think those tears caught Mama more off guard than you and I fighting had. I don't think Mama had seen me cry since I was a toddler and who knows if I even had then.

"How long?"

I was surprised by her question. I'd expected a lecture on being sure to give you the privacy you deserved or using bad language or just about losing my temper, which had always been her favorite thing to nag me about.

But instead, that one question told me that she understood. Understood every single emotion that was raging through me and just wanted to be there to support me. Because, that was my mama. I was really blessed to have her.

She waited for me. Waited for my tears to slow down a little, and finally, when I could speak, it came out as a ragged whisper, "Forever."

She pulled me into her arms and let me continue to cry.

Chapter Seven

Mean

"And all you're ever gonna be is mean."

- Taylor Swift

𝓘 *guess that one word for* that one song says it all. That was Brittney. Especially after she didn't get what she wanted.

♫ ♫ ♫

The rest of the week after our huge blow out, I stayed late at dive practice and would send some newbie out to tell you that I was staying late and that Coach would drive me home. I'm kind of surprised you let it go. You were never one to let me sulk, but for some reason you did. Maybe because you needed the time and space as much as I did.

Coach though, he didn't leave it alone. At first, he'd just raise his eyebrows, and not say anything. Finally, on Friday, on the way home, he asked "What's the deal with your right arm?"

I looked out the window. "He's got a new left arm."

"I see," Coach said, and then he was quiet all the way to our house. He put his SUV in park in the driveway and put a hand on my arm before I got out. "You know, Cami. Jake's a whole lot older than you. Someday three years won't seem like anything. But right now. Right now, it might as well be twenty."

I nodded.

"But, all I can say is that there is something special between the two of you. Something that no girlfriend or miles will ever break apart."

I looked at him wide-eyed.

"So. Just hang in there. Remember, someday, that three years won't feel like anything more than a blink."

I smiled my thanks because the words wouldn't come, grabbed my stuff, and headed home.

♪ ♪ ♪

But come Saturday, I couldn't avoid you. It was our birthday party.

Our parents had gone all out, decorating our shared backyard with a maze of fairy lights strung over the top of us and all over the bushes and fences. They had prayed it wouldn't snow and rented outdoor heaters and a dance floor.

We both got to invite a boatload of kids from school and the neighborhood. Our daddies had been barbecuing tri-tip and ribs all day. Our mamas were making Tennessee specialties like Southern mac and cheese for me, mashed potatoes for you, and plenty of green beans loaded with ham hock fixings and butter. And of course, plenty of cornbread and sweet tea. We might as well have been our own meat and three that day.

There was a huge two-foot cake with both our names etched along the side, but we didn't really care about that as much as the pile of MoonPies that Mama had bought. You and I were MoonPie fanatics, even if you couldn't really eat as many as you'd like to these days. I made up for it. I always ate your extras.

But today, I wasn't sure I cared about the yummy dinner or the pile of MoonPies. I was still not feeling myself. Wynn had outdone herself when helping me shop for a dress. It was midnight blue to set off my gray eyes, and was tight enough to show off the little curves I had, but not so tight that it looked slutty. I had pretty sparkly heels that, for once, I actually liked.

Wynn came to help me get ready and to try to cheer me up. She looked beautiful in a purple dress that was perfectly girly and gorgeous and didn't make her look too pale or too red. She'd had a boyfriend all year named Zack who was coming to keep her company tonight. He was a tall, thin cowboy who preferred the rodeo to the football field, but was a kicker on the middle school team anyway. All Southern boys needed to be involved in football in some way, otherwise they didn't exist in Tennessee.

I was sure I was going to be your typical wallflower because, even though I could dance, it really wasn't my thing and Wynn had Zack and you had Brittney. I guess it was a good thing there were MoonPies because I could sit in a corner and stuff my face till the midnight blue dress didn't fit anymore.

Just as I was letting this depressing thought register fully into my brain, Wynn came into my room bubbling with enough excitement to fill a glass of champagne.

"Did you hear?" she said, eyes sparkling with mischief.

My oblivious look said it all, so she continued.

"It's all over that Brittney and Jake broke up."

"Not funny."

"I would never tease you about Jake. She's been bitchy and griping to everyone that she's still coming tonight because anyone who's anyone will be here, but that she's really not looking forward to it."

"Well, butter my butt and call me a biscuit!" I said, too surprised to really think of anything better. As I let the idea settle in on me, my insides were flipping over like I'd already eaten too many pies.

And in this state of reverie, I let Wynn do me up. I even let her pull my dark hair into this sort of half updo with curls. And I hate curls. With a deadly passion. Almost as much as P-I-N-K. But when I looked in the mirror, I knew she'd done a good job. I looked…well…girly. And somehow, in this dress, my boobs looked bigger than the nubs they were.

When we hit the kitchen, my daddy stopped dead in his tracks with the barbecue tongs in his hands. "Andrea!" he called in a panicked voice.

My mama came up behind him, "What?"

And then she saw us too. She whistled. My mama did. It was hilarious to hear her wolf whistle like a construction worker.

"That's not funny, Andrea," my daddy said.

"Our little girl is growing up, Carter. You can't stop it. Just roll with the punches, sir."

She slapped him on the rear end with her kitchen towel and went back to work. Daddy's eyes got all squinty, and he pushed a hand to his head.

"I think I need a beer," was all he managed out before he led us out into the backyard.

The yard was already flooded with people. Wade and Blake were there with their girlfriends on their arms, and half the sophomore class was there for you. The seventh-grade crowd was a little smaller, just because I was a little prickly and not everyone liked the tomboy with the quick tongue.

Blake smiled big in his puppy-like way when he saw me and started over, but got sidetracked as the band started unloading their equipment. Blake still liked to think of himself as a budding musician. He wasn't bad. But he was no Jason Aldean.

Zack made his way through the crowd to tell Wynn how fantastic she looked and then was off again to fetch us some sweet tea. Wynn was going to make the perfect Southern wife someday. She knew exactly how to order her man around.

That's when I spotted you. You came out your back door and stopped to take in the whole shindig. You looked handsome as hell in tight jeans and a button-down that accented every single one of your muscles and made your eyes so green that I could catch the emerald from the other side of the yard. My heart banged so hard against my chest that I thought it would leap out of my mouth.

You saw me, too, and your smile reached your eyes. I swear those emeralds sparkled across the grass more than the fairy lights did. You were almost to me when Brittney intercepted. She was dressed in a black dress with red accents that barely left a smile between her and the Lord… or Satan. That night, her dress just seemed like the perfect echo of her fiery self.

You and she exchanged words. I don't know what they were, but then you went off with her into your house. I looked at Wynn and her smile faded. She'd seen too.

"It's okay. It is what it is, right?" I said with a shrug, but inside, my nonexistent pile of MoonPies turned to a solid mass.

Blake finally made it over to me, and he picked me up and swung me around like a doll. "Well look at you, Super Girl, finally playing in the big leagues," he said with warmth. He was the first boy to tell me that I looked nice that really mattered at all. I mean, he'd been in my life almost as long as you had, so it went a long way to picking up my scattered ego.

Blake's girlfriend, Kathy, was the nicest thing on earth. She didn't get jealous or catty, she just came up and hugged me and agreed with Blake about how nice I looked. Probably because she was secure in Blake's affections. And she wasn't threatened by me at all, probably because being five years older than me was more than enough distance for her. Probably because she knew I only had eyes for one boy.

The crowd seemed to thicken as more people showed up. Plenty of people followed Kathy and Blake's lead, and I was paid a lot of compliments that I wasn't quite sure how to handle.

Our parents dished out so much food that it could have fed an entire posse. We ate, drank sweet tea, and laughed. When you did come back shortly before dinner, Brittney followed, but she didn't look happy, and she didn't stay by your side which should have made me happy, but somehow did nothing to the solid feeling in my gut.

The band started up and between Wynn and Zack, and Blake and Kathy, I was never left alone. Not, at least, until after everyone had sung "Happy Birthday," and the cake had been served. It was when I had broken away to go get more tea and catch my breath that Brittney found me. She placed a hand on my arm, and I looked down at it debating whether I wanted to slam it back into her face or whether I'd play nice, as you and my mama would want me to do.

"Jake obviously didn't truly love me, but all I can say is Lord help whoever he really falls in love with because you'll always be there biting at her heels like the little bitch you are, ruining his life like a rotten fish ruins an icebox."

Blake came up from behind us. I guess he'd heard it all, or at least enough. He took one look at my face as I teetered between enough anger to put her under and enough heartache to do me in, and he swept in like the knight that you normally were.

"I think it's time for you to hit the road, Brit."

"You can't tell me to leave," she said, tossing her beautiful, silky hair.

"You're right, but Jake can, and I'm sure if I let him know what's going on, he'll be the first to show you the door."

She turned as red as her sleeves, but she just marched out of the yard and off into the night.

"You okay, Super Girl?" Blake asked.

I nodded, but the night had lost the limited shine it had for me. I made an excuse of hitting the bathroom, and Blake, thankfully, seemed to understand and turned back to the crowd. Instead of heading into the house, though, I moved toward the back of the yard to our tree house. I removed my sparkly shoes, left them on the ground, and climbed up into our hideaway.

I lay down and stared at the stars peeking through the branches and the "skylight" we'd added years ago. The music below was happy and the laughing was smooth, but it had started to die down as people began to say their goodbyes in the polite, Southern way that they always do. My mama would be mad as heck that I hadn't stayed to say goodnight and thank all the good people for coming to my party. But I didn't care. Mama was usually mad at me for something.

The cold air worked its way into my skin and bones without the heat lamps nearby to keep the winter at bay. But it kind of felt like my heart. Cold. Waiting to be woken back up.

Once the yard had dwindled to just a handful, I heard the tree creak as feet hit the ladder, and I didn't have to look up to know that you had joined me. You stretched out right next to me, the length of your body pressed against my side.

The warmth of you fighting against the cold that surrounded me.

After a while, you said, "Sorry about Brittney."

I had known all along that Blake would tell you what went down, but I thought maybe I'd be spared it tonight.

"Yeah. Me too."

"God, she required a lot of energy." And with that comment, I knew you were broken up for sure. Even though I should have been celebrating, I wasn't. I knew there was still that long line of girls waiting in Brittney's wake, and that I was still only a seventh grader.

"Why are girls like that?" he asked, truly bewildered.

I pushed my shoulder against his.

"Not all of us are."

He laughed like I'd told a brilliant joke.

"You require a lot of energy too. But maybe I'm just used to it. It doesn't bother me as much."

I couldn't help but smile to myself at that. You knew me. You knew me just like I knew you. That's why it didn't seem like work or energy. Even when we were mad at each other.

You placed a little package on my stomach. "Happy Birthday, Cami."

And my heart beat faster at your words and the Cami than at the present on my tummy. "You too, butthead," I said, but it made you laugh, which is what I had wanted.

I didn't make a move to open the gift, so you shoved your shoulder into mine. "Open it."

I reluctantly sat up, feeling the warmth of you drift away from me, and picked open the pretty little package which looked a lot like the polka-dotted underwear I'd been wearing earlier in the week when you'd thrown me over your shoulder. I truly hoped you hadn't seen them, and that it was just a coincidence.

It was a jewelry box, and no, I didn't get all girly and expect it to be a ring professing your undying love or anything. I mean, I was thirteen, and we weren't living in Shakespearean times. But when I opened it, I fell in love with you all over again. It was a necklace. A broken heart held together by wings. Beautiful and delicate. It made me think of the time in that same tree house that I'd told you that you were breaking my heart. You'd heard me. I knew you had, but this was your way of telling me that I had wings to fly above it all.

Okay, maybe I read way too much into it and did act a little girly. Maybe you just liked the necklace. Maybe your mama or Mia had picked it out. Regardless, it meant a lot to me. I think you knew that. I want to think that you'd bought that necklace as a peace offering for repeatedly breaking my heart.

You took the necklace from my hand and placed it around my neck. And no, you didn't kiss my neck or remark on the beauty of its slenderness. But at that moment, I didn't need that. I just needed you. I just needed to know we were still friends. That you'd still be there for me. And you were.

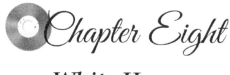

Chapter Eight

White Horse

"I'm not a princess, this ain't a fairy tale…
This ain't Hollywood, this is a small town."

- Swift & Rose

I love this country song. Because it's really about a hope that you have, that you've always had, that you have to let go of. It's about knowing that the thing you were dreaming about could never really be. There were many years, while I was pining away for you at the same time I was running to keep up with you, that I thought that there could be an "us." That it could work. That somehow the Disney-like magic would make its way into our lives. And then…then, there were a few years in there when I knew I'd never be a Disney princess. Not only was I definitely not typical princess material, but you weren't looking to be my knight in shining armor. You were really looking the complete opposite way.

I think it got a little easier for me once I accepted that you were out of reach. You weren't going to be my happy ending. Not while I was still in middle school anyway. I wanted to believe that, once I was in high school, things would change. I mean, lots of seniors went out with freshman girls, right?

But that January that you broke up with Brittney, I knew you'd have a new girl on your arm by the end of the month. At the latest, by the Girl's Choice Dance in February for Valentine's Day. And I was right. I almost felt bad for Brittney when it ended up being Amber. I mean, Amber had been the one she'd fought with you over the most. So, I guess Brittney had been right in a way.

Brittney didn't lose any time herself, though. She found a new boyfriend who was also a friend of Wade and Blake's. The thing that made me laugh was that when we were all out on the street throwing the football around (well, I was coaching from the sides), Wade and Blake would make all these snide comments about her and what a piece of work she was. Their friend was counting the days until he could get in her pants.

I watched you as they talked about her. And you didn't even seem bothered. It was like you had put her behind you like a pair of last year's shoes. It did make me wonder, though, if you'd gotten into her pants. I knew it was something you'd been trying for. You were a teenage boy after all, but you never let on in all of Wade and Blake's teasing about it. You were a gentleman. It made me proud of you. Even though I secretly wished you hadn't gotten that far.

Back to Amber. The thing about Amber was that she was actually nice. I hated to, but I liked her. She was smart and had ambitions other than being on the arm of a famous football player. She wanted to get her psychology degree and work as a school counselor. She was already planning on attending Brown. The thinking school.

And she never minded me being around. She always included me in the conversation. When we were all studying in your room, she'd help me with my homework and would swat your straying hands away with a purposeful look in my direction. She never rubbed it in my face that you were a couple.

So, you can see why I hated her at the same time that I loved her for saving me the pain. At a minimum, it allowed me to start doing homework with you again after school. Amber was usually the one to invite me. I guess that could have been weird. Her inviting me to your room, but it wasn't. It was her way of letting me know that she didn't think I was a fly buzzing around. Maybe that's why she lasted the longest of all your high school girlfriends. Maybe, because she wanted to be a psychology major, she did a little psychology on all of us and realized pushing me away would only push you away. Like it or not, I was part of your life.

The bad news about you getting your license was that you could head off to things like the drive-in and have make out sessions in peace and quiet. No me. No Mia. No Mama to interrupt your boy hands from roaming wherever they wanted. I didn't like thinking about it. Well, I did like thinking about it, but not with Amber on the receiving end.

Wynn said I took it better than she'd expected. And I did. Sometimes we got to tag along to the drive-in, or the movies, or the mall. Wherever you guys went, but a lot of times, you went on your own with Amber.

I had all this free time, and I didn't know what to do with it. I could only do so much diving. Coach had finally opened up his dive school, so I wasn't even practicing at the high school anymore. A lot of times you still picked me up in the Camaro on your way home, but sometimes my mama or daddy did.

I think my mama was secretly relieved to see that you and I were not joined at the hip as much as we had been. I think my admitting to her how badly I loved you had freaked her out a little. Anyway, I had free time on my hands. So, what did I do? I took up horseback riding.

What the heck? Do you remember saying that to me when I told you what I was going to do? Do you remember that I told you that we lived in Tennessee, after all? Sure, we didn't live on a farm or a ranch, but there were plenty in the area. You just shook your head at me like my mama normally did when I came up with something so foreign to her that she lost words.

Wynn joined me. It was good for our friendship to find something that was completely ours. Our coach for the end of my seventh grade year was Blake. Yes, Blake lived on our street, but he worked out at his granddaddy's ranch and taught us the basics. It was fun, and he got to tease me a lot about being Super Girl. He kept asking me if there was anything I couldn't do. Of course, he already knew the thing I was worst at: football. But I could sure as hell referee it, and he'd been on the losing side of my smart tongue many a time when it came to that.

I think he was particularly hard on me as my coach because it was payback. After we'd learned a lot, Blake taught us how to jump the horses over little obstacles. Wynn panicked and wouldn't do it, but for me, it was natural. When I was jumping the horse, I got that same floating experience as I did when I was diving. It was a bit of freedom from the things that bound me to the earth.

There were times, when we knew we'd be doing a lot of jumping, that Wynn wouldn't bother coming at all to the ranch and then it was just Blake and I. We didn't say much. We didn't need to. There was just us and the horses and the countryside.

One time, when we were out and about, my horse was in mid-jump over a creek when she got spooked by something and, all of a sudden, I was flying through the air, and diving into the creek like it was the pool. Blake was off his own horse and at my side as quick as a lightning bug flash.

His surfer boy face was scrunched up in concern until he saw that I was just pissed off at having been tossed, and not at all hurt. Then, he burst out laughing so hard I thought he'd pee himself like a dog marking its territory.

I punched him in the shoulder, splashed his face, and he just laughed more and hauled me up out of the water.

"You're something else, Super Girl." It reminded me of the time I dove off the cliff, and he'd swum out behind you to make sure I was okay. It was kind of nice knowing there were people out there willing to look after me when you were looking the other way. I guess, if I really looked around, there were a lot more people than even him that were willing to bat at my side. Truth was, I just never really wanted them there. I wanted my side empty until you chose to show up.

Blake got accepted to Ole Miss (scowl). I told him he was a traitor. Who could possibly go to Ole Miss when they had University of Tennessee knocking on their door? He laughed and said there was more to life than football. I gasped and pretended that he'd made the ultimate sin. But once summer hit, Blake had to turn over our instruction to someone else.

Blake turned it over to his brother, Matt. Haven't even talked about Matt up to this point, right? Probably because you know that we were both thoroughly unimpressed with Matt. He'd been invisible like all boys were that didn't play football. He never was out on the street playing with the older boys like you were. This was, come to find out, because Matt was quite the rodeo man and spent more time at the ranch than on the block. He knew Wynn's boyfriend, Zack, from the rodeo circuit and from around school. He was a year older than Wynn and I, though, so he hadn't been on our radar, just like we hadn't really been on his.

One time, you came to pick Wynn and me up, and Matt was laughing at us, pulling his cowboy hat off to hide his big grin. He was a little like Blake in that shaggy, blonde-haired kind of way. Almost like they both would be better off on a surfboard on a California beach instead of under a cowboy hat on a ranch.

Anyway, we'd made him laugh, which wasn't all that hard because he was a bit of a ham himself, and Wynn and I were laughing too, big belly laughs. I don't remember why or what the conversation was. What I remember was the look in your eye as you approached us. You came up to Matt and rubbed your knuckles on top of his head like you still did with me. You were easily 6'1" by now. Matt wasn't short, but he was still a couple inches under you.

"How's it goin', kid?" you said to him. Matt's smile broadened because he thought you were being funny, but I saw the flash of something close to anger in your eyes. Like when you'd punched Paul for talking smack about me being with you.

It made my stomach all squishy, that you didn't like the fact that he was flirting with me. It had to be because of that. You didn't wait for any more conversation. You turned to Wynn and me and said, "Gotta jam, ladies. Big celebration at the lake tonight, and we gotta get set up."

Wynn waved to Matt and headed off on your heels. I started to follow but then couldn't help myself. I turned back to Matt and said, "You're gonna be there tonight, right, Matt?"

Matt scratched his neck and seemed a little puzzled to be included in things he'd never really been included in before. You stopped in your tracks and turned on me with a look that could kill.

I mouthed, "Be nice," to you. You didn't look like you wanted to be nice.

"Well, I'm not sure. We'll see. Thanks for the invite though," was Matt's response.

The best thing was, you didn't speak to me the whole ride home. I know. You'd think I'd have been devastated by that, but it was like nectar to the gods. You cared enough to not like other boys flirting with me, even if you couldn't bring yourself to flirt with me.

Ha!

♫ ♫ ♫

That night at the lake, you had Amber at your side the whole night. It was one of the first times the two of you flaunted your "togetherness." Amber had had a few beers. I know. Beers. But you were going to be a junior and you were taking over from Blake and Wade as the party king, and we grew up in the middle of Tennessee, so, to all you disapproving parents out there, yes, there was beer.

Amber, with a few beers, didn't seem to care so much about me seeing your hands on her. My high from the whole Matt thing didn't last very long with the two of you hanging on each other.

Wynn, Zack, and I swam out to our makeshift dock that was still anchored in the lake. We jumped and dove and swam while you and the high school crew partied it up on the beach with a bonfire and music. It made me realize how you must have felt when you were in middle school and Wade and Blake had been leading the shindigs, and you'd been stuck with the fifth grader. You must have felt like I did right then, torn between wanting to be cool enough to hang out with the big kids but also more interested in the sky and the lake and the crickets.

We'd been out there for quite a while, when a splash in the water made us realize that someone was joining us on the platform. Matt stuck up a wet head. He'd hauled a cooler out with him and put it up on the dock first before dragging himself up behind it.

He was muscled and tan like Blake had always been, but a little skinnier. Not as broad-shouldered. He looked good. He wasn't you, but he looked good. "I come bearing gifts," he said proudly.

We opened the cooler, and it was full of MoonPies, RC Cola, and Doritos. A teenage feast. We all dove in, thanking him profusely. We laughed and flirted and had fun. Zack and Matt started talking about horses and rodeos, and Wynn and I went back into the lake.

We floated far enough away that the boys couldn't hear us before Wynn spoke.

"So, Matt, huh?"

"I guess," I said.

"What's it with you and high school guys?"

"I'm sure that Amber would associate some Freudian daddy issue with it."

Wynn gurgled.

"He's a nice guy. I don't think anything is gonna happen though," I told her honestly because, even then, I knew that there wasn't any guy that I could ever date who would ever hold a candle to you.

Eventually, Wynn and I made it back to the dock, and we were all just getting cozy, lying out on our backs with the stars above us, and Matt's feet finding their way to mine, when the music on the shore stopped and you hollered out to us, "Time to go, love birds!"

I laughed so hard I almost peed my swimsuit because I knew exactly what you were doing. You were bringing me back to that night that Blake had done the same thing to you and me. Of course, the three of them thought I was off my rocker. And I guess I sort of was. Because you would always make me a little crazy.

♫ ♫ ♫

When we went back to school in the fall, the thing with Matt went by the wayside. In truth, I only saw him twice a month for horseback riding lessons, and he seemed caught up with rodeos and school and just being a freshman.

I was caught up in diving and managing to stay afloat in a geometry class that I'd been assigned I didn't know how. Somewhere along the way, my teachers must have thought that I could do more than I ever demonstrated with my grades because they assured my parents I was more than qualified to take the course.

So, it was back to your bedroom for geometry lessons this time. Amber was good about it. She even added her two cents in whenever I'd get frustrated with you and start tossing paper snowballs instead of studying.

♪ ♪ ♫

You led the football team to the state championships as a junior that year. You didn't win. Mostly because your defense sucked, and you got hit so hard it knocked you out in the last quarter.

I felt it just as I saw it happen. I knew you were going to get hurt. I was already halfway down the bleachers before you'd hit the ground and your parents realized what had happened. We were on the sidelines when they brought you off. By this time, you'd woken up, but no one would let you back on the field. That pissed you off to no end. You fought everyone tooth and nail.

But your parents and the football coach won out, so I got to ride with you to the hospital where they did a CT scan and checked your brain for any issues. I could have told them there was nothing wrong with you. You were perfect.

As always. The god that could not be shot down by a mere human.

You did have a flaw, though. Your diabetes. And while you mostly had it under control, it still played havoc with you on occasion. Of course, because we'd spent so much of our time apart the last couple years, I hadn't been able to continue to be your personal food cart. Instead, you stocked yourself up. You had these little sugar tabs that you placed under your tongue when you needed it.

I remember one time you had a little spell with Amber in the room. She went white as a sheet and froze. All I could think was, some psychologist she's gonna make if she can't even handle a little diabetic episode.

I just got the orange juice and forced you to drink it until you came around on your own. Embarrassed, because Amber had seen you. Not because of me. You were used to me being there. I made some lame excuse after to leave because I could tell that Amber was feeling all girly and mushy and wanted to kiss you all better.

It had given you the perfect excuse to get all the way in her pants. Which I knew was where you most desired to be. And your parents weren't home. There was some big event at the dealership that both our parents were at, sparing us, of course from attending, but poor Mia had been dragged along. She was such a good kid.

I went home, called Wynn to come over, and we watched some sappy girl movie together. I was getting to the point where I didn't mind sappy girl movies so much. I mean, I'd still prefer a good football movie like *The Replacements, Invincible, Friday Night Lights, Varsity Blues,* or *Remember the Titans,* but I could kind of get into the whole happily ever after, even if I didn't think it was ever going to happen for me.

Chapter Nine

The Way I Loved You

"He says everything I need to hear and it's like

I couldn't ask for anything better."

- Swift & Rich

The beginning of this song is true. I had a boyfriend. A boyfriend that all my friends were jealous of because he seemed so perfect. Even my parents thought he was perfect. And maybe even you thought he was perfect. I couldn't really tell. The only one who didn't think he was perfect was me. But…it's still a good story. A story that, as always, has everything to do with you and very little to do with the other boy. Because it could never be the way that I loved you.

My eighth-grade year had gone by with me in a holding pattern. That's how I felt. And I didn't know then that life would be a continual holding pattern for me. You'd waited for me in the womb. That was only nine and a half months. I felt like I waited nine years. Life may be moving along, I may be winning dive competitions, having folks asking me if I would try for the Olympics (ha, I wasn't that dedicated), and having teachers asking me if I was ready for high school, but I really felt like I was waiting. Waiting for the alarm to go off and wake me up. Waiting for the three-year gap to disappear like I thought it would, magically, once we were both at the same school again.

So, you can understand that I was nervous and very, very expectant the day I entered high school. We'd spent another summer at the lake, but you'd also divided your time between a job at the dealership and Amber. You two were definitely sleeping together. I could smell her on you sometimes when I'd come over to your room, and we'd lay on your bed listening to music and talking about the scouts coming to look at you at football practice.

Your bedroom was some of our only alone time. At the lake, we were hardly ever alone. You were celebrating your last summer as a high school student. Your last year. You had everyone out there celebrating with you.

I was biding time for my new beginning.

That first day that I walked down the halls of our high school, all I could think about was how long it had been since we'd actually been able to see each other at school. I almost cried from happiness at seeing you. Which is saying a lot, as you know, I don't cry.

But…Amber was on your arm. And you were surrounded by Paul and Craig and their lady friends and a wake the size of a soccer team. You smiled and waved. But it was from the other side of the hallway, and you didn't come to say hello. You didn't come, sweep me off my feet, and say, "Finally! Finally, it's okay for us to be together."

I know. Really insane of me, right? I don't think I ever really THOUGHT that was what was going to happen. And

I certainly hadn't forgotten Amber. But…I don't know…just but.

Wynn saw my expression and took pity on me, hurrying me into the girls' bathroom so I wouldn't cry. But I didn't feel like crying. Instead, I punched the bathroom stall with my fist and then kicked the door repeatedly. Wynn just stood by and waited. What a good friend, right?

"Cami, you're scaring me."

I leaned on the sink and breathed heavily, trying to calm myself. I looked in the mirror and saw a girl. Yep. I'd become a girl. Dark,, wavy hair. Blue-gray eyes. A dress. A dress. I was in a dress. With my cowboy boots, true, but a dress.

"I'm fine. Really. I'll be fine."

Poor Wynn had been dreading freshman year, whereas I had been all bottled excitement. Zack's dad had been transferred to New Orleans, and so she'd had to say goodbye to her boyfriend of almost two years. I thought it was a good thing because he had been too gentle for Wynn. He did everything she wanted and never questioned it. I just didn't think Wynn needed that quiet of a life, but she'd been so sad for weeks. I didn't feel like I wanted to add to her emotional issues, so I calmed down—or did a good job of faking it—and we headed off to class.

The next time I saw you, it was the end of school and you were headed off to football practice. And in typical Cami fashion, I didn't think, I just reacted. Big surprise, right? I pulled on the t-shirt of the closest guy I could reach, shoved my lips at him, and kissed him like no tomorrow. At least, I thought I did, since I'd had actually no, none, zip experience in this area.

The guy I was kissing, after the first shock, realized his advantage, and stuck his tongue in my mouth, surprising the shit out of me, before pulling me up tight against his body. I fought an urge to slap the hell out of his face because I could feel your eyes on me. I could feel them boring into my head. I wanted to see that black smoldering anger that I'd seen when you'd approached Matt and me flirting at the ranch a summer ago.

When I dared to open my eyes and pull slightly away from my unsuspecting victim, I saw you approaching. But there was no smolder. Instead, you had a grin on your face. A grin. Like you thought the whole thing slightly hilarious.

I watched you approach with a sinking feeling in my stomach. Sometimes your smile hid a death wish. But, no. Not this time. You get angry when I'm merely flirting with a guy, but you see us exchanging spit and feeling each other's tonsils up with our tongues, and you don't even blink an eyelash? Come on!

It was as you reached up to tousle the hair of my victim that I let out an audible gasp. My victim was none other than Matt himself. How the hell could our school be so small as to have allowed my one-time victim to be the only other guy at the school whom I'd ever really shown the least interest in?

"How's the ranch, cowboy?" you asked with a smile. I pushed myself away from Matt's very firm chest and dragged the back of my hand across my mouth.

You turned your smile from Matt to me. Then I saw the flash. It was so brief and was so quickly replaced by your wide, beautiful smile that I could have imagined it, but I didn't think so. My heart skipped a beat. You looked back to Matt.

Matt grinned back, but he shifted his feet too. Like he was unsure how you'd react to his lips on mine. I felt bad. Matt was a nice guy. And I'd just used him in the cruelest way. "Ranch is good. How's football?"

You smiled, "Like always."

You stared into Matt's eyes for a moment. Like you were sizing him up, then with a quick smile at me, you sauntered away. You called back over your shoulder, "You two have fun now. Just be careful Mr. Leonard doesn't catch you."

And then you were gone. Mr. Leonard was our vice principal. And even though I was only a freshman, I knew his reputation for ruining the lives of any kid caught doing anything that might be considered even slightly offensive. I'm sure our PDA would definitely have been offensive.

Matt turned his eyes to me. They were green. And pretty. Not like they could bore into my soul like yours could, but they were pretty. I felt like a cad.

"I'm sorry," I said.

"What for?"

"Attacking you like that."

"Because you didn't mean it?"

And I looked at him and realized that there was no way in hell that I could be that harsh. I wasn't Brittney. So, just like that, I had myself a boyfriend.

♫ ♫ ♫

I wondered sometimes if that was what had happened with you and Kayla. Or even you and Brittney. A little tonsil hockey leading to the assumption that you two were a couple. Because that's just what had happened to me.

Matt called me a lot. Texted me more often. Nice things like, how was your day? Did you get that new dive you've been working on? Stuff that was completely sweet and made Wynn sigh because she was in boyfriend withdrawals.

I'd never cared about that stuff. I'd always rolled my eyes at you having to "play nice" with your girlfriends, and here I was all of a sudden having to do the same thing.

Matt became a regular in the car on the ride home. So, now it was a foursome. You and Amber. Matt and I. It was two teenage couples. He'd hang out in your bedroom with us doing homework. And the truth was, it was nice to be the center of someone's attention again. It was good for my ego.

For a while, many years ago, I'd been the center of your attention, but that was long gone. So, it just felt damn good. Matt would fetch me soda and chips. He'd play with my hair when it escaped my ponytail, and show up at my meets with signs that said, "Go Super Girl."

He'd picked up on Blake's nickname for me: Super Girl. I'm not sure why Blake had always called me that, but Matt said that he was calling me it because I was the strongest, smartest, wickedest girl he knew. Maybe he was just trying to get into my pants. But he wasn't even pushing it to third base, so I felt like I was safe.

The bad thing about having a boyfriend, is that it takes time. And I had to go to rodeos. I know I'm from Tennessee, and I like country music and football—I even got a high off jumping the horses at Matt's granddaddy's ranch—but rodeos bored the crap out of me.

All that male testosterone on display. Gag. But I went. I didn't hold up a sign like he did at my meets. And Matt never complained about it or said anything negative. It was like he was just happy to be along for the ride. And I realized that's what Wynn must have felt about Zack.

She said it wasn't. She said she loved Zack and as soon as she could, she was going to find a way to move to New Orleans and be with him, but I knew that she'd move on. Maybe that's what everyone thought had happened with me and my feelings for you, because my mama and your mama didn't seem to watch us so closely anymore.

They were relieved my crush had gone away.

But it hadn't. Every time I kissed Matt, I wanted it to be you. I wanted to open my eyes and not see his gentle green ones but the intense kaleidoscope of yours. I'm sure Matt sensed it. I tried hard not to let him realize he was second fiddle, but Matt wasn't stupid. A goofball sometimes, but definitely not stupid.

I tried not to stare at you when you were head to head with Amber, talking all hush-hush about plans for the weekend. But sometimes when I'd look up from staring at you, I'd see Matt staring at me, and I'd wonder how long it would last. How long he would put up with it.

And sometimes, I wondered if it bothered you at all. To see me engaged in my own little bit of tonsil hockey with Matt. Once in a great while, when Matt would kiss me goodbye and you were there and I turned to you, you'd have an odd look on your face, but it was never the deep, lake-green angry look in your eyes. It was a wary, thoughtful look.

♫ ♫ ♫

Matt and I did have fun. It wasn't like I didn't enjoy being with him. I got to go with a date to school dances, and I actually laughed my ass off through the whole thing because Matt was such a goofball and could make me laugh by doing the silliest things, like the Robot or the old-fashioned Mashed Potato. Always done poorly, but with much enthusiasm.

And we always went to funny movies. Never girly dramas or stupid shoot-'em-up action movies that were your favorite. So, I got to laugh a lot. And that was good. Laughter fills your soul, right?

But as the school year went on, after football was over, and the scouts had all been on your doorstep. After you'd made an informal pledge to the University of Tennessee, I started to panic. I literally started having panic attacks. I'd be perfectly fine one moment, and then the next, I was shaking so hard that I couldn't breathe. And the lack of breath would cause my vision to go spotty and my head to spin.

The day you got your official letter from UTK, I actually passed out. I know you never knew that. It would have been extremely embarrassing for me to have told you. I'd left your house to go home for dinner. Matt was walking with me. He was having dinner at my house, like he did a lot. My parents liked him. Who wouldn't? He was a parent's dream. Polite. Good to me. Never pushy.

Anyway, I was still reeling from your acceptance as I walked and, all of a sudden my eyes went all spotty, and just like that, I passed out. Matt caught me before I could go headfirst down the steps. When I came back around after the split second of darkness, he'd sat me down on the steps and pushed my head between my legs so that I'd get some air back into me. We sat there for a few moments before he spoke.

"You knew he was leaving," Matt said to me gently.

All I could do was nod from my bent over position, gasping for air.

"You'll be okay without him, you know." My head bounced up quicker than a horse flicks a fly with its tail, and looked into Matt's face, and I saw the writing on the wall.

"You're Super Girl," he said with a gentle smile and pushed back a strand of hair from my face.

"I'm sorry," I said to him.

"Me too," he said quietly.

"Why are you sorry?" I said in bewilderment.

"Because I knew that first day of school when you kissed me exactly why you did it."

I think my mouth probably hit the ground. I couldn't help it. I had just assumed he'd been oblivious to the whole thing that day. Sure, he'd realized some things over our six months together, but I didn't think he'd known that day.

Matt laughed, like he always did. At himself. At others. At life. "But it was one hell of a kiss."

I grinned like crazy at him.

"It was my first ever."

"Really?" His turn to be shocked. "Anyway, kissing you like that, for any reason, was sure worth it."

I nudged him in embarrassment.

"So, this is it, I guess?" I asked quietly.

"Probably. The horse is out of the barn, so to speak."

And just like that, I didn't have a boyfriend anymore.

Chapter Ten

Change

"And I'll do anything to see it through
Because these things will change."
- Taylor Swift

So Matt was gone. And I was back to same old, same old. Me tagging along with you and a girlfriend. I was a little sick of it. But somewhere inside of me, I just knew these things had to change. That there would come a time when those itty-bitty three years separating us would disappear and fall away just like Coach had predicted.

Wynn thought I was insane for giving up Matt. And in truth, I was. But as I've said before, I already knew I was insane. From the very first time when I was little, sitting on your porch and drawing your hand into my sticky one so that you'd take your eyes off the boys playing football, to the time I'd pulled Matt into that kiss just to see your reaction. I'd been crazy my entire life over a boy who still wouldn't even register the fact that I was anything more than the next-door neighbor kid that tagged along with him no matter what.

I told Wynn she should go after Matt herself, but she was too loyal for that. I think she thought about it. Her obsession with Zack had faded, and she was looking around campus at the other cute boys, and Matt was definitely one of the cutest. But somehow, that Southern honor got the better of her. Later, after she had her own trauma, I'd wished she'd taken my advice and picked Matt. But I'll stayed focus on this story for now.

After Matt and I broke up, my parents, you, and Amber were all worried that I'd go off the edge into a great depression or something. It was kind of ridiculous because when had I ever gone over the edge crying about a boy? Well… other than you. But it was kind of sweet, and I loved that you became especially worried when I wouldn't tell you why we broke up. You threatened to beat the crap out of him if he'd been forcing himself on me, and I just laughed like hell because wasn't it really the other way around? We'd started it all by me forcing myself on him.

But you were all watching me like you thought I was going to suddenly fall off the edge. And the truth was, I did feel like I was falling off a cliff, but it wasn't because of Matt. It was because of you. I had started counting down days. Days until you left. Days left with you. I was trying every day just to breathe. Trying not to get lost in the terror that was the thought of not seeing you at the end of almost every single day.

But somewhere near spring break, a new fear entered me. You were having a lot more of your "incidents" again. You liked to brush them aside just like you had before your eighth-grade year, before I'd gotten you to go to the doctor by agreeing to dive with Coach. I started carrying stuff with me again. I even raided your needles and insulin to keep a spare in my bag. I could have gotten in a lot of trouble at school if I was caught with them, but when had I ever cared about a little trouble? Especially when it was related to you.

♪ ♪ ♪

One day, that weird connection between us, the one that had brought you running the day I nearly fell off the ladder by the tree house, made you look at me on the cliff, and made me run down the bleachers before you'd been knocked out, came back into play. I always walked a certain way to my fifth period class. It was a way that avoided both you and Matt, killing two birds with one stone, so to speak. Not that Matt had been anything but nice, but I felt awkward around him at the moment.

So, Wynn couldn't understand it when I insisted that we go the way that would guarantee I'd hit both of you in one fell swoop. But something inside me was just begging me to take that hallway. So, we did.

That's when we saw the crowd. A crowd in high school usually means a fight, right? But this time, I saw Mr. Reed, the moron, standing nearby wringing his hands. My heart fell. I just knew it was you. How? How, you ask? I can't answer it. The same way you knew that I needed you that day on the ladder.

I ran forward, elbowing my way to the front of the crowd, and there you were. On the floor, shaking, babbling. Everyone was looking a little aghast at the football god having a seizure or something. Thank God I had my supplies. I grabbed one of the sugar tabs from my backpack and placed it under your tongue and then cracked open a Gatorade, getting it ready. I had your head in my lap, and even though I was shaking a little, I was crooning at you to drink it. I forced the drink into your mouth, and you gagged, but swallowed.

Mr. Reed stepped forward as if I was trying to kill you. I looked up at him with hate in my eyes. "Call 911, stupid, he's having a diabetic seizure."

"The office has already called," he said, ignoring my name calling.

I returned my focus to you. "Jake, Jake, come on. Drink a little more for me," I soothed, trying so hard not to panic. You'd never been this bad. Never. Dizzy, blurry, a little stumbly, but you'd never passed out shaking with eyes rolling back.

I heard the siren. Heard Mr. Leonard clearing the crowd as he came from the office, but I still wouldn't let you go. Eventually, the paramedics made their way to us. They took one look at me with the drink and you with dribbles down your chin and quickly determined what had happened.

"Diabetic. How long?" they asked me.

"Four years," I said.

They were pulling out an IV and finding a place to stick the line while talking with me.

"Ever had a seizure before?"

"No. Some lows. More lately," I told them honestly, not caring if you got mad at me later, only caring about having these two men save you.

"Okay, miss. You can let him go. We're going to put him on the gurney now."

I wouldn't let you go. I still had the Gatorade at ready, your head in my lap. They were trying to take it all away. They were forcing my hands from around you.

"Miss. I promise you, we're going to take care of him."

I let them take you from me, but as soon as they had you on the stretcher, I had your hand again. No one even prevented me. Not the paramedics. Not Mr. Leonard, or even Mr. Reed whom I'd insulted.

As we were rushing through the corridor with them pushing you and me jogging alongside, I saw Amber, her eyes wide, frozen in the doorway of the classroom near where we had been, and somewhere it registered in my mind that she must have been there for a while and not known what to do. I was disgusted, but I didn't let it sidestep me from tagging along with you.

No one stopped me from getting into the ambulance with you. I wonder about that now. Most of the time, they only let family go. Sometimes not even that. A lot of times, they make the family trail the ambulance. Maybe it was because we were both so young or maybe they assumed I was your sister because there was still such a gap in our ages. I don't know, but I am grateful they let me go because if I'd had to stay back at the school, I think I would have had to have an ambulance come back for me. But being there with you, having to be strong for you, made me stronger.

When we got to the hospital, I had to let you go for real. The doctors and nurses weren't as nice as the paramedics had been. They simply forced me to stay outside the swinging doors of the ER. I stood there like I was in one of those hospital dramas, staring at the doors.

Your parents and my parents came through the automatic doors a few minutes later. The school must have called them. My mama had me in her arms, and Marina and Scott were asking me what had happened.

I don't even remember what I said. I must have said enough that they knew the gist of it and went off to find a doctor or nurse. My mama had me sit down. My daddy paced in front of me. It seemed like hours went by. I'm sure it wasn't anywhere near that long. Eventually your parents came back, and they had a look of relief on their faces that told me everything I needed to know.

"He's fine. Awake. Angry as hell. Already trying to pull the IVs out. Come on. They say we can see him."

They led us to the room they'd placed you in. And as soon as I saw you, I ran over and hugged you. My head on your chest the best way I could get to you in the hospital bed. You put a hand on my hair.

"Cami, I'm okay." Your voice sounded tired. But I knew you were telling the truth. Like we always knew that about each other. Except later, when you wouldn't tell me anything at all so that I wouldn't know you were lying. But that's later again.

At that point, I didn't move, not right away. I hugged you for a good ten or fifteen minutes before the side of the hospital bed pushing into me caused me enough pain to register in my thick skull, and I let you go reluctantly.

Marina was on the other side of you, and as I lifted my head, she smiled at me.

"Okay, now will someone please get me the hell out of here?" you grumbled.

"Not so quick, young man," your daddy said. "Doc Wilson is on his way. He wants to evaluate you and maybe keep you overnight to run some more tests."

"No," you said fiercely. "I have that meeting tomorrow with UTK."

But Marina and Scott could be as stubborn as you, and they said they'd simply reschedule it. This set off an argument about you not wanting to worry the coaches at Tennessee that you couldn't deliver what you'd signed up to deliver, and them saying it was part of life and that if Tennessee gave you up because of this, then it was their loss.

In the end, you won. Sort of. But then, you and I had always had a way of getting what we wanted with our parents. Especially if we worked together. We'd break them like glue that had been iced. I dove in and sided with you, and they couldn't fight both of us. You agreed to see Doc Wilson and stay for the eval as long as you were released by ten the next morning, in plenty of time to meet with UTK.

After, when you were smiling again, relief washed over me because I knew you were back to yourself. You were being stubborn and were getting your way with your smooth talking. With the relief came fatigue. I was suddenly so, so tired. Probably because I hadn't been breathing very well for several hours and lack of oxygen can be very exhausting.

My mama saw me drooping. "I think we'll just take Camdyn home now." And as much as I wanted to refuse, I knew that it was okay. You were safe. You were in good hands, and I needed to get myself together.

"I'll walk you out," Marina said.

We walked in silence to my parents' car. Marina hugged me. "Thank you," she said quietly.

"I…I thought I was too late," I told her honestly, tears springing from my eyes.

"You weren't. You were there. Like you always are," she said and squeezed me again before letting me go and watching me get into my parents' car.

But honestly, I was terrified. Because, in a little over two months, you were going away, and who would be there then?

♫ ♫ ♫

When you came home, not much was said about the doctor and your sugar levels. But you were watching them a lot more, and so I was watching you a lot more. I was almost afraid to let you out of my sight, even during class. Any thought I had of recruiting Amber to help went out the door because when you came back to school, Amber broke up with you. She said that it was too hard to be with someone that she had to worry about constantly, and that you would have had to break up anyway with her going to Brown and you going to the University of Tennessee.

Even though I'd liked Amber, I suddenly didn't. How could she say that to you? How could she walk out on you just like that? But you said it was an amicable break up. You were still going to senior prom together. Still going to be friends, but it was time for you both to move on.

You didn't seem upset. That was strange to me. Strange that you just took it in stride like you'd taken Kayla and Brittney, even though you'd dated Amber the longest. Even though I knew for sure you'd slept with her. But maybe it was because you'd already let her go in your mind, too, just like you'd let the others go. You'd already seen the writing on the wall. Or maybe it was because, like me, you hadn't been able to get overly attached to anyone. That gave me hope. Hope that also scared me because I hadn't hoped in quite a while.

♪ ♪ ♪

We fell back into an old, long forgotten habit of coming home from school together, just the two of us. Sometimes we'd pick Mia up at the middle school. But a lot of the time, it was just the two of us.

We'd ride in silence, listening to our private mixed-up playlist of country, alternative rock, blues, and classic rock. It was always a comfortable silence. But one that seemed bittersweet too, like we both knew it was the last of the days.

One day, we were lying on your bed studying for finals, and you'd just taken a sugar reading and placed it back on the nightstand when you stopped me dead with a confession. You weren't big on confessions. Or weakness.

"I'm scared, Cam."

I rolled over onto my side, propped my head on my hand, and waited, watching you. You wouldn't look at me right away.

"I'm scared that I won't be able to control this anymore. That it'll ruin my football scholarship."

"There's more to life than football," I said, speaking the deadliest sin a Southern girl could ever say. Saying the words that Blake had said to me not many years ago. You raised your eyes to me enough to roll them in my direction, saying "stupid girl" without words.

"And your parents would pay for you to go to school," I continued.

You nodded. You knew I was right, but I also knew that you were feeling out of control. A feeling you hardly ever encountered. A feeling you would never like. The football god, who could will everything to go his way, wasn't sure what to do with something that didn't bend to that will.

"But...what would I do then?"

I shrugged and tried to lighten the mood with some teasing, "Anything. You're a god among men."

You flipped my ponytail into my face, and I shoved you, and we started a good wrestling match. One we hadn't had in a long time. But this time, even though you were stronger, you were limited. There were places on me you no longer felt okay to touch, and I completely took advantage of every ounce of your hesitation.

It still ended with me on the bottom, and you sitting on my stomach with my wrists in one hand. I was trying not to laugh, and you were smiling which was all that mattered to me at that moment. But as you stared down at me, with my hands above my head, and my chest heaving from laughter and exertion, the mood suddenly changed. It felt charged with electricity like the air after a lightning storm that precedes a twister. We both stared at each other, our smiles fading a little, playing with that charge, daring it to hit us. You caved first. You rolled off of me before I had a chance to whisper, "Give."

You got up, switched the iPhone to a new playlist and then left, saying you were grabbing some food. I had already returned to my Algebra II when you came back. You had a water and some trail mix, but you'd brought me a Dr. Pepper which you tossed at me. You rolled up next to me, and we just went back to studying like nothing had happened.

Chapter Eleven

Tim McGraw

"When you think happiness,
I hope you think that little black dress."
- Swift & Rose

So, I guess we can get back to the question now. The question, "When did you and Jake become a thing?" It was easier to explain the "not a thing" first. And, God, the thought of that first sweet summer brings to mind only one song, "Tim McGraw." It's so full of every last star-filled memory that I have of that day. The day you graduated. The day we fell asleep together…twice. The summer wind. My black dress and, later, my blue jeans. The water. The air. Charged. Full of every expectation I'd ever had. Some songs are like that. Can bring you back to exactly that amazing moment. Don't you think? I wonder, does that song make you think of that day too?

After that charged wrestling moment on your bed, everything seemed to build up toward what came next. The last week of school was a whirlwind. We had special night rallies and award assemblies for the seniors. We had a school carnival, and all the work that came with it. Plus finals. So, we were exhausted by the time the last day came. I hardly saw you on Friday. You were out with the boys, but on Saturday morning, before graduation, you and I went for a bike ride out to the lake and back.

When we got home, we grabbed a snack from the kitchen where your mom and Mia were busy making food and planning for all the grandparents. Just a close family "dinner" early in the afternoon at the house, because you'd said you didn't want a big to-do made out of the graduation thing. Instead, a bunch of the graduates and high school kids were having a party at the lake later that night. I still can't get over what a good kid Mia was—is. I would never have thought to help. I wanted to be with you, not chopping vegetables in the kitchen. And I don't think your mama would have even given two breaths at the thought of asking you to help. While you were awesome with a football, you were helpless with a knife. That would bite us both in the butt later… but that's still for later.

That warm Saturday morning, we were pretty wiped out, the muggy day tugging at us like a current in water. You and I collapsed on your bed with one of our favorite playlists running. One minute we were debating the guitar skills of Keith Urban and the next, I'm not sure what happened, but we had both fallen asleep. Knocked out asleep. Deep. We only woke up to Mia pounding on your door saying we had thirty minutes to get ready.

We both looked at each other startled. You had an arm flung over me. We both had hazy, sleep-filled eyes. You pulled your arm back and jumped up like you'd been bitten by a brown bug. I rolled off the bed, grabbed my bag, and turned toward the door at the same time as you pulled off your pants. You were standing there in your boxers. They were really cute boxers with footballs on them. You didn't even seem to think about having done it because you were pulling a pair of slacks off a hanger trying to hurry.

But I froze, staring at you. You didn't see me still as a statue until I'd somehow breathed out, "Geez, Jake."

You barely glanced my way. "It's not like you haven't seen me in my swim trunks, Cam."

But, God, did you look incredible. Way different in your underwear than in your swim shorts. I don't know why. I had seen you in your swim trunks a million times. But…these were thinner. Clinging to parts of you that made my heart spin like a top and other parts of me jump to attention. Maybe it was because we'd just woken up from a heady, midday sleep. Maybe it was because I knew you were leaving me. All I knew was that, that very moment, right then, was a life-changing moment. I could feel it right down to my toes.

What did I do? Would I ever back down from that kind of a challenge? I shrugged ever so nonchalantly and said breathily, "Fine, I'll change too," and I stripped down to my bra and panties before bending to pull out my little black dress from my bag.

You stopped dead still at the sight of me in my lingerie. You had one foot in your slacks and nearly fell over. My heart flipped again. And I was happy as hell that I'd put on the "I'm wishing for something more" undies that morning.

I swear your expression was worth way more than the eighty dollars I'd forked out of my own money to buy them so that my mama wouldn't know that I had this set that all but screamed sex.

I pretended to fuss with the zipper on the dress while you stared. I was still trying hard to act like I didn't care, but every single nerve in my body was standing at attention. Definitely not asleep anymore. Finally, you dropped your pants and said, "Shit, Cami, you're beautiful."

And you'd called me Cami so I knew you wanted my attention. I looked up into your mosaic eyes, and it was like a million stars bursting into existence. I'm not sure which of us moved, but I was in your arms, and you were smothering me with kisses. Good kisses. Kisses that moved my heart right up into my throat and made every part of me turn to little fireflies of light. They weren't like Matt's kisses which had been gentle and soft. These kisses were intense, like your eyes, and demanding, like you needed to get every little breath that you could out of my body.

You had one hand on the back of my neck and the other was on my bare back near the top of my panties, and when you moved that hand to caress the top of the silk, I felt every breath inside me evaporate.

I felt like I had come home. Like this was the only place I was ever supposed to be. I don't know how long we stood that way, locked in a kiss so powerful that I didn't know what was going to be left of me when it was done, but somehow you came to your senses before I did. Maybe you'd had more experience stopping yourself. Lord knows, I wouldn't have ever stopped.

You pushed me away and ran a hand through your dark hair, and I knew right then that you were going to apologize. I could see it written all over your face, like you were guilty of stealing the last MoonPie. But I wasn't going to let you. I would have jumped your bones right then if your mama hadn't saved me by knocking on the door, "Everyone okay in there?"

We both scrambled for our clothes, and you shouted out in a somewhat normal voice that we were just coming down. Thank God she didn't come in, but I still sent her a silent thank you for keeping you from having a chance to apologize aloud.

♫ ♫ ♫

Wynn found me at the beginning of the graduation ceremony. She was there with her family because Kayla was graduating too. Somehow, her step-dad and her mom had survived the Kayla years. Wynn wasn't sorry to see her stepsister heading off to college. The Kayla years had been tough on all of them. Now, Kayla was going down to Louisiana, and Wynn would be the only child in the household.

The graduates started walking in, and we were all searching them for you. Your parents, my parents, your grandparents. I spotted you first. Big surprise, right? I screamed your name and jumped up and down like the crazy woman I would always be for you. Somehow, you heard me even though we were in the football stadium. And you winked. At me. Well, okay, probably at everyone, but I felt like it was at me. I jumped up and down some more, about ready to burst inside. Our families started hollering your name and taking pictures. You did a little bow that made everyone smile and laugh. When you turned your back to walk up the aisle, everyone sat down. Wynn and I were a row behind the family, and I whispered, hardly loud enough for even Wynn to hear me, "He kissed me."

She slapped my arm, "Holy crap! No way!" My mama turned around and gave Wynn "the look."

"Sorry, ma'am," Wynn said with a smile.

I was all smiles. And I could feel again every nerve ending that had come alive when you'd looked at me in my bra and panties, and the heat that had swarmed my insides when you'd kissed me.

"What are you gonna do?" Wynn asked quietly.

"Stop him from thinking about it," I told her.

"How are you going to do that?"

I just met her gaze, and she mouthed, "Oh!"

Then we turned our attention to the ceremony.

I watched the ceremony, watched you get your diploma, and then, when it was over, I watched your friends and the girls that had been in and out of your life hug you, take pictures with you, and then leave you.

But today I didn't care. I felt a nervous anticipation in the pit of my stomach that wouldn't be calmed.

My mama was confused. She'd expected to have to practically drug me to get me through the afternoon. But instead, I was smiling and happy. Bubbling like a pot of grits. And God knows I never did bubbly.

Maybe she suspected something was up because after we'd done the family dinner, and the presents, and we were getting ready to head out to the lake where the graduates were throwing a bonfire party, she pulled me aside.

"Camdyn," she started and then stopped.

"Yes, mama?" I said with a smile.

"I love you. Always."

I looked at her funny. "I love you too, Mama."

She looked like she still wanted to say something more, but she either couldn't find the words or changed her mind. So, I squeezed her in a big hug and then bounded out to your daddy's truck that you'd borrowed so you could haul food and sodas and firewood out to the bonfire.

Of course, we didn't have the beer then. That was being brought separate. Even though I'm ninety percent sure our parents knew what was going to happen, they wouldn't have bought the beer or supported it in any way. They knew we were always safe though. You never drove if you were drinking—at all. And I'd never get in the car with someone who'd been drinking. So, the worst that could happen at the lake… well that was still a lot, but they knew we were both smart about things. Okay. Well, maybe you were smart about things. I was the unpredictable one.

When we headed out, the sun was just setting. It was warm already this year, but we had the windows down instead of the air conditioning on. It was exhilarating to feel the air blowing around us, bringing in the hint of flowers and grass and, somehow, the wildness of nature. And it was invading my soul.

I put my bag on the seat and pulled off my dress. I was pleased as a peacock when you almost went off the road watching me change into my jean shorts and a tank.

But you didn't say anything. I pulled my hair out of the updo and let it fly in the breeze. Tim McGraw was singing something infectious on the radio. And we rode to the lake like that. My stomach doing flips like I was diving from the platform, and you unable to stop yourself from looking at me. And I was smiling. Smiling, smiling, smiling until my face might break from the effort of it all.

When we got to the lake, we were swamped with people and work. We unloaded the truck and started the bonfire, but it seemed like every time you went by me, you'd touch me with your shoulder, or lifted things out of my hands just so you could let your fingers entwine with mine.

I was a bundle of nerve endings that were begging to be put out of their misery and there was only one thing that was going to do that. It was if you kissed me again. Long and hard. It took a while. Longer than I'd been hoping for. But after the bonfire was roaring, the beer was flowing, and the music was pounding, one of the guys in my class, Pete, came by and started flirting with me. I flirted back. Harmless stuff, but it was then that I felt you wrap your arm around my waist and pull me back into you, chin on my head. Just like you'd done with Brittney all those years ago. Just like I'd ached for you to do to me for more years of my life than I could count.

Pete looked over my head at your eyes and got the picture. He took off to find someone else to flirt with. At that point, I was happy to see it was Wynn because I thought Pete was nice. And while Wynn had forgotten Zack, there really wasn't a new boy in the picture yet. If only I'd known then… ugh.

When he took off, I lifted my head and sort of twisted to look up at you because I wanted to know what was going through your mind, and I could always tell by looking at your mosaic eyes. But I didn't get a chance, because when I moved, your lips came down on mine. And you thoroughly kissed me. You were kissing me like you'd kissed me in your room. Like you meant it. Like you were never going to stop.

My heart was soaring. If Coach had asked me to do a backward, three-turn somersault off the platform right then, I know I could have done it without even a pause. I was high. High on you. That chocolate cookie, grassy, boy smell of you that I'd been missing like the bear misses honey in the winter.

You came up for air first, and when we looked back out at the bonfire, there were some astonished faces looking at us. Or trying not to look at us. Brittney and Kayla were whispering with "Gross!" looks on their faces. Matt was smiling at me as if he'd been rooting for me all along. And Wynn looked almost as happy as I did. She really was a great best friend. She'd seen me through years of wanting you. Waiting…on the sidelines. And now, she was celebrating with me.

I wanted to jump up and shout from the rooftop that you were mine. But I didn't. Partly because I didn't want to move from your arms. And partly because I felt like, if I even took a breath, you'd changed your mind and decide you were out of your frickin' mind.

Eventually, you had to move. Paul was calling to you to help with another keg, and I really had to pee. So I was brave when you removed your hands from around my waist. I went off to the outhouse. When I came back, you and Paul were in the shadows of the truck. I had planned on sneaking up on you, unsure what I'd do when I got there, but I stopped when I heard Paul say my name.

"You and Cami, huh?"

"Christ. I don't know. What the hell happened? When did she turn into that beautiful creature?" My heart jumped into overdrive at those words.

"Shit, man, she's always been beautiful," was Paul's nonchalant response.

You were silent and then breathed out, "I feel like some incestuous perv. Isn't she like a kid sister or something?"

"Hell, you and her have never been like siblings."

"What?"

"Look. Even if you didn't notice, she noticed you. God, she'd spread her legs for you as soon as you waved your pinky. I don't know why you haven't tapped that before. I would have loved to!"

Your response was a right hook to Paul's jaw. It was the second time you'd hit Paul over me. I ran forward from the shadows and grabbed your arm before you swung at him again.

"Jesus, Jake!" Paul said, rubbing his jaw and picking himself up from the ground.

"You're drunk, Paul. You're lucky I know you're drunk," you answered in return.

Paul looked from you to me, and then just sauntered off to the bonfire. I held onto your arm as you tried to follow.

"What the hell was that?" I asked. Even though it'd been a shitty thing to say, Paul was Paul. He'd always been a player. Would always be a player. It wasn't any big secret. So, I was surprised that you had actually hit him.

You didn't realize that I'd heard the conversation, and just said darkly, "He was just getting out of hand."

I brought your bruised knuckles up to my lips and kissed them. "You don't need to defend me. Everyone will think I'm a wuss and can't defend myself."

You smiled. The shadows of the fire playing across your face. It was so close to what you'd said to me after I'd hit Brian outside the locker room all those years ago that you couldn't help but smile.

"Come on," I said dragging you toward the water. "Let's go out to the dock."

"We don't have our swim suits," you complained. I think you were nervous of being by yourself with me. I didn't care.

"Can't keep the dolphin out of the water," I laughed and pulled off my tank top, but kept my shorts on. Then I turned to you and pulled off your t-shirt, my hands hitting your warm skin all the way up over your head. I threw it on the ground with my top and my flip-flops.

You groaned, but removed your shoes, and we swam out to the dock in our shorts. Well…and my bra. I beat you. I did that a lot lately. My five foot eight height was still shorter than the six foot two you'd finally topped out at, but I was in the water practically every day. And I had lots of muscles from all the diving. I could hold my own with you in this one place: the water.

I pulled myself out and lay down looking out at the stars. You were just two seconds behind me and rolled up right next to me. When you put your hands behind your head, I scooted up tighter against you and rested my head on your inner arm, like I had when I was in fifth grade, and you were going into middle school.

"God, Cami," you breathed out.

"Stop making this so difficult," I said back.

"I knew you were beautiful. I did."

"I know."

"You knew?" I could hear the teasing indignation in your voice. "Never the humble one, are you?" You were up on your side looking down at me in a flash, my head hitting the dock with a thump, but I didn't care.

I laughed up into your face, "Says the football god, himself."

"That's totally different."

"Shut up and kiss me."

And after one long look at my face, my lips, and my body, you did just that. And God did it feel good. Again. I was on fire. Even though the night had cooled and our skin was wet, all I could feel was heat. Your heat. My heat. You rolled so that you were on top of me, your bare chest rubbed against the thin silk of my bra and my stomach turned to liquid.

You let your hand wander to my breasts and touched them through the silk and I arched up into you, and you groaned again. I could feel you through your shorts, rubbing up against my thigh. I'd never thought it could feel like this. Like I was going to explode if I didn't get closer to you.

Your hands wandered everywhere and ended up at the button of my jean shorts. You tugged at it, and it flew open with a pop. It was the pop that seemed to bring you back to where we were and who you were with.

You stopped, and I opened my eyes to find yours boring into me like a drill. The moon shining on us. The stars above us. The crickets singing. It was a song being sung for us. The noise from the bonfire seemed miles away.

You rolled off of me and pulled me close to you again. This time, my head was on your chest, my hands on your stomach, inches away from the button at the top of your shorts, and I twirled my hand in a thoughtless pattern, light and soft.

"You have to stop that," you said with a husky voice that I'd never heard, but was thrilled to know that I had brought out of you.

But I stopped. I wasn't so much afraid of what would happen if I didn't stop, but of moving into something that you would regret. I'd never regret. I knew that from the tip of my head to the bottom of my toes.

"Jake? Where the hell are you, Jake?" It was Craig calling you. Drunk Craig who was going to the University of Tennessee with you while Paul was heading off to some East Coast school.

I wanted to kill him for ruining our mood.

"Come on," you said, and you pulled me up.

You stared at me for a long time, and then laid a gentle kiss on the top of my nose, before turning away. "Race you to shore," you said, before diving in and taking off.

You had a good head start because you'd surprised me, but I just smiled, dove in, and started stroking at a pace that always seemed to beat you.

Except, I didn't win. Maybe because you were fueled from pent up guy stuff, or maybe because I was slowed by your kisses. Either way, you were smiling like you'd won the lottery when I reached the shore a few strokes behind you. We replaced our tops and shoes and headed off to find Craig.

The rest of the bonfire passed in a blur. You never let go of my hand. We danced, slow and tight up against each other, and fast and crazy. Wynn joined us for a dance but was pulled away by Pete to do a slow dance. People were drunk and happy and celebrating the end of another year. I wasn't drunk. I didn't even have one beer, but I felt like I'd had a million of them. Everyone else may be celebrating an ending, but to me, it was the celebration of a beginning.

By about two in the morning, everyone had filtered away in their cars, heading home. You and I had agreed to stay and make sure the bonfire went out without starting a fire. The night got cold. I shivered, still wet. You threw me a pair of sweats from the truck, and I changed out of my wet bottoms into them. And with barely a thought, left the wet panties behind too. I felt bold, like I hadn't felt in years.

You had opened the sleeping bags, zipped them together, and rolled them out into the back of your daddy's truck. I crawled up and joined you inside them. You were quiet. And I started to worry a little.

"Jake?"

"Hmm?"

"You don't have to be sorry you know."

"I know."

"I've wanted this for a long time."

162

"God, I am an idiot. You always told me I was."

"Well, you are. But just when it comes to girls."

"You're not supposed to be a girl. Dolphin, maybe. Definitely not a girl."

I chuckled. And you did too.

"You knew I was. Remember. You told my mama I was a girl when I was in her tummy."

More thoughtful silence.

"I know. And if I had any doubts, I really knew you were a girl that time at the lake. You know. The time we had to go to the Quick Stop."

I smiled against your chest.

"I think that's why I was so happy that Brittney showed up. I didn't want to think of you that way. It was easier to think of her that way."

My turn to be quiet.

"But Cami," you said, and I got nervous again, because you were saying my name in that way that made sure I was paying attention. "We're still a mile apart."

"I don't care."

"But I do."

"Why?"

"Because it wouldn't be fair to you. To have you pining away over some guy who's away at college when you should be going out, making high school memories, and shaking your butt at all the guys, making them drool."

"Cuz that's so me," I said dryly.

"Well, it could be you."

What I should have said right then to you was that I loved you and that there would never be anyone else but you, whether you called me your girlfriend or moved on without me. But I didn't because I was scared that if I pushed you, we wouldn't even have this time together. Instead, I said the thing that I didn't really mean.

"Let's just have this summer then. This last one. Together."

I felt you nod. We were both so tired. The emotions of the day. The make out sessions. The euphoria for me of it all. So, we fell asleep again. My head on your chest, our feet intertwined, and the stars and the crickets singing our song.

♫ ♫ ♫

We woke in the cool predawn light. There was a mist that had formed on the lake and made it seem a little dreamlike. It was the second time in twenty-four hours that we had fallen asleep together. I pulled out my iPhone, and it read five a.m.

My parents were going to be pissed. I mean, they knew I was with you, but the way my mama had looked last night, I wasn't sure she was going to trust me with you anymore.

We scrambled out of the truck, kicked some dirt over the bonfire that still had some coals, and then headed out for home. We pulled into your driveway and shut off the engine quickly, both of us hoping that I could sneak into my house from the back.

I looked over at you. You were so serious. Like you'd just broken a thousand state laws. I leaned over and kissed you. Just a small kiss, not intending it to be more, but you pulled me up close to you and devoured my lips again.

A knock on the window scared the shit out of both of us. My mama was wrapped in a blanket with tired eyes, and a not too happy look on her face.

You opened the door, and we both slid out the driver's side. I didn't even have the grace to look ashamed. I was happy. So, so very happy. But I did block the view of my panties lying on the seat of the pickup.

"Jake Carter Phillips," my mama started.

"Yes, ma'am," you said, trying to sound contrite, but my mama didn't take it that way.

She shoved her finger into your chest and finished off, "You. Will not. Be staying out all night with MY. Fifteen. Year. Old. Daughter."

I think she said it to bring home to you our age difference. And maybe that you were eighteen and that I was considered jailbait.

But somehow, looking at my smiling face got the better of her. I'm not sure she'd seen me this happy in a long, long time. Maybe ever. She pulled me out from behind you and hauled me off toward our house. She called out over her shoulder, "Later, we'll set some ground rules."

When I looked back at you, you held up my panties and winked at me, and my stomach flipped happily.

My mama, luckily for me, let me go to bed. I was kind of surprised that I got off that easily, but after she'd let me sleep the morning away, she came in, pulled the blinds open, and sat on the edge of my bed with a searching look on her face.

She stared at me like that until I shifted uncomfortably.

"I think you've always been more his than mine," she finally said quietly.

"Mama," I protested, but she shushed me.

"But Camdyn...he's going away. And he's got a life right now that is going to be even more different from yours than when you were in middle school, and he was in high school."

"I know," I said with my heart in my throat.

"I just don't want you to get hurt, or..." her voice trailed off. "Well, I don't want you to do anything stupid."

"Mama. You're talking about Jake. When have you known him to ever do anything stupid?"

"I'm not talking about Jake. I'm talking about you."

"Well..." because I knew she was right. I'd done plenty of stupid things. Some she didn't even want to know about. Like diving off a cliff.

"But it takes two to tango, right?" I tried to laugh it off. She responded by placing a box on my nightstand. It took me a moment to realize it was a box of condoms.

"Mama!" I exclaimed at the same time hoping to hell she really hadn't seen my panties in the truck. Not that anything had happened... but well...

"Look. If I know you, you've already been thinking about it. You've always been five steps ahead of me. I just want you to be safe. I don't want you to end up with any regrets."

I just stared at the box. And I knew that if you had wanted to go all the way last night on the dock, or in the sleeping bags in the back of the truck when I'd already been panty free, I would have. Without a thought in the world. I'm pretty sure you would have been safe about it. I take that back, I know you would have been safe about it. You were a gentleman. You cared about me too much not to be, but this made me realize that my mama wanted that too. That she knew that this decision was mine. And the thing was, looking at the box of condoms made me realize what a big decision it really was. Maybe that was half her point.

She leaned over and kissed me on the cheek. "I think you're too young. I think that you aren't ready for the emotions that come with this, but I also want you to know that I realize that I don't have any control over this or, really, any of the decisions you make for you and your body."

I just nodded as she confirmed what I already knew. She'd made her point. She got up and headed for the door.

"And you bring him and his parents over here for dinner. We're going to have to have a new set of rules if you two are going to be dating."

And she left. It took me a while to realize how she'd said "him and his parents" in a way totally different than she normally talked about your mama and daddy. We were a family.

I lay there for a few minutes longer, and then couldn't stand it anymore. I picked up my phone, ready to call you. But at the last minute, I changed my mind and called Wynn. I knew she had news to share as much as I did. At least Pete wouldn't be disappearing in two months. He was still going to be there as we entered our sophomore year.

But I wouldn't think about that right now. I'd been thinking ahead my whole life. To this moment. To knowing that you were mine, and for right now I was going to bask in it. Take every moment as it came and simply enjoy.

Chapter Twelve

Our Song

"And when I got home ... before I said amen
Asking God if he could play it again."
- *Taylor Swift*

I started this whole thing with a song, and it just seems like, one after another, they roll together to make a film in my head of our life together. The moments that made us, us. But that beautiful summer before you left, it was one of our best memories. It was truly an example of "Our Song." We had more than this one song. We did. But that right there was the first of us truly together. The late night talks, the first tangled kisses, the firsts. The many, many firsts. Not all. We saved some firsts for later. These were still ones that could never happen again.

When you and your family showed up for dinner that night after the bonfire, it was really weird. My mom had set the table like she did when Daddy had business folks over. She was being all formal, and she'd even had Daddy barbecue tri-tip like he did for Grandma and Papa.

When your mama and daddy showed up, they looked things over and gave each other a scrunched up, "What's going on look?" Then, you did that thing that made my heart zigzag like a race car, which was grab me by the waist and pull me up against you, chin on my head.

"Andrea's worried about setting the tone for how Cam and I are to proceed now that we're dating." You said it so casually and with such a grin in your voice that I couldn't help but smile.

Both your parents' mouths went, "Oh," at exactly the same time. Mia made a "gross" face. And that kind of took the steam out of my mama. She placed the mac and cheese on the table and then slumped into the dining room chair.

"Well," your daddy said, clearing his throat. He looked at us and then looked away as if it was too painful to watch.

My daddy came in from the barbeque pit and almost dropped the tri-tip when he saw your arm around me. Apparently, my mama hadn't said anything to him either. It was priceless. I felt like I could fly, and God knows that was always something I strived for.

Everyone sat down, and you held the chair for me. It was slightly uncomfortable. Not the part of you holding my chair, the whole family thing. I looked at my mama and couldn't tell, like with the condoms, if she'd done it on purpose to continue to make it feel like more of a big deal, or if she just hadn't known how to handle it.

My daddy started the passing and everyone was quiet. Again, abnormal when we were all together. Normally no one could shut up and everyone was talking at the same time about who knows what. Once we'd all dished up, your daddy broke the silence.

"So, someone going to enlighten me on just when this happened, and what we're supposed to think about it?"

My daddy, winking about boys and genitals just a few years ago, looked like he was regretting every comment he'd ever made about it.

"This is your fault," your mama said, waving her fork at my daddy and yours, making them both blanch.

"How do you figure?"

"All that talk about white weddings when they were little, and she was holding his hand."

Both our daddies looked abashed thinking back to two little kids on a porch step with sticky Popsicle fingers.

"If it helps, I think Jake was as surprised as you all were," I said with a smile. You messed up my hair and smiled back.

"I think I'm going to puke," was Mia's response as she looked to a text that came in on her phone.

This distracted your mama who immediately got on Mia about texting at the table. And everyone breathed, and all of a sudden, we were eating and joking and being completely normal. When I looked up at Mia again she winked. Your wink, and I smiled and mouthed, "Thank you."

Your sister was cool. Just like you.

After dinner, though, it couldn't be avoided. We got this long list of no's. No more doors shut on rooms, preferably no rooms, no staying out past eleven o'clock, no ignoring our families or our chores, no, no, no, no, no.

It went on a long time. When it was over, we excused ourselves to hit the Dairy Queen for milkshakes and left them to dissect this issue of us dating to the parental nth degree.

When we got to the Dairy Queen, you got my door, and paid for my milkshake and fries. It felt weird. "I'm not sure I can handle you being this nice to me," I told you.

"Whatta ya mean?" you asked.

"Door, paying for me, you know, the royal girlfriend treatment. It's not me."

You leaned over, scooped some of my shake up with a finger, deposited it on my lips, and then moved in to flick the milkshake off of my lips with your tongue. My stomach fell to my knees. And my voice went away.

"If I'm gonna be able to do that, then I'm gonna give you the royal girlfriend treatment."

I just stared into your eyes. And even though I really, really liked it when you kissed me, and I really, really, really wanted that girlfriend label, it kind of hit me for the first time what we'd done to our relationship. This wasn't something we could just shrug away like the time I'd slugged you in the stomach for stealing the fish right off my hook.

"Hey, love birds," Paul's voice broke into our thoughts. He slid in next to me and stole a fry that I wasn't eating. "What's up for tonight?"

You didn't look happy to see him. In fact, you looked like you had last night when you'd hit him. Paul's face wasn't bruised up at all, so I knew you hadn't hit him as hard as you could have. But it was still interesting to see that look. I wasn't sure whether to be proud or sad. I certainly didn't want to come between you and Paul. The two of you had been friends almost as long as we had been friends.

"Nothing that includes you," you said with a guttural growl.

Paul ignored it. "Lake?"

You shook your head.

I knew why. If there wasn't a party going on, the lake was reserved for make out sessions and… well… the rest of the stuff that follows. Last night I would have been all over that thought. Today, with a couple condoms in my bag, I wasn't sure how I felt about it at all.

"I was thinking bowling," you said with a shrug, and when I met your eyes, I could tell that you were nervous about being alone with me too. I wondered if it was for the same reason.

"Bowling? Shit, we haven't been bowling since we were…" and Paul's voice faded away because he all of a sudden realized that I was exactly what he'd been about to say. A freshman. Well, technically, I was a sophomore now, but really who's counting a day or two?

We ended up at the bowling alley anyway. And a bunch of the guys and their girlfriends showed up, as well as Wynn and Peter. We played girls against the guys, and it was so much fun both flirting with you and teasing you at the same time. What was really fun was the way you tried to distract me by kissing me when it was my turn, or playing with my hair, or doing anything you could to make that zing go through my body and make me tingle in places that I'd never really thought about too much. Unfortunately for you, the tingle set me on fire which made me do really well.

Bowling was the one exception with ball games and me. I couldn't play football worth a squat, but I could aim down the alley. Maybe it was because I wasn't really a team player and bowling was more of a one-on-one thing. Who knows? Anyway, the girls did pretty decent, and for a while I was leading them to a win, but we didn't win. Who would expect us to against a bunch of jocks?

After, you took me home. And we sat in your car for a long time. Music on, you played with the hair at my face, and ran a finger down my cheek, and just stared at me with those intense, mosaic eyes of yours. I felt like I couldn't breathe, and yet, like I was breathing a million times a minute.

"I really am an idiot," you said.

"Yep. One hundred percent, prime time, idiot," I said all breathless.

"But, Cami..." You paused, and I just nodded. "I'm terrified of screwing this up. Of hurting you. Of being the bad guy. I'd be able to beat up anybody else that messed with you, what do I do if the bad guy is me?"

"Just kiss me, idiot," I said for the second time in two days.

And you did. You pulled me up close and kissed me in that way that you'd kissed me the day before. Like nothing else in the world mattered but the two of us. I think I fell in love with you all over again. For the third time? Or the fourth? Does it matter? I would fall in love with you many more times. I could have stayed there all night, in your arms, kissing you.

But my mama flicked on the porch light. It was kind of funny. It was at five minutes to eleven, but it made us realize she was serious about the eleven o'clock thing. She'd never really been serious about my curfew before because she'd known I was always with you, and that you'd take care of me.

Now, I bet she wasn't sure she wanted to think about what that meant. It made us both smile and chuckle a little. You walked me to the porch and the door. Not that you hadn't made sure I made it home safely before, but it just felt, well, different. You kissed me one more time. That was definitely different. You squeezed my hand, winked, and said you'd see me later.

I'd barely washed up and climbed into my pajamas when my phone buzzed at me. It was on vibrate so it wouldn't wake Mama, but I smiled when I saw it was you.

I answered it. You asked what I was doing. I said something silly about just getting back from a really good date, and you asked me to tell you about it just like you would have if we were just friends.

We talked for a long time. I don't know about what. Stupid stuff I'm sure. And I don't remember when it happened, but I fell asleep. Talking to you. Listening to you.

♫ ♫ ♫

You know, when you look back over your past, there are moments that you can remember with crystal like clearness. And no matter how much time goes by, you think of that memory, that moment, and it's like you are right there. Like no time has passed. Your body remembers it, too, because you feel the same emotions and tingling inside. Your breathing changes, you feel like you are right there all over again. And then, there are times that you can barely recall. They are like the flickering lights of an old black and white movie. Images without sound that fade in and out.

That first summer with you. I remember all of it. Crystal clear. Every date. Every kiss. Everything you said to me. It's burned into my body like a tattoo. It won't ever leave me. It was like heaven on earth. There are other memories we shared, later, that are the same way. But maybe because that summer was the first time we were ever together that way, it holds a special place in my heart.

We spent that summer like we had all summers, mostly at the lake. But I still had dive practice, you still were working out, keeping in shape for football, and you were still doing some part-time work at the car dealership. I think our daddies were still hoping you'd want to go into the family business. So, our days weren't always spent together.

But, the ones that were...well...they were happy dreams. We'd still race to the dock in the middle of the lake like we did before, but when we'd get there, you'd kiss the hell out of me and then toss me into the lake when we got too hot and heavy. You'd still race me to the shore, and I still won a lot which would make you grab me and kiss me like there was no tomorrow.

We stayed out late at the lake with the usual crowd. Barbecuing, playing loud music, and dancing. I'd never really been into dancing. It had always felt kind of stupid. Like people trying to act like lemurs or something. But with you, God, I loved it. Because even when it was a fast song, you found a way to touch me. And let's face it, I loved you touching me. I'd always loved you touching me... even with your eyes.

It was magic. Pure and simple magic. The whole summer. I think I smiled more in those eight weeks than I smiled my entire life. What I would love to do is write down every single moment, but...you know those moments. You experienced them too. So... what's the point? I can't share with you anything new, anything you didn't know. Except maybe...maybe, that those were the first times in my life that I felt truly and completely whole. When you were there, holding my hand, wrapping your arm around my waist, and tucking me close up against your body where I fit like the last piece of a puzzle.

♫ ♫ ♫

A weird thing did happen that summer though. All of a sudden, there were a lot more guys flirting with me. Guys that had graduated with you, guys that would be seniors when we went back to school in the fall. A lot of football players.

You hated it, which of course made me love it more. I didn't ever start the flirting. But I could keep up with it. And you know that I was always about getting your attention. And flirting with other boys definitely did that. As soon as you saw it, you'd get all possessive with your hand around my waist and your eyes going that deep, lake color that scared the hell out of the guys.

It was like you'd broken some kind of invisible barrier that had surrounded me before. Maybe it was because I'd been off limits in a way that Mia still was, when I was viewed as "Jake's responsibility." Like a "little sister." Now that you were dating me and kissing me, it somehow made it okay for everyone else to see me in that light too. There'd been that brief time, when I'd first found my girl clothes and you'd found Brittney, that the boys had tried some, but since then, they'd all abandoned ship. Partly because of me, but mostly, I think, because of you.

Or maybe they were attracted to me because I was glowing. And smiling. And nice. And let's face it, I wasn't usually very nice. Most people would still describe me as prickly. And I had been. Still was. But now you'd lit me up inside. So, it was like I was an open flame and the boys were the moths drawn to it, as cliché as that may be.

♫ ♫ ♫

For eight weeks, we were enchanted with each other in a way that hadn't been possible before, but, then, the enchantment wore off some because you started packing. You had to get to Knoxville early to start football practice, and that reality hit us both hard, smack in the face, like water hits your stomach in a belly flop.

We were quieter in our times alone. My smile faded some. My mama noticed it, but didn't say anything. She'd been watching for it. She'd known it was coming that first night when she reminded me you were going away.

It wasn't that I had expected you to change your mind and stay. God, I didn't even want that for you. I wanted you to go and be the football god that you were. To take the world by storm the way you'd taken our town and my heart. But I couldn't stand the thought of life without you.

My panic attacks came back. The twisted pain in my stomach returned. I tried to hide it. Tried not to dim our time together with the blind fear that would take over when I thought of you leaving.

The weekend before you left, we ditched all the friends, and headed for the lake. You'd borrowed your daddy's truck again. Thank God Mama didn't know that.

Instead of parking in our normal spot, you four-wheeled it out onto the grass until we were parked under our favorite tree with its arms outstretched. The tree we laid under when Blake called out to us all those years ago. The tree you'd been under when I'd walked out of the lake bleeding for the first time.

It was our tree.

I could almost see it stretching its arms higher in a victory dance for me tonight. Like it had all summer. It had silently cheered me on.

We'd packed a cooler full of food, and you'd loaded the back of the truck with sleeping bags and blankets. I hadn't really given much thought to it all, other than the thought of being able to be with you. Like I always wanted to be with you.

The sun was almost gone, and the sky was that deep purple-gray that's there before the black, when we crawled into the back, sharing my mama's potato salad and your mama's fried chicken. We'd done this kind of thing a million times in summers past. But it was like tonight was set aside from the rest in some way. You had the music going in the background. Some of our favorite songs that were now in a list called Cami. Cami…

"Just think. In a week, you'll be stuck in the city hardly being able to see the stars," I said casually.

You lay back and looked up at them. I joined you, in my favorite position, my body tucked the length of yours, head on the arm that you had behind your head.

"Everything will change," you said a little wistfully. If a macho guy can be wistful, I guess.

"Stop being a wuss," I said to lighten the mood. And that did the trick, for a while. You started tickling me, and we were wrestling, me trying to get away, and you trying to get every spot that you knew was ticklish on me. I'd lost my advantage because you weren't afraid of touching me pretty much anywhere anymore. Which was a thrill and a curse.

As always, it ended with me on the bottom, and you on top. This time, you didn't roll off to go get a snack. Instead, you stared at me for that same long, intense moment, but then started kissing me slow and delicious like there would never be another moment like this. And, in some way, there wouldn't be.

The heat of you soaked into me like the sun on the dock in the summer. You touched my face, my neck, and stroked my breasts. I couldn't help my body's reaction to you, I arched up into you, and I felt your hardness on my leg.

And right then, right then, I knew that I didn't want you to go away without us having gotten as close as two people could possibly get. I pulled at your t-shirt and it came off, followed by my t-shirt. I was wearing my sexy underwear again. Well…pretty much all summer I'd been wearing them or something similar.

You ran a finger under the lace of my bra, and I felt like every part of my body was going to explode. You removed your lips from my mouth and kissed me all the way down to the button on my jean shorts. Those shorts were gone in two seconds flat. I'm not sure how you did it. But you'd obviously had lots of practice. I think I should have sent a thank you card to the Kaylas, Brittneys, and Ambers of the world.

Your hands were so warm and did such delicious things to my body. At first, you didn't react when I undid your button and tugged at your jeans. When I tentatively moved my hand into them, and stroked you through your boxers, you kind of came to your senses.

You pulled my hands up and kissed them and rolled away from me. We were both breathing hard. I felt the cool breeze touch my skin, and I shivered.

I didn't want you off of me.

I moved up close and kissed your bare chest all the way down past your belly button to the top of the boxers, and you groaned. But you shifted away from me and pulled me up to hug me against your chest.

"Why do you keep stopping me?" I asked.

"We have to stop," you said with a voice so husky and low that I could hardly hear it.

"I don't want to stop," I told you, honest as I always was with you. I looked into your eyes in the dark, and I swear they flashed like lightning.

You kissed me hard and intense, but it was different. More like a kiss of reverence or adoration.

"I know. But we need to."

"I have protection if you didn't bring any," I said a little confused.

Then the flash in your eyes was anger.

"Do you think I would ever consider doing that with you without having protection?"

I was more confused than ever. Why were you angry at me?

"I'm just saying. I'd like to do this. I've thought about it a lot. I want you to be my first," I told you, putting it all out there.

You pushed me away, buttoned your jeans, and pulled on your t-shirt. I could tell you were angry by the way you held your back so tight. I sat up and hugged you from behind.

"Why are you mad?"

You stopped and held my hands that had surrounded you from the back, but you didn't turn to face me.

"You're insane if you think I'll do this with you. God, Cami, you're fifteen."

"So! How old were you?"

"That's totally different."

"Why, because you're a boy? Haven't I always been more boy than girl?"

"I'm leaving."

"Yeah."

"I'm not going to take your…well…and then up and leave," you said with anger and bitterness.

"Not even if I want this? You wouldn't do it for me?"

You were quiet for a long time, but then you shook your head no. And then I was angry. I felt like you were treating me like a kid again. Like the next-door neighbor that needed protection. Like you had to look out for me to save me from myself.

I pushed away, tugged on my clothes, and climbed out of the bed of the truck.

"Cam?" you called out to me.

I ignored you and walked to the edge of the lake, debating whether I'd dive in to take out some of my anger in a good long swim or just storm around some more. I kicked at the dirt and threw some pebbles, skipping them across the jewel-like surface of the still lake.

I heard you climb out of the truck. I heard you walking toward me, crunching the grass with your boots. You tried to pull me into a hug, but I wouldn't let you.

"Don't be mad at me," you said.

"Then stop trying to protect me from everything."

You were quiet.

"If I don't, who will?"

I pushed you. "God, I don't need a big brother. I wanted a boyfriend tonight. Not some god damn hero."

"What are you really mad about? Is it so bad that I'm not gonna screw your brains out and then leave you here while I go play the college kid?"

"I'm sure someone else would oblige me."

"So that's all you want? Just to have sex for the first time? Like diving off the cliff, Cam's just got to prove she can do something?"

"You're an idiot!" I yelled at you, partly because I was embarrassed to think that maybe some of what you said was true. I did want to prove that I wasn't a kid anymore, and having sex with you was definitely a step in that direction.

"No. Tonight, you're the idiot!" you said looking down at me, eyes flashing.

And then I did something that surprised us both...I burst out crying. In the middle of a fight? I was more a punch-you-in-the-face kind of girl. And here I was crying. You tried to wrap your arms around me, but I pushed you away and stormed back to the truck. I slid into the passenger seat and slammed the door.

It took you a while to join me. I was in the middle of a good cry—hiccups, blubbers, and snot—by the time you joined me in the truck cab. You handed me some tissues from God knows where but didn't say anything. You started the engine and drove toward home. I didn't slide over to the middle of the cab seat like I had all summer when we were in your daddy's truck. I sat at the passenger seat, crying and fuming at myself for crying.

When we got home, it was still early. Mama hadn't turned on the porch light. But I didn't want to face you. I felt humiliated and embarrassed. I'm not sure if it was because you'd turned me away or because you were right, and I'd been doing it for all the wrong reasons.

All I knew was that for the first time in eight weeks, I couldn't face you. Couldn't bear the thought of you kissing me good night on the porch in the gentle way you'd come to do all summer. I thought if you kissed me, I might scream in anger and frustration and sadness.

Instead, I ran inside, up to my room, and continued to cry while I destroyed more pillows in frustration at you and at me.

♫ ♫ ♫

When I woke, I felt like my head might explode. I wasn't used to crying so much. I felt like I had the flu. My eyes were all puffy and my nose felt like I'd need a gallon of Nyquil in order for it to feel normal.

I wasn't sure what had woken me because it was barely gray outside. The sun hadn't quite come up yet, but it was light out. Maybe it was just the enormous headache I had. I sat up and fought off a wave of nausea while trying not to think about our fight.

That's when I heard it. A clack on my window. I went to it, pulled back the curtain just in time to see a pebble hit the glass and startle the heck out of me. I gave a little squeal, dropped the curtain for a second, and then went back to it.

My window looked out into our backyards. And I could make out in the early morning light, red petals strewn under my window. And the petals led all the way from the window to our tree house.

I couldn't see you. But I knew you were out there. My heart flipped over and began to beat a steady rhythm. I dropped the curtain and ran to the mirror. I looked like shit.

My hair was a bird's nest. My nose was red. My eyes were like little slits in my face, but I didn't have much time. A pebble hit the window again.

You weren't going to leave me alone until I came out.

I pulled my hair back into a ponytail, slipped a lightweight sweatshirt over my camisole pajama top, and headed barefoot to the stairs.

I knew how to hit every stair without making it creak, and I did so. No way did I want Mama to know I was heading out at the break of dawn to meet you in the tree house. Although, let's face it, having sex in the tree house with our parents two yards away wasn't a likely possibility this morning.

I opened the back door quietly, shut it just as quietly, and flew on the dew and rose petal strewn grass to the tree house ladder. I made it all the way up to the last rung when your hand reached out to help me up the rest of the way. You swung me into your arms and were kissing me in that gloriously intense way before I could even catch my breath.

After a long moment, I pulled away and rested my head on your chest. Your arms were around my waist, and I was pulled up so tight next to you that an ant couldn't have found its way in between us.

You had your chin resting on my head. Peace.

"I'm sorry," you said.

"Me too," I agreed.

You lifted my face with your hand, and even though I was very self-conscious of my hideousness this morning, I let you stare down into my face. You kissed both my puffy eyes and then, somehow, drew me into an even tighter hug. I went back to resting my head on your chest.

"I love you, Cami," you said.

"I love you too," I said back.

"I don't want to hurt you."

"I know."

"But I'm leaving."

"I know."

"I don't want you to wait for me."

I didn't respond. I couldn't. Hadn't I been waiting for you all my life? Would it be any different with you a couple hours away in Knoxville? Wouldn't I still be waiting for you?

"I mean it, Cami." And of course, I knew you did mean it because you were using Cami. "I want you to be a normal sophomore girl. I want you to flirt, and go to dances, and date boys, and just worry about being a high school teenager."

"Why?"

"Because," your voice broke like you were trying hard to keep it together. "Because if you don't, I won't be able to forgive myself for being so selfish."

"You're n—"

But you cut me off. "I was selfish enough to think I could have this summer with you and that it wouldn't matter. But if I leave, and you don't have the normal high school experiences that you should, I'll know that I'm responsible for you missing out on a huge part of life. Your high school years can't be done again. There's no do-over. You deserve to live it to the fullest."

I couldn't believe it, but I started to cry again. At that time, I didn't know that one person could cry that much. "I don't want to have any experiences that don't include you."

You squeezed me. "God, Cam. I know. And that's exactly what makes me hate myself more."

You held me tight like that for a long, long time. Till the sun had already come up, and our mamas were wondering what had happened to us. And the thing is, if I had known how much your words were true, about the no do-overs, I wouldn't have agreed with you that morning. I would have forced the issue more. But…I didn't.

You'd think my mama would have thrown a tizzy fit with me coming into the house in the early morning in my pajamas, but when she saw my face, she knew she didn't have to worry about my body. Instead, she had to worry about my soul.

Chapter Thirteen

Superman

"I swear I'll be with you someday…
'Cause I loved you from the very first day."
- Taylor Swift

My superman. My gorgeous, mosaic-eyed Superman. I had to watch you spread your cape and fly away. With your mother's beautiful eyes, and your father's calm. How could I ever say anything but "I love you?" You were flying away. On the wings of, "I love you."

It was that very next Wednesday that we drove you to college. Your daddy and mama drove in your daddy's truck loaded with your stuff in the back. You and I drove in your Camaro. We had the music turned up loud and the windows down.

We both tried to be lighthearted. I think I especially tried to hide my pain because I wanted you to enjoy college. Every aspect of it. I didn't want you to be worried about some little girl back home with a broken heart. And I realized that was probably what you were thinking about me. You wanted me to go back and enjoy every part of high school too. Like I didn't have a broken heart. A heart that you'd broken. Again.

I could have easily put the song, "Tied Together with a Smile," here because that's also how I felt. Like I was putting on my smiley face for you and the world, but inside I was broken, and not sure how I was going to get through.

But let's face it, you were a god among men. I had to let you fly. I had to let you move away. I was scared as hell that you'd find some sexy college girl, and that she'd earn your heart in a way some silly fifteen-year-old never could. Hadn't our mamas and daddies found each other in college?

But...I also knew, as my mama was fond of reminding me, that if I tried to hold on too tight to you, that it would just make the string brittle, and that it'd break. Just like if you tried to hold a horse too tight, it shied away.

So, my brave face was on.

We moved you into your dorm. We got to meet some of your football teammates as you were all in the same building together. Your roommate seemed nice. Not a dumb jock at all, even though he mistook me for your little sister. It was then that we both felt our age difference again. Like we'd been able to deny it all summer, but now, in the cold hard world, it was still there.

We went to lunch with Craig's family who had moved him into his dorm too. At least you had a friend somewhere on campus. And before I was ready, it was time to leave. You walked us out to the truck. You kissed me in front of your parents. Hard and long. As if you thought it was our last kiss. As if it was going to be the only one you'd ever get from me again.

Your parents got in the truck. I think it was still hard for them to see us like that.

"Cami."

I nodded, afraid to speak because the smile was just barely there.

"Promise me you'll have fun."

I nodded. "Ditto."

You nodded too.

"Just make sure you find someone better than a cheerleader to fool around with," I said, trying hard to have my old Cam sarcasm that I used to tease you with.

You smiled, hugged me tight, kissed me on the top of my nose, and then walked away. I watched, knowing you'd look back, and you did. You waved and winked at me. I loved your wink.

I climbed into the cab. Your mama put her arm around me and handed me a family-sized box of Kleenex, but I didn't cry. That wasn't me. What I wanted was the water so I could swim myself to exhaustion, where I wouldn't have to think. And when we got home, that's exactly what I did: biked to the lake and swam until I was shriveled and beyond tired, beyond thinking. Until my shriveled body matched my shriveled heart.

♫ ♫ ♫

I had two weeks of summer left before school started. Coach was happy you'd left. Well, I mean, he wasn't HAPPY, but I certainly turned my focus onto my dives which did make him happy. I got a few new dives that I'd been practicing, and that was something good in a pile of misery. I'd missed qualifying to zones that year because I'd not been very focused during the summer at the regional events. Let's just say, I'd had some other things on my brain. I still had some chances to compete better through the winter, but Coach and I were really focused on getting ready for the spring season.

I also got my driver's permit. I'd been eligible to get it in July… but I hadn't needed to drive. I'd had you. Anyway, Daddy was thrilled that I got my permit. Probably because he got to teach me something. I never realized how much you'd taught me. How much I hadn't let anyone else but you teach me things. And the truth was, I knew that if you were home, you would be teaching me to drive. So, it made it all bittersweet. But I tried to be nice, for Daddy's sake.

When I wasn't diving or driving, I was out riding horses with Matt and Wynn, or hanging out with my gang of friends that had somehow popped out of nowhere at the lake.

What I'm saying is, I kept busy. And I talked with you. We still texted each other and called each other every day. Multiple times a day. But…we both had a wall up now. We were afraid to tell each other too much. We didn't want to be moving on, but we didn't want to appear to not be moving on because we knew that was what each of us was hoping for the other.

Complicated. Backwards. But it was what we'd moved on to.

♫ ♫ ♫

School started, and I had a lot of offers for dates. It was weird. Your dating me and then leaving gave this huge opening for all the boys. I continued to flirt and smile. If nothing else, it made Wynn happy. She had Pete, and Pete seemed nice enough. But sometimes he reminded me a little too much of Paul. And somehow Wynn was always looking for a double date. I don't think Pete liked that part.

I slipped into this weird routine of studying with Mia. Probably because we used your room, and it still smelled like you. Chocolate cookies, football, and boy. Mia didn't seem to mind being the center of attention, even though she knew it was only because you were gone. She didn't mind being your replacement. I was lucky to be surrounded by really good people. Wynn. Mia. Our families.

I got better grades because I wasn't distracted by you and your girlfriends. Or drooling over you. Mia was a good distraction because she'd become extremely popular with the boys. Her size D's probably didn't hurt. Weird that your little sister had boobs double mine. I'd never advanced past a B. Anyway, all of a sudden I was the smart, older sister with a worldful of advice for the younger sister starting her ventures into the boyfriend world.

I missed your first football game. Not that you played much. You were on the bench, backup QB. You were only a freshman. Tennessee already had a superstar QB. But you got to throw a couple passes at the end of the game because they were winning by 28 points. I missed it. Your family went. I missed it because of a meet of my own.

I tried not to care. Mia came back bubbling with having had a chance to hug you, and she gave me a hug that was supposed to be from you to me. And I love your sister, but it isn't the same hugging her. She doesn't smell like you or have your strength in the arms.

She also told me that you had a dozen girls crawling all over you after the game. Flirting, saying hello. I asked her what she told you about me, and she laughed and said basically the same: I had boys crawling all over me, saying hello.

I asked how you took it. She shrugged, couldn't say. But you were going to an after party at some fraternity that a lot of the jocks belonged to. I couldn't really see you in a fraternity. I mean, I could see a fraternity wanting you. You were a god among men, after all. Easy on the eyes, superstar arm, girls flocked to you like ants to chocolate cake. But you were pretty independent and not into the hazing and club mentality.

I made a choice after that not to go to any of the games your family went to. I didn't think I could bear to see you and be one of the fan club again. To not have any claims on you. To have the super lionesses consider me the sister's friend.

♫ ♫ ♫

Homecoming came, and I went with a boy named Luke. He was tall, blonde, and blue-eyed. Pretty much your opposite. Other than the tall and built thing. My mama was thrilled to buy me a pretty dress and shiny shoes. They let Luke drive me to the dance.

The dance was good, but Luke's hands on me made me feel like screaming. They seemed soft and clumsy compared to yours. The thing was, he was a really, really nice guy. So, I let him hold me, and I let him kiss me good night on the porch. But his lips were wet and soft and not at all the intense, demanding kiss that I was used to from you.

I think he knew that I wasn't that into him because he was going out with another girl by the end of the week. I wasn't upset. Wynn thought I might be. His new girlfriend thought I might be. She came up and stammered an apology to me, like I was going to go off the rails and hit her.

I did have a reputation for knocking out my enemies. News of the locker room incident from your freshman year was still going strong. I just smiled and wished her well. I think that made her more nervous, like I was waiting to pounce. It was then that I realized that, to her, I was the lioness… weird…to have others consider me like that.

I was "living high school" like you'd asked me to. Mia must have sent you a picture of me and Luke at Homecoming because you sent it back to me with a note that told me you thought the dress was perfect and wished you'd been able to… see me in it. I wondered if that was what you really had been going to write.

You were "living college" too. You'd had a date to your first Homecoming as a Tennessee Vol. But Mia hadn't sent me a picture. I just heard she was someone from your bio class. Interested in being a doctor. Smart. Pretty, no doubt. But I didn't want to hear more about her. Mia was good to me. She knew I couldn't bear even the thought of you with another girl.

♪ ♪ ♪

It wasn't until Halloween had come and gone that I felt life start to trickle back into me. You were going to be home for Thanksgiving. Thanksgiving. I could count the days now.

I hadn't seen you in person in almost three months. I'm not sure how I survived it. Skype and FaceTime just aren't the same thing. My mama saw the change in me. She saw the nervous energy that came out instead of the full-force dedication to forgetting you.

But then you ruined it. You decided not to come home. I was so irritated with you. You told all of us that it was because you were doing extra training and trying not to fall behind with your courses that were harder than you expected.

I knew the truth. You were avoiding me.

I felt like I'd had the wind knocked out of me just when I was starting to breathe again. It must be like how an asthmatic person feels when released from the hospital after a severe attack, only to find the grass and tree pollen at an all-time high.

I wanted to stay in and grumble all weekend, but finally, on Saturday, Wynn and Mia wore me down and dragged me to the movies. We were standing in line for the popcorn when I felt a strong arm go around my neck and shoulders and someone tall rub the top of my head with knuckles. My heart skipped a beat until I heard a deep, "Hey, Super Girl."

You never called me Super Girl. Dolphin. Cam. Cami. Never Super Girl. I turned around to see Blake smiling down at me with that shaggy hair of his and his dimples. I'm sure my disappointment radiated off of me because Blake one-arm hugged me even as I called him, "Traitor."

"I'll forgive you that as long as you promise me you aren't here to see that stupid girly chick flick," Blake teased back without letting me go, and at the same time, referring to the poster of two teens holding hands as they jumped into the ocean.

"As if," I said with my typical growl. I pushed at his side, and he let me go with a grin.

I looked around for his entourage and there was none. Not even his brother Matt.

"So, I see that no one else could stand to be seen with you."

Blake chuckled at me. "I'm on my way to the music store and caught a glimpse of you in the doorway. Just wanted to say hi."

He tried to rub my head again, and I punched him playfully in the arm. "Matt says you've still been riding and that you're getting so good at jumping that you hardly ever end up in the creek any more."

I wanted to hit him again at the same time I felt myself turn as red as a turnip. I mean, I had gotten pretty good, but I didn't know that Matt and Blake talked about me at all.

"Well… I am me," I said, trying to project a little of my little-kid sass that I used to use on this big guy.

"But Matt's such a liar," Blake said at the same time, and I went to punch him again, but he dodged me.

"Wanna bet?" I groused.

He laughed heartily at me. I kind of missed his laugh. He'd always been the one to lighten the mood on the street or at the lake when anyone was starting to go at it. No one was around anymore to stop all hell breaking loose. Not even you.

"Okay. I'll pick you up at eight. You can show me your moves," he said as we moved up toward the register.

"In the morning?" I pouted.

"I'm heading out in the afternoon so it has to be early. What? Are you too much of a princess these days to get out of bed before noon?" Blake said with a casual hand toward the miniskirt and flouncy top I had on. I still had my boots.

I snorted. "Hell no."

"Okay then, I'll see you at eight, Super Girl."

And he was gone out the door of the theater before I could give him another sassy retort.

The next morning, I was in my riding gear and out on the porch before Blake even pulled into my yard. He jumped out to open the door for me, but I had already scrambled into the passenger seat before he got around the hood.

He just shook his head and climbed in. We rode in silence for a few minutes while he played with the radio dial. "How's Ole Miss?" I asked with a growl.

He burst into a smile the size of Texas. "It's awesome. I'd recommend it to you as well, but I have a feelin' you'll be following someone to UTK."

"As if I'd ever be traitor enough to go to school in Mississippi!"

Blake just laughed and shook his head and turned up the radio. I'd forgotten how much he loved music. Any kind, but especially country rock.

"You still playing?" I asked him.

"Got a band together. We're shit, but it's fun."

"And gets you lots of ladies, I bet."

Blake just chuckled.

We pulled in to his granddaddy's ranch and parked near the barn. I was used to being here now, and we got the horses hitched up and ready to go in no time.

The air was chilly and fog drifted from the ground and up into the trees as we started out. The leaves had mostly fallen and as we trotted, the horses' hooves tossed them into the air like small tornadoes. It was peaceful and quiet except for the sound of the horses' breath and hooves pounding through the countryside.

I followed Blake's lead, but didn't bat an eye as he made some tough jumps over hedges, bushes, and fences. He always waited on the other side and watched me as I jumped. It was like I was in eighth grade again because he was always criticizing me on the other end. But he did it with a smile.

The morning went by in a slow, dreamlike state. It was beautiful outside, the horses were calm, and Blake was one big smile under his cowboy hat dipped down low over his eyes. It was a good morning.

It wasn't until we were almost back at the ranch that I realized I'd hardly thought of you while Blake put me through my paces. It had been a reprieve of sorts because my body and mind seemed to ache constantly for the thing I was missing most.

As we rubbed the horses down, I teased Blake, "So, Matt's a liar, huh?"

"Well, damn, I can't say he is regarding this," Blake waved at me and the horse with his smile that never stopped.

"What's that supposed to mean?" I said with eyes narrowed.

"Oh just something he said about you attacking him at school one day that I'm sure was not true." But he was already grinning in a way that made me know he knew all about Matt and my short-lived dating endeavors.

I threw the towel I was using at him, and he caught it deftly and tossed it back.

He drove me home with the same big, carefree smile on his face that he always seemed to have. As we pulled into my driveway, I opened the door and then looked back at him.

"Thanks for today. I really needed it."

Blake's smile lowered a notch. "I kind of figured. You've never been really good at having Jake gone."

Funny how well he knew me considering how little time we'd ever truly spent together. I tapped the brim of his hat and jumped out. He drove off with a wave and a toot of his horn, and for a moment, I wished I could be back out riding with him in the fog with the horses so I wouldn't have to feel the king-sized hole that was my heart.

♫ ♫ ♫

When school started on Monday, it hit me how much my novelty had worn off with the boys at school. I didn't really care, but as everyone was being asked to the winter formal, I didn't even get a "let's go as friends" offer. I think it was mostly because I wasn't able to show much interest in much of anything that the boys did. And let's face it, teenage boys may not be all about long-term relationships, but they want a long enough one that will get them into someone's pants. They weren't getting anywhere near mine. So, they moved on. I was still good to flirt with, I guess. Wynn said she'd overheard Luke tell someone that I had a wicked sense of humor and sarcasm that bit anyone near me in the butt. And I guess that was true. I was as good at putting on that front as I was at putting on the makeup Wynn had taught me to use oh so long ago. But Wynn and I both knew that it was just on the outside.

Anyway, I didn't have a date for our winter formal. That upset Wynn. She wasn't going to be able to avoid being alone with Pete. It also upset you. When I got home every day, I usually sent you a text. You usually sent me one back after practice. The day before the dance, you sent me this long note about how I'd promised to participate in normal things.

I ignored it.

It was the first time I'd ignored a text from you all year. I'd fallen into a bit of a funk since Thanksgiving, and I hadn't quite shaken it when you'd started scolding me, and I wasn't sure even how I wanted to reply to you, so I just ignored you. I went about a whole week without texting you. Can you believe it? It wouldn't be the last time I did that. But it was certainly the first. I hate myself for that now. For my stupid, almost childish, holding out…but…at that point, it was just my way of saying that you weren't the only one who could disappoint or who could avoid the contact.

That week, though, I had a good distraction. Wynn had gone all the way with Pete, and then he'd promptly dumped her. It was sad. Traumatic for her. And I'd always thought Pete was a nice guy, if a little used car salesman-ish, up until that point. No more. We were on a "Smear Pete Campaign." Hell hath no fury like Cam scorned. Someone should have told Pete that.

Anyway, our smear campaign was working pretty nicely. Luke and Matt were doing a good job of beating Pete up in gym, careful not to get caught. Girls were warned to stay clear. In the end, it made everyone a little more afraid to mess with me than they had been before, but it was worth it when Pete decided he was moving to Nashville to live with his dad. Don't mess with Cam!

♫ ♫ ♫

Just about the time I couldn't have avoided responding to you, you were coming home. This time for real. You couldn't miss Christmas. I think your parents would have disowned you. I wasn't sure how long you'd be home. UTK had a bowl game a couple days after Christmas, so you'd be home for a short time but then be heading back out to practice with the team.

Wynn, Mia, and I walked home from school the last day before break. It was a long walk, but we still did it sometimes when we all wanted some space and didn't have a lot of homework to do. Normally, one of the many guys in Wynn's and my little group would have driven us, but today, we wanted the time to ourselves.

When we turned the corner onto our street, there was your car, sitting in the driveway. I froze. I couldn't breathe. Couldn't take a step forward. I almost lost the grip on the books I had in my arms.

Mia saw the car and looked at me and saw my expression and took pity on me. "I thought you knew?" she said quietly. Of course, she didn't know that I hadn't spoken with you in a week.

Then we heard your voice from the porch. "Is that my ragamuffin of a sister?"

And there you were. Gorgeous. Lean. More muscular, if that was possible. Or maybe I just hadn't seen you in so long that I forgot. My heart was beating like a race car ready to take off from the start line, but my body was still immobilized.

I watched as Mia ran up the steps and hugged you tight. You ruffled her hair and pushed her around a little like you used to do with me. God, I was jealous of her. Your sister. Being able to touch you. Mia looked back out at the sidewalk where I was still standing unmoving. Wynn, the ever good friend, was at my side.

Mia punched your shoulder one more time and headed inside. You leaned up against the porch pillar looking too damn good. Like you really did need tights and a cape. How did the girls at UTK have a chance against you?

"Hi, Jake," Wynn called out and then turned to me. "I'm gonna head on home." And she physically pushed me toward the steps which caused me to stumble a little. "Call me later," she whispered and then headed down the street to go down the block to her house.

I felt like my feet were being dragged in the mud at the lake as I slowly walked the couple feet to the porch. You watched me the whole time. You didn't have your lazy smile. You didn't wink. You just watched me take every single step. You looked me over from head to toe and watched me climb the stairs until I was even with you.

I was suddenly very glad I'd worn my miniskirt and combat boots that Wynn had insisted I buy. They looked good on me, my legs still tan from a summer that had slowly disappeared into the coldness of winter.

"You've been ignoring me," were your first words to me. You crossed your arms over your chest. I'd been longing for a hug for four long months, and you were denying it to me. Probably as repayment for the ignoring you thing. But hey, you'd started it.

"I was mad at you."

"I gathered."

We stared at each other for a long time. Your eyes flickered with light and emotions. I could smell you. That wonderful scent that was like Ritalin to my soul.

"Are you still mad at me?" your voice was making me heady. Like I'd drunk too much beer.

"Yes," I barely whispered out.

"Hmmm. I wonder what we should do about that?"

God, could I think of a million things for you to do about that. But we'd put this wall up between us, so that we could pretend to move on and enjoy our separate lives that were so far apart in the span of years and experience, but seemed to be running alongside each other like the creek and the creek bed.

"Just give me a hug, damn you," I said all grumpy and irritable.

And you laughed at me, like you always had at my prickles. It washed over me, smoothing my ruffled feathers. You pulled me into a hug, and I almost cried. It was like what I imagine a drug addict must feel when they've been denied drugs for way too long. It was just a hit. I knew I was going to have to go through the withdrawals all over again, but I didn't care. I just drank in every moment of being held in your arms.

You didn't kiss me. I wanted you to, but you didn't. And I didn't force it. We went inside, and your mama had baked sugar-free apple spice cookies that made the house smell like Christmas. We helped hang ornaments on the snow flocked tree that she'd brought home that day. We strung popcorn and berries on thread like we had when we were kids. We laughed and talked about school and football and diving like we had for years.

You pulled out your insulin kit a couple times in the couple hours we were helping decorate, and I didn't say anything. I just let it slide. The fact that you were watching it so much didn't bode well. But at that moment, I was just so happy to see you that I didn't want to disturb it with talk of diabetes and sugar levels. To see you seemingly so happy and—most importantly—home, was all I wanted at that moment.

My parents came over for dinner, and our daddies drilled you with talk of football, parties, and classes. They were reliving their own college days through you. Lots of "remember whens" went around. Our mamas rolled their eyes and cut off stories they felt weren't appropriate for me... or maybe Mia? Who knows?

After a while, you and I made hot chocolate—yours was sugar free—snagged some blankets, and made our way out back to the tree house. We climbed to a place where we knew no one would disturb us. It was our house after all.

We huddled together wrapped in the blankets, the bare skin of my leg rubbed against your jeans and made my nerves come alive. But we were silent, ignoring the electricity in the air. Instead, we just drank our hot chocolate, watched our breath materialize in the cold night air, and stared at the stars like we used to.

"How was Homecoming?" you asked finally.

I made a grimace. You laughed.

"I didn't know boys could be so slobbery."

You chuckled again. I think I would have preferred it if you'd gotten all possessive and angry.

"How was your Homecoming?"

You shrugged and got serious. That worried me.

"Do you like her very much?" It came out of me like a paper being torn from a notebook. Raspy and rough.

"Who? Kate? Nah," you replied, and I felt like someone had lifted a shackle from my heart just a little. But you'd known immediately who I was talking about, so that wasn't good either.

"You were so serious. I thought maybe you... her..." I couldn't finish.

You looked into my eyes for a long time. Like you wanted to say something to me and were debating it, but whatever it was you let your brain win out over your heart.

Instead, you looked out at the night, took a slug of hot chocolate, and then moved on to a new topic. "My lows and highs have been all over the place."

I knew you meant your glucose. My heart stopped.

"What do the doctors say?"

"Stress. Change. That it'll balance out after football season is over."

"What does your coach say?"

"As long as I'm good to throw, he doesn't really care. I mean, he's a nice guy, but he's all about the win, you know?"

I nodded and put my head on your shoulder. It wasn't sexy at all. It was more like what I would have done when I was eight and you were eleven.

"Promise me you'll take care of yourself," I said with a lump in my heart.

You nodded and laid your head on top of mine.

♫ ♫ ♫

You were only home five days. Five days. But I saw you every day. You took me driving so I could practice some more before my driving test in a couple weeks. We went to the lake and did some fishing. We biked in the rain and came home soaked through to the skin. We just hung out. Like we always had. Like there was nothing between us, even though there was a wall of cotton. Not once did you try to kiss me. Not once did I try to kiss you.

But it was really good to be near you. To have you hug me once in a while. To just be able to sit next to you in front of the TV and make fun of the ABC drama shows like we always had.

But then you were gone.

♫ ♫ ♫

UTK's quarterback got cracked up in the first half of the first bowl game. They brought you in. We watched on TV as you battled it out. You got beat up pretty good. Your offensive line sucked. I was screaming at the screen, jumping up and down like a madman, so angry that they were letting the other team slaughter you.

But even though you guys lost, I saw that when you took your helmet off, you were smiling. That gorgeous, heart-stopping smile of yours, and it got you a photo in the national papers. Your face was plastered all over the place. And let's face it, you'd made some amazing passes. And UTK had made two touchdowns because of you. You were a god among men again. That day, the team was clapping you on the back, and the coach was looking at you in that thoughtful way that coaches do when they think about making drastic changes. It didn't really matter though because the season was over for your team.

Chapter Fourteen

The Moment I Knew

"And what do you do when the one who means the most to you

Is the one who didn't show."

- Taylor Swift

I called you on your birthday. You were at a party the football team had thrown for you. It was hard to hear you. All I basically got to say was "Happy Birthday" before you were dragged away. I hoped they knew enough not to get you drunk with your glucose levels all over the place. But then, you had never been the one to do the spontaneous thing. You would be smart if no one else was. You'd practiced a lot being around me.

My parents were doing a big ol' "Sweet Sixteen" thing for my birthday. I hadn't really wanted a party, but Wynn convinced me to let them do it. I think she wanted a party. She was still recovering from the whole Pete fiasco. Trying to pretend like she didn't give a rat's patootie about him or what had happened, while we both knew she'd been devastated. But what put me over was the chance of seeing you. You hadn't exactly promised. You wouldn't promise anything unless you were sure. But you said you'd try to come home for it.

My real birthday was two days before the party. I passed my driving test the day I turned sixteen, and you called to say happy birthday and congratulations. We were right in the middle of cake and candles and the birthday song. I pretty much just got a "Happy Birthday" before I had to go.

On Saturday, I got all dressed up, excitement bubbling up in me like Mentos in a soda bottle at the thought of seeing you again. Of having you near me. It was a repeat of your sixteenth and my thirteenth birthday party with the backyard lit up with fairy lights and a band and the barbecue. If I closed my eyes, I'd be right back to that time you'd crawled up into the tree house and gave me my broken heart necklace that was still pretty much the only jewelry I ever wore. I wasn't really a jewelry type of girl. But your necklace was never far away from me.

The turnout for the party was good. My flirty obnoxiousness still made the boys like me enough to want to hang out, and I clearly wasn't a threat to the girls because they all knew that I was just about the flirtation and nothing more. And I was honest to the core, so everyone could expect me to tell it like it was. My quick tongue, for the first time in my life, paying out for me. I guess it made me original. I'd never thought I'd be popular like you or Blake or Wade had been, but…it was a role that fit me. I wasn't a follower. Didn't really care to lead either, but I could hold my own.

That night, every time the back door opened, I'd look to see your face bursting around the corner. As the night wore on, and you didn't show, the Mentos bubble ran out. I still smiled and danced with my friends and guys who were my friends like Matt, but inside, my heart was crumbling like MoonPies left out too long.

I should have known. It shouldn't have been a surprise. But…I couldn't help it. I was waiting for you. The sparkly lights were up. I was in a gorgeous dress. It was for you. But I should have known…

Once most of the people had left, I crawled up into our tree house like I had on my thirteenth, after Brittney had tortured me with her cruel words. My heart started pounding when I heard footsteps on the ladder, but it was Mia's head instead of yours that popped up.

"Sorry to disappoint," Mia said with an apologetic, knowing smile. I just gave her a weak smile back.

"Jake sent me a text. Told me where to find this to give to you." She handed me a present. I noticed that she didn't make excuses for you. Didn't tell me why you weren't here. I guess I kind of knew why. It was the same reason you hadn't come home at Thanksgiving.

When I opened the present, it was a star certificate. You'd had a star named after me in the Delphinus constellation. The dolphin constellation. Next to the certificate was a pair of dolphin earrings with our birthstone in them. I just stared at all of it for a long time. Thinking of all the stars we'd watched together. Thinking of you. Thinking of you telling me that I was like a beautiful dolphin when I was in the water. God.

You'd obviously remembered it all too. The dolphin. The stars. And you'd put it all together to have a stupid star named after me. And sent me stupid dolphin earrings. It was the stupidest, most perfect gift and only one that you could have given to me. It made my eyes sting and my heart break which made me want to punch something. Instead, I crumpled the wrapping paper until it was a tight ball that I could smash back and forth at the ceiling. My poor parents, the used Jeep they gave me to drive around in couldn't come close. You were always the winner when it came to me.

♫ ♫ ♫

I didn't see you again until you came home for spring break. But this time, you came with baggage. You came with Kate. You said that the two of you were just friends, and that her parents traveled a lot working for the government, I read into that that they were CIA spies. And I hated her. More ferociously than I'd ever hated Kayla or Brittney. Kate was dangerous. Because she was smart, beautiful, connected, and miles more mature than I was. The only good thing about her was that she wasn't scared away by your diabetes like Amber had been. She was often the one asking you if you knew what your levels were. She wanted to be a doctor, so I guess it was understandable, but I knew better.

Truth was, you may have just been friends with her, but I knew she had her claws dug in deep. And I knew you'd told her about me by the way she watched me. Especially when I was around you. But we'd gone back to our easy, kidding around selves the best we could. You weren't holding me by the waist and kissing my neck.

This, of course, made our parents happy. I think they were secretly hoping that we'd gotten whatever had been there between us out of our system. So, I'd smile and tease and be my old Jake sidekick. But inside, I felt like all the old stab wounds to my heart had been kicked open and were slowly bleeding.

It was awful. And I think it was then that I realized that when you hadn't come home at Thanksgiving or my birthday, it had been as much for me as it was for you. It was almost easier to have you gone than to have you there. Just like I was almost glad when you left. Almost.

♪ ♪ ♪

When school ended, I was deep into dive season. And I was doing really well. You didn't come home. That seemed to be the new status quo. You took on a summer resident advisor (RA) job in the dorms in preparation for being an RA in the fall. How they chose you to be an RA when you'd be on the football field most of the time, I don't know. But you were always a smooth talker. So, you probably had smooth-talked some woman interviewer into it.

In June, I competed at regionals and made it to zones. I was happy, for the time I was in the air and in the water at least. In those moments, all I had to worry about was the feel of the air around me as I twisted and flipped and landed in the coolness of the water. The dolphin at work. And that's what I did my best to focus on — the moves, the air, the water.

We had to travel to zones. My parents allowed me to bring Wynn. It was fun to have someone in the stands to cheer me on like you used to. You still cheered me on. But a text and voicemail weren't the same thing.

I felt like our worlds really were far apart these days.

Chapter Fifteen

Dear John

"Wonderin' which version of you,
I might get on the phone, tonight."

- Taylor Swift

To everyone and anyone, I swore I was fine. I tried not to have my life revolve around thoughts of you. I did. I swear to God, I did. I remember when my mom said that I was too young for all the emotions that came with sleeping with someone. And yet, I felt just as tied to you as if we had gone that far. And sometimes. Sometimes I did feel too young to love you like I did. Do. Sometimes… sometimes I wished it would go away. I can't believe I can even say that now. But they were just brief moments. Seconds. Nanoseconds really.

A happy, or unhappy, coincidence came when the Junior National Dive Championships were announced. They were to be held in Knoxville. How the gods decided to grant me that one, I'll never know, but my parents booked a hotel for the five days. And for the first time in a very long time, you were in and out of my meets. You had to twist it around your own schedule, but you were there when I made it to the final round.

The sad thing was that you usually brought Kate with you. You did it to be safe. To put a barrier between us. Afraid the cotton wall would disappear. Kate was always confident and happy about being there. About being included. She'd put her hand through your arm and cling to you like a puppy to a rawhide bone. I felt like I'd been through all this before. Seemed like we'd gone back three years instead of forward.

Because you hadn't seen my dives all year, I was determined not to let Kate being there ruin it for me. I wanted to show off for you. I wanted you to see me dive as you'd never seen me dive before. I was on the young end of my new age group of 16 to 18-year-olds. But it didn't matter. I'd been doing this a long time. I wanted to be your beautiful dolphin.

When I came out of the water after my last dive, you were there on the side of the pool, and you hugged me so tight. You didn't care that I was dripping wet, and that I was ruining whatever clothes you had on. You whispered, "I'm so proud of you," in my ear and it sent shivers of delight through my body. It was all I cared about.

I didn't make it to the top six. I was one spot away from the alternates. But the girls who made it were older than me. More experienced at zones and nationals. I was thrilled that I'd made it that far. Probably helped that even though I usually didn't care about competitions that way, lately, all I'd wanted to do was dive because it helped me forget for a few hours.

My parents took us out to dinner that night. Our last night in Knoxville, and Kate couldn't come. Darn. She had to go do some sorority thing. I couldn't believe you were dating a sorority girl. And I razzed you about it when my parents had gone back to the room, and we were sitting poolside in the Tennessee humidity.

"Dating?" You look truly puzzled.

"Puh-lease!" I said with disgust.

"Really. She's just a good friend."

"With benefits?"

You at least had the decency to look a little chagrinned.

"She thinks she's your girlfriend."

"No," you said with vehemence.

"You really are still an idiot when it comes to girls."

And that's when you pushed me into the pool. But I was quick, and caught your t-shirt as I went over, and you ended up coming in as well.

We came up spluttering and laughing.

"Idiot!" I called and took off for the other end of the pool as fast as I could with my summer dress tugging at me and my sandals weighing me down. You caught up to me faster than I thought you would. I hadn't been able to race you in over a year, and you'd been working out tons with the football team.

You pulled at my dress and caught me back to you, and when I turned around laughing, you kissed me. It was the first kiss we'd shared in over a year. But it felt just like it always had. Hot and zingy. Just like I'd come home.

I reached up and wrapped my hands behind your neck and tugged at the hair at the nape of your neck. It was long. Longer than you usually wore it. I moved myself tight against your body. All my nerve endings came painfully awake as if they'd been hibernating, waiting for you to reclaim them.

When we came up for air, you looked angry and disgusted.

"I am an idiot," you said. And I laughed.

You lifted me up onto the side of the pool effortlessly, and then pulled yourself up beside me but a little bit away, and you stretched out on the cement in the heavy night air instead of continuing where we'd left off in the water. You didn't look at me. You looked up into the sky. I drank you in and eventually came to the realization that you weren't going to continue kissing me, so I just lay down next to you.

"I'm sorry I kissed you, Cam."

"Don't be. It reminds me what kissing is supposed to be like."

You laughed. "Not dog slobbers?"

"Definitely not dog slobbers."

We lay out in the warm air for a long time till the Tennessee summer night air dried us off, and I could head back to my room with some respect. At the hotel room door, you looked at me for a long time.

"You're amazing, Cam. Don't ever forget that." And you flicked my nose with your finger and strolled away.

I didn't know whether I should be crying, screaming, or laughing. I felt like I was on a roller coaster ride.

I went back to school my junior year more confused than ever. I knew that you wanted me. I knew that you still had feelings for me, but were purposely denying both of us happiness because of some stupid thing about our age and where we were at in life. Stupid.

Your coach had you playing about half the time. The senior QB wasn't very happy about this because he was looking to get drafted, and you were inching in on his stats. This made football tough for the first time in your life. The team was divided between the two of you. He was the team leader who'd earned his spot and put in his time, and you were the new talent who almost always led the team to a win. Not always an easy win because your offensive line still stunk, but they were wins.

And on top of the team tension, your glucose levels were still all over the board these days. You were having a harder time managing and controlling it. Some days you told me that you even had tingling and loss of feeling in your left hand. At least it wasn't your throwing hand.

Your doctor wanted you to go on an insulin pump. But that would mean the end of your football career. You can't go careening around a football field with a pump and a needle in you. Even Kate had mixed feelings about this. I think it was because as a wannabe doctor, she knew you needed the pump to stabilize your levels, but she'd started dating you as a freshman because of the status of dating a superstar QB.

All of this made you super moody. If I talked with you on the phone, I never knew what mood you were going to be in. Sometimes you were normal, happy, teasing Jake.

Other times you were this person I felt like I'd never met. This dark, thoughtful Jake who I still loved but pulled at my heart in a completely different way.

You were struggling. Drowning. And all I wanted to do was to help you. I wanted to be the dolphin bringing you to the surface. To make sure you were safe. And I couldn't. Not only because we were two hours apart in miles, not only because we were three years apart in age, but also because you wouldn't let me.

On the outside, I was still doing what you'd asked. I was living the high school life. I'd been selected to the Homecoming court. And Mia was selected to Homecoming court as a freshman too. Even though she wasn't an athlete, Mia had your easy way of smooth talking everyone, and your smile. And your wink. It was fun having her at school with me.

Anyway, I got all dressed up and did the homecoming thing. My daddy used the '58 Corvette that was the icon of our car dealership to drive Mia and me in the parade. She was good for me. It was like I had a little piece of you with me when Mia was there. She could keep me sane like you used to be able to do.

I went to the dance with a guy named Keith who was the Junior Homecoming Prince. He was nice. Polite. But honestly, I thought he was gay. He'd never had a girlfriend that anyone could remember, dressed nice, and had the best taste in everything. That might be a stereotype, but it seemed to fit for him. Of course, as part of the football team, living in Tennessee, he'd never admit to being gay in high school. Regardless, he was a lot of fun.

Before the big day, the Homecoming court and leadership teams had been working hard on the floats and stuff. Keith and I were having a great time leading the group in laughter and adventures. We started water fights, food fights, and wrestling matches that made me think of you with longing. Keith was just a good guy. Maybe he felt as safe with me as I did with him. Neither of us wanted anything to come of the relationship. Mia took lots of pictures and pasted them all over Instagram the morning before the big game and dance.

You called me that morning right after she posted the pictures. You were crabby as hell. I asked what was wrong, and you said nothing, life was just peachy.

"It doesn't sound like it."

"Well, guess what, Cam, you're not always right."

"I'm never right when it comes to you these days."

"What's that supposed to mean?"

"Why are you angry with me?"

You sighed. "I'm not."

"You are. Did you call because you need someone to fight with? Or have you not checked your levels lately?"

"God. Not all of my moods have to do with my goddamn glucose levels." And I knew you were in a rotten mood because you hardly ever swore around me anymore. Not since middle school when I'd picked up your bad language. You hated it when I swore.

"I'm hanging up," I said.

"Fine. Go have a good time with Keith." And you were so sarcastic, I could tell you were jealous. I wanted to laugh because Keith was so obviously gay, and I could easily tell you that, but the stubborn side of me was tweaked by the whole conversation and glad that you were jealous. So instead, I egged you on.

"Isn't this what you wanted? You wanted me to go get a high school boyfriend and do all the things a high school girl is supposed to do."

You didn't say anything. I could tell reality was hitting you. I could imagine you sitting there cursing yourself and wanting to apologize because I was throwing back at you every last thing you'd been saying to me for a year.

"I gotta go," I said.

"Cami."

I froze. And you knew I was still there. That I would never hang up on you when you called me that.

"I'm sorry," you said.

"I know."

"Have a good time tonight."

And I did. Sort of. Because Keith was fun. And not threatening. But at the back of my head I was thinking about you and worried about your moods and what the hell was going on with you.

You didn't come home for Thanksgiving again. I guess I had expected it this time. But when you came home for Christmas before the bowl games started again, you were not yourself. You were shaky at the drop of a hat, and you'd drop things from your left hand. You'd growl at Mia or me over the stupidest things.

The night before you left to go home, I confronted you again. We were in the tree house. Hanging out, looking at the stars. My star wasn't out tonight, the best time to see it was really in September. When we were never together.

"Jake," I breathed out as we snuggled under a blanket together.

"Yeah?"

"I'm worried about you."

You didn't answer right away. But finally, it came out soft and emotional, "Me too."

I turned in the blanket so I could look at your face. You wouldn't look at me. Eventually, I took your chin in my hand and forced you to look at me. Like you had done to me all those years ago when I'd admitted that you were breaking my heart.

"What are you going to do about it?"

You looked into my eyes with that intense look that still made my heart skip beats. Today I could see more than just desire in those eyes. I saw pain. Fear. I wasn't used to you being afraid. It rarely came out. Only around the stupid diabetes because you couldn't control it.

And instead of replying, you kissed me again. Strong and hard and full of so much more than just the teenage longing that we'd shared so many times. It was like you were trying to draw strength from me. I was usually the one relying on you for strength. It freaked me out at the same time it made me feel important. Needed.

You were the one to push away. You always were the one to push me away. It was so ridiculous. The stupid, dramatic ups and downs were killing me. I felt like we were in an ABC Family drama that we'd always made fun of before now. I stood up and threw the blanket at you.

"What the hell? I'm so tired of being a ping-pong ball. You want me. You don't want me. You want me, but you feel like you shouldn't want me. Make a goddamn choice and stick with it."

I stormed out.

I felt guilty as hell. You were hurting. You needed me, or rather, you needed something. And I had not only walked out on you, but I didn't even talk to you through the whole bowl week. But a girl can only take so much. And I was irritated. And stubborn. And you know when I get like that there isn't much that can bring me around. Usually it was you. But as I was mad at you, there was nothing to stop me from being the Cam that both our mamas had wanted to lock in a closet.

When I think about all of that now…I hate myself. What a waste of time. We wasted so much time. Both of us. God! We were both idiots, weren't we?

UTK did pretty well at the bowl games, but you weren't quarterbacking most of the games. Your coach was finally trying to help that senior QB to the draft too. When I saw you on the sidelines, you looked pale. It twisted a knife inside me. Maybe I was partly keeping away because if you told me again that you were scared, I'd be running to Knoxville to try to save you, and I knew that you'd be as happy about that as you were the time I punched Brian in the face.

I called you on your birthday. You were pretty short with me. You called me on my birthday, but it was brief and to the point. We'd put up yet another, thicker wall. It felt like, even though you'd been gone for a year and a half, that this was the first time I really felt without you. Like you were truly leaving me. I had forced you to leave, and you'd taken me seriously. It made me easy prey for everything that followed.

Chapter Sixteen

I Knew You Were Trouble

"Once upon a time, a few mistakes ago
I was in your sights, you got me alone."
- Swift, Martin, Shellback

Where does that deep frustration lead a person? To mistakes. Mistakes with boys who are there and who can make you feel good for a while. And the truth was, in the end, it was only going to end up bad. For me. For everyone. So... I guess I knew it was trouble from the moment it started. But I wanted it. Needed the trouble to lead me astray from you. It was self-defense, but ended up with me on the ground in a whole new way.

Trouble's name was Seth, and he showed up just after Christmas my junior year. He'd moved in from New York City. And the rumors came with him. He'd been in and out of trouble back East. His parents had sent him to live here with his grandparents, yada, yada, yada. Your typical bad boy. It wasn't normally my thing. After all, you were truly my only "thing," and you were the opposite of a bad boy.

I will say this. He was gorgeous. Dark like you, but in a totally different way. I think his family was Cuban or Puerto Rican. He was muscled too. But more like I'll-beat-the-crap-out-of-you muscles than jock muscles. Your five o'clock shadow only appeared at the end of a very long night and was all scruffy Southern farm boy. His five o'clock shadow seemed a permanent fixture.

He rolled in on a stereotypical bad boy motorcycle complete with a black jacket and black combat boots. He had a tattoo of a tiger on his arm that peeped out below his black t-shirt and made every single girl in the parking lot that day sigh a deep, lusting sigh. Not many high school boys in our Southern town had tattoos. And he replaced his helmet with dark glasses that made you wonder constantly what was going on behind them. He rarely took them off. Mostly when teachers demanded it, and even they seemed to be too intimidated to ask him sometimes.

Maybe it was fate that I wasn't there when he first pulled up. I pulled up after him. And he was in my spot. We had assigned spots. He probably didn't know that being his first day and all, but I'd paid good money for my spot in the parking lot, and I'd be damned if I was going to let him take it.

So, he was just walking away from his bike when I hollered out the window of my Jeep at him, "Yo, stupid!"

And he turned back and gave me the laziest smile I think I'd ever seen. He lowered his glasses to show off a pair of brilliant blue eyes that contrasted with the rest of his heritage and gleamed like sapphires hit by a ray of sunshine.

He sauntered up over to my Jeep and put his tan, muscled arm on the windowsill. He had his leather jacket flung over his other shoulder in a careless manner that added completely and absolutely to his I-don't-give-a-rats-ass-about-anything persona.

"What can I do for you little lady?" And his attempt at Southern manners with his New York Bronx accent just made me laugh. Right in his face. This made his smile lower a level, and I saw a glimmer of something in his eyes before he hid the brilliant blues behind his glasses again.

"You're in my spot," I said with as much condescension and Southern-daddy's-girl attitude as I could muster.

"There's a lot of you I'd like to be in. Your spot is just one of them."

I rolled my eyes at him and pushed his arm off the window.

"Move your bike, or I'll have someone move it for you."

Seth laughed. He had a good laugh. Not the baritone, tummy-rolling laugh that you had, but a sarcastic, devil-may-care type of laugh. He just smiled and started walking away.

Thank God Keith showed up with a bunch of the football team crammed in his SUV. I jumped out, explained to Keith that some a-hole had parked in my spot, and the team obliged me by picking up his motorcycle and storing it on top of one of the school's planter boxes.

Seth watched from the steps of the school. I thought he'd be pissed, but he wasn't. Or at least, he wasn't showing it. He was smiling, like it was a game that he was very much amused at. When I had parked my Jeep, and got to the doorway of the school, he stepped in alongside me.

"So, I guess you're the one," he said.

"Pardon me?"

He just snickered and walked away. Later, I realized that that had been both a promise and a threat.

Seth was in a couple of my classes. Girls were fawning all over him like they used to fawn over you. It was sickening at the same time as it was a challenge of sorts. And I needed a challenge to sidetrack me from you. From the lack of you. We were barely texting each other a couple times a week. And they were always brief and full of stupid, faraway nonsense.

And even though Seth was a good challenge when he was around, I just played it off like I didn't care an inch about him. But I'd watch him when he didn't know it, and I knew he was watching me because I could feel his laser blue eyes, even through his dark glasses, watching me walk the quad.

You were smooth like a milkshake. Seth was slick like baby oil. And he was probably the only guy who'd made me look twice at anyone other than you in my entire life... and maybe Matt. But Matt had been more about curiosity and making you jealous. And I'd never looked twice at you. I'd stared with complete and utter idolization for seventeen long years.

By the end of February, Seth had already left a small chain of used and slaughtered hearts and bodies behind him. Girls were licking their wounds and yet not being able to say anything bad about him because they would have jumped back into his arms as quick as a water bug into the lake if he'd snapped his fingers.

He reminded me of Danny Zuko without the nice side. So, when he asked me out, I knew he didn't intend for it to end well. That he didn't intend the chain of broken hearts to end with me. To him, I'd be just another link in it. But I felt safe because there was no way he was ever going to get my heart. My heart had already been carved out and given to you years ago. Probably the day I was born.

The first day he asked me out, I said, "Hell no." And he didn't even care, he laughed and walked away. The second time he asked me out, I just shrugged and told him that if he could come up with something entertaining, I was in. Then I called and cancelled on him at the last minute. By the look he gave me on Monday, I could tell I'd started a battle that he was determined to win. It thrilled me a little. To know I had some power over someone when I had no power over you.

He started leaving little sayings on the windshield of my Jeep. They were sort of philosophical and poetic for a guy who looked like he was ready to knife you for your iPhone. It made me a little curious. What was behind the glasses and leather jacket? What had he done in the Bronx that had gotten him sent here when he had this side of him that seemed so wistful? True, at that point, I was thinking that he was raiding some poetry website, but he still had to find the saying to write out for me, right? Later, I found out that it was his own poetry. He was a dichotomy.

One day, he was listening to some rock band on his phone outside homeroom, and I said I liked it and asked who the band was. He told me and then plugged in earbuds so that I could hear it better. This made all the girls in the hall glare at me. Well, at least the ones who wanted to jump his bones, or already had and been dumped. The next day, he left me a CD on my windshield.

That Saturday morning, he showed up on my doorstep with my favorite Starbucks Frappuccino. I don't even know how he found out what it was. Maybe Wynn? Maybe he'd tailed me after school because it was an addiction of mine? I don't know. But it was my favorite. With the chocolate drizzle and everything.

When he knocked on the door, my mama eyed him up and down and I think would have said, "Hell no," just like I had said, but I didn't let her. I slid past her, grabbed the cup from him, and then curled up in my fuzzy slippers on the porch swing. Seth sat up on the porch rail looking completely at home, as if he'd been here a hundred times doing the same thing. He was like that a lot. Completely at ease. Or at least, like the tiger on his arm, making it look like he was at ease when really he was about to pounce.

"You're a puzzle," he told me.

"How's that?"

"Well, I hear that you're a little edgy and crazy. Willing to punch out a guy twice your age, but you look all girly and soft."

I rolled my eyes even though I was kindof thrilled inside. To know that someone, who hadn't known me my whole life, thought I looked like a girl. Hadn't that been what I wanted from you for so very long? To be treated like a girl. Well, to be fair to you, I'd wanted the best of both worlds, but it was still thrilling to know that what he saw made him look twice. At least, that's what I read into what he said.

"And that," Seth went on after my eye roll. "You do that, and it just drives me crazy. Like you think I'm just some annoying little flea."

"I just think you're predictable."

Seth smiled at that. It wasn't a warm smile. It was actually a smile that said I'd dared him, and that he'd accepted it. But it was also a really good-looking smile. I felt like I was playing with fire. It was an adrenaline rush. For the few moments I was with him, it made me forget about you. It was like diving. For those few seconds I was in the air, it was always just me, the wind, and the adrenaline.

"Let me take you out tonight. It won't be predictable."

I got up off the swing and headed for the door. "Promises, promises," I said and went inside.

But Seth showed up at six o'clock. On his bike. I wasn't sure my parents were going to let me get on the back of that thing with him. Mama was a little panicked. I bet she was wishing that she had you back in her living room instead of this boy from the Bronx with a leather jacket and a motorcycle.

They had a hushed conversation in the kitchen, but I could hear it anyway. Daddy knew better than to tell me a direct no. He knew that if they refused to let me go that I would be only too happy to defy it. It would be a new challenge for me. He knew my stubborn side just as well as you did. I think he thought that I'd wise up and figure out Seth wasn't the thing for me all on my own. And he trusted me. Probably more than he should have, but he did.

Anyway, in the end, they let me go and I waved at them as I put on the helmet Seth handed me. "What, no complaints about it messing with your hair?" he asked sardonically.

I grinned because he obviously didn't understand how little like a girl I really was. "Maybe it will be an improvement," I said. He laughed and helped me buckle the chin strap.

We got on his bike and rode off. And the truth was, that date wasn't predictable. He drove like a crazy man which was thrilling and scary and very much like flying through the air, but when we pulled up to a stop, it was outside the junkyard. What guy takes a girl to the junkyard on a date? Especially a first date?

I didn't ask why we were there, which I think had to surprise him a little. How many times had I been to the junkyard on a date? Or at all? But he didn't comment either. Instead, he greeted the guy at the gate with a handshake and a shoulder pat which made me realize he'd been there a lot. Then, with me tailing him, he started gathering different pieces of scrap metal, glass, and junk. He told me my job was to find something green and shiny. So, I wandered around for a while on my own until I found this broken plate that looked like an antique my grandma had in her house. I brought it back to him all excited like a hunting dog bringing back the duck to its owner. He took it from me, flipped it over a few times, and then shoved it into the saddle bag of his bike not seeming impressed at all.

I almost asked about it, but then he turned around, grabbed me around the waist and kissed me. And I tell you, it wasn't soft like Matt or slobbery like Luke. And it wasn't like your kiss that would reach my toes, but it was demanding and hard. And angry in a way. And I liked it. And I kissed him back with my own fierceness and anger. Probably directed at you, like I could get even with you by kissing this boy in the way I really wanted to kiss you.

He laughed when he pulled away. "I knew it. All fire inside," he said and handed me my helmet.

I got back on, put my arms around his waist, and he drove crazy, like a madman again, back down the country roads to his grandparents', house. It was a ranch not far from Matt and Blake's grandparents. We never went in to say hello to grannie and pappy though. Seth wasn't that kind of kid.

He drove to a barn out back, flung open the doors, grabbed his bags and went in. I followed. Not like a puppy dog this time, but because I was curious.

Inside was crazy. Like a museum gone haywire. He had statues made of wire and gems, and a whole mountain with a waterfall he'd crafted out of stone and metal and glass. It was incredible. He was a junk artist. I'd heard about it in Art 101, but never really seen it. I strolled around looking as he unloaded our new finds onto a table at the back.

"Where'd you learn to do this?" I asked.

He shrugged.

"Some of it's amazing."

That got his attention. He leaned against his workbench, legs crossed at the ankle, arms crossed against his chest with a sardonic smile, "Some of it?"

"Well, you know, I don't really like the piece with the urinal. It's kind of gross."

He laughed. "That was a tribute to Marcel Duchamp."

"Who?"

He smiled again and crossed the room to me. "He was the one who started all this." He waved his hand at the room. Then he picked me up by the waist, carried me over to the workbench, and plopped me down on it. He ran his hands over my legs and then dragged my head down to his and kissed me hard. My teenage hormones that had been longing for you, jumped up and down quite a bit. He was a damn good kisser. Not you. But close.

I pulled back and grabbed the broken green plate I'd found in the junkyard from the pile on the workbench. "What are you going to do with this?"

"I'm doing a bird in a gilded cage trying to break free. This will probably be part of the bird."

"Is it supposed to represent you?"

"No. You."

I looked at him so surprised that I almost dropped the plate. He laughed and took it away from me like it was a precious stone he didn't want to lose.

"Let's go get some pizza," he said and led me out of the shed.

♫ ♫ ♫

And that started my new relationship. Mia and Wynn hated him. They'd seen the long trail of girls he'd left behind him. They didn't like the way he could be callous and cruel with his words to me, to my friends, to everyone. I just took it in stride. He was just Seth. Honest. Direct. Not really any games. Or at least that's what I thought at the beginning. So... like me. He didn't promise to be faithful. Didn't ask me to be. But we were. But I also knew it wasn't a requirement. If he was interested in someone else, he would have moved on.

And as I got to know him a little better, I realized he was driven by his own pain just as I was being driven by mine. I liked the adrenaline rush of a dive to help me forget. He liked the adrenaline rush of speed. The bike was always going way too fast, and it scared me to death sometimes, but I didn't stop him. I just let him drive. Because I understood the need to do so. In that moment's adrenaline rush, there was momentary peace. For me, it was from thoughts of you. For Seth? Not sure.

I think the whole school was waiting with bated breath for him to dump me and find the next bit of skirt. But when he didn't, it became an interesting thing to talk about. What had I done that had snagged him when the others had been left bleeding behind him? What on earth interested me about him when I could have had any of the good Southern boys who'd wanted me?

There were a couple things I think I had done. One, was I could make him angry in a flash and didn't back down when he was that way. I got just as angry. Sometimes it made me think of you and Brittney. The way I thought you used to argue with her just so you could make up. Because when Seth got really angry, he'd responded by kissing the hell out of me. It was weird. We'd be screaming at each other about me not calling him or him not picking me up from dive practice like he said he would, and the next moment, he had his hand at the back of my head dragging me into a kiss that said he didn't give a rat's ass about any of that. He only cared about kissing me.

The other thing that kept him wasn't anything I had done, it was the thing I hadn't done. I hadn't let him get all the way into my pants. Not that we hadn't gone far. We had. And God did it feel good to be touched and stroked and demanded of again. And I kissed him back hard and touched him in places you often hadn't let me touch. It was a good exploration. I felt like I was gaining good experience. That someday I could use it to surprise the hell out of you. And I think that's really what stopped me from letting him go too far. Your face popping in my head. Because at the end of the day, I still needed you to be that first one.

The more I said no, the more it seemed to drive him to try. Not in a violent, threatening way, but in a tiger pursuing its prey kind of way. I knew that if I gave in, I'd be like Wynn with Pete. Like the long list of girls Seth had left behind him already.

So, we played this game, Seth and I, of pushing each other, driving each other, challenging each other. He taught me how to drive his bike, which was thrilling and crazy. I taught him how to dive off the platform at Coach's dive school. He told me about the Bronx, his psycho dad, and the scary-as-hell life he'd lived there. I didn't tell him much. I think he'd heard a lot of it anyway, or maybe he didn't care. Maybe he was so wrapped up in what was going on inside his own head that he didn't have enough room to learn about someone else's pain. He was a twisted soul all on his own. And he was driven by so much inner creativity and anger. You could see it in his work. I could see his genius. But I could also see his dark side.

As the winter faded into spring and the air became warm again, he became my new racing partner at the lake. He didn't fight fair. He'd cheat any way he could and declare it a win. At first, when I complained, he just laughed and said, "Little girl, haven't you learned that life isn't fair? Get used to it."

But it was another good challenge for me. He had way more upper body strength than me like you had, but the same as you, he couldn't compete with the dolphin in the water, so I could still beat him a lot. That drove Seth crazy. Sometimes, he'd get angry about it, and one time, he left me at the lake before coming back for me an hour later. Sometimes, he'd just push me into the lake off the dock. Sometimes, he'd kiss me till neither of us had any breath left.

A lot of Saturday nights, there was a big group of high schoolers partying out at the lake just like there had been with Wade and Blake, or you and Paul. But instead, Matt and Keith had kind of taken over as the party kings. We were all the cool juniors and seniors now. Seemed strange, somehow to have Mia there as a freshman looking to all of us to learn the ways of the lake-going teenagers.

But it was at these parties that I realized probably the worst thing for me about Seth was that he drove my risk-taking side to its peak. He was always daring me to do something. Drive his motorcycle, beat him to the dock, swing from a tree, drink more beers in sixty seconds than him, etc. Sometimes I went along with it. Sometimes I didn't. Drinking really wasn't my thing, but with Seth, I found that when I drank, I could forget about you. Especially if I was drinking and then Seth was kissing me. You were really far from my head on those days. But truth be told, I didn't like the out-of-control feeling I had drinking. Like I wouldn't quite be able to stop anything that happened to me, and with Seth... that could be anything. So, it was a scary challenge. An adrenaline rush of its own.

The other bad thing about Seth was that when he was drinking, he could be particularly snarly. He was anyway. Snarly. Especially with the guys. All the guys kind of kept their distance from him, especially if he had a drink in his hand, because they could say "dude," and he would see it as a challenge. It was usually me kissing him that would bring him back down. None of the guys, Wynn, nor Mia quite understood why I was with him. But it was exactly because he wasn't the gentleman you were. He wasn't a nice Southern boy. He was different. And at that point, I needed different.

So, he was snarly when he drank. The biggest problem was that he drank a lot. He could put away more beer in an hour than I'd ever seen anyone do. Most of the time, you couldn't tell he was drunk other than the fact that he became really obstinate and ornery. He didn't lose motor control or puke or do goofy things that most Southern drunk boys did. He held it really well, except that his leash was even shorter than normal, meaning it was miniscule.

One Saturday in early April, I'd had a few beers myself and was chatting with Keith when Seth joined me, drink in one hand. He hated me chatting with the other guys. It was like I was challenging him. Or they were. Or both. But I'd been more boy than girl my whole life so I got along better with the guys in my group of friends. Seth saw that too. But he didn't like it. He'd always find some way to take possession of me.

This Saturday, he pulled at my elbow, and said "Let's race."

I didn't really trust him in the water at this point. Wasn't sure I trusted myself either, but I didn't feel like ebbing his flame into a full-blown fire. So, I let him pull me out to the lake. We stripped down. Him to his tighty-whities, me to the bikini that I almost always wore under my clothes to the lake these days because of times like these. We raced to the dock and clumsily climbed out of the water, heavy with exertion and the buzz we both were feeling.

"What do you see in that gay guy?" he asked.

"Keith? He isn't gay," I said even though I knew he was. I also knew there was no way Keith wanted anyone in high school to know that.

Seth laughed his cruel laugh. "Sure he is, shall I go ask him?"

I caught my breath. I knew that if I made a big deal out of this, Seth would easily take the challenge and go announce to everyone on the beach that Keith was gay. He'd add some nonsense to it, like Keith having made a pass at him or something, just to make it seem more real and exciting because Seth wasn't afraid to cheat to win. I wasn't sure how to proceed without challenging him either way. I tried to just let it die away.

Then Seth caught sight of the cliff overhanging the lake. The cliff that, all those years ago, you'd so angrily made me promise never to jump off of, and even in the night, I could swear I saw his blue eyes glimmer.

"Dive queen, I'll make a deal with you. You dive with me off the cliff, and I'll keep quiet about your friend's sexual tendencies."

My heart did a flip flop. Just thinking about the cliff could make me feel you shaking me. I could still hear you begging me never to jump off of it again. But right then, I felt like I was on another cliff. A cliff that had its own adrenaline pull, and its own dangers. Plus, I'd had enough to drink to not want to think about you and promises I'd made to you. Seth took my silence as fear.

"Scared?" Seth laughed scornfully.

"No," I said shaking my head because I was never scared, and to hell if he thought I was. Well, I was only scared when it came to you.

"Then jump with me."

He pulled my wrist, and it hurt. I tried to pull away, but he wouldn't let me. He pulled me into the water, and when he let me go, I followed him toward the cliff. Some of me felt like I didn't have a choice. Some of me was pushing at the image of you and wanting to hurt you. Some of me just liked being crazy and alive for those moments I did the insane with him.

My heart was pounding as I climbed behind him. Not sure if I'd be able to do this. To break my promise to you. When we reached the top, I grabbed Seth and kissed him hard. He kissed me back, pulling at the string on my bikini top that I'd double knotted on purpose. He cursed at it, but I just pushed him away.

We stood there, eyeing each other, breathing hard from the swimming, the climbing, and the kissing. "God, I'm a little sick of this," he said and walked to the edge of the cliff.

"You gonna jump or wuss out?" he said, looking back at me. I stared at him and then stomped my way to the edge to join him. I looked down. It really wasn't that far. The first time I'd jumped, it had looked like a million feet. Now, it looked almost too close.

"Take the leap, Cam. Let everything else go. It's worth it," his voice had lost some of its hostility. Instead, it had a silky, seductive tone to it. Before I could decide, he pushed me.

Thank God I had my diving experience. I tucked myself up and hit the water as smooth as glass, but also hit the bottom hard on my rear. It hurt, but at least I didn't break anything. When I surfaced, he was laughing, and before I could stop him, he jumped too. He had to have hit the bottom harder than me because he wasn't as graceful or experienced as I was, but when he came up, he was all smiles. He kissed me hard, and then we swam to shore.

There, Keith and Matt were waiting for us. Matt pushed Seth on the shoulder, "You asshole, you could have killed her."

Seth doubled up his fist and leaned forward, but I stepped in between them. "I chose to jump," I lied.

"Bullshit!" Matt said angry.

I could feel the rage in Seth behind us. He was begging someone to let him let it loose, and I didn't really want it to be Matt because as much as Matt had muscle, Matt had a code, and Seth didn't. Seth would slaughter him.

"You calling her a liar?" Seth asked, pushing at me, but I held my ground.

"It doesn't matter," I turned and pushed Seth away. "Let's get out of here."

I kept pushing him until he grabbed me and kissed me hard. Sometimes I thought he knew that he would do something terrible if he let his anger out, and he chose to do the kissing instead. After my lips felt thoroughly slaughtered and abused, I pulled him to the Jeep.

By the time we got in, I was sober. Dead sober. So, I drove us home.

♫ ♫ ♫

You were pissed. You'd heard about my jump off the cliff. Probably from Matt or Mia. It didn't matter. You texted me a text that I knew you'd done with eyes that deep, deep pond color. It said two words: "You promised." I knew just exactly how angry you were.

I also knew I was in the wrong. I think that made me crosser. I responded with six words: "You don't control my life anymore." I could imagine you getting that text. I could almost imagine the tone in your voice to be the deep one that you'd used with Brittney the day she wouldn't get in the car after you'd flung me back inside.

Your response was that it wouldn't be a life if I kept putting it at risk and that you'd personally come lock me in the closet if I kept up this insane behavior. I dared you to try. And then I stopped looking at your texts. They kept coming, and I just turned the phone off.

I knew I was wrong and just didn't care anymore. Or more exactly, I didn't want to care anymore. And maybe, subconsciously, I was hoping you'd come home and lock me in the closet. At least you'd be home, right? At least you'd be touching me for the few minutes it would take you to wrestle me into that dark space. And maybe...maybe I could swing it so that you stayed in the dark space with me.

After the cliff incident, though, I was a little wary of Seth. After all, he had pushed me. Before, I'd always felt that even though he was wild and took chances, that he wouldn't do anything to purposely hurt me. I wasn't so sure anymore, and that caused us to fight even more. Mostly on the phone at night when he sounded drunk or drugged or something. When he'd see me at school in the morning, he'd kiss the hell out of me and apologize. He said he was just f'd up. That life had f'd him up, and that I was his breath of fresh air. His bird in the cage he wanted to set free. But really, I thought maybe, he wanted to set himself free.

But as April turned into May, the cool Seth hardly ever surfaced any more. He seemed more the drunk, angry, tortured Seth, and it made me a little nervous. On the Thursday before prom, I drove over to his grandparents' after dive practice. I found him in his barn, and he'd completely destroyed the bird in the cage statue. It was scattered in pieces all around the workbench, and he was hammering out something new in metal. He'd known I was coming. I'd called and told him. So, it scared me a little. Because he'd known I'd see it and because he'd told me the bird was me, right? But I also was angry that he'd destroyed something so beautiful. Something he'd put so much effort into.

"Damn it Seth, that was stunning. And you destroyed it."

He laughed coldly, stared right into my eyes and said, "I destroy everything in the end."

"It doesn't have to be that way," I said, and I tried to touch his arm, but he pushed me off.

"Right. Cuz you're Super Girl," he taunted me with Blake's nickname that Matt had continued to use. He was bitter and sarcastic.

"Because I know you."

He laughed really cruelly, "You don't know me at all, darlin'."

I left in anger and disgust. Not at him. He wasn't anything that I hadn't known he would be. I was disgusted with myself for being so stupid to have been taken in by someone in more pain than I was in. To think that two people in pain could somehow help each other forget. But the next day, on Friday, Seth was apologetic again. I felt like I was back on a roller coaster, and this roller coaster didn't have safety belts or harnesses like the roller coaster I'd been on with you. I hated it. I wanted something to forget you, not make me feel the drama all over again.

Saturday, we got all dressed up for the prom. Somehow I felt like I was playing a part. There was a group of us going together in a limo. I'd convinced Wynn and the boys to let Seth come. I promised he'd be on his best behavior. Which was something I knew I really couldn't promise, as I am sure they all did too. But they did it for me. It was nice to have a group of friends that you could count on.

Mia was going with one of Matt's friends. Mia was with us a lot. She didn't really stop me from doing anything crazy. She hadn't even stopped me from drinking myself silly when I was with Seth, but sometimes, she would look at me with your eyes, and it was enough to make me stop.

Tonight, I wasn't drinking. Mostly because I wasn't sure how things with Seth would go, and I wanted to be in control. After the prom, we abandoned the limo, and Seth drove his grandparents' car out to a party at one of the seniors' houses. For me, this was the final test. Would I continue to put up with Seth and his drama, or would I cut him loose?

He was his normal self. Drinking. Leading a pack of younger kids in drinking games. Daring folks to do stupid things that they would lamely follow him in. At about midnight, I knew I was done with it all. I tapped him on the shoulder and said, "I'm leaving."

Seth grabbed my hand and stood up, not letting me go. He pulled me up against him and kissed me with alcohol breath that I suddenly found nauseating. "I'm not ready to leave, Cami."

"Don't call me that."

"What? Cami? Cam. Cami. Cami. The beautiful yet elusive Cami. The one who's saving herself for a man who will never take her."

I pushed away from him, but I grabbed at the keys that were in his pocket. He twisted them back out of my hand.

"I'm not ready to leave yet," he said and shoved the keys down the front of his pants.

I stared at him. His gorgeous self. But all I could see was a guy bleeding from the inside. He'd constantly be living this dual life of the misunderstood artist and the psychopathic teenager full of pain.

"Goddamn it, Seth, give me the keys."

He pulled me back at him and kissed me hard. "Come and get them, sweetheart."

"Go fuck yourself."

"That's what I have to do all the time. You don't put out."

I reached out to slap him, and he caught my wrist in his hand and gripped it hard. "You don't want to do that. I hit back."

But I brought my other hand up and slapped him hard. It took him by surprise, but not enough to let me go. Instead, he used his other hand and slugged me back.

My head flung backwards, stars flew in front of my eyes, just as he let me go. I hit the ground. Tears stinging my eyes from the pain and from anger. Anger at myself. At him. At everything in my life that had pushed me to this.

That's when Seth hit the ground next to me. Hard. Blood pouring from his nose. Strong arms wrapped themselves around my waist and pulled me up against a body I knew like the back of my hand.

"Let's go," your voice was deep and angry too.

Seth started to get up, but Keith and Matt stepped forward, and I think he knew he'd lost. Mia ran up with my bag, and you almost ripped it out of her hands. "You need a ride?" you asked her. She shook her head, "No, Matt's driving Tim and I home."

You shoved me into your car and didn't say a thing. I didn't know how you'd gotten there. I didn't even know that you'd come home. I just knew that you were there. And I was a mess.

You stopped at the Quick Stop, and I stayed in the car. When you came back you had a Dr. Pepper, some MoonPies, and a bag of frozen peas. I looked up at you with teary, puzzled eyes. You took the peas and placed it against my cheekbone. It hurt like hell. I hadn't realized that it hurt like hell.

You were so gentle holding the peas to my face, but when I managed to meet your eyes, I could still see anger there. A lot of anger.

"You're killing me, you know," you said to me.

And my own fury soared back to life. I remembered your words from ages ago when I told you that your make out sessions in your room with your girlfriends were killing me, and I threw them back at you. Seth had taught me to fight dirty.

"I'm not trying to kill you, I'm just a teenage girl trying to get laid."

You cussed under your breath and slammed the car into gear. You sped out to the lake, drove out over the grass to our tree, and parked.

I slammed my way out of the car and ran to the shore. You let me go. I stormed back and forth for what seemed like forever. Cursing you. Cursing Seth. Cursing me. Eventually, I took off my fancy shoes and sat down with my feet in the lake, the edges of my prom dress seeping in the water.

I don't know how long it was before you joined me, but when you did, you wrapped yourself around behind me as if to protect me from the world and never let me go. Tired, I leaned my head back on your chest. You put your chin on my head, and I finally felt like I was at home again. Safe at home in your arms.

"I'm sorry," you said.

"Why are you sorry?"

"For being an idiot again." I knew you were trying to make me laugh, but it just brought back tears and made my swollen cheek hurt.

"I thought I could go on and not need you. I thought I was doing the right thing. For both of us. But I can't know that you are with other guys and not want to beat the crap out of them. All I think about is you."

"Welcome to my world," I said softly.

"Was it really this bad? For you. When I was with the other girls."

"Yes."

You squeezed me so tight that I thought you were going to knock me out. You buried your head in my neck and kissed it. And I knew that you weren't letting me go again. And finally, I felt like Seth's gilded bird. Like I'd finally escaped my cage.

Chapter Seventeen

Ours

"And life makes love look hard...

But this love is ours."

- Taylor Swift

Mary's song. Our song. Ours. Special moments that are embedded into a country song that can speak volumes to a person about their own lives. Ours is definitely that way. Lord knows there were plenty of people who didn't think we should be together. But God, did it feel right to us. Life had made our love look hard. But we found out it was really very easy. You just had to give in. We had to not care about the three years. About others talking. About college or high school or what was next.

After we'd sat by the lake for a long time, and the mist of the early morning started to settle it, I began to shiver. You helped me up from the ground with my soggy prom dress clinging to me and you'd kissed me again. For the first time since Christmas, but it was the first kiss that I felt like you meant without wanting to take it back in a really long time. And your kisses were nothing like Seth's kisses. How had I ever compared them? It reminded me that the intensity of your kisses were all about the two of us. Not about anger or pain or apologies.

You did draw back, but it wasn't in sorrow or regret this time. It was because it was damn cold and time to take me home to face the music.

When my parents saw my bruised cheek, they wanted to press charges, but once I pointed out that I'd hit him first, they grew quiet. I'd always been in trouble for hitting. Being aggressive. At that point, I think everyone was just glad that you'd shown up. Like always. To be my hero.

When I asked about it, how you'd known, you'd said that you'd been fuming about the cliff dive for two weeks, and when I hadn't responded to you the last couple days, you'd wanted to come home and read me the Riot Act. You'd been about five minutes from home when Mia had called and told you things were out of control, and that she was worried about me.

This time, when you had your arm around my waist, promising my parents you weren't going to let Seth ever hurt me again, I think my parents were relieved. Maybe they realized that I'd always be reckless without you, and that you there, pushing the hair out of my face and looking at me with adoring eyes, was a hell of a lot better than me driving on the back of Seth's motorcycle and getting hit by a boy. I think they thought that at least with you, I was safe.

And I was.

You were good to me; good for me. That next day, I decided to take you on a horseback ride out at Matt's grandparents' ranch with a group of my friends. We were just getting ready to leave when Seth's motorcycle pulled into the driveway.

You were down the steps, blocking his path to me so fast that the June bugs wouldn't have been able to keep up. Seth set his helmet on the handlebars and eyed you and me. You had your arms crossed, legs spread out, and were ready to block any move that Seth made to get to me.

I guess I had been expecting this. Seth always came back to apologize. Always. This time, though, I wasn't in the same place I'd been every time he'd said sorry before. I had you. God. I had you. That was all that mattered, but as I looked down from the porch to Seth's bruised face, I did feel something. It was sorrow and guilt because I knew this was my fault.

I knew when I'd started all this with Seth that I could never be what Seth wanted or needed. I'd never have been able to give him the piece of my heart that was reserved for you, regardless of how he'd treated me. I slid down the steps and under your arm as you tried to block me from leaving your protection.

"It's okay," I told you as I walked to the motorcycle where Seth still sat.

"I'm sorry," I said just as Seth said the matching words.

He reached out to touch my bruised face, and I could feel you take two steps toward me. I turned to you, shaking my head. I had this. I didn't need you and Seth going all out testosterone when Seth and I both knew that this was it.

Seth's fingers dropped to the handlebars.

"I'm going back to the city," Seth said.

This surprised me. I thought of his parents and the bad place it had been for him, and guilt swarmed me. "Why?" I asked with sadness.

"I'm just as destructive here as I was there. I thought maybe…" his voice faded away with a shrug. "I got into an art school in Manhattan."

It was so like Seth to keep something huge like this to himself. It didn't surprise me, but it did kind of explain his over-the-top emotions lately. He'd been waiting for an answer and Seth was never good at waiting.

"I've been trying to decide what to do for about a week," he continued, grabbing at his helmet strap. "This," he glanced at me and then at you, glaring behind me, "just made me realize it's the right thing. My grandparents have agreed to pay for it. I won't have to see my dad…"

I hugged him. And you were behind me in a nanosecond. But I smiled at Seth. "I'm so happy for you, Seth. Really. I am."

Seth smiled that wicked smile of his at me one last time. "Yeah. I'm happy for you too." Then he looked at you, "Don't let her get away this time, dipshit!"

And I had to hold you back as Seth slammed his helmet on and took off down the driveway. Funny. All I felt was happiness for him. I wasn't angry at him anymore, or me, or at any of the stupid shit he and I had done when we were together. I was just happy that there was a possibility of life working out for him. And for me.

I turned into you, and you swallowed me into your arms with a hug so tight that I knew I'd never have to say goodbye to you again.

We were silent on our way out to Matt's granddaddy's ranch, and it reminded me briefly of the drive Blake and I had made what felt like a lifetime ago now. When we pulled up to the barn, Matt and the gang were ready and waiting. He had his girlfriend with him. They were quite the matching pair in a way Matt and I had never been. Matt had my typical horse saddled up, and he had a gentle mare that he handed off to you. It was kind of funny because you weren't really a horse-riding guy. Football: fine. Horseback: not so much. Which was your own sin being from the South and all.

I laughed my ass off as you tried to get into the saddle, which of course, just challenged you to do it with a smile and some panache. But let's face it, horses and you might just have been like footballs and me. Opposing forces. So after about an hour of you sliding around in the saddle, I finally took mercy on you and told Matt that we were going to stop and head back. Matt laughed a knowing laugh and went on with the group.

I dismounted and you followed suit with a look that was almost pure relief, and you didn't even get upset when I laughed at you. Instead, you wrapped my fingers in yours as we walked the horses back, and I felt like I'd come home after being out in the cold and rain for a very long time.

"I gave up football," you told me. We'd been together almost 24 hours, and you were just now dropping this bombshell on me?

"What?" I exclaimed and pulled away to look at you.

You fidgeted with the reigns. "I had to make a decision in April. Coach needed an answer so that he could recruit a strong quarterback for next season. I was going to start…"

Your voice trailed away. I wrapped my arms around you and you buried your head in the nape of my neck. We stood there forever. I kissed your cheek and your eyelids, and then you were devouring me. Like we'd never kissed before. Like it was the first time and the last time and every time that we'd missed in between. Your hands were all over my body. I couldn't keep up. But we were standing in the middle of a ranch in the middle of the day, and it wasn't going to go anywhere. We kissed until you seemed to expend the sadness and the anger at losing something that meant so much to you. And for that one time, you had a little of Seth in you. But you weren't punishing me like Seth had, instead, it was like you, too, were coming home.

After a long, long time, you stopped, and looked into my eyes and smiled. Then, you grabbed my hand, and we made our way back to the ranch where we left the horses with Matt's granddaddy, and drove home.

♫ ♫ ♫

You had to go back to school the next day. I had four weeks left, and you had just two. When you went back to school, you had to give up your scholarship and your position on the team. And your status changed. You became, for the first time in your life, a spectator. Your parents weren't upset about the scholarship. They were happy. It meant that you were getting the insulin pump, and that, hopefully, you'd be regulating your levels better. Which meant we'd all have to worry about you less. Or so we all thought.

We Skyped and talked every day. You'd tell me about your classes. I'd tell you about stupid school stuff. And even though we were three years apart, and in different worlds, it didn't seem to matter anymore. It was almost like we were on your bed together doing homework and talking about the stuff that happened that day.

There were people who talked smack. You robbing the cradle, me being jailbait, on and on. But the thing was, I think most of those same people would say it had been inevitable. I had known all along that you belonged to me. You were mine. And for the first time in a couple years, I was at peace again. Truly smiling again, not the pasted smile that I'd used for two years to make you think I was living it up. This was a real, happy smile.

What I didn't know was that, even with the insulin pump, you were having a hard time regulating things. Your levels were jumping up and down. You were having bouts where you couldn't remember what had happened for the last hour. You didn't tell me that. But I found out when you came home for the summer.

♩ ♩ ♩

We had gone camping. Just the two of us. I know. Seems weird that our parents had gone from "no rooms, no alone time, blah, blah, blah," to "go ahead, go camping by yourselves over the weekend." Especially as I was still only seventeen. But somehow, being with you made me seem more grown up. And I was going into my senior year of high school, and after that, I'd be out on my own. You were twenty. You'd already been out on your own for two years. They could have said no, but they didn't. Don't judge them. Remember, I wasn't an easy child.

We didn't go far. Just an hour away from home. We'd brought our fishing poles and cards and plenty of food. And though I thought about the possibilities of what the time alone with you could mean, sleeping next to you in a tent with no one on earth around, I hadn't really thought it all through. I wasn't sure if you'd gotten over the whole "you're younger than me" thing enough to go the next step. So, for me, it was just about having time with you after we'd been deprived of it for so long.

As I helped you put up the tent, I kept teasing you. I was wiggling my butt in my short shorts, and laughing at every mistake you made. I'd throw things at you, and purposely not get close enough to let you touch me. When you tried to grab my hand or kiss me, I would skip out of reach and smile at you. I knew I was playing with fire, but I'd learned a few things from Seth.

You waggled your finger at me when you went inside to put down the sleeping bags and the blankets, and for the first time, I was a little nervous. I kept the picnic table between me and the tent while I put out the beach chairs and fishing gear. When you came out, I looked up and you had this look on your face that made my heart go thud louder than before. Your eyes were that dark, pond color. But you weren't angry. It was another emotion that was there. One that I was just starting to learn.

You came over to my side of the picnic table. "Payback is hell," you said and inched closer as I inched away.

"Jake..." I said, trying to sound like my mama scolding us as kids, but it came out breathless and my chest was heaving, and you noticed and smiled a knowing little smile.

I moved in a flash, but you chased me down, threw me over your shoulder like you had that time I'd escaped your Camaro after tossing Brittney against the dash, and you threw me into the tent.

It wasn't the most comfortable place in the world. Hard ground with sleeping bags, blankets, and pillows, but you didn't seem to care. You pounced on top of me and wrestled me to a standstill with my arms above my head. And you started kissing me in a way that made me moan all the way down to my inner core. Your lips touched every soft place on me that they could reach, and when you felt the fight go out of me, you let my arms go and I got to touch you back. I'd learned a few things from Seth that made you groan, too, and eventually reach in your bag for a condom box.

I went gladly over the edge with you. No one needed to push me. I was happy to have my legs wrapped around you. Happy to be as close to you as I could possibly get. It was like this was what I had been created for. To be with you. And I'd waited two long years for you to come around to the fact that this was where you belonged too. Well, really, seventeen long years, but I'll give you some of those because I'd been just a kid.

We didn't fish much. We didn't play cards much. We didn't even leave the tent much. Except for food. And bathroom breaks. And to dive in the lake to cool off. But for most of that glorious weekend, we couldn't keep our hands off of each other. There was always some part of us touching the other. A knee, a leg, a foot, a finger.

It was perfect and beautiful, and I think my mama had known what was going to happen, because she'd packed a box of condoms in my bag, too, when I hadn't realized it. When I showed you, you grinned like crazy, and said you'd never be able to look my mama in the eyes again.

On Sunday, we were packing up to go when you started acting funny. Like in the old days. Sort of delirious and saying stupid things. I asked you what your level was. You griped at me to mind my own business, which wasn't a good sign. The truck was loaded when you hit the ground.

I pulled out the sugar tabs that you had stored in a bag and put one under your tongue and coaxed you back some. But you were still really out of it.

I drove like hell to the nearest hospital. By this time you were throwing up, and I was truly panicked. When we got to the hospital, I was practically screaming at the ladies in the ER. The doctor, a woman, came out and tried to make sense of what I was saying. She asked if I knew your last levels. I didn't, but the pump stored some of that information, but you'd had it off a lot while we were involved in… other activities. They wheeled you away and wouldn't let me go with you.

I flashed back to my freshman year, but this time I was way more freaked out. I knew the vomiting wasn't a good thing. I called Mama first. My teeth were chattering so hard that she couldn't understand me. I went up to the nurses' station and handed the phone to someone behind the desk. The nurse explained to Mama what was happening. Mama told the nurse that she and your parents were on the way.

It took almost an hour for them to get there. And when they did arrive, Scott and Marina were wild-eyed. My mama had driven. Daddy was out of town at a car show. I told them that the doctors hadn't told me anything. Wouldn't let me see you.

Eventually, the woman doctor joined us. She said that your ketones were extremely high. Asked if we'd known how high they had been and for how long. None of us knew. You'd been taking care of things on your own while you'd been away. We knew things were bad enough for you to give up football. But no one had known just how bad things had gotten because you hadn't wanted us to know.

She explained that the ketones might come back in line as they got your glucose level under control and flushed out your system, but that it was also a possibility that you had some permanent kidney damage from your levels being out of whack for too long. I didn't really understand what that meant. She left. Marina and Scott seemed to understand though.

"What does she mean?"

"It means his kidneys could be gone," Scott said, deadpan. No emotion. Just the facts.

"What?" I looked at him incredulous. Kidney failure was something that happened to old people. Alcoholics and people who were far, far older than you.

Mama put her arms around me. I pushed her away and went to the nurse, demanding to see you. Surprisingly, she told me where you were. I stormed in on you. You were hooked up to wires and machines, but I didn't care. I came right up and punched you in the shoulder. Repeatedly.

You let me. Finally, you said in a really tired voice, "Coach Daniels is going to be pissed if you break your hand with regionals coming up."

Tears stung my eyes, but I refused to let them fall. Instead, I crawled into the bed with you, laid my head on your chest, and you put your arm around me. "You're a shit," I said.

"I know," you said back.

♫ ♫ ♫

They held you for two days. Mama made me go home and shower and change, but then I went back and wouldn't leave until they released you. I drove you home. You were exhausted. You slept for another couple days. I hung out in your room. Brought you food. Made you get up and go outside and enjoy the summer sun.

Later in the week, you went back to Doc Wilson so he could check your ketones again. They had gotten better, still weren't great, but were more in line with what they needed to be. They ran some more tests. They were still worried about your kidneys, but thought they'd be okay with the pump and keeping your levels in check.

They said that you'd just gotten out of whack over the weekend because of all the hiking and activity. I tried really hard not to blush at the thought of the activity that we had primarily been engaged in and the reason you'd had your pump off so much.

Life went back to normal as much as it could. You took to working out at the gym and swimming with me instead of football practice. We spent evenings together at home or at the lake. Sometimes we'd be with my friends or any of your friends that had come home for the summer, which was less and less as they got lives away from our little town.

Even though we often couldn't find the right place to truly be together like we had in the tent, camping, there were moments when no one was home, or no one seemed to care what we were doing, and we could be together. The way we both wanted to be together. I was more careful though. Sometimes I didn't even want you to remove the pump, and I always made you put it right back on. I think you were embarrassed at first because you'd always been the perfect god, and now there was this thing hanging on to you that proved you weren't. But mostly you just did it. Because you knew you had too.

We definitely had lighter moments. Do you remember the one toward the end of summer? One day at practice, I told Coach I had to wrap it up as you were picking me up.

Coach winked at me, "God, I love it when I'm right. Those three years are nothing but a blink now, aren't they?"

He was gloating. I threw a wet towel at him, "Stop being such a sniveling know-it-all."

"I believe that cost you twenty more laps," he said, his smile remaining. I ignored him. But he easily blocked my path and pointed to the pool.

You sauntered in to find out what was taking me so long. "What's the hold up?"

"Coach wants me to do twenty more laps." My hands were on my hips in defiance.

You smiled at Coach and me. "What'd you do?"

I threw a towel at him, too.

"Coach?" you directed the question to him.

"Just called me a sniveling know-it-all. I've heard worse. But she still owes me twenty."

You grinned at me. "Hell, I think she owes you fifty."

"No way." My arms were crossed but you slowly made your way to me. I was wary. And put some distance between me and the pool.

When you reached me, you kissed me. I pushed away a little. "Did you like that, Cam?"

I didn't know how to respond to this attack.

"I hope you did, because that will be the last one you get until you decide to do the fifty laps," you continued.

I moved toward the pool, looking back at you with a sly smile. "Okay, buddy. Be that way. Side with the old man, but you know that won't get you what you want either."

And I dove in, splashing you. It took you a minute to follow me. You had to disconnect the pump, but it was still a lot faster than I would have expected.

Coach watched all of this, busted out laughing, and then tossed the keys to the school on a table and left.

After that, you focused your athletic energy into me, and Coach let you. You were way tougher on me than he ever was. Of course, you didn't have all the knowledge that he did, but you were a quick learn. And you'd been watching me dive for nearly eight years. And you knew my body in ways no one ever would. So, it kind of made you the perfect coach.

By the time I got to regionals, I was in really good shape. I got to zones, and at zones, I made it to nationals. At nationals, I made the team of six that would represent the USA at the worlds in England.

We were going to Europe! It was crazy. Coach said that he should have had you coaching me all along. But you and I smiled and knew that it would never have worked back then. You and I were different now. We were a team in a way that we hadn't quite been a team before.

You had already decided to take the fall off of school. You were still battling with your glucose levels and ketones on a daily basis, and everyone agreed that you should take the semester off. So, the good thing for me was that you were going with me to Europe.

♫ ♫ ♫

I missed the first three weeks of my senior year going to worlds. There were five of us that went: Mama, Daddy, Coach, you, and I. We got to explore London and stroll along the Thames. You shared a room with Coach, and I was wishing that I was just a year older, and I could tell my parents to go to hell, that I was sharing a room with you. But… I don't think my mama or my daddy would have appreciated that as a senior in high school.

I was nervous as hell at the worlds. I normally didn't think of the meets as competition. Mostly thought of it as time in the air, flying through the sky like it didn't matter. But you'd put so much energy into me that I didn't want to disappoint you.

You were there every time I came out of the water. Telling me what to do different. And I didn't even try to kiss you even though I wanted to. You were in your business mode. Like when we were little and you were teaching me anything, you'd never let me fool around.

In the end, I came away with the bronze. A bronze! At worlds! Sure, it wasn't a gold, but I was thrilled. I couldn't contain my smile, and this time I could kiss you, and you kissed me back. Of course, that made the papers. Diver kissing coach. It was kind of laughable, but the USA Diving Committee didn't think so. They told Coach that you wouldn't be able to be at the poolside anymore. You didn't care, you were already talking about next year.

Chapter Eighteen

Stay Stay Stay

"And I'll be loving you for quite some time

no one else is gonna love me when I get mad, mad, mad

so I think that it's best if we both stay."

- Taylor Swift

𝓘 *just heard this song the* other day, and it made me remember my senior year and college recruitment and us. We didn't fight very often. Even if we did, it mostly ended in a wrestling match with laughter and kisses. I think it helped that we both knew, deep down, that we'd already been apart and that it was hell, and that the best thing that could ever happen to us was to be together. But... there were still times. Times when loving me wasn't easy. Times when loving you wasn't easy, but where we both made the choice to hang in there together and just stay.

When we got back from worlds, colleges came courting me. It felt weird to be the star like you had been. It was a heady feeling, and I could hardly believe that your ego hadn't ever gotten bigger than it had with all these people telling you what a superstar you were. I was thrilled at the attention, but I wasn't going anywhere. The only place I was going was wherever you went. If that meant we went back to UTK, then that was fine with me.

One day, after Texas A&M had left our house because I'd basically told them there was nothing they could offer me that would make me accept them, you got really mad at me.

"What the hell was that?" you asked with those lake-colored eyes.

I shrugged.

"Why would you blow them off like that?"

"I'm just being honest. I'm not going to Texas."

"Why?"

"What do you mean, why? Do you think I'm going to go that far away from you? Now? After all we've been through?" I yelled back.

"I'm not going to let you throw away your future because you think we can't be apart for a few weeks at a time," you stormed at me.

"I've wasted enough of my life being away from you," I told you back.

"Cam, we have our whole lives ahead of us," you told me and tried to pull me to you, but I pushed you away and stormed out.

It wasn't you that came and found me in the tree house. It was Mama. I was a little surprised by that.

"You know, Camdyn, if you're going to have a grown-up relationship, you can't go running to a tree house every time you have a fight." But she sat down next to me. After a few moments, she pulled my hair back and began braiding it like she used to when I was younger and would fight her tooth and nail because I hated sitting there that long while you were already out on the street playing.

"What is it that you're afraid of?" she asked me.

"I'm afraid that he'll move on without me again."

"Do you really think he ever moved on?" When I didn't answer, she kept going, "Camdyn. He's been waiting for you since before you were born. He's not going anywhere without you."

Just then you hollered up at me. I stood up and looked out of the tree house to see you with your old shoulder pads on over your t-shirt.

"Come down here and fight me fair and square," you said. I couldn't help but laugh.

"How is that fair?" I said, referring to the pads.

"Are you kidding? I've felt your right hook. I figure if you're going to hit me, I need some kind of protection."

I looked over at Mama. She was smiling too.

She stood up and rubbed my face with her hand. "You've always been more his than mine."

It was the second time she'd told me that. I hugged her, and then jumped out of the tree like I used to when I was little, from the window. You picked me up and squeezed me, and I punched your padded shoulders. We were wrestling on the ground by the time Mama climbed off the ladder.

"Get a room, you two," she said as she went into the house. That stopped us dead in our tracks. We looked at each other in shock, and then just busted up laughing.

In the end, you accepted that I wasn't going anywhere without you. And I accepted that you didn't want me to give up my chance of a college scholarship to tag after you. We talked it over and decided that you'd transfer to wherever the best offer came from. Whichever offer came in that was a place we both wanted to live and would accept your UTK credits.

I guess most parents would never have agreed to that; to let their teenage daughter move away to college with some guy. But you weren't just some guy. And everyone knew that even if they paid for two apartments, one for you and one for me, or if I lived in the dorms, and they paid for that, the place I'd really be was wherever you were. Hadn't I grown up in your bedroom? So, they all came to accept that you and I were together. There was nothing that was going to break us apart. Nothing. At that time, that's what it seemed like.

♪ ♪ ♪

You took some extension courses for the second semester. UTK was glad to let you do it because you'd been a football hero and because of your health issues. All I cared about was that you were there every day when I came home. My senior year didn't seem so important anymore. It was just a means to an end. A means to getting us into our own place together.

In January, the college that I accepted was Virginia Tech. It wasn't necessarily the highest ranked. But it had made the most generous offer, and would accept most of your units and you. And they wouldn't make me live on campus which suited us to a T.

Coach was devastated to be losing me. But he liked the coaches at Virginia Tech better than the coaches at Texas A&M, so that was a plus. He felt like it was a better fit as well. He also knew that you were going with me and wouldn't let anyone push me into things that I shouldn't be doing.

♪ ♪ ♪

The high school wouldn't let you attend prom because you were 21 and that just seemed way too old to be going to prom. And the truth was, it was. Prom was like child's play for you. And it suddenly seemed that way to me too. I didn't really want to participate in it at all. So, instead, we took a trip. We flew out to Virginia Tech and went apartment shopping. Just the two of us.

It felt weird to be walking through the airport, holding hands and being able to kiss each other all we wanted without people staring at us like we were a bit , as folks at home had been doing for the entire year.

We found this simple little one bedroom that was close enough to campus for us to walk or ride our bikes, but wasn't overloaded with partying teenagers. If the landlord was surprised by our ages or our moving in together, he didn't say anything. He'd probably seen just about everything in a college town. We signed the lease for a move in date of July 1st.

♪ ♪ ♪

When graduation came, it seemed really anticlimactic. My family was there to cheer me on, but you were the person in the stands that I had eyes for. Wynn cried so much after that, I thought she might become a rain cloud. She was going to Tennessee State in Nashville. And my one true girl friend and I just didn't know how to say goodbye.

Two weeks later, you and I were packing up the Jeep and the Camaro with our things. We'd shipped some furniture out that you'd been using at UTK, but most of our stuff was in our cars. My mama cried almost as hard as Wynn had. Even my daddy got teary-eyed.

But somehow, the fact that you were going with me made it not so hard for them. And maybe because I was with you, it was easier for your mama and daddy to let you go, after the struggles you'd had all year keeping everything in balance. We'd look out for each other, like we always did. At least, that's what I thought would happen. It turns out that you were better at keeping secrets than I thought.

Chapter Nineteen

Treacherous

"And I'll do anything you say
if you say it with your hands."
- Swift & Wilson

God, this song makes me think of you. Of those times in our apartment. The slow, warm nights. Your hands. My hands. Us. Together. The song is sexy and slow, like it always felt like we were when we were together, hidden away in our apartment in Virginia.

It didn't feel like we were playing house. I'm sure to people older and more experienced than us, that is what it would appear to be. You were taking summer classes to get caught up on a few things. That's why we'd come out early. Well, and so I could start training with my new coaches.

We almost always walked together to campus with our fingers entwined, like we'd always been this way. Sometimes we'd bike together, but that didn't seem as fun anymore because we couldn't touch each other as easily biking. And no matter who was done with class or practice first, we waited for the other so that we could go back to our little piece of heaven together.

I mean, it wasn't really heaven. It was just a grungy college apartment. Clean. But old and bare bones. Neither of us were really decorators. Or as it turns out, were we very good cleaners. Or chefs. We ate a lot of pizza. And take out. And mac and cheese. You had to be as careful with carbs as you were with the sugar, so we had veggies and protein in there. But to us, it was heaven. In many ways, we lived our life in a bubble. We didn't make friends with the neighbors. Didn't make friends with people in classes. We had eyes only for ourselves. As if we hadn't known each other all our lives. As if we were two strangers who had fallen in love and needed to get to know all there was to know about each other.

When I was gone, all I could think about was getting back to you. To the feel of your hands on my skin. And if you were the one gone, you were the one racing back to me. And the first thing you did was pull me to you and kiss me like you'd been gone for months. We were making up for years of lost time. We were making up for the year we'd had to live in our separate houses even though we'd wanted to be like this. Next to each other. Skin to skin. I guess that summer was like being on a honeymoon. I guess we could have been a newly married couple. We might as well have been because we did everything together.

When we went grocery shopping to pick out our meager supplies, knowing that we wouldn't cook much of anything, you wouldn't wander far away. You'd be near me, touching me, reaching past me to grab something and kissing me on the way back.

Completely disgusting stuff. I know.

Girl stuff. Romantic stuff. Stuff that I never thought I'd care about, but that you showed me that I did. That it mattered to me that you thought I was beautiful, and that my limited curves were all you needed and were lovelier than any other person you'd been with.

Sometimes, when I'd open my eyes in the morning, you'd be there staring at me with a leg over on top of mine, a hand resting on the curve of my waist. I'd say, "What?" thinking I had snot or drool or something down my face.

"You're just so damn beautiful," you'd tell me with a smile. With those mosaic eyes lighting up like fireworks.

And all I knew how to do was kiss you. Because I still wasn't very good with compliments. Even if they were from you. Even if they were words I'd wanted to hear from you since I was nine years old.

♫ ♫ ♫

My poor mama. I think she must have thought I'd forgotten her because I hardly ever called or texted, and completely forget an actual snail mail letter. The truth was, I had forgotten her. I had forgotten everything but you. Summer was a Hollywood movie. A romance that didn't seem to end, and that I didn't want to end.

When classes started in the fall, and I had more consistent dive practice, we were drawn apart a little more. And when we were home, we both had a boatload of schoolwork to do. We had to set ground rules, because if one of us touched the other, it was all over. There'd be no studying.

It was kind of fun though, for me, to break the rules. I'm smiling as I write this because, when had I ever been a rule follower? What made you think this would be different? You'd always get mad at me, remember? But it was in that cute way you'd come to get mad at me. Hardly ever with dark, pond colored eyes, but more an exasperated, I-know-you're-gonna-win kind of eyes. Eyes that knew it was gonna be fun to have me break the rules, and you try to stop me. With eyes lighting up like fireworks.

To punish me, you tried studying at the library. But I knew where to find you there too. And really, I knew exactly how to get what I wanted now. I knew exactly where to kiss you and touch you. You'd flush a million shades of red when I was really bold in the library. Who knew that Jake Carter Phillips could actually blush? And I loved the fact that I could make you do it. I loved that Seth had taught me ways of not playing fair. And… I could win a lot this way. It was intoxicating. I felt like I had a whole lot more power over you than I ever had before. Sex. Guys are putty for sex. Too bad I couldn't have used that when I was twelve.

One day, a couple weeks into the school year, the sororities and fraternities came out of the woodwork, advertising rush week. We were in the quad, studying together between classes, but the chaos in the quad was demanding our attention. We both gave up studying and stretched out on the lawn. I had my head on your stomach while we watched. I could feel you watching me. I always knew when you were. Hadn't I always?

Finally, you pulled my hand up and kissed it, and then said, "I feel like an ass."

That wasn't what I had expected, so I rolled over to look into your eyes. "Why?"

"Because of me, you'll miss out on all that."

"It's not because of you. I wouldn't be doing that anyway."

"But you'd be going out and partying with your teammates and chugging back beers and winning hearts."

"You said pretty much the same thing when you went away and left me in high school and look how that ended up."

You were silent, looking at me, searching my face for any regret of which there was none.

"I don't want any of that. Not even a little bit," I told you, meaning it with all my heart. You stared a little longer. I finally pulled your head down and whispered, "Shut up and kiss me."

And you did, long and hard, before pulling back.

"I guess it's good," you said with a slow grin, "because I've learned my lesson. I sure as hell wouldn't be letting you ride away on the back of some damn motorcycle."

I reached up and kissed you again before popping open the button on your jeans and then making a break for our bikes with you chasing after me. I wasn't going to make it to biology today. I had better ways to learn about the human body.

My life with you did make me stand out a little from the rest of the dive team who were leading the normal party lifestyle of most college students. I probably did miss out on stuff that was normal and important to developing your own sense of self. But it was worth it every time I rolled over in bed and felt you next to me. Every time I got to curl up next to you at night and fall asleep with your arm thrown across my body in that protective way that you'd come to do without even knowing it. All of that would never, ever leave me. All of that was forever worth any loss of anything "normal" I should have been doing. I'd give anything and everything up for those minutes together. They were the most precious moments in the world. Ingrained in my memories more than any other moments in my life.

♫ ♫ ♫

When we went home for Christmas, it felt like a splash of reality. Like we'd been living in that Hollywood movie for so long that we didn't know how to react to a normal life. The only thing that had ever burst into our bubble at school had been your diabetes. You'd found a local doctor, and you were there regularly, but it was still a struggle to keep you on an even keel. Of course, the way we'd been eating hadn't probably helped. Not that you ate MoonPies for dinner or anything, but we weren't exactly representing the food pyramid.

The first confusion when we got home was where were we going to stay? I mean, we'd been living together for almost six months, and it didn't make any sense for me to go to my room and you to go to yours. But it was also a little hard for our parents to watch us say goodnight to them and climb the stairs to your old bedroom hand in hand.

I mean, they KNEW what was going on, but to SEE it going on was a little different. Eventually, everyone adjusted. What surprised the hell out of my mama more than that was me showing up to help in the kitchen. I'd never, ever helped in the kitchen. Unless it was by her demand to unload the dishwasher or clean up the PB&J mess I'd left on the counter.

But six months of mac and cheese and hamburgers had made me realize that you couldn't sustain your levels eating like that. So, mama became our teacher. I say our teacher because you were hell-bent on not being apart from me for any length of time, even if it was for a good cause. Even if we'd pretty much been side by side for six months. Regardless, it never got old to me, the fact that you didn't want to leave my side. It felt fair. Like I'd been doing that for so long, and you had a lot of catching up to do. Anyway, Mama ended up teaching us both how to cook the best she could in a couple short weeks.

It was hard to be in her kitchen and not ours though. You were always wrapping your arms around me and trying to take the knife so that you could chop with me still trapped in your arms. And I'd tease you the whole time. We both knew where we would have ended up if we weren't in Mama's kitchen. Probably on the floor, but all mama had to do was glare at you and you'd at least slow down.

But she couldn't stay mad at you because you were still smooth as a milkshake when it came to women. You'd say something nice, and she'd glow, and we'd be back to throwing vegetables at each other.

Before we left to go back to school, Mama pulled me aside. She looked into my eyes and said, "How is everything, Camdyn?"

"Good, Mama," I said with a smile that was the size of Texas.

"We worry you know. All of us." And I knew that she meant more than just her and Daddy. She meant your parents too. And I knew somehow that she meant that they worried about more than the normal college work and even your diabetes.

"Why?" I asked.

She looked like she was trying to find words. Like she'd been thinking about it for a long time and still couldn't figure it out. She shrugged. "We shouldn't. You were always more his than ours."

She smiled at me, and I hugged her. But later...later I knew why she worried. It was because we were each other's whole world. More so than ever before because, really there was nothing separating us anymore. Nothing tugging at the fabric of us so that we were forced to be two separate people. Instead, we were one. And what do you do when you get split in two again?

♫ ♫ ♫

The first day we got back to school, we made a big deal of shopping for our first "grown up" dinner. You went out to buy a bottle of wine, and I stayed home to finish up. What a disaster! By the time you got home, I'd burned the vegetables and turned the steaks into dust.

I can laugh at it now. You did, which made me mad, of course, and I burst into an extremely rare batch of tears because I'd ruined it all. Which made you know how serious I'd been about it. I didn't ever just cry, did I? Only over you, and even then, it took a lot.

You kissed the tears away and said we'd just have a salad. And wine. And cheese and crackers. And that we'd celebrate with a touch of each other for dessert. That was so you… then. The hard edge of you had melted some. You were softer. And yet, at the same time, more focused. More focused on what was important right then and there. At least that's the way I felt. Maybe just because you were only focused on me. And as we both know, that's all I'd ever wanted.

♫ ♫ ♫

It happened just as the Virginia winter had begun to let up, and the air was full of cherry blossom smells. I got out of a class at dusk and went to where you were always waiting for me at the bike rack. You'd been early lately because there was a guy in the class that gave me the creeps. So, you were always there. Except…that today you weren't.

I waited. My heart pounding. My stomach churning. And I just knew. Something bad had happened. It wasn't just you being late or getting stuck in traffic. You weren't there, and I knew I had to find you. Like I knew in the hallway my freshman year. I got on my bike and started out the way I knew you would have come. When my cell phone rang, I almost crashed. I dropped the bike to answer it.

"Hello?"

"Camdyn Swayne?"

My heart fell into the pit of my stomach. "Yes."

"We have you listed here as an emergency contact for Jake Phillips."

My knees buckled, and I sat down hard on the curb. Waiting for the worst. I was breathing hard and yet not breathing at all. It was weird. "Miss Swayne?"

"Yes?" I croaked out somehow.

"We have Mr. Phillips here at Montgomery Regional. He's had a diabetic seizure."

"I'm on my way."

I flew back to the apartment on my bike, jumped into the Jeep, and was at the hospital in under twenty minutes. In that time, I'd called home, left messages on both our parents' cells, and sent Mia a text.

When I scrambled into the ER, the nurse took pity on my ragged look, and let me up to your room right away. You looked like you always did after these episodes. Hooked to wires, pale, tired. But today, when you looked at me, there was something else in your eyes. Something you were trying to hide.

We didn't get to say anything, I'd just barely grabbed your hand when the doctor came back in. He looked at me and stopped and then kept coming. "I'm Doctor Wong," he said with his hand outstretched. I took it and shook it, "Cami Swayne. I'm Jake's girlfriend."

"I've heard a lot about you, Ms. Swayne. Dive champ, right?" And he smiled. It was a nice smile. Now, thinking back, I wish I could have wiped the smile off his face. I wish that I could have somehow prevented the words from coming out of his mouth, but I couldn't. And the words came anyway.

"Jake's collapse is not just related to his diabetes. His kidneys are pretty shot."

I looked at this strange doctor as if he was an alien creature for a long time. We'd been down this road before. Everything was going to be okay after a few days of fluids and intense glucose monitoring.

"You knew about his kidneys, right?" the doctor continued talking to me.

"He's had some issues with his ketones for about eighteen months, but we thought we had it under control," I acknowledged.

The doctor looked surprised.

I looked at you, and I knew. I knew that you'd been having a harder time than you'd admitted to me. You hadn't wanted me to know. Hadn't wanted to burst my... your... our bubble. You were still protecting me.

"God damn it, Jake," I said.

The doctor was even more surprised. He put a hand on my shoulder, but I shook it off.

"I'm going to get some air." And I left you. I left you there.

I was furious. So very, very angry. Angrier than I'd ever been at anyone, even you, before. Angrier than I'd been at Seth. Angrier than I'd been at myself with Seth. How could you not tell me? How could you lie beside me every night and put your arm around me and not tell me that your body was giving out on you?

It took me at least thirty minutes of pacing and storming and kicking the tires of the Jeep before I could calm myself down to go back. When I did, the doctor wasn't there. You had your eyes shut, but as always, you knew that I'd walked in.

You opened them and looked at me hesitantly. Like you rarely did. Your normal, confident self on the wayside. No longer godlike. Slowly, you'd been giving in to your mortal side without telling me. I sat on the bed by your feet and curled my knees up to my chest, staring at you.

"I'm really mad at you," I said finally.

"I know. I'm lucky I still have a shoulder." You smiled weakly.

"How could you keep this from me?"

You shrugged. But I knew. You couldn't stand for me to see you as weak. You couldn't stand to be the one needing help.

"We weren't sure it would happen this fast," you said by way of an apology.

"Who's we?"

"Doctor Wong and I."

"Do your parents know?"

"No."

I just looked at you. Fuming still, but unable to keep the force of it while looking into your mosaic eyes that looked tired and afraid.

"What do we do now?"

"Dialysis, and they put me on a transplant list unless we can find a donor that matches me in someone we know."

That was easy. I mean, I had to be a match, right? Hadn't everything in my life been for you? So, why would this be any different? I almost smiled because it seemed so simple.

But it wasn't.

I wasn't a match.

I couldn't believe it when the results came back. I demanded they start them that very same day. They couldn't because the lab that did them wasn't open. They only take 45 minutes to an hour, so I went the next day, while your family was still driving up to see us. The result of the crossmatch was positive, which I thought was a good thing when they first told me, but then they told me that in this test, they actually want the results to be negative.

I felt like I'd failed you.

And the truth was, even if I'd been a match, you wouldn't have been able to have a transplant right away. Your panel reactive antibodies (PRAs) were too high. You had to have some transfusions and a procedure called plasmapheresis before anyone could really be a donor for you. I learned more medical terms in those few days… months… than I ever thought I'd want to know. Science had never really been my thing.

When your parents showed up, they were furious, not just with you but with me too, because they thought I'd known and not said anything either. Then they were mad at me because I hadn't been watching you like I knew they thought I should have been. Like I knew I should have been. But when they realized how livid I was at myself, I think they caved a little.

That, and my mama reminding them that it was you who hadn't told any of us what was going on. All I know was that all of this permanently ended our Hollywood movie.

Maybe, in the end, that is why you didn't tell me. You weren't just protecting me. You were being a little selfish too. You wanted to live that little bit of Hollywood before everything went to hell in a handbasket.

Chapter Twenty

Sad Beautiful Tragic

"Distance, timing, breakdown, fighting
silence, the train runs off its tracks."
- Taylor Swift

Not all the words to this country song match ours. But the tone of the song. The fact that everything was lovely and sad and goddamn tragic. That's true. That we both broke down in very different ways. I still can't hear this song without thinking of those times. Watching this giant among men slowly fade away.

They kept you in the hospital in Virginia for a week. We found out that the best live kidney donor for you was actually Mia. Which was a good thing and a bad thing. The good thing was that we didn't need to wait for you to slowly move your way up the transplant list. The bad was two things really. First, with your PRAs still all over the place, you couldn't have the transplant yet. And second was that Mia wasn't 18. The doctors recommended, even with parent approval, that the donor be 18 before a transplant take place. So, it wasn't going to happen for a while. Instead, they put a tube in your abdomen and sent you home with a dialysis machine. The dialysis machine and a boatload of meds. To keep you healthy. That was a joke.

You were exhausted. Tired. You tried to keep up with school, and it was a failing battle. We fought a lot because you didn't want me to drop classes or dive practice to take care of you. They were stupid fights. Not serious. We didn't throw things or and walk out. Our fights were more like we just couldn't agree to disagree.

Your parents had gotten a hotel room and stayed for another week after you'd gotten out, but they could see you were trying hard to go back to normal, and they didn't think their hovering over you was going to help. So, they went home. Reluctantly. I think they would have preferred to take you back home right then. But you were being stubborn. You didn't want to leave because you didn't want me giving up ANYTHING for you. So, it was you and me. But… the truth was, I didn't feel like I could leave you. Like when I was ten and stored up all those supplies in that dirty pink backpack just in case. Like I'd watched from the sidelines while you played football in case you needed a Gatorade.

You finally dropped your classes for the semester. But you'd drive me to and from school as best you could. You were trying to still be the strong, perfect, godlike Jake, but one who just happened to need a new kidney. But that wasn't really working. Your grin had faded, and when you pulled me up against you by the waist, your muscles were noticeably less. You were still gorgeous. And your kaleidoscope eyes still thrilled me to the core, but my heart ached that you were appearing so… so… frail.

I couldn't concentrate on school or stupid math problems when the only thing that had ever mattered in my life was crashing to pieces right in front of me. So, it wasn't a surprise that I ended up failing a couple courses, lost my scholarship, and we moved home.

♫ ♫ ♫

It felt better being with people who loved us. I took some courses at the local junior college. Coach brought me in to teach at his dive school. And whenever I left the house, I knew you weren't alone because Marina was there.

♫ ♫ ♫

You hated the entire process of being ill. Of needing the machine in our room. Of not being your normal, athletic self. The drugs made you moody. Life made you moody. But I still got to curl up beside you at night, and you'd still throw your arm over me in a protective manner, and for right then, that was all that mattered as we got you sorted out so that you might have a chance at a good kidney transplant with Mia. Beautiful Mia, who was only a junior in high school, but would, without a question, give up an organ for her superstar older brother.

We still took trips to the lake, but you couldn't really go in because you didn't want to get some infection in your tube from the germs. But we could sun. And you could watch me swim. And we could hang out under our tree with the upstretched arms, reading books and talking about a life that we both weren't really sure was going to happen anymore. That neither of us really knew what we wanted from anymore, other than each other.

Our daddies were still holding out hope that you'd go into the family business, take over the dealership. But you thought you wanted to coach football. And what did I want? I couldn't name it. I had what I wanted. That was you. I was just taking classes to make everyone happy. I couldn't have cared less. I'd never really thought about me in that way. About what would Cam do with herself?

Overall, we were in a holding pattern again. Not one of our own making anymore. It frustrated me that we'd wasted so much of your healthy time that we could have had together because you'd been worrying about our age difference, and I'd let you.

♫ ♫ ♫

In the summer, the doctors thought that you were in good enough shape for the transplant. Mia wouldn't be 18 until December, and was only going to be a senior in high school, but between your parents and Mia, they convinced the transplant team that it was what everyone wanted. I guess you got your smooth talking from someone in your family.

I can't imagine what Marina and Scott must have felt like having both their children go under at the same time. I knew that, for me, it was hard enough to think about the risks Mia was taking, and yet at the same time, being so incredibly grateful to her for giving you the gift that I couldn't give you.

The day of your surgery, I woke with panic in my veins and your arm around me as normal, and I flipped over so I could stare into your face. You were already awake and staring at me.

287

"You know…this isn't what I wanted for us. For you," you said with that serious look in your eyes that you got when you were trying to do something for my own good that you knew I'd hate.

"I know."

"I feel like I've said that a lot to you over the last few years."

"Jake, I love you. You love me. That's all I want."

You played with my hair. "I know. But I thought we'd be at school. You'd be leading your dive team to great wins. I'd be getting my degree, looking for a team to coach, even if it was pee wees."

I nodded. Choked up a little because this hadn't turned out the way either of us wanted.

"You deserve better than this, Cami."

"Don't start," I said fiercely, bringing your lips to mine and kissing you hard. In a way that still made me tingle all over, and I knew did the same to you. You groaned and wrapped me hard in your arms that were still strong, but nothing like they'd been before.

"If it was reverse, you'd feel the same," you said into my hair.

"Maybe. All I know is that I love you. I've loved you my whole life. This is where I belong. This is home."

You nodded into my neck. I could feel wetness on my cheek. It was hard to believe they were tears. You didn't cry. The god among men didn't cry. But you were.

"It's so hard to not be able to have any say in this. To have my body doing something I can't will it not to do.

What I really want to do is take you away, make love to you, and forget the rest of the world."

"We will. We'll do that. When this is over."

"Okay… it's a deal?" you said, trying to gain hold of your emotions.

"Promise?" I whispered.

"Promise," you said. And God, I wanted it to be true. You'd never break a promise to me, would you? But sometimes, those promises aren't really ours to make. I had to learn that the hard way.

That afternoon, even though I was panicking inside, I hid it. For you. For your family. I kept up that false smile and laughter that I'd gotten really good at the two years you'd been away at school. I was making you laugh, and Mia too. Marina and Scott were glad I was able to pull it off. Don't ask me now what I said. I couldn't tell you. It was just stupid stuff. But that was the point.

When they took you both in, we all sat in the waiting room, staring at books or the TV or our phones, but not really seeing anything. My mama and daddy tried to be the strong ones, but really, Mia and you were just as much their children as I was. We'd all been one big family.

Three hours and twenty-five minutes. That's how long we waited to hear news on you. Mia was in and out sooner than that. We actually were just going to see her in the room they'd put her in after getting released from recovery when the doctor came in to see us.

He was smiling, and I felt like my heart was about to explode. Like it had many times at the sign of a doctor and you, but the smile reassured me just a little. He wouldn't be smiling if it hadn't gone as expected, right?

He told us it went well. That everything looked very positive, and somewhere in the back of my brain, I remembered the crossmatch test and that positive wasn't always a good thing, but I shook it off. He shook our hands, smiling. Said you'd be in recovery for a little longer, and then we'd be able to see you.

In the meantime, we got to see Mia and let her know that her sacrifice had gone well. That made her smile. And we promised her a milkshake as soon as the doctor okayed it.

♪ ♪ ♪

When I first saw you, you smiled at me and said, "We made it," weakly. It was hard to see you like that. Not the grinning, self-confident boy that I'd fallen head over heels for at the age of… well… all my life. But I knew you'd get back there. I knew that this was the first step. So, I nodded and kissed you.

You and Mia got to share a hospital room for a day. I stayed with you too. Not that the hospital folks really wanted me to stay, but they really couldn't make me leave without calling security, and my mama had an in, so they pulled in a cot that they usually used for new fathers, and called it good.

I helped the nurses with the basic things that I could do for the two of you. Mia was released, but I stayed for the rest of your week in the hospital. I'd leave to shower and change when your mama or my mama was there, and then I'd be back.

We went through the training sessions that the transplant team did together because I wasn't going to let you have any more secrets from me. They said that after you'd recovered, and after they'd cleared you, you could have a perfectly normal life. You still had diabetes. Still had to treat it with the respect it deserved and not ignore it, but you could get back to normal activities. Even sports. Just not contact sports.

I asked if sex counted as a contact sport and the transplant team got embarrassed. I laughed and said, just kidding. But I really wasn't. I mean, you and I were both athletic, and things could get pretty hot and heavy.

What they said was that you weren't cleared for any kind of physical activity yet. You made a joke about too bad they hadn't told me that last night, and the team got embarrassed again. I smacked you playfully, making sure the team knew that you were teasing. But God was it good to see you teasing. To have a smile on your face. It felt like it was the beginning of a new road.

♩ ♩ ♩

When you came home, I was still terrified. Like if I blinked you'd fade away. We had tons of doctors' appointments, and I went with you to all of them. Neither one of us was carrying classes over the summer. I still was coaching at Coach Daniels' school, and he was pretty frickin' amazing with the flexibility he gave me and still paying me for a job.

You. You were really trying hard to get back to your old, determined self. Like this was just some new playbook you had to learn. And you wanted your own space. Our own space. So, at about a month in, you and I started talking about moving out of your parents' house.

We wanted to have a place where our life seemed like a Hollywood movie again. The one where we got to make love wherever and whenever we wanted and there was nothing but us. Our parents weren't very thrilled. I think they weren't sure you were ready for it. So, in the meantime, we slowly got you back into an exercise routine, and got your meals into a really strict schedule that we knew would have to be a lifetime in the making. Just like the meds would be part of your life forever.

We weren't stupid. We knew that the ten-year survival rate for kidney transplant patients was only in the fifty percent range, but that was because so many of them were old. Or had serious illnesses that you didn't have, right?

So, we just plodded along, recovering. Trying to be happy again. Trying to find that joy and easiness that had slipped away.

♩ ♩ ♩

You were cleared for some more strenuous activity, which lit up both our lives because, to tell you the truth, it had been getting harder and harder to keep our hands off each other. We'd lived through such an intense six months, from the time you'd be hospitalized in Virginia until now, that we wanted to work that out through passion and sin.

But that first night, I was still a little afraid to damage you. You pulled me close and kissed me with all the intensity that you had kissed me with that very first night in that very same room when you'd been in your football boxers and I'd been in my sexy underwear. But we finished the night with a passion that was full of all the emotions we'd been storing up for six months. We were spent and tired. In a good way, finally. I told you how much I loved you. You looked at me in that intense way that only you could do, put both your hands around my face and said, "How was I ever insane enough to think I could ever live without you?"

I grinned. Happy. "Because you were always an idiot when it came to girls."

You kissed me and tickled me, and we actually had a wrestling match that we hadn't had in a long time. You still won. Even weak as you were. That's because I'm extremely ticklish, and you knew every spot. Some spots that you hadn't even discovered until we'd moved away to Virginia Tech together.

The next morning, as I was in the kitchen about ready to leave for a session at Coach's, you came in a little sweaty. I looked at you, and you seemed pale. I tried not to panic, but you were nauseous too. I called the doctor immediately. You said it was just that you were overly hungry. I didn't agree.

The doctor had me bring you in. You weren't thrilled. But I didn't care. You said you weren't going to live like this, with me waiting for something bad to happen every time you had a hiccup. I knew the meds were making you a little cranky. So, I just ignored it. And you did go with me. I didn't have to argue with you to get in the Jeep or anything.

♫ ♫ ♫

The doctor ran some tests. Blood, urine, etc. They didn't come back in so good. They immediately put you in for a biopsy of the kidney. Didn't even release you. Once again, I had to be the one to call everyone and let them know what was going on.

Your body was rejecting the kidney. We'd expected it. I mean, all transplant patients' bodies reject the new organ at some level. That's what a boatload of the drugs are for. To suppress the immune system. And acute rejection wasn't something that you were past the stage of expecting. It just meant more drugs. This irritated you again.

But they let you go the next day, and that made me happy.

You recovered for another day at home and then insisted that you and I go out looking for apartments. You were so damned determined that we be on our own. It's kind of funny, really, because hadn't we really been on our own our whole lives? We'd depended on each other way more than we depended on our parents or other friends.

In any event, I caved, and we went. It wasn't like we didn't know our little town like the back of our hands, but we'd never really paid much attention to the apartments and condos that could be rented. We weren't going out of town. We still needed to stay close. For our families. For your doctors.

It happened when we were out and about looking at those apartments there was no way we could afford. I know now that it was a failed attempt to reclaim some of our Polaroid moments of color and passion that had disappeared months ago with your kidneys. The sun streamed through a set of picture windows and highlighted you in a halo of light that captured my breath. In that moment, caught in the shimmery white, you almost looked like the football god you once were and not the weaker version of yourself you'd become. You gave me your slow, heart-melting smile as you grabbed my hand and twirled me around in the empty space until I was held tight against your chest, feeling at last like I was the only girl in your world.

You swayed me back and forth, slow and sensual, and for a second we forgot it all. We forgot the realtor, the year of doubt, and the harsh reality of the future. I let out a breath into your neck and thought maybe, just maybe, we were in the clear. We'd held onto each other through it all. You tipped my chin up, and I was caught, as I'd always been, in the sparkle of your beautiful, green and gold mosaic eyes. The only eyes that ever made me feel alive.

You kissed me, reaching down to the depths of my heart where you'd forever claimed every last tile on the walls of my soul. The realtor cleared his throat, but we just ignored him like we'd ignored everyone for that picture-perfect six months we'd been away at college. You smiled against my lips, and I couldn't help but smile back. You whirled me again, but out of your arms, and then dragged me up the stairs at a jog.

I was smiling, still caught in that precious moment, when you turned to me again and whispered, "Cami," and I listened because I always listened when you said my name that way and not the short version, Cam, that we both preferred. And this time, my heart melted for a totally different reason when your mosaic eyes turned to me with an indescribable look. It was like a switch had been thrown from that brief second of life below until now. Then you said something that would tear at me for the rest of my life. You said, "I love you, Camdyn," before you crumpled to the floor.

An ambulance ride later, we were at the hospital. Again. How many times had we been there this year? It didn't actually matter because I already knew. I already knew that this time it was going to be different.

You see, it was the only time in our entire lives you'd called me Camdyn.

♫ ♫ ♫

They wouldn't let me see you. That still pisses me off to this day. That I didn't get to see you. I'd ridden with you in the ambulance. I'd told you I loved you, but I wasn't sure you'd heard it. I just wanted you to hear me again. Wanted to be able to look in those mosaic eyes and know that you really saw me like no one ever could.

By the time the doctor came out, Marina and Scott had arrived. They were haggard, just as I was, from the constant back and forth. And on top of that, the doctor wasn't smiling. I sat down hard on a side table that swayed under my weight.

"It doesn't look good."

"What do you mean?" Scott asked. Always looking for the facts, your daddy.

"We can't get him to wake up or respond to anything we do. The kidney seems to be in full rejection. His body is going into shutdown mode. We aren't exactly sure why. We've loaded him up with a new round of immunosuppressive meds. We're hoping that they'll kick in and bring him back around."

We all just stared at him. Not sure what all of that meant.

"And if they don't?" It was Marina who said it. Your brave mama, asking the thing we knew in our hearts but didn't want to know.

"If they don't, he won't wake back up."

♫ ♫ ♫

I wanted to pound something. I wanted to pound something until my hands were bloody, and you had to wake up to kiss them better. And I wanted to run, but the only place I'd ever run was to you. They weren't going to let us in to the critical care ward, but I started screaming like hell that I wasn't going anywhere till they let me see you, and because everyone knew my mama, they let me in to see you.

You were on tons of wires and machines again. I didn't care, I crawled right up with you like I always had, and I moved your arm so that the weight of it was over me. And I begged and pleaded with you.

"Please don't leave me, Jake. Please, please, please don't leave me. You are all I've ever known. You are the only thing I'm on this earth for."

And then I started to cry. The tears I rarely cried but when I did, they were always for you. Your mama tried to pull me away, your daddy tried to pull me away, the doctor begged, but I wouldn't budge. I wasn't going anywhere. They couldn't move me. Not until the machines started flatlining, and I didn't have a choice because it was the only chance I had of them saving you.

My mama came and swept me into her arms, and I couldn't stop crying. I was crying and crying and crying. Because I knew. Like I'd always known the truth about you.

You were gone.

When they came out to tell us, I already knew, and before they could stop me, I'd pushed my way past them and back into the bed with you. A bed where you wouldn't ever reach over and hold me again. A bed that you'd died in without even waking up those beautiful mosaic eyes to let me reply to that last "I love you" that you'd given me.

I don't know how long I lay with you like that. Eventually, my mama and daddy came, and they pulled me away from you. Said I had to let them take care of you. But they hadn't. They'd already let you die.

♫ ♫ ♫

I don't know how they got me home, but they did. I, honest to God, don't remember it. I do remember walking like a zombie out to our tree house and climbing up into it and looking up at the stars. Somewhere out there was the star you had named for me. Would you be there? Would you be there looking at me? We'd never spent any time talking about God or life or after life. What did I know about it?

I cried again. More than I'd cried over you in my entire life. More tears than I thought a body could hold or make. But none of the reality of you being gone had hit me yet. These tears were for what would come. That future moment. Because right then in the tree house, nothing was really real yet. All I knew was that when it grew cold, there was no one there to toss a sweatshirt up that smelled like chocolate cookies and boy.

My mama brought me a blanket and a pillow. She didn't even try to get me to move. She just gave them to me, rubbed my face with her soft hand, brushed my hair away from my face, and let her own tears fall on me. Their salty water mixing with my own.

She left me there. Because she knew I didn't want her. I wanted the person who I'd always belonged to more than her. I wanted you.

♫ ♫ ♫

So many people came to your funeral. So many, many people. You were still a god among men. Except now you weren't among men. Now you were a legend. Everyone had Jake stories to tell. Stories of you throwing a football, or making a joke, or saving them from making a fool of themselves. They talked to me about how you'd always talked about me. About how they'd always seen us together.

What a joke.

Wynn came home for the funeral. She hugged me, and sat with me, and made sure I was presentable. In black. A little black dress that made me think of another little black dress and the grin on your face as you watched me change out of it in your daddy's truck with the air blowing around us. The day that I had thought was a beginning.

♫ ♫ ♫

The pain I felt. It was like no other I'd ever felt before. Breaking my toe or spraining my knuckles on Brian's face. Not even the twisted pain in my stomach of watching you kiss another girl. God. I think I'd have taken that then in a heartbeat. Just to know you were back. To know that I could watch you while you did that. Kiss another girl. Because at least it would mean you were here.

I honestly don't know how I made it through any of it. I went where they told me to go. I walked where they wanted me to walk, and I greeted the people they wanted me to greet. I don't even know who was there. All I know is that a lot of people came. I didn't truly see anyone. I tried to get up and talk about you at the service. To say something amazing because you deserved that. But I just ended up in front of all those people, crying my heart out for you till my mama came and got me. I made them play "Long Live" and then cried as the words washed over me because you wouldn't be there to fight off the pretenders or the dragons, and there would be no children to remember our name. And all I knew was that I'd had the time of my life with you. And that, that life was now over.

Long Live

"But if god forbid fate should step in
And force us into a goodbye…
I had the time of my life fighting dragons with you."
- Taylor Swift

Chapter Twenty-one

Red

"Losing him was blue, like I'd never known,

Missing him was dark gray, all alone."

- Taylor Swift

I know that Miss Swift didn't mean this country song to be like this. To be about the loss of someone who had died. But it was true. Loving you had been a race that I'd been determined to win. It had been passionate and free. Free like me diving from the high board. It had been all my colors. All my memories. But…the only regret I had…was when I let you stop loving me and touching me. Letting you walk away to college without the "I love you" meaning forever. Right then. And for all our time. Remembering you was never in flashbacks. It was right in front of me. Hard, painful memories that would make me laugh and cry all at the same time. Only Red.

Remember when you and Wynn and my parents were all worried when I broke up with Matt? You were watching like I'd fall to pieces or something. And now, I was falling to pieces and I had no one to watch out for me. That's not fair. It's not true. It was just that I didn't have you to watch out for me. I still had Mama, Papa, and Wynn. She'd gone back to school in Nashville. But she was texting and calling almost every day. She told me that when I was ready, she wanted me to come up there to school with her. See. Good friend. She'd always been. Even when I hadn't deserved it.

But the truth was, I didn't think I'd ever be ready to go anywhere again. I couldn't be. The one thing I had been born for was gone. So, nothing really mattered anymore. Because that had been all that mattered. I'd never wanted anything else for myself, remember? You'd been my only wish. My only dream come true.

Everyone was on a suicide watch. I mean, they didn't tell me that. But I knew it. I didn't have anything to live for anymore. But even though they were worried I'd take my own life, I actually didn't have enough energy to come up with a plan. Or maybe I was afraid that if I did, when I got to the other side of whatever is out there after death, that you'd be mad as hell at me with those lake-colored eyes. And thinking about you just made more tears come.

Coach came to see me and told me the kids at the dive school were looking for me. But he was so choked up when he said it, when he looked at me, that I wanted to hit him. I didn't. You'd be proud of me. I didn't. Instead, I just acknowledged him without committing to anything. But truthfully, I wasn't moving anywhere. I was in dead stop mode. I had on a sweatshirt of yours that I never wanted to get out of. I'd go into your room… our room… and just lie there crying and trying to get the scent of you, pretending that I could still feel you in the bed with me.

For a couple weeks, I took to living in our room. I'd emerge once in a while because my body was demanding the bathroom, but that was about it. Marina or my mama would leave something on the bedside table for me to eat, but I didn't care for any of it. Which is saying a lot because you know I'd always been a horse. Able to keep up with all of you boys. They tried to get me to shower and do normal things. But I felt like if I lost the scent of you, it would be like there was nothing left. Even though I was in our room so much, I was barely sleeping. I couldn't sleep. I missed your body and warmth. I missed the weight of your arm around me. I missed your breath on my face, and your mosaic eyes looking into mine. I was in agony. In a pain I didn't know how to surmount.

One day, several weeks after the funeral, Marina came in and lay down next to me on your bed. I was curled up in a fetal position. Crying. I couldn't stop crying. I'd gone from being the tomboy who never cried to that drama girl who never stopped. I hated it. I knew you would hate it, but I still couldn't stop. It seemed like whenever I'd cried in my life, it had always been over you. Only you.

Your mama was crying too. "Cami."

Her voice was deep with emotions and tears, and I could just catch a hint of you in it even though she was a woman. "Cami, he wouldn't want to see you like this. It would break his heart. He'd be beating something to a pulp trying to get you out of here. He'd drag you down the stairs and throw you into the lake himself."

I knew she was right. I knew you would be so pissed at me for acting like this. For coming to a complete stop. For not living a life that you'd want me to live just like you'd wanted me to have a full high school experience. But I couldn't go on without you. I didn't know how to go on without you. Since I was born, I'd been looking for your eyes on me. Later, for your touch on me. I didn't know what to do without those things. Without the prospect that someday you'd be there looking at me again.

"I know," I sniffled so that she didn't think I was ignoring her, which was my normal protocol when anyone tried to talk to me about you. About what you'd want for me.

"Live your life for him."

"I was," my voice cracked as I said it, and she put her arm around me. It wasn't you. But it was in your room. Our room. And it was as close as I was ever going to get to you again.

♫ ♫ ♫

After that, they made me go see a shrink. A "therapist" who helped people with grief and traumatic experiences. So, for the first time in a while, I showered, but I put on another of your shirts that still had your scent. The smells were fading faster than a summer sunset, but I was keeping them as close to me as I could.

The shrink asked me how long I'd been with you. I told her twenty years. She looked puzzled, as I was only twenty. See. It's just hard to explain to someone who hadn't known our story. That's what I told her. That she couldn't understand our story.

So, she told me to write it down. To write it all down. That maybe somehow it would help me both be with you and to get on without you.

♫ ♫ ♫

So...that's what I did. I wrote this story for you. Yet another thing I've done in my life for you. She says it's not for you whenever I tell her that. She says it's for me. But I don't see that. I want you to know out there wherever you are that this is still about you. Nothing in my life can be about anything else but you. Right?

♫ ♫ ♫

That fake smile I'd learned when you left me to go to college became handy again. I knew that if I didn't do something soon, somebody would commit me to an insane asylum. Maybe that wouldn't be so bad because then nobody would interrupt my thinking about you.

♫ ♫ ♫

I rode my bike to the lake the other day. Passed the Quick Stop, and it made me think of that day I'd started my period and you'd found Brittney. I rode to the lake and threw my bike under our tree and lay down looking up at its branches reaching toward the sky like I imagined I was reaching out for you even now.

Sometime in those last few months, when we'd gone down there and you'd had to stay on the beach while I swam, you'd carved our names in the trunk. I'd never noticed it till now. It was a big heart with Jake and Cami. Not Cam. Cami. It made me smile weakly and also want to cry, but I was fighting the tears these last few days. Trying hard to choke them back in.

I stared out at the other side of the lake and the cliff. I marched around the lake, dug my fingers and my bare toes into the earth and reached the top. I stared down into the water from the edge. I remembered how angry you'd been the first time I'd jumped. Could almost feel you shaking me and bruising my skinny arms. I also remembered how irate you were the second time, when Seth had pushed me, and I stopped talking to you, and you came to find me and picked me up when Seth hit me. And I thought about how furious you'd be out there wherever you were if I jumped again.

Then I thought, "Good!" Maybe you deserved to be pissed off. I was pissed off. I'd broken one promise to you in my whole goddamn life. One measly damn promise. And I was so very angry that you'd broken the biggest promise you could have made to me. You'd promised me we wouldn't be apart again. And you hadn't kept that promise.

Across the way, there were some kids partying. I flashed back to thoughts of Wade and Blake. Later you and Amber. Later you and me. I remembered the thrill of the water and racing you to the dock. And instead of jumping, I climbed down, and raced your memory to the dock, and pulled myself up, tired and breathing hard. I was out of shape from weeks of inactivity. I tried to warm up in the weak spring air that was threatening to bring on summer. A summer I didn't think I could do without you. Summer had always been some of our best times.

What else do I say? It was a tough time. Those words seem so trivial. So understated, but I'm not sure I could find another word to explain it. Hell? Maybe. Living hell? Closer. There were times where I just wanted it to end because I kind of figured we'd be together again that way. There were times that I knew you'd kick my butt all the way to the lake and back if I didn't get going. But I was stuck. You'd always been my path out, and I couldn't see those eyes leading me anymore.

♫ ♫ ♫

My therapist said I needed to move out of our room. That it was holding me back. When I refused, Marina and Scott had my mama take my things out and bolted the door shut. I just gave them all the evil eye, went out to the garage, grabbed a screwdriver and a hammer, and headed back up the stairs. All four of them, my parents and yours, stood in front of the door.

"I'm not going to let you keep me from him."

My mama was crying. "We're not, honey. He's gone. We want to keep you from becoming him."

I lifted the hammer and tried to shove her out of my way. My daddy got as furious as I'd ever seen him get. He tossed me over his shoulder like you used to, threw me into the shower, and turned on the cold water. It was so something that you would have done that I was stunned.

I looked up at him with a tear-stained face. "That was for Jake," he said.

Then he stomped out of the bathroom.

I lay there for a long time. Under the cold, cold water. No one came to turn it off. No one came to save me. The only person who would have, was gone. And truth be told, you would have left me there for a long time before you came in to get me. But you would have. You would have brought me towels to wrap up in and hugged me and made it all better by just letting me breathe that scent of you. That chocolate cookie, grassy, boy scent of you that I could hardly smell anymore.

Eventually, my teeth were chattering so hard I had to climb out. I wrapped some towels around me, kicked off my soggy shoes, and went to stare at the bolted door. No one was there blocking my way anymore. I could have unscrewed the bolts and gone in.

I stared at it for a long time, fighting my inner self.

Then I marched down the steps, across our yard, into my old house, and climbed the stairs to my old bed. The bed I hadn't slept in, in almost two years.

But now I did sleep.

I slept for a long, long time. Longer than I had since you'd gone, because for all those weeks, I'd still been waking up every hour or so reaching out for you in an empty bed.

♫ ♫ ♫

When I woke up, I continued to work on this story for you. But I finally knew my therapist was right. It was also for me.

Chapter Twenty-two

A Place in This World

"I'm alone, on my own, and that's all I know.
I'll be strong, I'll be wrong, oh but life goes on."
- Swift, Orrall, Angelo

I listened to this song for a long time the other day. On repeat. Because I was heading down a path with no direction. An airplane on autopilot. I couldn't see through the tears. The grief. I hadn't known what I wanted before you died. I really didn't know what I wanted now that you were gone. I was alone in the world. I know you'd yell at me and say I wasn't. I know my family would protest. That includes your family... my family... our family. So, what did I do? I let Wynn force me into a direction, a path. It wasn't one I chose, but it was movement.

In the fall, I joined Wynn at Tennessee State. It was far away from the memories of you. It was some place that you and I had never gone or done things. But the best part of it was that it was a place where I could go through the motions of living without anyone overanalyzing it like both our parents and my therapist had done for months.

Wynn had joined a sorority her freshman year, and was living in the sorority house to which I was granted access because of my sob story. There was no hazing. No rush week. I guess they felt like I'd already been through enough. Or maybe they felt like my tragic love story was good drama. Gave them points in the sorority race to be the best. You and I would have laughed at it just like we did all the ABC tween dramas.

Regardless, I had a room with Wynn, and she kept me going. She always had a list of things for us to do. Football games were off limits, obviously. But there were plenty of other sports to go to and watch muscled boys that she would flirt with mercilessly. She wanted me to go swimming at the pool and maybe start diving again, but I didn't have any desire to swim anymore. Or dive anymore. I didn't have anyone to show off for. I didn't want the adrenaline rush anymore. After that one swim at the lake, when I'd pulled myself back from the cliff, I hadn't been swimming since. It was gone. I'd left it at the docks. It was my past. Just like you.

I had classes. I honestly don't know what they were or how I passed them. Do they have some non-stated rule about not failing someone who'd just watched the love of their life die before their eyes? Maybe they do, maybe they don't, but somehow, I passed. Not with As, but I passed. I was still undeclared because I didn't have a clue what I wanted to do with the rest of my life. Hell, I could barely get through each day at a time. The rest of my life seemed impossible. But as Mama pointed out whenever she texted me, at least I was going through the motions.

I had some boys flirt with me in a class or two. But they were repulsed with a glare that would have only made you laugh. It was kind of funny. And inside, that made me smile. Knowing that you would have laughed at my glare while they were scared away. That you would have simply pushed my shoulder and started a wrestling match that I wouldn't have been able to stop from smiling at.

Slowly, the fake smiles would sometimes turn into real smiles when someone made me laugh. Wynn or Mia. Beautiful Mia who had graduated and moved to UTK and would send me goofy videos from all over the school with "Jake was here" signs. They were funny in a bittersweet way. She'd grin and wink, your wink, and it broke my heart but made me smile too. No one would really ever talk to me about you. They were afraid I'd break. Or maybe I was afraid I'd break, and they sensed that, but Mia felt somehow safe enough to text me something about you or send me those pictures, but she'd never say anything about you in person. Not to me.

Sometimes, when I'd smile, I'd feel guilty. Like a real smile was somehow betraying you. But then I realized, it was just betraying my loss of you. I know that you certainly wouldn't have wanted me to stop laughing or smiling or living. I knew that. And I was trying. Trying to find my old self or some semblance of it, if only because I knew that that was what you'd want. There were moments, when I thought I couldn't do it, that I'd shout up at you, "God, Jake, I'm trying, okay?" Wishing for a sign that you'd heard.

But the deep-down truth was that I just didn't want to be happy without you. I didn't want anything without you. I wasn't anything without you.

♫ ♫ ♫

I don't know how long one can write about the same thing. The misery, the unhappiness. The going through the motions so the people who love you will think that you are okay. But I think that's how I survived that first year in Nashville.

That first year without you was the worst. Then, the fog started to clear just a little. I didn't always feel like I was under a rain cloud. I started looking about me for something to hook onto, to get myself involved in, hoping that it would pull me back to life.

Coach Daniels knew some folks with dive schools in and around Nashville, and he said he'd make a few calls for me if I wanted to go back to coaching kids, but the truth was that diving was still too painful. It still reminded me of you too much. I didn't think I'd ever be able to do that again.

Wynn and I got our own apartment. She was almost finished with school, whereas I was a couple years behind her. I'd lost a lot of time. She was getting her nursing degree and wanted to work in an OB ward, or preferably, a neo-natal ward. She was interning at Vanderbilt University Hospital. She wasn't working with patients yet, but was working on the administrative side, checking in patients, that kind of stuff. One day, she asked if I wanted to tag along just to see if anything piqued my interest because she knew I was still floundering around for a direction.

I went with her. She left me to go to work, and I wandered around the hospital a bit. I came across a sign that said "Diabetes Support Group." I don't know why I did it, but I ended up following the arrows, and coming upon a conference room with a small group of people of all ages sitting around a table.

I stopped at the door. A pretty, dark-haired woman, obviously the leader of the group, in a pencil skirt and glasses, asked if I was looking for the diabetes group and would I like to join them? I certainly didn't have diabetes. But I wanted to join them. And I did.

For the first few minutes, everyone was just introducing themselves and talking about whether they'd been newly diagnosed or had been living with diabetes for a while. They were talking about the lifestyle change and how it was impacting them positively and negatively. I just sat there for a long time. Quiet. Listening.

Finally, the leader turned to me and asked if I'd like to introduce myself and share my story.

I froze for a second. It wasn't my story. It was your story. Our story. But then I started. I told them my name, and I told them about you. I told them how mad I was at you and myself for not forcing you to get your condition diagnosed earlier and to take care of yourself sooner. How mad I was that you and I had both let a game come between you and your health. I blamed myself. If I'd thrown a fit, you would have done something earlier, for me, right?… Maybe.

I hadn't realized that I was harboring that anger. Toward both of us, for screwing around with your life. But I guess when you're ten and thirteen, it doesn't seem like those things are so very critical. You feel like you're going to live forever. We didn't understand that not taking care of yourself then could end your life in just a few short years.

I have to say, the group was really nice. I mean, here they were for their own support, trying to find a way to make themselves feel better about this disease that they had been diagnosed with, and here I was, dumping on them the most painful realization of the worst that could happen to them.

After I'd blurted the story out, with no tears shed, just anger and tears in my eyes, the group remained quiet for probably a whole minute. Then, the woman next to me hugged me. And then they were all surrounding me and telling me how brave I was to share that story, and thanking me for reminding them that the small choices they made every day were making a difference, if not to them, to the ones they loved.

They broke up to get snacks. Veggie tray. No cookies for this group. The leader, Anne Pavilotti, came over to me and introduced herself with a handshake.

"I'm sorry I ruined your group," I told her honestly.

She stared at me in a way that reminded me a little of your stare. "I think that must have been a long time coming. How long has Jake been gone?"

"Eighteen months, five days six hours."

She stared at me a while longer.

"Would you be interested in sharing that story again?"

I laughed in a very sarcastic way. "God, you'd want me to torture more people with that?"

She smiled. "I'd especially like you to come and talk to our juvenile diabetes group. I think your story could really make a difference for them."

"Really?"

"Really."

314

It's funny. Because, in a way, you had found a path for me again. It was like you'd shown me the way one more time. I was moving in a new direction. Anne set me up volunteering with the diabetes and endocrinology department and talking with groups. I wasn't leading groups, but I was sharing our story... a briefer version of our story, and I was listening to kids and teens talk about their struggles. I got to keep reminding them about the importance of taking care of themselves right then.

I realized at that point that I wanted to continue to do this. I didn't want to be a nurse or a doctor. I wanted to be a counselor. Not a psychiatrist. I wanted to be Anne. I wanted to lead groups through life's ups and downs. To help them make better choices. Better choices than the ones we had made.

Anne told me about the coursework that I should take as an undergrad and recommended a graduate program. She became a mentor. It was good to have someone to direct my energies again. To keep me on a path going in a right direction. Like you had. Like Coach had tried to.

It meant more college than I would have ever have expected me to have the patience for. But my mama and daddy were glad to pay for it because they were relieved I'd found a road to go down again. And somehow I knew that you'd be happy too. That our story would lead me somewhere.

♫ ♫ ♫

Wynn graduated, passed her nursing exams, and got a job at Vanderbilt. We'd commute together if our schedules overlapped, but that wasn't often because as a newbie nurse, she often got the worst shifts. She was dating a guy who was getting his PhD in philosophy. He wanted to be a professor. I laughed at that. You would have enjoyed Grant. He was funny but so serious. I guess that was good because Wynn was sort of serious too.

She was happy though. And it showed.

And I finally realized that I'd like to feel happy again too. I had a purpose now, but I wasn't filled with happiness yet. I wasn't sure I could be, but I'd like to try. For you. For me. For the memory of our story.

♫ ♫ ♫

But at that point, I was just putting everything I had into school and the groups I was part of at Vanderbilt. I was doubling up classes and trying to catch up from backpedaling for so long. I was more me. A me on a mission. I was going everywhere fast like I used to. Like when I was racing to get back to you or racing to beat you. But now, it was just me, racing to be the new me.

It was good. Not great. But better.

I even went out on a date. It didn't end so well. And I realized that that step was maybe too much. That for right now, having a career direction and helping others was going to have to do, because even if I wanted to be happy, I wasn't really ready to let anyone take your place. I wasn't ready to open my heart up to someone who might end up leaving me again. But at least I tried, mama said.

On your birthday, your mama came to see me. It was strange to have Marina come instead of my mama. My mama had been the one to make the drive to Nashville the most. Checking in to make sure I wasn't feeding her a line of BS, and that I was really navigating this world without you.

I took Marina to the hospital to meet Anne. Anne hugged her tight and said how sorry she was that Marina had lost her son. She told Marina how proud she was of me and that I was really making a difference for dozens of kids by sharing Jake's story with them.

After, Marina and I went to dinner, and Marina got quiet.

"You okay?" I asked her.

She nodded, but I could see the tears threatening to burst through. I knew if she cried, I would too. I was better. Maybe only shedding them once a month these days instead of forty times a day, but if she cried, I'd lose it completely.

"I never forced him, you know? Sometimes I hate myself for not forcing him," she finally breathed out, dabbing her eyes.

"To give up football? To get the pump earlier?"

She nodded.

"You couldn't have."

"I could have. I was his mother."

I shook my head and reached for her hand.

"Marina, I don't think even I could have made him give it up. He had to come to the realization that he wasn't a football god on his own."

She reached for a Kleenex and squeezed my hand.

"I love you, Cami. No matter what, you'll always be my daughter, and I want you to know how very proud of you I am. I know that he'd be proud of you too."

And then I did cry because I couldn't help it.

Chapter Twenty-three

Begin Again

"I've been...thinking all love ever does
is break and burn and end,
but on a Wednesday in a cafe
I watched it begin again."
- Taylor Swift

Never would I have thought that this song could be anything I'd relate to after you were gone. Never. But I guess that's what makes amazing artists amazing. Their songs are written for all kinds of times and places. Things that you thought were the weak part of me, someone else might find fascinating. Things that I thought I'd never find interesting about someone else all of a sudden strike me as just that. So eventually, this song did mean something to me.

I hadn't written in a long time because, well, I didn't think our story had any more to say. We'd spent the entire gamut of emotions. Our lifetime together had been twenty short years, right? But then something happened. Something that made me think of you. Not something sad or something I'd remembered about you and me, but something that made me scratch my chin and think, "What would Jake have thought about this?" So… I wanted to think about you as I wrote it. In the end, I think you would have liked it. Maybe you would have laughed and reminded me about that summer I was going into fifth grade. It makes me smile thinking about it, and what you would have thought.

♫ ♫ ♫

It happened just after I'd been accepted into my graduate program at Tennessee State. I'd taken on a paying part-time job with the counseling department at Vanderbilt, and Wynn had convinced me to chop my hair for the first time in my life. It was a sharp A-line. Super short in the back and angled long in the front. It made me look different. Grown-up. I wondered every time I looked in the mirror what you would have thought of it. Would you like to run your fingers through the short, crisp layers at the back? Would you like that I'd had them bring out the chestnut highlights and that somehow they'd made my pale eyes stand out more?

Speaking of, my eyes didn't look so bloodshot, and the darkness underneath them seemed to have improved. I started wearing makeup again. Not much, but enough to show that I was putting effort in. I got some new clothes. More trendy. More grown-up than teenager. Wynn was as excited about my new transformation as she had been that summer when I'd bought my first miniskirt for you, and you'd promptly found Brittney.

Wynn had just gotten engaged to Grant. She was moving in with him in about a month, so I was looking for a new apartment. I kind of wanted one of my own. One that I could pay the rent on so that I could stop leaning on Mama and Daddy quite so much and become the grown-up that I was trying so hard to be. That I'd been trying so hard to be for years without really ever realizing what that all meant. I did now. Or at least, I had a better notion than I had at twelve.

Anyway, none of that was what really made me think of you in a way that made me want to sit down and write to you. It was this other thing. The thing that happened while I was in a Starbucks perusing the apartment rental sections, circling away, that made me want your opinion. That's when I heard a smooth voice say, "Super Girl?"

My heart did a flip of sorts. Not the kind of flip when you said my name, but a flip that took me back for a moment to all those summers longing for you, and I looked around, hair swinging about my face, trying to find the person who'd said it. Only two people had ever called me Super Girl.

It took a second for my eyes to land on him, because he looked so different, but I couldn't help the smile that emerged when I did. It was Blake. Still shaggy and baby-faced, but somehow also grown-up with a scruffy chin and an expensive suit that seemed incongruous together. I could tell he'd been walking out when he'd caught sight of me because he was in this weird posture of half going and half coming.

"Blake!"

He came over and hugged me. A good, long hug that reminded me a little of your bear hugs before you'd fallen in love with me and before your hugs had taken on a totally different context.

We stood staring at each other for a moment.

"I almost didn't recognize you!" he said with that sheepish grin that had always been him as he eyed my hair and grown-up dress. But today, I still had my cowboy boots on and that felt a little like the old me.

"Says the pot to the kettle. Can't believe you're in a suit!"

He laughed.

"Can I join you? Or are you waiting for a hot date?" he asked.

My turn to laugh, and I waved him into the chair.

"How are you?" he asked. It was usually a question I dreaded because it always came with a silent, how-are-you-now-that-Jake-is-gone kind of tone, but Blake's didn't seem that way at all. Just seemed like a normal question he'd ask anyone. But I still gave him my canned answer.

"I'm good."

"You're looking a hell of a lot better than the last time I saw you."

I was both slightly offended and puzzled at the same time, trying to think back to the last time I'd seen him. Had to be years.

"At Jake's funeral."

I grimaced. "Honestly, the president could have shown up, and I wouldn't have known."

We kind of let that settle down in between us. And it wasn't uncomfortable, which surprised the heck out of me again.

"So, Nashville?" he asked, moving on but not in a way that felt like he was trying to avoid the discussion, more like he was really interested in asking me.

"Well, I figured with all the moody, starving musicians in this town, I'd fit right in."

He laughed at me. Right out loud. No one had laughed so hard at me in a long time. "You always were a little firecracker."

I threw my napkin at him. He grinned again as if to say that I'd just proven his point.

"How long you been here?" he asked.

"Almost three years."

"That's unbelievable. I can't believe we haven't run into each other before now."

"And you, what happened to Mississippi?"

"Graduated. Came home. You were right, of course, Mississippi can never compete with Tennessee."

I looked puzzled again.

"Don't you remember calling me a traitor for going to Ole Miss?" I suddenly did remember. And I blushed a little because I'd been so brash about it. How the hell did I ever think that I could tell people what direction their life should take?

He was all grins again. I wondered if he ever stopped grinning. Had he always been this way? "I see you do remember! Ha. Who knew a skinny-ass kid like you would be right. Anyway, I've been here about two years."

"Doing what?"

Impossibly, his smile turned even bigger. So big that I thought his face might break open, "Entertainment lawyer, specifically music."

My turn to smile. "Well, now that does fit. Except I always imagined you'd be the starving musician."

"Nah. I knew early on that I wasn't good enough. Doesn't mean I don't know when someone else is though."

"That's pretty cool. You're all grown up."

"Sometimes. I still like a good race though." I looked into his smiling eyes with a little wonder. I almost thought maybe he was flirting with me, but that didn't seem to fit. I'd always considered Blake way older than me. Not like you. Blake had a good five years on me. If your three years had been a mountain back then, Blake's five years would have been an entire planet.

His phone beeped, and he ignored it, but when it beeped again a few minutes later like an impatient kindergartner waiting for a snack, he sighed. "I'm going to be incredibly rude for a minute, do you mind?"

It was so gentlemanly, like you would have done, that I couldn't help but nod with a smile. He stood up, stepped outside, talked on the phone for a minute, and then came back in. When he sat back down, he caught me circling another apartment listing. He took the paper and looked at it. "Apartments?"

"Well, Wynn... do you remember Wynn?"

"Is she the one that played tonsil hockey with my kid brother, or was that you?"

I about choked on my chai tea I laughed so hard, and I had to wipe the spray down. It was embarrassing and yet still funny at the same time. He was grinning like a kid who'd just had Christmas early.

"That was me. God. I'd wondered where I picked up that term. Must have been from you. Jake hated it."

"Probably because you were always teasing him about doing it with his long line of fabulous women."

I loved how he hadn't shied away from my bringing you up, how he dove right into the story and added on. And what he said was true. I felt my smile widen again. I don't think I'd smiled so much in an hour since… well, before Virginia even.

"Sorry. We got sidetracked, so what's the deal with Wynn?" he asked.

"She and I have been living together, but now she up and got engaged and is moving in with her fiancé."

"How dare she do something so terribly predictable!"

This time I tossed a grape at him, but he was prepared, caught it, tossed it in his mouth, and ate it. I noticed for the first time that he had really nice lips. Not too small or too big. Like they'd be just right for kissing.

Embarrassed at my own thoughts, thoughts I hadn't had in forever, I looked down at the circled listings to escape. I could hide behind my swinging A-line, which made it an advantage these days.

"Anywho, I decided it was about time for me to get a place on my own."

"Big step."

I couldn't help but glance up to see if he was teasing me again, but he wasn't. He was all seriousness. He looked down at the ads and handed them back. He put in his own two cents about which ones he thought I should or shouldn't call on.

"God, I had the most horrible experience just down the block from this one, so with much prejudice, I say don't ever rent on that block," he said it with much drama, and of course, he expected me to ask about it, so I did.

"Okay, mama's boy, tell me what happened."

He threw a grape at me, and this time I caught it, but he stole it right back out of my hand which I wasn't prepared for. Whenever you teased me, I knew exactly what you were going to do before you did it. With Blake, I kept being caught off guard. And… I found I liked it.

"Blind date that went psycho," he told me.

"No? With you? The Southern gentleman reincarnated?"

He grinned again. "Yep. We'd just left the Italian place on the corner, and I was asking if she'd like me to walk her to her car, and she went all feminist on me. Screaming about how women nowadays didn't need big, burly men like me to throw down their clubs and lead them by the hand."

I was laughing again. It felt so delicious. Like candy I'd denied myself for too long.

"So, I guess I'm down to these two, as you've declared everything else a disaster area."

"You going to call them now?"

"Was planning on it."

"Would you like me to tag along? You know, as your lawyer and all?"

"Because I need a lawyer with me to rent an apartment?"

"You never know," he teased back.

So, I called the two numbers, and they both could see me. Blake tagged along. He was wrong though, they didn't like to see him coming at all. They thought that he was renting the apartment for me. You know, like a sugar daddy thing.

It was hilarious. They were both a bust.

We stopped for lunch at a meat and three.

"That's it. You're officially fired as my apartment lawyer," I told him mockingly.

"Thank God. I hate looking for apartments anyway."

"It's your fault. You offered. I was perfectly content to go on my own."

"But then I would have had to say goodbye a lot sooner."

When I looked up at him, in surprise yet again, I could tell he was serious. And this time, I knew that he was flirting. Or at least that there was a lot of meaning behind those words. I blushed, probably right down to my chestnut roots and hid my face behind my hair again.

He reached across and brushed my hair aside. I didn't know how to react, I jumped a little. No one. No guy anyway, had touched me that closely in a long time.

"Hey, did Super Girl just blush?"

I brushed at his hand, and he withdrew it.

"Well, times change."

"Yeah." It was the most somber he'd been all day. I knew he was thinking about you. Like I was thinking about you.

"Jake would have dug this place though. Has all his favorite things: girls, food, and football." I looked around and saw that there were a lot of pretty college girls in the diner. And a lot of football pictures. I hadn't really realized it. We were close to the campus, so it made sense, but I'd kind of been oblivious to it.

I smiled. "You aren't afraid to say his name around me."

His turn to look surprised. "Are people still afraid to talk to you about him?"

I nodded.

"They shouldn't be. Makes you hold onto it more. Like you're afraid everyone's forgetting him, and you're the only one who will remember, so you have to remember twice as hard."

The wisdom of his words really settled in on me. He was right. I'd been trying to remember you for everyone. Everyone that wouldn't mention you or anything you liked or what you'd done.

We were interrupted by the check. Blake wouldn't let me pay for lunch, or even my portion of it. Those Southern gentleman manners coming into play again. I thanked him politely. I still had my Southern girl manners too. We got in his car that we'd taken on the apartment hunt, and he asked, "So, where to now?"

I looked at my iPhone for the time. "I have to get to Vanderbilt. I have a meeting at two."

"AA?" he teased.

I chuckled. "No, I'm leading a teen diabetes group."

"Wow!" he said and then added, "that's impressive."

I shrugged.

"Really," he added with meaning.

He drove me to the hospital. I wanted to get out, but wasn't sure what to say before I left.

"Thanks. For everything today," was all I could come up with.

"I enjoyed it!" And I could tell he was being honest, but I still couldn't fathom why. So, I reached for the door handle, and he stopped me with his words, "Hey, I have to go in and deal with the client I left hanging earlier, but I could pick you back up. We could go to dinner?"

I just stared at him for a moment. I didn't know what to respond to first. The fact that he'd blown off a client for me or that he was sort of asking me out on a date.

He grinned. "Too much? I monopolized your whole day and now you're wondering what kind of psycho I turned out to be?"

I smiled. "I don't think you could ever be a psycho. You're too much of a teddy bear."

He looked wounded. "Geez, does that suck."

"What?"

"No guy wants to be the teddy bear. They want to be the rock star."

I just stared at him. His eyes were twinkling with humor. I still didn't know how to respond to this new version of Blake. Flirting with little ol' me.

"I'm being pushy, right?" he was laughing at himself now, "God. Always that way. I see something I want, and I just go after it." When he said it, I thought that it sounded a lot like the old me. Doing before thinking.

"I think I'm just trying to adjust to the fact that Blake Abbott just asked me out on a date," I tried to reassure him.

He was still grinning when he added, "Technically, since I paid for lunch, it would really be our second date."

I smiled back at him, "I don't have anything to throw at you."

"Your right hook. That was always a good one."

I was laughing while I opened the door, but I looked back in at him and tried to inhale some confidence, "I'm done here at seven, is that too late for you?"

"Any single man in their twenties would have to be committed if they said no to you."

"I never knew you were such an outrageous kiss ass."

He grinned more, "See. That's the Super Girl I remember. I'll see you at seven!"

I swung the door shut and watched him drive away in his sporty Cadillac, which made me realize that he had to be doing pretty well for himself. Even I knew those cars weren't cheap. When he was out of sight, I turned back to the hospital, and I still had a smile on my face. It felt good. That smile.

I texted Mama. And Wynn. But in truth, I wanted to text you. I wanted to know what you thought about Blake asking me out. I could imagine your eyes flashing possessively and angrily if you were still here. I could imagine you putting your arm around my waist and pulling me close if he'd smiled at me that way with you around, just so he'd know that I was yours.

But now. Now that you knew you were gone, what would you think?

♫ ♫ ♫

Anne was appalled that I wasn't going home to change for my date with Blake. She said I should have made him pick me up at Wynn and my apartment. I told her I was new to this whole grown-up dating thing.

"What? You haven't gone out on any dates since Jake?" she said, even more appalled.

"A couple. College boys. Wasn't the same. And didn't work."

She pulled out what she called her "emergency kit." It had makeup, a scarf, shoes, and a cute leather jacket. I looked at her like she was a little insane. She sighed.

"I'm a single woman in my thirties. We are always prepared."

The shoes didn't fit, thank God, but the jacket and makeup added a lot to make my plain summer dress look like I had at least spiffed up a little. She and I went back and forth on the scarf. "Trust me, you want the scarf!" she said strongly.

So, I let her wrap it around my neck, and when I looked in the mirror in her private bathroom, I realized that I looked good in it. It was a different me. Different like the haircut and the lines that I'd earned around the corners of my eyes at twenty-three, but it kind of all fit.

When I walked back into Anne's office, Blake was there, shaking her hand and dwarfing the office with his height and breadth. After all, he'd been a football player just like you. And he'd obviously kept in shape. It had to be a single-guy-in-the-music-industry thing, but he looked good. Fit, strong, blonde. Like he should still be on a surfboard in Cali. That's what I'd always thought about him and Matt.

When Blake saw me, his eyes lit up, and his polite smile turned into a full-on, shit-eating grin. It made me tingle in a way I hadn't tingled in so, so long. My tummy even did a little backflip. I liked that he liked what he saw.

"Every time I look at you, I can't believe how fabulous you look," he said.

"Kiss ass," was the only response I could give him without betraying how much that compliment had meant. But Anne knew. She was smiling, and she even wiped her eye. I rolled mine at her. It felt good to roll my eyes at someone again.

"Where are you taking our young Cami?" Anne asked in a way that would have made my mama proud.

"The 1808 Grille, does that meet with your approval?" He smiled broadly at her with a knowing look that only supremely confident men can do.

Anne tried not to be astonished, but was. She just nodded.

"Okay, well, be off you two."

He held the door for me, but I waited for him on the other side, and we walked through the hospital in silence. He had changed his clothes. He wasn't in a suit anymore. Instead, he had on comfortable jeans and a really nice, modern button-down that still spoke volumes of how he was all grown up. But on his feet were a pair of worn in cowboy boots. Not the kind you used on the ranch to muck out horse stalls, but the kind you wore to nice occasions. He looked a little more like the Blake I remembered.

He held the car door again. He'd done that all day. I slid into the leather seat and tried to take in the whole concept of Blake owning the car and having enough money to do these grown-up things. When he slid behind the driver's wheel, I turned to him.

"You know, the 1808 Grille, it's pretty pricey. I'm not really a pricey kind of girl."

He smiled at me. "Jake would kick my ass if I didn't give you the star treatment."

I swallowed hard. It was kind of sweet and poignant that he'd been thinking about you and our date just like I'd been thinking about you.

"I hope you don't mind, but after dinner, I need to stop by this club. There's a singer there that my partner wants me to check out. Just the look of him makes me think, 'No way in hell,' but my partner says he's got the voice of an angel."

"That sounds good. You...you own your own firm then?"

He nodded with a proud kind of look in his eyes. One he probably had every right to have. I couldn't imagine Blake doing anything at less than the 100% effort he'd always given football. Or racing me to the dock. Or playing his guitar.

"Yeah. My partner, Wil, he'd been in the business for a while already when I joined a firm he was at here in town. We quickly realized that we worked well together and didn't like some of the politics of the office, so we decided to go it on our own. It was tough at first, but we've got some big clients now, so we're all good."

"Like?"

"Band Perry. Thompson Square."

"No shit?"

He grinned again that grin that said he was proud of himself and kind of embarrassed at the same time.

"Who'd you stand up today when you went apartment shopping with me?" I asked, expecting him to say no one, but he got all bashful which I thought was kind of sweet.

"Blake Shelton."

"Holy crap!" I was stunned.

"Well, when he first started talking to me, it was because he thought our names being the same was something of a joke. I don't represent him at all. He's got a team he's had forever. But he's heard some nobody and thought we might like to take a look at them."

"Holy crap!" I said again. This time Blake laughed loud and hard. "What the heck were you thinking putting Blake Shelton on hold to go apartment diving with me?"

His smile went away, and he looked at me with all seriousness, "I'd choose you any day."

I didn't know what to say to that. Kiss ass had already been used too much. I was thrilled to my toes, and yet baffled at the same time. I hadn't seen him in years, even counting the funeral where he may have seen me, but I certainly hadn't seen him. It seemed a little overwhelming. And fast. And heady.

It seemed a little bit like me. The old me, who ran fast and hard at what I wanted. Most of the time. Except, sometimes, when I'd had to wait for you to catch up. To stop being an idiot.

♪ ♪ ♪

Dinner was good. People knew Blake there. It was obvious that he brought a lot more famous people than me there. The waiters looked at me a little wonderingly, and I smiled, thinking that maybe they thought I was Blake's next hidden gem being thrust into the music world that was Nashville. Little did they know that I could barely carry a tune. Not even for songs I'd known my whole life.

Blake asked if I wanted wine, and I didn't. I'd never really been a wine drinker. He sighed happily, "Thank God. I didn't want it to ruin my image of you. How 'bout a beer?"

I nodded yes. It made me think of the kegs by the lake. But he ordered some local brew. It was good. Definitely not the watered-down Bud Light we used to buy.

We talked about summers at the lake. The swimming races. We talked about you. With laughter and good memories. It wasn't as painful as I thought it would be. The thing was, Blake didn't let me bask in the old memories. He had a way of weaving them into our current lives and what was going on right then. It was a good mix. Making me feel like I could be this person I was right now, with all my memories and heartaches, and my new beginning.

"You know, back then, everyone always knew there was something between the two of you."

"Everybody but Jake. God, he could be an idiot when it came to girls."

Blake chuckled. "Maybe to your face. Truth was, I remember many times we'd come out of the locker room, and he wouldn't budge until you'd joined us. He'd kind of be tense and on alert until you showed up, and then he'd relax and suddenly be himself. The normal, confident, joking Jake that he was when you were there."

"No!"

"Yep. I think that's why none of the guys made a move on you. Even when you were a freshman."

"How would you know? You were away at Ole Miss by then," I said, but there was a lot of sarcasm when I said Ole Miss and that made him beam again.

"I had a brother with a big mouth." He winked at me. "You know, he was scared as hell when you decided to kiss him in front of Jake. Thought he'd get dragged to the lake and drowned."

I looked at him doubtfully. "You told me this morning that you didn't even remember who it was playing tonsil hockey with Matt."

He looked sheepish. "Caught. I knew. I wanted to see how you reacted."

"Why?"

"Curiosity."

"About?"

"Your feelings for Matt."

"Poor Matt," I said, thinking back at how badly I'd used him to get Jake jealous.

Blake threw his head back laughing. "Exactly!"

"You know, Jake used to tease me about liking you."

"No shit!"

"Yep. Summer before fifth grade. He thought I had a little girl crush on you."

"Did you?"

I shook my head, "No. I didn't have eyes for anyone but Jake."

Blake nodded, but he didn't seem upset by that.

"What about now? Do you think you could have a grown-up girl crush on me?"

"You are not humble, are you?"

"Where do you think Jake learned it from?"

"His godlike status."

"Well, yes. And me!"

I couldn't help but smile at him. I felt so relaxed with him. Like everything was just going to run its course. Like I didn't have to make anything happen, and I didn't need to look over my shoulder for the women waiting in line, although I imagined that Blake had his own line of women out there somewhere. They weren't visible or waiting on the porch by his door.

"So? You didn't answer me. You avoided it." His eyes were twinkling and serious at the same time as they looked into mine.

"Do you always move this fast?"

"Unfortunately. It's what Wil is always complaining about. And you are still avoiding my question."

I took a deep breath and breathed out. "Yes. Yes, I think I could very much have a grown-up girl crush on you."

That made Blake's face-splitting grin come back out.

"Good! Let's go then." And he dragged me out of the booth, and out of the restaurant.

He took me to Tootsie's Orchid Lounge, or just Tootsie's as the locals call it, where he was clearly known again by the bouncers. We avoided the front room which was packed with both residents and tourists and headed up the stairs to the back room where he said the local guy his partner wanted him to hear was set to play in an hour.

The bartender already had a beer extended to him by the time Blake reached him. "What would you like?" he asked me.

"Honestly, just a sweet tea."

He grinned, but didn't bat an eye ordering it like the college boy I'd gone out with had. He'd wanted me to drink. Be drunk. Like him. But Blake wasn't drinking to be drunk.

We found a seat at the back and listened to the music. Blake was different here. Still confident and grinning, but you could tell he was really listening in a solemn way to the music being played. I didn't doubt that he was really good at his job. He looked like an expectant father, waiting for the baby to shoot out so he could catch it on the first good note.

"So, you don't really get to make musicians' dreams come true, right? I mean, you just sign the contracts for them. You're not an agent or a producer."

He put his hand to his heart like I'd shot and killed him. "Now that's hitting where it hurts."

I smiled, "But it's true, right?"

"Yes and no. I definitely make sure that the deals people sign are fair. To all parties. I don't want a studio making more than they should or an artist. And on the other hand, launching a new artist takes a lot of bucks on a studio's part. But I also know people in the industry, and I like to think they respect my opinion, so if Wil and I find someone we think is good, we have a few ways to open doors for people."

It was a little humbler than he'd been before, but that's what made me take it as truth. He wasn't really bragging about it. Just stating it like it was. I realized that I wouldn't be able to tell for sure if Blake was lying to me like I'd always known if you were, but I could tell when he was serious and when he was just having fun. And that was good too.

We listened to the guy that Wil had recommended. And I thought Blake was right, his look was a "hell no," but looks could change, wasn't I living proof of that? But I also wasn't sure he had the voice of an angel.

When we got in the car, Blake asked my opinion. And I liked that. No one had asked my opinion in a while. Not even you, usually. Probably because you already knew what my opinion was, but still.

"Eh," I said, waving my hand trying to explain that I thought it was just okay.

"Exactly!" he exclaimed back like I'd just said something completely brilliant. "I knew you'd be on my side!"

I laughed at that.

He started the car and then turned to look at me with a funny look on his face.

"You know, I don't know where you live."

We both chuckled at that. It was kind of funny, seeing as he'd been helping me look for places to live all morning. I gave him the address near the hospital, and he knew where it was and took off.

When we got there, we had to find street parking a couple blocks down. Wynn and I lived in the second story of an early 1900s home that had been converted into apartments. There was really only street parking. It was a reason I used my bike a lot. But, heck, I would have used my bike a lot anyway.

Blake opened the car door and walked alongside me down the sidewalk in the direction of my apartment. I felt oddly nervous for the first time all night. It wasn't nervous like I was scared, but like I had pent-up energy kind of nervousness. A way I hadn't felt in a long time.

The streetlight lit up our stone steps pretty well, and I noticed the light was on in our apartment which meant Wynn was waiting to see how things had gone. I hit the first step and turned back to Blake to say good night. It put us almost eye-to-eye.

He tugged at the scarf that Anne had made me wear, and the motion pulled me closer to him. Before I could even think about it, he was kissing me. A good kiss. Not slobbery. Not quite as intense as yours had been, but still demanding something back from me. Not just sitting there whimpering. Not angry like Seth's. It made my insides, that I thought had died, twirl. It knocked my nerve endings awake after a long, long sleep.

He stepped back a little, still holding onto the scarf so that I wouldn't run away. And I had completely conflicted emotions toward Anne and the scarf. On the one hand, I felt like I should thank her profusely for suggesting it, and on the other hand, I felt just a bit panicked. I hadn't let anyone kiss me. Not since you. And Blake had just done that. And it had felt good. Really good, to be honest. My brain was saying I'd betrayed you in some way, but my body was doing a silent high five with my lips.

Blake looked down into my eyes, and he was somber, but there was still a smile on his face.

"I really liked that," he said.

It made me laugh. I think, now that I am writing this, and now that I know him a little better, that he'd said it just that way on purpose so I would laugh because he'd known I was feeling conflicted.

"I'd like to do that again sometime. Maybe even tomorrow?" he continued.

I pushed at him with my hand, trying to pull Anne's scarf away, but he wasn't letting go yet. "You're such an egomaniac. What makes you think I'd like to do it again?"

He grinned lazily. "Let's just say that I am not an idiot when it comes to girls."

And it didn't even make me mad. The fact that he was making fun of you; saying that he was better at something than you. I was relieved that someone could actually joke with me about you. Tease me about you without fearing I'd break down into hysterics.

I tried to pretend that I was offended though, "You'll have to call me in the morning. Maybe I'll have changed my mind by then."

I tugged again, and this time he let me go, but he was still smiling that confident smile. He took my key from my hand, mounted the steps, and unlocked the door for me. See. Complete gentleman. Then he bopped me on the nose with his finger like you'd done a million times as he headed down the steps.

"Sleep tight, Super Girl."

And he was gone in the night.

♫ ♫ ♫

So…what would you have thought? That's my big question now. If I'd told you this story maybe when we'd both been dating other people? Would you have thought it was sweet? Would you have warned me away? Or would you be happy because it was Blake and Blake was good people? Had come from good people.

Wynn said it was good. That he was perfect for me because he knew you. That he knew our story. That I didn't need to explain to him the things that I couldn't possibly explain to another guy. Things like the fact that no one could ever take your place. I'd never love anyone the way I'd loved you no matter how cliché that was. The way I still loved you. That I wouldn't have to explain that I was going through life as if my right arm was missing. Would always be missing.

But people without arms can live complete and happy lives, right? Blake already knew all of my history. He'd lived much of it too. He'd seen us together. He knew that I wasn't completely me without you, but he made me feel like the me that I was, was still enough.

Chapter Twenty-four

State of Grace

"This is a state of grace,

This is the worthwhile fight."

- Taylor Swift

I never would have expected Blake. Could never have seen him sweeping into my life. But it was kind of nice to feel like there was someone out there willing to force me into a brand-new world. Into something that could feel good and happy and true.

After that first day, Blake and I saw each other every day for another week. We'd catch dinner and a movie. Or go to a club so he could watch some up-and-coming. Or go bowling. Do you know how long it had been since I'd been bowling? And he even took me riding out of town where he had a horse stabled. It was good to do something with him that had always been just mine. Something you'd never been good at, and funnily enough, the thing that Blake himself had taught me.

On one hand, it felt fantastic to be that competitive girl again. To be the girl some guy was trying to beat. It felt like

I was a little more myself than I had been since you'd gone. On the other hand, it was bringing up different thoughts of you that I hadn't had in a long time either. I felt good, but sad at the same time.

One night, about a week into our new thing, we were at my apartment watching some stupid show about white trash lottery winners that Blake thought was hilarious. We were on the couch, but we weren't really watching it. We were fooling around a bit. He was touching me in ways that I hadn't thought anyone would again. And my body was on high alert, when his phone rang.

He'd been waiting all night for an important call about a contract he was trying to sign with some folks in L.A. So, he groaned, rested his head on my chest for a moment, but then looked at the screen. When he saw the picture of the person calling, he chuckled and tossed the phone on the side table.

"Just Matt. I can talk to him later," he said and moved as if he was going to return his lips to mine, but I pushed his chest and turned my head.

"Matt! What have you told Matt about us?"

"Everything," Blake said with that lazy, knowing smile that both made me want to strangle him and hug him.

"What?!"

"He's jealous as hell by the way. Told me that it was incredibly unfair that I ran into you. I told him I was closing the deal he was unable to close."

I used all my force to push him off of me, and he hit the floor laughing.

"Egomaniac!"

He was still laughing. "I'm just kidding! Matt's happily married. A beauty queen from Texas just as into the ranch and rodeo thing as he is."

I sat, legs crisscrossed, arms across my chest, glaring at him.

"He was still jealous though. After all, you're Super Girl."

"Kiss ass!"

"Yep! That's me," he reached up and yanked on my leg so that I fell, sprawling onto him. "But it's all for a good cause."

And he kissed me hard, thoroughly leaving me breathless and still wanting more. His hand was up my shirt and had undone the clasp at the back of my bra, in two seconds flat. And I was just debating in my head how far I was going to let this go, when his phone rang again. He tried to ignore it, but I pulled away and reached up to grab the phone. It wasn't Matt. No Matt picture on the lock screen, so I handed it to him.

He answered it, and I took the time to put myself back together; hooking my bra back up, moving away, and going into the kitchen to get two more beers.

When he was done with his call, he found me there. Took the beers, put them on the counter and pulled me close, kissing me again. But this felt more like a goodnight kiss. Like he was trying to cool us both off instead of heading in for the kill like he had been before. And I knew very well that I would have been the kill.

"I guess I'm leaving for L.A. tonight," he said with his hands on my hips, pulling me closer into him while he leaned up against the counter. I was between his legs, trapped a little, but in a good way.

"That's great!" I said, truly happy that he was going to get to close the contract.

"Hey!" he said, pretending to be offended.

"That way my other boyfriend will get some time in," I said, playing back.

"Did I ever tell you that I have complete access to a full-time hit man as part of my work in the entertainment industry?"

"Ha ha."

"Well, I might have to do the job myself because you're not famous, but I'm definitely not willing to share you."

It pleased me. A lot. That we'd only been seeing each other for a week, and yet he had kind of claimed me as his own. I didn't even know very much about his past relationships. What other women he'd been seeing before me. Just that atrocious blind date that had led him to hate an entire neighborhood.

"So, you're leaving," I said breathless as he ran his fingers along the top of my jeans on the skin by my hip bones.

"Unfortunately. I do travel quite a bit in this job. L.A. and New York mostly. When I get there, it'll be all crazy hell for twenty-four or forty-eight hours."

"But you love it."

He grinned a little. "I do. I did. But right now, I'm thinking there's actually a place I'd rather be." And he stared into my eyes and then was kissing me again with a passion that felt reckless and deep and a little over the edge. I was definitely the kill. He was going to make sure he had me just where he wanted, and I wasn't sure I'd be able to stop it. But then, suddenly, he pulled back, "Wait. Do you want to come with me?"

He looked eager. Like a kid waiting to be rewarded with a gold star. But I shook my head and laughed at him. "No way. I have things to do here. Apartments to look at. Teens to save."

"That's right, Super Girl to the rescue." He smiled his self-assured smile at me but seemed to be searching my eyes as well. "Maybe next time? If I give you more warning?" He looked like he really wanted me to say yes. Like he was counting on it.

I nodded. Not really ready to commit to anything. It seemed weird to be thinking that far ahead. Blake and I hadn't really been about that. We'd just gone like green-light-go and not really stopped to think about anything further ahead.

He kissed me again and then sighed. "I guess I better get going then. Gotta go pack a bag and get a flight."

I stepped out of his legs, and he let me, but he held my hand all the way to the door. He turned back and smiled at me. "God, you look good," he said and then flicked my nose playfully, and was off down the steps in a bound. He was so full of energy and life. Life...

♫ ♫ ♫

With him gone, I got to really pause and reflect. And the truth was that I wasn't just thinking about you in my quiet times now. I have to say, that my thought might start with you, but it almost always ended up with Blake. When my phone vibrated, my heart would jump and soar a little, and when I heard his voice, I got excited. Yep. Excited. Smile and everything.

It made me realize that while, to Blake, this might be some lighthearted fun, it was quickly becoming more serious for me. And I wasn't sure I could do that again. Serious. It hadn't really ended well for me the last time. I'd spent twenty years on you, only to have you up and die on me.

But it was still nice to hear his voice. He'd tell me who he was meeting with and something funny that had happened, and he always asked about me. How my day had gone, how had the meeting with Johnny been? It amazed me that he'd remember these little minute details of my life that sometimes I might have forgotten even myself if he hadn't asked about it.

And he always ended the call telling me that he was missing me, and that he couldn't wait to get back to Nashville to see me again. That he was thinking up something good for us to do so that I wouldn't think he was predictable.

Seth hadn't been predictable either, but that hadn't been good. With Blake, I was thinking unpredictable might be a whole lot tamer. He was offended by that when I mentioned it. Like calling him a teddy bear that first day.

♪ ♪ ♪

When he got back, Blake showed up in swim trunks on my doorstep. He had a t-shirt on too, but swim trunks, really? I let him in, and he told me that he couldn't get it out of his head how I'd always beaten him at the lake. Which was a lie. I hadn't always beaten him. He'd been five years older than me, and an all-muscle, testosterone-driven boy, but he said, in his head, he always had me winning.

I laughed at him and said I wasn't going swimming with him. He said he wasn't taking no for an answer. That he'd already got a picnic lunch in the car, and he was planning on taking me out to a lake. Not our lake, but a lake all the same.

I got stubborn. I'm not sure why. Lord, I was happy to see him. But you know how I can be. I crossed my arms over my chest and placed my hips apart in my I-don't-think-so stance. Blake just burst out laughing at it. "Oh my God, that is exactly how I remember you!"

He didn't even bat an eye. He just tossed me over his shoulder like a bag of cornmeal and started toward the door. But I just couldn't. His holding me like that reminded me of you. The lake made me think of you. Racing at a lake was you. And all of it was something I couldn't do. Not without you. I just couldn't.

All of a sudden, I was hyperventilating and crying and pounding on his back. It took him a couple of seconds before he got that I wasn't playing around, and when he put me down and looked at my tear-stained face, I could tell he felt like a total cad.

He wrapped his arms around me and pulled me to his chest. "I'm so sorry, Cam. I didn't mean to. God. I'm sorry."

I just kind of clung to him for a moment. Then I sniffled and got hold of myself and stepped away to look up at him.

"No. I'm sorry. I'm just still a little messed up sometimes."

He looked like he'd just run over a puppy.

"I didn't think about it that way. About the racing and the lake…"

And I knew he hadn't.

I was ready for him to try to beat a hasty goodbye. I'd just thoroughly embarrassed him and me both. But he didn't. He lifted a hand and wiped away a tear, which only made more tears come because it was so something you'd do too. And all of a sudden, I was mad. Not at him. At me. I hadn't cried like this in so long.

Then he bent his head and lifted mine and started kissing the tears. He pulled me close again, and in that moment, a switch was clicked, and I wasn't thinking about you anymore. I was thinking about Blake. And the way he smelled nothing like you, but he still smelled like country and boy. And the way his lips felt so soft and yet rough on my cheeks. How he was there, and how it felt good to be held and kissed.

And I reached for his lips and was kissing him back. Fervently, like I had found something I never thought I'd find again, but that, somehow, I had found in him. I ran my hands down his arms and his back and let them make their way to his blonde hair that curled at the nape of his neck.

He pressed his body tighter against mine. And his gentle kisses became needier. More demanding. And he was pulling me into him. And it felt good. It wasn't you, but it was some place that I could also belong.

I started tugging at his t-shirt so that I could feel his skin against mine, and he obliged me by removing my t-shirt at the same time. We were breathing heavy, and for the first time in years, I felt alive again. Truly, one hundred percent alive. Like every nerve ending that had been asleep, and that Blake had started to reawaken, was truly and fully awake; hurting from lack of use and wanting to be used.

I pulled him toward my bedroom. He picked me up and was kissing me everywhere. I wrapped my legs around his waist and we banged laughingly into the pictures on the hallway wall. We reached the door that was mine, and we made our way in, never removing some part of our bodies from our lips.

He tossed me onto the bed and then stopped at the foot of the bed and watched me.

"Look. It's not that I don't want to. God help me, but I do. But I don't want this to be about Jake."

I loved how he wasn't afraid to say your name or bring you up or remind me of you. I knelt up on the bed and pulled him toward me, kissing him hard, full of longing.

"I promise you. This is only about you."

"And you."

I laughed, "And me."

And he placed his hands on either side of my waist and pulled me into him. He was strong and muscled. Broader than you in many ways. And he knew tricks you didn't. Sorry. But he did. Maybe because he was older and had been single for so much longer. All I know is that when I was with him it was good in an entirely new way. A way that I could never compare to you. I didn't want to compare it to you. I wanted it to be about Blake.

♫ ♫ ♫

Later, we ordered in Chinese food. And I realized that it was kind of nice not having to worry, really, about what Blake was eating or not eating. That I could tantalize him with my MoonPies, and he'd fight me over them. It was… a relief. God, I felt guilty even thinking it, but it was true. And it made me feel bad about how hard I'd been on Amber when she'd dumped you your senior year after your seizure in the hall. I got it now.

Wynn came home and caught Blake in his boxers in the kitchen. I laughed to see him use his Southern manners in apologizing, but at the same time, not being in the least bit self-conscious by his nakedness.

Wynn looked like she was going to shed her skin she was so happy. I mean, not at Blake's nakedness, but wow, that was a good sight too. She was happy for me. Happy that I was smiling. That he was making me smile.

♫ ♫ ♫

Later that night, he had me sprawled out on my stomach while he was massaging my back in ways that were certainly not going to be allowed in any legitimate massage parlor, when he dropped a bombshell.

"I was just thinking. Maybe instead of looking for your own place, you should move into mine."

I rolled over to look up at him.

"What?!"

"Too soon?" He grinned at his impulsiveness. "But I mean it. I don't regret having said it."

I didn't know what to say to that. It was something he did to me a lot. Take my words away. I knew that I didn't want to move in with Blake just so that I wouldn't be alone. Hell, truth was, I was good at alone now. But I didn't want anyone else to think I needed Blake to fill the gaps in my life. That I wasn't strong enough to stand on my own.

"I take it by your silence that you don't think it's a good thing?" He looked a little crestfallen.

"I just…" didn't know what to say. "I don't think I was expecting you to make me that kind of an offer."

"Shit! Did I offend you? Should I have proposed first?" He was half teasing and half serious which scared me more than his offer to move in with him.

"God, no!" I threw back.

"But I do want to be with you. All the time. I think about you constantly. I feel like you injected me with some Super Girl spell or something. The whole time I was in L.A., the only thing I wanted was to get back on the plane and come right here to your house."

"Kiss ass."

And he flipped me over and did kiss my… well. Anyway. It was funny and lightened the mood that turned into something more passionate. So, it was a long while before we came back to the subject.

"I'd really like it," he said while we were making root beer floats in the kitchen.

"I'll think about it," was all I could commit to at that time.

"Okay." And I loved that he didn't push me. That he knew when to back off even if you would never have backed off or let me breath till I answered you. You would have pushed me to a yes. That was what made Blake different, and also lovable.

♪ ♪ ♫

Wynn understood my dilemma. She even agreed to extend our rent on our apartment by a couple weeks in order to give me time to figure things out. And Mama and Daddy came to Nashville. I think Mama was worried about how fast things were going with Blake. I think she thought that I was tying myself to him because of his connection to you.

I greeted her with a hug and a smile. It was a real smile that reached my eyes, and she saw it, and she kind of took a sharp breath and then hugged me so tight that I thought she'd break me.

We met Blake at a restaurant we both liked that was walking distance from Wynn and my place. Blake saw me first and came up and kissed my cheek and said, "Hey babe," in a way that made me thrilled down to my toes. Then he turned to my parents and stuck out his hand and shook both of theirs.

"Mr. and Mrs. Swayne. It's been a long time. How are you?"

My daddy was eyeing him up and down. Blake had on his expensive lawyer suit. He'd just come from work.

"We're good. Sounds like you've been doing well for yourself too," my daddy said, and I was surprised to see Blake flush a little, both in pride and awkwardness.

"Yes, sir. I've been lucky."

As Daddy and Blake started talking business, Mama watched. She was like a hawk. She watched the way Blake's hand would find its way to mine, and the way he rubbed my pinky soft and slow. She watched when he got my chair for me and the way he pulled my hand into his arm when we walked down the street to get cappuccinos at a local coffee shop.

And she watched me. I'm sure she was more worried about what was going through my head than what was going through Blake's. She could read him a mile away. He wanted me. And it showed. Even in front of my parents.

He didn't flaunt it the way you had by wrapping your arm around my waist and pulling me tight up against your body, but the way Blake touched me, the slow, sensual pinky rub, the way he'd bend his head toward mine like he wanted to kiss my cheek, but didn't. All of that, screamed how he felt. It was sweet. Endearing. And made my heart flutter. It made me smile at him. And that…that my mama saw… the smile that I had.

After the coffee, Blake made his excuses. "I know that you really came to see Cam and not me. So, I won't hog your time with her."

"Please. Don't be silly, come back to the apartment with us," my mama protested in the Southern, polite way that she was supposed to do.

But Blake knew Southern manners as well as anyone. "Thank you, but I'll have to decline, ma'am. I have an early appointment. It was a real pleasure seeing you again."

He shook both their hands. "I hope that I'll get to see a lot more of you if this woman would ever agree to move in with me."

He pulled me close and kissed my cheek again. Then flicked me on my nose and made his last goodbyes.

We were all silent at first, walking home to my place. Daddy looked like he wanted to say something, but Mama was giving him the evil eye. Me. I was smiling still.

Daddy hugged me. "It's good to see you smiling again, honey."

"I know!" I said with a lot of my old sarcasm and attitude which made my mama smile too. "So, don't hold back now. Tell me what you think," I said to both of them, but mostly Mama. If I'd never listened to her while you were alive, it had almost been the opposite since. I listened to her all the time.

"I think he likes you a whole lot," she said and she actually choked up.

"Because it's pretty hard to like me," I said with a smile again.

"Well…" my daddy teased in a way he used to tease me but hadn't in a long time for fear I'd break.

"I think the bigger question really is, what do you think?" Mama asked.

I was quiet. Considering. "I think at first I liked him because he remembered me the way I was. And then I think I liked him because he wasn't afraid to fold Jake into our conversations. But now..."

I didn't know how to put it into words.

"Now?" Mama prompted me.

"And now I think I like him because he's Blake. I like his smile, and his charisma, and his Southern charm. And I like the way he makes me feel, and the way that I don't have to pretend to be anything I'm not around him. I don't have to pretend to not have loved Jake."

Mama hugged me. "That sounds like a lot of reasons."

"I miss him when he's not with me. And I think of him more than I think of Jake."

I breathed out shakily. That sounded disloyal to me. Saying that aloud about you. But Mama got all teary-eyed.

"Those are all real good things."

"But..."

"But nothing. Don't you know by now, Camdyn, that life is too short for buts? If this is how you feel, and he wants you to be with him and you want to be with him, then just do it. Worry about the rest as it comes up. Enjoy what you have. If it lasts, great; if it doesn't, then you'll have some more beautiful memories to add to your life story."

And you know what? Mama was right. I can see you pretending to have a heart attack at me admitting she was right. I can see you tousling my hair and rubbing it in. But it didn't hurt so badly like it used to, because I knew that I'd get to tell Blake Mama was right too. And he'd be happy in a whole different way.

♪ ♪ ♪

When I told Blake, he sent Mama a bunch of flowers. Right then. He stopped kissing me, took out his phone, dialed 1-800-FLOWERS, and had them deliver flowers to my mama's house. It was kind of hilarious. And sweet. And so impulsively Blake.

He was bouncing off the walls with energy. He started pulling things out of my drawers and throwing them on the bed. I laughed at him and told him I wasn't moving in that day. And he asked why not?

And you know what else he did? He went out and got boxes. Right then. He said Mama was right, life was too short not to make every moment the moment you wanted to live. Right then.

Of course, I didn't move in that day. I started packing though. And every day for a whole week, when he'd get off work and I'd get out of school or work, he was there with takeout and boxes. It wasn't that I had that much stuff. Really, it was an apartment, how much could there be? But we'd get sidetracked. You know, like you and I used to get side tracked studying. I was good at sidetracking people. I'd forgotten how good at it I was, and I was enjoying remembering and getting more practice at it.

But even though I could sidetrack Blake, he never let me lie on my butt and do nothing after. He had me up and packing again. He said I could relax once I'd moved in.

He actually owned a house. A very grown-up kind of thing to me. It was on a quiet, tree-lined street that reminded me a little of our street. Except that it was in the city. Way more cars. Not a street where kids could really play football. But that was okay too.

I'd only been to Blake's house twice before I moved in. So, it seemed a little like I was going to stay at a hotel, or sleep over at a friend's. But Blake wanted me to make it my home too. He said he didn't give a rat's ass about anything that was in the house. So, if I didn't like something, toss it. If I wanted to add something, go right ahead.

Blake had paid someone to move my stuff. Not because he didn't have the muscle to do it, but because he said he didn't want me to have to do it. Sweet, right? He was always sweet. After they'd gone, leaving the boxes strewn about the places we'd directed them, Blake said, "I have something to show you."

And he led me down the hall to his bedroom. Well...our bedroom. He had this massive king-sized bed in it that made me wonder about how many women had been in it, and made me realize that I really didn't know very much about Blake. Or rather, grown-up Blake, but also that I didn't really care. I was here now. I thought he had one thing on his mind, and when I went to kiss him, he kissed me back, but then pulled me to the nightstand.

He looked down at it, and that's when I saw that there were two pictures on it. One was Blake and me. Some stupid picture he'd snapped with his iPhone that first night that he'd taken me out, and I'd worn Anne's scarf and jacket. But we both looked happy. I had a real smile on my face, not my fake one. The other picture was a picture of you and me. My mama must have given it to him. It was you with your arm wrapped around my waist, chin on my head. And we were both so blissfully happy. In the background was the Tower Bridge in London. It was from the time you'd gone with me to worlds. It felt like a lifetime ago.

I looked at the two pictures, and I got all teary-eyed. I wasn't really crying. Just emotional. Blake pulled me into his arms and hugged me and then looked down at me.

"I want you always to remember that I love you right now for who you are. For all you've been through. But I also want you to realize that I never, ever want to take Jake's place. Your love for him is there. Will always be. I get that. Our love can be here, separate. Our own thing. Just like the two pictures."

"You love me?"

"Who wouldn't?"

"Kiss ass."

"Super Girl."

He flicked my nose, and I smiled up at him.

"I love you too, Blake."

"I know."

"Egomaniac."

And then he kissed me and made me forget all about you for a while. For a long while. It was longer and longer each time, but it would never be forever. You were mine and I was yours and that wouldn't change. But for now, I was also Blake's and he was mine. And I liked that too. And I know, somewhere out there in the stars in the Delphinus constellation, you are thinking that it's good too, and that you are happy that I am happy. And for right now. That's enough.

♫ ♫ ♫

I hope you loved Cam's story. I hope your heart is full now. But maybe you want a little more of Blake's part of the story? You can find out when he first fell for the tiny referee with her braids askew and blue popsicle stained lips in an exclusive short called *THIS LIFE WITH CAM* that's in the *4 book box set of the My Life as an Album series*. It has over 2100 pages of southern charm and is available on Amazon (and FREE in Kindle Unlimited): https://amzn.to/3aEHEgS

Want to check in with how Cam and Blake are doing in the future? You can do so for FREE when you download an *EPIC bonus epilogue* for the entire *My Life as An Album series* when you sign up for my newsletter:

https://BookHip.com/WZVAFM

Maybe you have enough of Cam and want to figure out how Jake's little sister, Mia, dealt with his loss? She's kind of stuck until she meets a soulful musician that changes her entire world.

You get her HEA story in _MY LIFE AS A POP ALBUM_ in the box set or available on Amazon (and FREE in Kindle Unlimited): https://amzn.to/2vLBetR

OR just keep reading here to see the first two chapters.

My Life as a Pop Album
Prologue
Hello

Hello. I'm Good Girl Mia. Mia Andrea Phillips. You probably don't know me, but you might know my brother, Jake. You might know Jake because, for a short while, he was plastered all over the sports channels and magazines as the future of the NFL. That was when he was the superstar quarterback for the University of Tennessee, and before his diabetes and his bad kidneys forced him to quit.

My brother Jake was the first one to call me Good Girl Mia. It was his way of teasing me about never getting in trouble. And it's the truth. I am a good girl. There's nothing I can do about it. I have always been the good girl. I've been the friend, the helper, the one you could count on. The one to drive you home if you drank too much. The one to stop you from making monumental mistakes. The one who never gave her parents *any* problems because her brother and his girlfriend gave them enough.

In fact, I've been so good at helping others that I actually gave Jake a kidney. Yep. An actual body part. Unfortunately, that didn't end very well, so maybe I'm not as good at helping out as I'd like to be…

If you are a Good Girl also, then you know how it goes. You know that Good Girls never break rules and that they never, ever run off with the bad boy.

Well then, how in holy potato peels did I end up here, with a sexy-as-all-get-out musician lying naked next to me? Well…that's the real story, isn't it?

Chapter One
The Meet

I'M A MESS
"I'm a mess right now,
Searching for sweet surrender."
-Ed Sheeran

My best friend, neighbor, and almost sister, Cam, once told me that her life could be played out in a series of Taylor Swift songs. And I understood what she meant because her life with Jake was like all the old Taylor songs. Angst and heartache and yearning.

After I had graduated from the University of Tennessee and moved back home to run the family business, my life became a series of Ed Sheeran songs. "I'm a Mess" seemed to resonate with me at first because I felt like I was just going through the motions while secretly looking for a sweet surrender. And I definitely couldn't figure out how everything was all going to work out.

I guess that wasn't completely true as I did have one thing going right for me and that was working at my daddy's car dealership. The one he planned on handing over to me in the fall. Contrary to most people's opinion of me, I liked running the dealership. I loved the vague idea that we might be starting a tradition where someday I would pass the dealership on to my kids. Not that there was any chance in the near future of me having children.

Because, let's face it, my personal life was the part of my life in all sorts of disarray. You'd never know that by looking at me. I prided myself on the fact that very few people knew about the emotional turmoil that rolled like waves through me on an almost daily basis. My mama once told me that if you went into someone's house and the place was nice and tidy but the cupboards were a disaster, that it said something about them. I knew exactly what she meant because that described me to a T. Neat and tidy outside, chaos on the inside.

My life wasn't going to get any easier that July because that's when HE entered my world, flipping it on its axis even more.

That day, it was hotter than blue blazes with the humidity like a wall you could almost see if you squinted hard enough, and I contemplated lying down on the tile showroom floor to cool off like our dog, Sparky. Instead, I lifted up every last hair on my head and stood under the air conditioning vent trying to dry the sweat off my neck.

And, of course, it was then, when I had my hair, bangs and all, swept up like a Conehead, that he sauntered into our dealership. While I was a sweaty puddle, he looked like a Jamie McGuire book boyfriend come to life.

He was lean and muscular in a blue t-shirt and just-tight-enough ripped jeans that accentuated every sculpted line. Lines of gorgeous muscles that belonged in an underwear ad. He was tall, but not too tall, around about six feet, and had sexy, bed-tousled looking brown hair that highlighted his pale gray eyes. Eyes that were the color of the winter skies right before a tornado. I was a sucker for a boy with tattoos even if I thought I'd never date someone who had them. And this piece of gorgeousness had them.

There were words wrapped around each wrist and some sort of bird on his neck. None of it was easy to make out over a distance, but that made me think about how, if I was close enough, I could brush aside those curling ends and investigate more. I suddenly wanted to do that very much. Every fiber in my body was aching to drop my grossly sweaty hair and sweep up his, just so I could get a good look at him and his tattoos while inhaling his scent.

Of course, this had me rolling my eyes inwardly at myself. And it was then that I remembered how ridiculous I must look with no hair and a sweaty grimace. So, I slowly, ever so slowly, let my dark hair drop down, wishing I wasn't as absurd as I looked.

On most days, I was proud of my hair. I'd just spent thirty minutes in normal Tennessee two o'clock humidity, however. So I was pretty sure it was flat where I didn't want it to be and curling funny where it shouldn't. But better down than cupped in my hand like a swim cap.

"Ms. Phillips?" he asked in a voice that was lyrically smooth, like a chord from an Ed Sheeran love song. He sounded just like he looked: sultry and intoxicating. The Good Girl Mia side of me was screaming to back away from the boy.

"Yes?" I was surprised to hear my own voice sound so normal while looking at this stunning human being. I've read a lot. I mean hundreds upon hundreds of books, and this guy could certainly be on any cover and attract sales like flies attract fish.

He proved that even more when he smiled, and the smile took over his entire face. It was a smile that showed off the cleft in his chin and eyes that sparkled like rain hitting those clouds inside them.

"Really?" he asked while his smile spread more.

"Um. Yes, why?" I asked.

He threw a thumb back over his shoulder. "Those folks back there said I should talk to the owner. They sent me to pick up the car for the charity auction at the Abbott farm tonight."

I didn't know what to address first. That he didn't believe I was the owner, which—to be fair—was a completely normal mistake as I was only twenty-two, or the fact that he was supposedly picking up Jake's cherried-out Camaro. The Camaro that my family and Cam had agreed to auction off for the American Diabetes Association.

I wasn't expecting a dark-haired bad boy to be picking up Jake's Camaro. I was surprised that Daddy or Cam would let anyone drive it. They were having a hard enough time giving it away. But then, I guess it shouldn't really be a surprise as none of us wanted to drive it. It was still too emotional for both our families. It had sat in the dealership's showroom since his death. The mechanics kept it running, but that was it.

"Who exactly told you that you were to pick it up?" I asked, making a beeline for the management offices in the back with him tagging along behind me.

"Blake. Well, I guess it was Cam. But Blake said to take her orders as if they were his own. I kind of think it's really the other way around with those two sometimes." He winked at me. "Do you know them?"

Again, I didn't know what to respond to first. The wink that left my still upside-down heart pattering like a kitten who'd just chased a bug, or the absolute nonsense he'd asked about me knowing Blake and Cam.

"She's pretty much my sister," I told him flatly as we reached the office. And she pretty much was. We'd grown up next door, and our families shared everything, including Sunday dinners. And if Jake had been alive, she would have married him and made the sister thing legit. Instead, she was with Blake who was also from our town but lived in Nashville now as an entertainment lawyer.

I pulled out my iPhone from the desk drawer and texted Cam.

ME: *There's some moron here who says you told him to come get Jake's car?*

I waved the book boyfriend into a chair, buzzed the intercom, and asked Mary Beth for an iced tea. "Would you like anything?" I asked the man.

"Sure, iced tea sounds great."

My phone buzzed back.

CAM: LOL So you've met Blake's pride and joy?

I stared at the text like it should make sense. She hadn't really answered.

Mary Beth, who'd worked for my daddy for almost as long as I'd been alive, brought in two sweet teas. She fluffed her hair that was ratted tall like she still belonged to the eighties while she took in the BB—the book boyfriend—in front of her.

"Thanks, Mary Beth."

"That's such a southern name." The BB's grin returned with the cleft in his chin stretching in a way that made it seem like it was smiling too. "I'm really glad I came to Tennessee."

He took a big gulp of the sweet tea and choked almost as if he'd slammed back a shot of whiskey. "Holy shit, that's sweeter than cotton candy."

Mary Beth smiled politely at him. "Thank you." Then she turned to me. "Anything else you need?"

Mary Beth seemed to think that any time the parts manager, a mechanic, or one of the male salesmen came into the office, she had to chaperone me like a debutant. It was both pleasant and smothering at the same time.

"I think we're good. Thanks. I'll buzz if I need anything," I said as I texted Cam back.

ME: *You're telling me the moron is allowed to drive Jake's prize possession?*

I took a sip of the tea and turned to find the keys of the Camaro on the wall behind me. When I turned back to the BB, he was watching me carefully, and I literally fought the urge to wipe at my eyes and fix my hair. I'd never been a girl overly concerned with the way I looked. I didn't go overkill with the makeup. I fixed my hair in the morning and typically forgot about it until it went up into a messy bun at the end of the day. But this man, this BB, made me want to appear as good as any book girlfriend could look.

My phone buzzed.

CAM: *Maybe you're right. Can you bring it? And bring the pride and joy back with you. Blake will never let me live it down if he gets lost.*

I sighed. "They've had a change of heart. I'll give you a ride."

"What? They don't want me to pick it up or the car isn't being donated?"

"Don't take it personally. The car. It's just… special," I said with a pang of emotion in my voice that I hadn't expressed aloud in a long time.

"But the dealership is donating it anyway?"

"No. My family is donating it."

He grinned. "Oh. I see."

"I doubt it."

I finished my sweet tea quickly. I suddenly needed to get all of this over with. The car and the BB would both be deposited safely, and I could go home where, hopefully, they would both stop pulling at the scabs inside me.

"I've been asked to give you a ride back out to the ranch. Seems there is some fear of you getting lost," I told him.

The BB chuckled. "Damn Blake. He never lets anything slide, does he?"

The BB's laugh made my insides go squishy again. I suddenly resented it. I didn't want this temptation to Mary coming into my life and stirring up the pot. I had enough on my plate with taking over the dealership, starting my MBA classes in the fall, and trying to recover from a broken heart. I didn't need him here making me feel anything. Especially not the desperate longing that hit me when I watched him.

"Let's go, Lost Boy," I said as I grabbed my purse, my phone, and the Camaro keys. I stopped by Mary Beth's desk.

"I'm off. I'll be at the Abbott's ranch if you need me for anything." I looked over at the sales folks that were waiting in the air-conditioned room for a new customer that wasn't going to show in the summer heat. "I guess I'll have to leave Denise in charge for now. She's the only one that can sign contracts while Ben is on vacation."

Mary Beth patted my shoulder. "Don't you worry, sugar. We'll keep this place rolling. Remember, we're closing early, anyway. Everyone in town will be at Jake's fundraiser."

I swallowed back the lump in my throat, nodded, and walked out of the showroom with the BB following me.

Chapter Two

The Camaro

HAPPIER

"Promise that I'll not take it personal baby,

If you're moving on with someone new,

Cause baby you look happier, you do."

-Ed Sheeran

As I rounded the corner of the building, I stopped suddenly at the sight of Jake's Camaro. It wasn't like I hadn't expected it. I'd come out to drive it for goodness' sake, but it was still hard to see.

Daddy had had the body department take it out and detail it. It looked sparkling red in the shimmery sunshine. It was so Jake that it was hard to even look at, let alone drive. Jake had loved this car. Even more, he'd loved Cam sitting next to him in it.

"You okay?" The BB seemed to sense that he had stepped into the middle of something but wasn't quite sure what.

I nodded, unlocked the door, and slid into the driver's seat. I reached across and unlocked the passenger side, and the BB got in as I adjusted the seat. Daddy was pretty much the only one to drive it after Jake, and they'd been close to the same height at a lean, mean six feet two inches or so. My short frame made it a stretch even with the seat as close to the dash as I could get it. The truth was, sixties muscle cars weren't made for short girls.

I adjusted the mirrors and then finally, unable to delay it anymore, turned the ignition. It roared to life and instantly brought back memories of me in the treehouse with a flashlight and the sound of Jake coming home from the lake. You could hear the car all the way down the street, typically, with the music blaring. And yet, our neighbors had never complained. No one had ever told my parents that he drove too fast or had his music too loud. They all looked the other way. I guess that was mostly due to his superstar status in town.

"You sure you're okay?" the BB asked.

"Stop asking that," I said with a huff that I didn't really mean. It was bad enough that I had to drive Jake's car. I didn't need some perceptive hunk delving into my emotions.

"Okay," he said with a grin that said he found me slightly humorous, and I didn't know if I hated that or liked that.

I pulled out of the lot and headed down the street, making the turns automatically till we got out to the pastures and farms. We passed the turnoff for the lake, and I couldn't help but let my head be drawn that way ever so slightly; wondering if Jake was watching over us all from his place by the tree with branches like a goalpost that he and Cam had loved.

"So, you know Cam well then?" he probed further.

"We grew up together," I said, not wanting to be rude, but definitely not wanting to talk.

"So, you know Blake then, too?"

I just nodded.

"Don't feel like you have to elaborate or anything," the BB said.

I didn't want to elaborate, but I could also sense my Southern manners kicking in. It wasn't polite to let your guest do all the talking. Not that he was really my guest. I hadn't invited him to Jake's fundraiser, but if Blake and Cam had, then it was pretty much the same thing.

I sighed. "I'm sorry. I'm just a little emotional today. This was Jake's car."

I could feel the BB's eyes boring into me, but I didn't look over. "Jake, as in the guy the fundraiser is named after?"

I just nodded.

He seemed to be putting it all together, which meant I didn't have to spell it out for him. "You're his sister?"

I nodded again. I am his sister, but it still felt like it should be said in the past tense. I was his sister. He's dead. God, I couldn't believe I had tears in my eyes. What in bejesus was wrong with me? I hadn't cried over Jake in a long time, and especially not openly in front of another human being.

"Wow. I'm sorry. That sucks," he said.

As we neared the ranch, I tried to get my emotions back under control by turning the attention back to him.

"So, who are you exactly?"

"I was hoping you'd ask," he said with that infectious, knowing smirk that simultaneously made me want to wipe it off and join along. "I'm Derek Waters. Musician. Songwriter. My band is playing tonight."

Of course this beautiful BB would be a musician, I thought to myself with a whole pile of sarcasm. Cam had said he was one of Blake's protégés so I should have put two and two together instead of being stunned brain-dead by his gorgeousness. Blake did specialize in writing contracts for up-and-coming musicians after all.

"I can't believe they were going to let you drive Jake's car," I groused before I could help myself. Then I flushed in embarrassment because that was definitely not something a polite Southern girl was supposed to say.

To my surprise, he laughed at me. A big laugh that seemed to come from his belly and had me glancing in that direction, taking in how awfully good he looked in those snug jeans of his. This made me want to rip my eyes off and stuff them away where they couldn't do any more damage.

I pulled into Blake's grandparents' farm and was taken aback by the volume of trucks and cars. A massive tent had been put up near the barn, and people were busy hanging twinkle lights and setting up tables with flowers.

Somewhere in the middle of all that would be Cam, going a mile a minute even though she was eight months pregnant. It hadn't been a planned pregnancy. She and

Blake weren't even married yet. Like all things Cam, stuff happened before she thought about it. She appeared to be taking it in stride, which seemed so not the Cam that Jake and I had grown up with that it made me sad once more.

Old Cam would have been kicking walls at the idea of carrying anyone's baby, and especially the idea of carrying anyone's but Jake's.

"Shall I go see where they want the car parked?" the BB asked, and I realized that I needed to start thinking of him by his real name, Derek.

"That would be great," I said.

He jumped out of the car, and I literally sighed with relief. I thanked God that I could go back to being my normal self instead of the drooling Neanderthal girl I seemed to have become around him.

Blake found me sitting in the car. He leaned his shaggy, blonde-haired head into the window to give me a half hug. "Hey, Mia! Why don't you get out, and I'll drive the car over to where we want it set up?"

"You don't trust me?" I asked, teasing.

"She seems completely trustworthy to me," Derek said, coming up behind Blake.

I couldn't help the visible eye-roll. Blake saw it and grinned his joyful smile that was never far from his face. I could tell why Blake and Derek got along. They both seemed like generally happy guys. I wondered what it must be like to be that happy all the time.

Blake turned to Derek and waved his finger at him. "No."

Derek grinned. "I didn't—"

"No!" Blake cut him off.

"Hey!" I protested because I was a good driver. I was as careful driving as I was with almost everything in my life.

Blake took me in and then started backpedaling, "That's not what I meant. Honest."

I realized I was missing something, but I wasn't sure I wanted to know what it was. Not with Derek belly laughing again. It made my stomach flop like when you flipped backwards over the top of the monkey bars for the first time.

I got out of Jake's car, grabbed my bag, and headed for the tent. "I'll leave you two children to whatever it is you're doing. I'm assuming Cam's inside?"

I didn't wait for a response. I could still hear Derek laughing, and it sounded like Blake punched his shoulder, but I didn't bother to look back. I was glad to be leaving gorgeous with gorgeous behind me.

In the tent, I found Cam going a mile a minute like I had expected, which was still good to see because for a while after Jake had died, she'd come to a full stop like she never had in her whole life. Now, with Blake and the baby, she was almost back to normal, except that it was a different normal.

Her dark hair, with its chestnut highlights, was shorter than it used to be when we were growing up, but she still had it in a ponytail in acknowledgement of the heat. She was in a t-shirt dress which, again, was so anti the old Cam that it was hard to take in. It was probably much more comfortable than jeans due to the little round ball sticking out of her middle, though.

"Cam!" I said and hugged her. She hugged me back, and this stupid, emotional me got teary-eyed, causing Cam to notice.

"Hey, kiddo!" She pulled back, taking me in. "What's wrong?"

I waved her off. "Nothing."

"Did the moron upset you?"

"No. No. I think it was just driving the Camaro."

As I said it, Blake drove it up onto the grass near the tent, and the beefy engine got to us both. "He really loved that car," Cam said quietly.

We both stared for a moment, taking it in. Cam had ridden in the car way more than I had. She'd been Jake's sidekick and soulmate from the time she was born, and even my birth, two years after her, had never come in between them.

Blake exited the car, smiled at her, and then went off in a different direction once Cam had smiled back. It made me wonder, like I had a million times before, what Jake would think of Cam and Blake. Would he be like Ed Sheeran in "Happier"? Would he be happier to see her with someone new rather than with no one? I thought he would like to see her being taken care of and with someone that knew them as well as Blake had. I thought he would like to see her able to smile once more, but I also thought he'd hate the idea of her in anyone's arms.

Cam was never one for tears, and even though the Camaro had momentarily gotten to her, she'd already turned back into her normal, bossy self which was good because it kept her from punching something instead. She handed me a box of mason jars filled with candles.

"Here, they go on all the tables, according to the event planner."

"Okay, but I have to leave soon to get ready. I'm sweaty as sin," I told her.

"You'll just get sweaty all over again. We've got the misters and fans set up, but today had to be one of the muggiest days of July, didn't it?"

"Are you wearing that dress?" I asked her.

"You don't think it works?" Cam gave me her mischievous smile that used to mean she was plotting against Jake, but now was aimed at me.

"Yes! You look beautiful. I'm just trying to decide what I should wear."

"I'm just teasing. I have a purple dress in the house."

She was referring to Blake's grandparents' house here at the ranch. She and Blake were staying with them for all the fundraiser shenanigans. Honestly, though, they stayed here a lot when they visited from Nashville. Blake's grandparents had more rooms. Plus, I think it was easier for Cam to be here than at our house or her house where everything reminded her of Jake. Or, really, of her and Jake—the one being they used to be.

I took the box as instructed and placed the jars on the tables near the flowers that were already wilting in the heat. When I'd made it about halfway through, I was surprised to find the box lifted out of my hands.

I turned to find Derek smiling at me again. "Let me help."

"Don't you need to be practicing or something?" I asked with a wave to the stage because the last thing I needed was this BB by my side again.

"Won't make any difference this late in the game. We'll either suck or be a hit," he said. He gave a self-deprecating shrug accompanied by yet another sexy smile.

For some reason, this time the smile reminded me just a little of Hayden's smile when he wanted something. And I was trying to forget all of Hayden Hollister's smiles, even though they lived with me most nights. This had me narrowing my eyes at Derek in a way that probably wasn't fair to him but I was sure was well deserved anyway.

"I'm sure you have something better to do than help me put out mason jars, unless I'm not trusted to do that either."

"I'd trust you to do anything you wanted to my... tables," he said. My stomach did that monkey bar flip again because he was definitely flirting with me. It had taken me awhile to really figure it out for sure because I wasn't used to guys flirting with me.

Well, that wasn't exactly true. I was used to slimy guys hitting on my size E's and talking to them more than my face, but gorgeous BB musicians weren't normally the kind to do anything with me, much less flirt.

I tried to grab the box back, but he easily shifted it away from me and moved to the next table where he handed me a jar. There wasn't much I could do unless I wanted to make a huge scene, so I just took the jar and placed it on the table. Thankfully, we were done in no time.

"What are you doing now?" Derek asked as he twirled the empty box in his hands. He seemed wound tight with inner energy. It was like Cam and Jake, and even Blake. But never me. I was a read-a-book-and-bake-cookies kind of girl, not a run-until-I-broke kind of girl.

"Going home to shower and change," I said with a shrug.

His grinned widened, if possible, cleft stretching even more, and then he said, "You can't say things like that to me."

He gave me a once-over, and I suddenly hated my dark pantsuit with a passion, even though just that morning I'd loved it as much as I'd loved Hayden. As president of our business fraternity, Hayden had been all about business fashion, setting the tone with his custom-made suits.

I was just about to say something sarcastic back to his sexy innuendo when the box he was spinning flew out of his hands, and the corner hit me in my right breast before falling to the ground.

"Holy profanity!" I gasped, covering my injured part with my hand.

"Shit!" he said at the same time. He reached out to touch me and then stopped, realizing where I was hurt.

"I'm..." He didn't even know what to say as he stared at my hand and the breast it was covering.

Blake and Cam took that unfortunate moment to come up to us, with me clutching my boob, and Derek acting like he had permanently maimed me.

Blake put his arm around Derek's shoulders. "I thought I made myself clear on this matter."

Blake was smiling, but there was a tone to his voice that was deadly serious.

Cam took it all in.

"No way in hell, Derek. She's off limits," Cam said. Suddenly, I got what it was all about earlier with Derek and Blake.

I was used to Cam protecting me. She'd been my shield when it came to boys ever since I'd entered high school and Jake had gone off to college. The only boy to date me then had gone through her, which was no easy feat. But I wasn't a fourteen-year-old virgin anymore, and their protectiveness was just humiliating.

"You guys are embarrassing," I said.

Cam looked dubiously at my hand on my breast. I removed it even though it was still smarting. "It was an accident."

Everyone stood there for a moment, Blake sending "back off" vibes to Derek, me still mortified, and Cam looking like she was ready to start a fight, baby bump and all.

"You guys are awful. Anyone able to give me a ride back to town?" I asked, changing the subject.

"I have to go back to the hotel and get ready too. You can ride with me," Derek said. The three of us groaned.

"It's just a ride," Derek said with a smirk that really suggested it might be something else entirely. It seemed that he was egging Blake and Cam on because it wasn't like he was going to attack my sweaty, suit-clad body in the back seat of whatever vehicle he owned.

"You have the rental here?" Blake asked.

"Shit, no. Owen dropped me off at the dealership on his way back to the hotel."

Blake sighed. "Take my truck."

Blake fished the keys out of his jeans pocket and flung them at Derek, who caught them deftly. I would have dropped them. I was not anywhere near the athlete that Cam and Jake had been. Jake had gotten his football scholarship to UTK, and Cam had won a diving medal at the World Championships before she'd been recruited by Virginia Tech, whereas I could barely stand on a treadmill without falling over.

Cam's eyes narrowed at Derek as he swung the keys in a circle around his slender fingers. "She's my sister, dipshit, got it?"

Derek looked all innocent, but his eyes were flashing a challenge that said otherwise. It made me tingle all over in a way that was not normal for me. Because, butterbeer, the thought of him treating me in a non-sisterlike fashion was enough to add another layer of sweat to my already sweaty body.

"God, Cam, I'm not twelve," I said before turning to Derek. "I'd appreciate the ride."

Derek and I walked away, but I could feel Blake and Cam's eyes on us all the way to the truck. The passenger door was closest to us, and Derek grabbed the handle and opened it for me. "Thanks," I said with a gulp. It felt too date-like for me to be comfortable with, even though I knew we weren't going on a date. The furthest thing from it.

He climbed into the driver's side, and we took off out of the ranch. I slyly tried to take him in as he drove. He had to be a little older than me. Maybe twenty-four to my twenty-two? But he had a youthfulness to him that made him seem younger. Maybe it was the sense of carefreeness about him. Even before Jake, I hadn't had a carefree bone in my body. But now…now that I was all that Mama and Daddy had left, I took even fewer risks, which meant literally none.

He turned and caught me staring. He lifted an eyebrow and grinned. "They told me no."

I flushed and looked out the window. "As if."

"I haven't heard anyone use that term since the eighties," he chuckled at me again.

"You weren't alive in the eighties."

"Well, I've seen a lot of eighties films."

"They are the best," I said with a sigh.

"Yep."

I turned toward him. "You really think that, or are you just appeasing me?"

"Two things I never joke about: music and movies."

"Those are the only two things?"

"I'm sure there are a few more things, but I can't think of any at the moment."

At least not any he wanted to share, because I swear I saw the first look of seriousness flash over his face. But it was gone as quickly as it had come.

"I get the music, but why movies?"

"Well, my brother is Dylan Waters," he said, as if that was supposed to answer my question.

"Am I supposed to know who that is?"

Surprise washed over his face. "Director. Producer. The Spy Network?"

He named a movie that had taken the world by storm last year. It was liked by fans and critics, and it had won a bunch of Oscars. I hadn't seen it because I'd been busy with senior year and Hayden, or rather, busy with not having Hayden. Instead, I'd been busy writing love letters to someone who hadn't chosen me, and burying my head in books as a way of avoiding my reality.

"I heard it was good," I said with a shrug.

He laughed again. "You haven't seen it?"

I just shook my head.

"I think you've surprised me at least twenty times since I've met you." This time, there was no smile to accompany the words. Instead, there was that quiet, thoughtful look on his face once more.

"Turn left here," I said as we approached town. We drove down the street in silence. "It's the one on the right with the green truck."

He pulled into the driveway behind Daddy's truck, and I felt like I was fifteen and my only high school boyfriend was bringing me home. As if I should be expecting something but wasn't sure if I wanted it or not. He turned to me. "Do you need a ride back out to the ranch?"

"Nah, I'll go with my parents."

I reached for the handle and was surprised as all get out when he stopped me. When his hand hit my bare wrist, heat seeped from his fingers into my skin like honey into a biscuit. And just like him, that feeling was smooth, silky, and dangerous. Yet it was also soothing, somehow. Like comfort food with a kick.

I thought maybe I needed to stick my head in an ice chest if I was getting this discombobulated over one touch from a boy band star. I looked down at his hand, and he pulled back as if he was as shocked as I was that he'd stopped me.

"I'll see you tonight," he said.

It was one of those sexy, more-of-a-statement-than-a-question kind of things that made me swallow hard and look away. All I could do was nod at him and then climb out of the truck, hoping that I hadn't left my pride on the seat along with the sweat stains.

I couldn't help but look back and saw him wave as he pulled out of the driveway. Suddenly, I was dreading tonight on a whole new level. And maybe that was good because it would distract me enough that I wouldn't break down. I'd be able to be the quiet, supportive Mia everyone had come to count on.

Keep reading

My Life as a Pop Album

(my life as an album series vol. II)

http://bit.ly/MLAAPAlje

EEK! I'm so excited to announce that **this holiday**, I'm releasing a collection of short stories based on the children from the original cast of the album series: MY LIFE AS A HOLIDAY ALBUM. Everyone might be smiling at the start of the holiday, but the secrets that have come home with them might just ruin the entire season for them all! Will they be able to keep them hidden, or will they be exposed with a bang that isn't at all the New Year's Eve fireworks that are planned? It's available on Amazon at special pre-order price that'll last until it releases on December 7th, 2020.

https://amzn.to/330h3bm

Second Message from the Author

Thanks again for reading my story. At the beginning of the book, if you even saw it, I told you I didn't want to fill your head with my social media sites, accolades, and other books because I wanted you to read the story and then decide how you felt about me and my words. I hope that you loved Cam's journey. I hope her strength and resiliency along with my mix of songs and story burned a memory into your soul that you will think of every time you hear one of these songs from now on.

We talk about music, books, and just what it takes to get us through this crazy thing called life a lot in my Facebook reader's group, LJ's Music & Stories. If you do nothing else with the links here, I hope you join that group. I hope that we can help **YOU** through your life in some small way.

I know that there are thousands (really millions) of books for you to choose from, so I am honored that you chose to spend a portion of your life with one of my book babies. If you liked it, I'd be honored if you took another moment (or two) to write a review on Amazon, Goodreads, or BookBub, but even more than that, I hope you enjoyed it enough to tell a friend about it.

I truly hope to hear from you!

Love Your New Friend,

LJ EVANS

♩ *where music & stories collide* ♩

About the Book

Regarding the medical topic in this book, I want to apologize in advance to the doctors of the world and those living with diabetes for any overt errors in the book. While I have known quite a few people with diabetes in my life, some more severe than others, happily, all of them have had their diabetes treated without incurring the severe consequences that the character in this book experienced. I have, however, been on the receiving end of someone I was close to who had Type 1 diabetes collapsing, experiencing "black outs," and needing immediate medical attention, so what I've written was drawn from my own fears in those moments. While the severity of the medical condition in this book may be slightly dramatized, I have been moved beyond belief by all the readers who have reached out to tell me how their personal stories shadowed this one in many ways. Those people lost love ones to Type 1 diabetes and have felt exactly the pain of Cam, Jake's family, and those who knew him. I hope that isn't you. I hope that you and all your loved ones never have to experience the crushing difference between Type 1 and Type 2 diabetes. They are completely different animals.

For more information about diabetes, please visit the American Diabetes Association at:

https://www.diabetes.org.

Acknowledgements

Thank you to Taylor Swift for writing music that inspires the creative in all of us. Thank you to my editors and companions who listened to me talk about these characters until they seemed a part of our family. Thank you for improving my story and making it more than I thought it could ever be. Thank you to Jenn at Jenn Lockwood Editing, Laura, and Brenda for all their edits and those who overlooked the mistakes the first time around. Thank you to all who believed in me and pushed me to make this book available to the public.

Thank you to every single person who has read Cam's story and reached out to me to tell me that this story moved them in some way. I'm especially grateful for Kelsey, Rachel, Leisa, Michelle, Lisa, Misty, and Emily who have done everything they could and beyond to get this story in the hands of new readers. I will always feel blessed that you were brought into my world.

About the Author

Award winning author, LJ Evans, lives in the California Central Valley with her husband, daughter, and the terrors called cats. She's been writing, almost as a compulsion, since she was a little girl and will often pull the car over to write when a song lyric strikes her. While she currently spends her days teaching 1st grade in a local public school, she spends her free time reading and writing, as well as binge-watching original shows like *The Crown, Victoria, Veronica Mars,* and *Stranger Things.*

If you ask her the one thing she won't do, it's pretty much anything that involves dirt—sports, gardening, or otherwise. But she loves to write about all of those things, and her first published heroine was pretty much involved with dirt on a daily basis, which is exactly why LJ loves fiction novels—the characters can be everything you're not and still make their way into your heart.

Her debut novel, *MY LIFE AS A COUNTRY ALBUM*, was the Independent Author Network's 2017 YA Book of the Year. For more information about the *MY LIFE AS AN ALBUM* series, or any of LJ's books, follow her at:

Website: https://www.ljevansbooks.com/

Bookbub: http://bit.ly/LJEvansBB

Amazon: http://bit.ly/LJEvans

Goodreads: http://bit.ly/LJEonGRs

Facebook: https://facebook.com/ljevansbooks

Instagram: https://instagram.com/ljevansbooks

Pinterest: https://pinterest.com/ljevansbooks

Twitter: https://twitter.com/ljevansbooks

 Books by Lj

My Life as an Album Series

My Life as a Country Album — April 2017
My Life as a Pop Album — January 2018
My Life as a Rock Album — June 2018
My Life as a Mixtape — November 2018
My Life as an Album Series Box Set – March 2020
My Life as a Holiday Album – December 2020

Standalone - Anchor Novels

Guarded Dreams — Eli & Ava, May 2019
Forged by Sacrifice — Mac & Georgie, October 2019
Avenged by Love — Truck & Jersey, April 2020
Damaged Desires — Dani & Nash, October 2020
Branded by Love — Brady O'Neil, coming in 2021
Unmasked Dreams — Violet & Dawson, coming in 2021

Coming in Some Dream World When LJ Has Enough Time

Untitled, magical realism — contemporary romance
Down on 4th – Historical Fiction
Untitled, Ezra and Elara duet —urban fantasy

Made in the USA
Monee, IL
03 December 2020